CROSSED BONES

Books by Carolyn Haines

Crossed Bones
Splintered Bones
Buried Bones
Them Bones

———

Summer of the Redeemers
Touched

CROSSED BONES

Carolyn Haines

DELACORTE PRESS

CROSSED BONES
A Delacorte Book / April 2003

Published by
Bantam Dell
A Division of Random House, Inc.
New York, New York

Library of Congress Cataloging-in-Publication Data is on file with the publisher.

ISBN: 0-385-33659-4

Manufactured in the United States of America
Published simultaneously in Canada

10 9 8 7 6 5 4 3 2 1
BVG

For Steve Greene

Acknowledgments

Many thanks go, as always, to the members of the Deep South Writers Salon. Stephanie Chisholm, Susan Tanner, Renee Paul, and Jan Zimlich gave time, talent, and creative insight into critiquing this book. These women have traveled to some strange places with me in the pages of my books, and I owe them much more than thanks.

Special thanks go to Fran and Mike Utley for their generous help with the musical aspects of this novel.

Steve Greene is a law enforcement expert who can also address the issues of plot—what a combination! I thank him for his careful reading and support.

I'd also like to thank my agent, Marian Young. Classy was invented to describe her.

And a sincere thanks to the entire group at Bantam. Liz Scheier is an editor to die for, and Jamie Warren Youll has created another masterpiece of a cover. From copy editing to publicity, this book has been a real pleasure thanks to the professionals at Bantam Dell.

CROSSED BONES

1

MY GREAT-AUNT CILLA WAS FOND OF SAYING THAT THERE'S nothing like the feel of a blooded animal between a woman's thighs. Of course with Aunt Cilla, that might apply to a Thoroughbred or a Southern gentleman with good lineage. Although most of the women in my family have been cursed with the Delaney womb, Great-Aunt Cilla was the only one of my female forbears who didn't bother to hide her affliction. She was exiled to Atlanta for her honesty.

Lying here in the porch swing with my hound at my feet and a mint julep in my hand, I can't help but think of my ancestors and the history of this land I love. I've just concluded an Old South tradition—perusing my cotton fields from the vantage point of a horse.

Tidbits of Aunt Cilla's wisdom are coming back to me. Her womb might have had a vociferous appetite, but it was nothing compared to her brain. It was she who pointed out to me the two most potent symbols of the Old South: King Cotton and blood.

On my morning rides, I see the past, present, and future of my home: the cotton, with its green leaves covered in early morning dew; the whisper of money, of times long gone and of a way of life that seems both a dream and a nightmare, depending on perspective. The wealthy settlers of the rich Delta soil in Mississippi understood the powerful combination of horse and land, the addictive pleasure of riding one's property on a healthy and responsive animal.

Aunt Cilla had her own uses for healthy, responsive animals—especially of the human species. An excellent horsewoman, she was especially fond of grooms. Horses, leather, a virile young man—Aunt Cilla's favorite aphrodisiacs.

"Sarah Booth Delaney, you are one worthless gal. Out here sittin' on the porch, fantasizin' about lettin' the hired help poke you. If you were worth a lick, you'd be wedded, bedded, and bred by some respectable gentleman."

The disapproving tone belied the soft richness of the voice. And voice was all it was. Jitty, the itinerant ghost of my great-great-grandmother's nanny, had yet to materialize.

"I would have thought you'd be glad to know I was thinking about anyone, hired help or gentleman caller, *pokin' me*, as you so delicately call it." I was far beyond getting ruffled at Jitty's nagging. We were on old, familiar ground. My lack of use of the legendary Delaney womb was her favorite topic of haranguing.

"If you were thinkin' of a real hired hand, like that Willie Campbell fellow, I might be interested. You let that man use your land, might as well let him plow your furrow."

I declined to dignify her bawdy remark with a comment. Willie Campbell had leased the land around Dahlia House, and he had a fine crop of cotton in the ground. Egyptian cotton and the new strain that burst into boles of fiber already tinted green and blue. Ignoring Jitty, who was wavering in and out of existence at the foot of the swing, I sipped my julep and rubbed Sweetie Pie's belly with the toe of my boot.

"You lookin' mighty self-satisfied for a woman whose inner thighs are sore from a horse. There's a better way to get that lazy look on your face." She crystallized to the left of the swing, effectively blocking my view of the driveway.

My eyebrows rose in an inquisitive arch. Only yesterday she was one hot mama in spandex and spikes. Now she looked like Sunday morning church in a black-and-white photograph. Jitty was once again hip-hopping the decades, searching for the era that best suited her current attitude.

"What gives?" I asked, indicating the shirtwaist dress and sensible flats. "Your space boots need new heels?"

"I've been giving our predicament a lot of serious thought. What we need around here is some conviction, a dream, something to work toward. I'm gonna get it for us."

On my last three cases I'd been stabbed, shot, and generally bruised on all body parts. None of that struck fear into me the way Jitty did. I sat up a little straighter in the swing, taking care not to spill my julep. It contained the last bit of scraggly mint I'd been able to grow. "What do you mean by that?"

"I'm talking about passion and a belief in something. Have you forgotten your mama, Sarah Booth? She believed in something, and she fought to have it."

I nodded. "Yeah, I remember. Folks around here refer to Mama as 'that socialist.'"

"She wasn't a socialist. She was a woman who saw inequality, and she wanted to change it. She wanted all people, no matter what color or gender, to have equal opportunity."

"And she started a commune on this land, which nearly sent the entire county into a convulsion."

"It was your daddy who started the commune. Your mama just went along with it."

"You know, Jitty, if I'd had normal parents and been raised to be a Daddy's Girl, I might have turned out more satisfactorily, from your point of view."

I was a bitter disappointment to Dahlia House's resident haint. It was an uphill climb for Jitty as she tried to force me into the role of MFF, manipulative femme fatale. She wanted me wed and bred, or at least bred, so there would be an heir to reside in Dahlia House. Delaneys had occupied this land since before the War between the States. Jitty had no desire to find a new place to hang out should I not produce the next generation.

"You don't have to be a Daddy's Girl, Sarah Booth, but it would be nice if you'd bathe and hold off on the drinkin' until after lunch." She pointed at the julep cup in my hand. It was fine pewter, engraved with my mother's initials in an intricate pattern of twining ivy. "Puttin' that devil's intoxicant in a fine cup won't change what it is."

I looked at her from under a furrowed brow. "You're not turning into a teetotaler, are you?" I'd endured a number of different attitudes from Jitty, but I wasn't about to tolerate someone who lectured me constantly on my vices—especially not when that same someone would put me in the most intimate of acts with a perfect stranger if it would produce a child.

"Nothin' wrong with a drink ever' now and again, as long as it don't rob a person of her dreams. Looks to me like you might be headed down the path to destruction, what with your heels hiked up on the swing and those skintight britches clingin' to your ass."

I studied Jitty closer. She was wearing a dress that looked like it had come out of my Aunt LouLane's closet. One thing I'd always admired about Jitty was her flair. She could carry off just about any look. She'd even straightened her hair and curled it under. All she needed was a sweater thrown over her shoulders and a Bible in her hand. She'd make a perfect minister's wife, circa 1960-something.

"What, exactly, is it you want me to do?" I asked.

"It's a toss-up between findin' you a man and findin' you some work. Either one will do at this point."

The bullet wound in my arm had healed just fine. There wasn't a reason I couldn't get out and beat the bushes for a client. The truth was, I'd given in completely to the joy of riding Reveler and feeling the rhythm of the passing summer days. There was plenty of time in the future to concentrate on what I ought to be doing.

Jitty took two steps away from the swing to face the front of the house. The shadows of the pink lemonade and coral honey-suckle vines that crept up the trellis beside the porch cast an intricate pattern of light and dark over her, and I was reminded again of a black-and-white photograph.

She took a deep breath and slowly began to hum. Deep, rich, and throbbing with emotion, the sound seemed to seep from her, as she stared down the driveway. I was transfixed. With all of her talents, Jitty had never confessed that she could sing. I was also jealous.

"Sum-mertime, and the livin' is ea-sy. Fish are jumpin', and the cotton is high."

I closed my eyes and let the words slide through me. It was a song that always touched me, and in Jitty's powerful contralto, I felt the hairs on my arms stand on end.

"Your daddy's rich, and your mama's good-lookin'." She stopped abruptly, forcing me to open my eyes and glare at her.

"Now that you've shown me you can sing, keep doing it," I commanded.

"Shush," she said, cocking her head in an age-old attitude of listening. "If you ain't got the blues now, you're gonna," she said as she vanished into thin air.

"Jitty!" I hissed. I hated it when she delivered one of those enigmatic one-liners and then disappeared. "Jitty, you're cheating. You can't just say something like that and take off." But she could. Jitty could not be summoned or dismissed. If she'd ever been servile, she'd long forgotten the basic deportment.

"Sarah Booth?" The voice that called out held some concern. "Who are you talkin' to?"

I recognized John Bell Washington's voice instantly. He was a blues guitarist I'd met on my last case, thanks to the cyber-intervention of a teenager. Nonetheless, J. B. was a nice guy who'd risked a lot to help me.

"I'm over here in the swing," I called out to him, rising to give him a hug as he came up the steps to the secluded shade of the small side porch. J. B. was every woman's dilemma—handsome and frequently unemployed. The work schedule for a blues guitarist was strictly seasonal. J. B. had another major talent as a masseur when he chose to work the day shift, which wasn't often as long as his mama supported his desire to play music.

He walked around the corner of the porch toward me, a puzzled look on his handsome face. "Who were you talkin' to?" he asked again.

"Myself, I guess." I blushed becomingly. For all that I'd disavowed the tactics of a Daddy's Girl, there were a few harmless maneuvers that I deployed when necessary.

The blush effectively derailed his curiosity. At a momentary loss, he thrust a newspaper toward me. "What do you think of this?"

Luckily, women of the Delta in the Daddy's Girl ilk aren't expected to read newspapers. In fact, being even moderately well-informed is a deadly sin and can lead to freethinking. I took the paper from his hand and read it with open curiosity. It wasn't easy to miss the article he wanted me to see. It was outlined in bold black ink.

"Blues Blizzard Scott Hampton Arrested for Brutal Murder." I scanned the story, which was a thumbnail sketch of race, music, and hot tempers that had plagued the nation since the sixties.

The dead man was one Ivory Keys, an acclaimed piano player who owned the most popular nightclub in Kudzu, a thriving, mostly black community on the west side of Sunflower County. Needless to say, Ivory was black. Scott Hampton, heir to the Michigan auto-manufacturing family, was white. Of interest was the fact that both men had served time in the Michigan State Penitentiary, their sentences overlapping slightly in the nineties.

Ivory Keys had been brutally stabbed in his own nightclub, Playin' the Bones, where Scott was the featured talent of the wildly popular club band. Keys had hired the white musician when he got out of prison after serving his time on a cocaine charge. Apparently, Keys and Hampton had had a rather unusual relationship dating back to their prison days.

The murder weapon and money, thought to have been stolen

They were very close, more like a father and son than . . . Scott loved my husband."

"Even people who love each other can do harm to each other," I said softly. In some cases, it was all the more reason for violence.

"Scott didn't do this thing."

"Why are you so certain that he's innocent?" It was a fair question.

"Why are you so certain that he's guilty?" she countered, but with a sad smile.

"The evidence—"

"I know the evidence," she interrupted, but with much less force. "Murder weapon, money, all of it. Anyone could have put that knife and that money in Scott's saddlebags. Anyone. And that's all they've got. A knife and some money. They don't have motive."

"They're looking at robbery and/or a desire to get out of the two-year contract Ivory signed him to." She had to hear it sooner or later.

"Hogwash. Scott didn't want out of his contract. He and Ivory loved that club. They sat up nights talking and planning about what to do next. That boy and that club brought my husband immense pleasure."

I couldn't argue with her view of things, but I could keep pressing my only advantage. "That still doesn't explain why you think Scott is innocent."

She reached down and picked up a ring I hadn't noticed on the coffee table. When she held it up, the light struck it golden. A wedding band. I noticed the silent tears running down her cheeks. For a moment, her age showed.

"I can't decide whether to wear my ring or take it off," she said. "Seems odd being married to a dead man, yet that's how it is. My husband, so alive and full of music and joy, walked out of this house Monday afternoon and now he'll never come home again."

I swallowed the lump in my throat.

"Let me tell you something about Scott Hampton. He saved

"Yes, ma'am." I really hadn't wanted to say that, but evasion, even born out of kindness, wasn't Ida Mae's style.

"Come in and sit down," she said, finally stepping out of the doorway.

I followed her inside the house. Neat and colorful, just like the yard. Sunflowers nodded in a large vase on the dining room table. Glancing out the window, I saw what looked like a two-acre field full of the big, yellow flowers with the black centers. Some of the blooms were at least eight inches wide.

"Beautiful," I said, gesturing toward the window.

"Yes, they are," she said slowly. "Ivory loved them. He said they were smarter than us humans because they turned their faces up to the sun to accept God's blessings and they never questioned the right or wrong of it."

I sat on the edge of the chair she indicated. I hadn't noticed at first, but all around me were religious icons. A crucified Jesus hung on one wall, along with a beautifully framed painting of the Last Supper. Mary, halo glowing, hung on another wall. There were also pictures of Jesus with the little children crowded around him, and one depicting the tomb with the stone rolled away and Jesus ascending above the tomb. Beside that was a pair of praying hands. The ceramic rendition was uninspired, and I could see it had been painted by a child.

"My son did that," Ida Mae said. "Emanuel. He made that at vacation Bible school when he was eight." She spoke with such sadness I wondered if her son had died. I didn't want to ask such a personal question, especially not when she'd just lost her husband to an act of violence.

I put the check on the coffee table in front of her. She looked down at it a moment.

"I want you to help Scott. He didn't kill my husband, no matter what people say."

"The evidence—"

"Damn the evidence!" She spoke so sharply that I actually jumped a little.

"I'm sorry," she said. "I just know Scott didn't kill my husband.

warding off evil. I couldn't remember if you were supposed to make a wish on the tree or if you placed the empty glass bottles on branches to keep the devil at bay. Although the sun was hot on my head and skin, chill-bumps danced over my arms.

Ida Mae answered my knock immediately. She'd obviously been standing at the window, watching me. She wasn't exactly what I'd expected.

I guess in my mind I'd been prepared for either a stout, matronly woman or a nightclub lady. Ida Mae Keys was neither. She was a tall, slender woman with gray-streaked hair that was carefully cut and curled. The navy suit said businesswoman, as did the sensible pumps. Instead of the sixty-something I knew her to be, she looked forty and in excellent health.

"I'm Sarah Booth Delaney," I said, holding out my hand.

Her handshake was firm and perfunctory, just as her question was direct. "Is Scott out of jail?"

"The bond hearing's set for Friday. It's going to be a high bond."

"I can sell some things and make it."

I took a breath as I tried to decide the best way to say what I'd come to tell her. "Mrs. Keys, I'm returning your check." I pulled it out of the pocket of my slacks and held it out to her. I'd already decided not to mention the noose. "Scott Hampton doesn't want my help or yours. He told me to tell you to keep the money."

Ida Mae looked at the check but made no effort to touch it. "Scott didn't hire you, so he can't fire you." It was as simple as that in her mind.

"He won't cooperate with me. Under those conditions, it wouldn't be right for me to take your money." I extended my arm.

"I'll have a talk with Scott. He'll come around."

I didn't think so. In fact, I didn't think even a personal conversation with either God or Satan would have much of an impact on Scott Hampton.

"I don't think I can help Scott."

She put one finger on her lips and stared at me. "Because you think he's guilty."

GROOMED WAS THE FIRST WORD THAT POPPED INTO MY HEAD AS I got out of the car in Ida Mae Keys' front yard. *Colorful* was the second. Zinnias lined the dirt walkway. Gerber daisies bordered the small wooden house, and daylilies in all varieties bloomed orange, pink, purple, and lavender. These were not just flowers that could be planted and left to fend for themselves. They required care.

As I walked to the steps, the tinkle of glass against glass stopped me. At the side of the house, I saw the branches of a bottle tree waving gently in the breeze. Coke, Nehi, Bubble-up, Dr Pepper, and Barq's soft-drink bottles had been slipped onto the stout branches of the tree. It was a sight from a high adventure of my childhood, when my mother had taken me to a palm reader in Memphis. The old woman had at least a dozen bottle trees in her yard. I'd sat on the steps and listened to the voices of the bottles as they brushed and touched each other in the wind, while my mother had gotten her fortune told.

The bottle tree was either a symbol of good luck or a way of

Mayhem met my gaze. The place had been trashed, and it didn't take me long to find the brownish stain on the floor that marked the location where the body had lain. A stool and table were overturned by the bloodstain. I could picture Ivory Keys sitting at the table, working.

Eyes adjusting to the dim light, I stood still and looked around. It was a very cool place. The bar was mahogany and looked as if it might have been salvaged from the old Sunflower Hotel when it was torn down. Tables and chairs, all heavy and comfortable, were scattered on three sides of the big dance floor, and up against the walls were thickly padded booths. An assortment of glasses hung from racks over the bar, which was fully stocked.

The stage where the band played was set with drums, an upright piano, a well-used amplifier on a chair, and mike stands.

When my eyes had adjusted to the dim light, I moved deeper into the club. According to Coleman, Ivory Keys had been stabbed with a homemade prison shank. The knife had been found in Scott's possession, wiped clean of prints.

Pretty stupid for a man who thought himself so smart.

The wreckage in the nightclub indicated that someone was hunting for something. The cash register was bashed open, the empty drawer hanging out.

Money—nearly three grand—had also been found on Scott. But why would Scott wreck the club if the money he wanted was in the cash register? The obvious answer was that he was looking for something other than money.

I took my time and fixed a mental image of the club in my head. Ivory's murder had been brutal. Coleman hadn't said exactly, but there was the implication that Ivory had been beaten before he died. The destruction of the club showed a form of rage. Scott Hampton, with his contempt for all around him, was most probably the man who'd killed Ivory Keys. It was time to talk to Ida Mae and make her see reason.

I walked out of the jail, determined to return Ida Mae's check and not to lose a wink of sleep over Scott Hampton. The sheriff's office was empty, thank goodness, and I left a message for Coleman to call me when he found out who'd put the noose in the tree.

THE COMMUNITY OF Kudzu was little more than a crossroads in the northwest corner of the county. Driving through the flat cotton fields, I scanned the horizon for the simple church steeple that would mark my destination. It was said that during the twenties and thirties, a nightclub at this crossroads had been one of the hottest blues joints in the nation. All of the greats had played there as they roved the South, all headed for Detroit and eventual fame.

During this time, clubs known as juke joints dotted the dirt roads of the Delta. Open mainly on weekends, these bars were often little more than shanties where the black folks could gather to drink and dance. From the burning sun of the cotton fields to the sweet heat of a summer night, the blues had been birthed to express the sorrow, desperation, and power of sex that told the story of a time, a place, and a people.

In the distance I saw the steeple and turned off the highway onto a dirt road that cut, straight and narrow, between the rows of cotton. In less than ten minutes, I stopped at Blessed Zion Independent Church. A small sign announced services for Ivory Keys at ten o'clock Saturday morning. Behind the church, two elderly black men were digging the grave.

From in front of the church, I could see the nightclub at the crossroads. Although I'd driven to Kudzu to return Mrs. Keys' check, I decided it wouldn't hurt to take a look inside.

Playin' the Bones looked like a small war might have been fought in and around the club. The front door was locked and remnants of crime-scene tape lay on the ground. The back door was closed but unlocked. I walked inside.

from the club, were found in Hampton's possession. He was in Sunflower County jail charged with first-degree murder.

"Do you know him?" I asked slowly.

"I knew them both. A better man than Ivory Keys never walked this earth."

"And Hampton?"

J. B.'s face showed his ambivalence. "He's one of the most talented guitarists I've ever known. Maybe better than Stevie Ray Vaughan."

"What's he doing stuck in Kudzu, Mississippi, then?"

"If I had to name one reason, I'd say attitude. He's got a chip on his shoulder larger than the Rock of Gibraltar. And he's always eager for someone to try and knock it off."

"Drugs?" I asked. After all, he'd been in the Big House once for possession. Many a crime had been fueled by a snoot full of white powder.

J. B. shook his head. "I heard he was clean. That was one of Ivory's demands before he gave Scott the job. No drugs."

"And Scott lived up to his promise, until he plunged a knife into Ivory's back." I sounded skeptical because I was. The picture of Scott Hampton in the newspaper showed an arrogant, angry man, with light eyes and pale hair expertly cut to look oh-so-disheveled. I could easily read the "spoiled rich kid" smirk. I was familiar enough with it on the faces of the young men my age from the Delta: the sons of Buddy Clubbers, who'd grown up to believe the entire world was their oyster. These were the men who were paving the rich Delta soil to create strip malls and other eyesores called progress.

"It may not be that simple," J. B. said.

The hint of doubt in his voice hooked me. "So you believe he's innocent?" I asked.

"What I believe isn't important. What Mrs. Keys believes is. And she believes Scott is innocent. She wants to hire you to find the real killer."

I motioned J. B. into the house. I'd already suffered a lapse as a hostess by not offering a cool libation. I was about to remedy that, as well as replenish my own drink.

When we were in the dim interior of Dahlia House's parlor, I poured the bourbon over ice and handed him his glass.

"To music," he said, and we both drank.

"Now let me get this straight. The widow of Ivory Keys wants to hire me to prove Scott Hampton, the man who was found with the murder weapon in his possession, not to mention some three thousand dollars in possibly stolen money, is innocent."

J. B. reached into his jeans pocket and pulled out a piece of paper. He unfolded it and handed it to me. It was a check for five thousand dollars signed by Ida Mae Keys.

"I told her your fee was ten thousand, and she said she'd pay the rest when you got Scott out of jail."

2

FRESHLY BATHED, MASCARAED, AND UNFORTUNATELY ENACTING
Truman Capote's description of ladies melting like marshmallows
in the summer heat, I drove to the Sunflower County Courthouse
with the roadster's a.c. on full throttle. A phone call to Ida Mae
Keys had confirmed the singular fact that she wanted Scott
Hampton out of jail and proven innocent. Ida Mae refused to ex-
pound on her reasons and had abruptly gotten off the phone, stat-
ing point-blank that she had no need to meet with me, just get on
with the job.

Her check was safely tucked away in the old pie safe at Dahlia
House, since I'd determined not to deposit it until I talked to
Coleman. In my past P.I. conduct, I'd slipped across the fine line
of ethics a few times, but I wasn't going to take money from an elderly black woman whose husband had just been killed if I
couldn't help her.

Coleman Peters, Sunflower County sheriff, was the logical
place to start. Besides, Coleman and I had something personal to
finish. Although neither of us had acted on it, a strong emotional

bond had formed between us. I'd come to rely on his honesty and good sense. There was more, though. Coleman didn't waffle. Not in what he thought or felt. He was rock solid, and that was sweet nectar.

Coleman was freshly separated from his wife, an event I had not played a role in. *Actively* not played a role in. For the last twelve weeks, while my shoulder was healing, I'd done my best to stay out of his way. He'd come out to Dahlia House several times to check on me, but I had not put myself in his path. He had decisions to make that no one else had a right to interfere in.

As I parked beneath a pecan tree beside the First Baptist Church of Zinnia, I scanned the courthouse lawn. Memories came, unbidden, of childhood summer days when my father hauled my bicycle to the courthouse in the trunk of his car. While he worked as a judge, I was free to ride the streets of Zinnia. It had seemed such a big place then, with so many exciting possibilities to explore. Unlimited potential. Only ten years ago, I'd still felt that way about myself. But my stint in New York had taught me some hard realities. Dreaming wasn't enough. There were a lot of other elements in the equation of grabbing success and happiness.

As I crossed the street, I was thinking about what Jitty had said earlier about dreams. Somewhere along the way, had I become afraid to dream? It was a question to ponder.

The heat was intense and I was glad to step inside the courthouse. When my father had served as circuit court judge, there had been no air-conditioning in the building. Though I often took the troglodyte, no-progress stance and rejected modern improvements, air-conditioning was a true miracle. I stood for a moment under a vent, hoping to dry up the rivulet of sweat that had begun to slip down my spine and into my underpants. Melted was exactly how I felt.

The sheriff's office door was open, and a sound bite of conversation caught my attention.

"He's guilty as sin," the dispatcher said in a country twang veneered with sophistication. "He sits in the jail cell, feet propped on the bars, cool as a cucumber. If he feels anything, it sure ain't, I mean, isn't, remorse."

"He's hard," Deputy Dewayne Dattilo agreed. Dattilo was a new addition to the force, as was the dispatcher.

"He can play the guitar. I heard him a few times when I was out dancin'. He could make a girl's bones melt, if you know what I mean." The dispatcher's voice carried grudging admiration, topped off with a portion of sexual hunger. "He had the women squirmin' in their seats, or those of them who could stay seated. And that one crazy gal, man, she all but jumped on his leg."

"She's gonna be trouble," Dewayne said, and not without a little eagerness.

I entered and was greeted with wary curiosity from one and dislike from the other.

"Is Coleman in?" It was a courtesy question. I could see him at his desk in his office.

"I'll see." The dispatcher, known as Bo-Peep because of her overpermed, blondeened hair, went into Coleman's office and closed the door. I couldn't help but notice that she had a great figure and a walk that was all invitation. Coleman had hired her while I was at Dahlia House healing. She'd worked as a temp last winter. In those brief two weeks we'd developed a mutual animosity club. Now she was on the payroll full time, permanent.

Within minutes she came out and swayed over to the counter. "The sheriff says he can see you," she said. Leaning closer, she whispered, sotto voce, "He's gone back to his wife, though, so don't get your hopes up."

I brushed past her, determined not to show the shock I felt. Once in Coleman's office, I closed the door, composing myself as I turned around to face him. His blue eyes held sadness, matched by the long line of his mouth.

"Ida Mae Keys has hired me to prove Scott Hampton is innocent," I said, wanting to immediately put the visit on the footing of officialdom.

Coleman shook his head. "I like that old woman, and I hate to see her waste her money and your time. You've got a perfect record for solving cases, Sarah Booth. This is one you might want to walk away from. The evidence we have is circumstantial, but it's pretty damning."

"Fill me in." Concise, professional, that was the tone I had to maintain. I focused on the lines at the corners of his mouth that hadn't been there two months before. He might be back with Connie, but he wasn't a happy man.

"Murder weapon found in his possession. Just over three thousand dollars, which we believe was stolen from the club, also in his possession." Coleman sounded more tired than convinced.

"What was the murder weapon?"

"Prison-type shank. Handmade."

"Where'd you find it?"

"In the saddlebag of Hampton's motorcycle. The bike was parked outside his house. He's renting a place on Bilbo Lane, way out in the sticks."

"Anyone could have put the money in the bag," I pointed out.

"He had a bad attitude when we went out to talk to him. He refused to talk to us, and we had to get a search warrant. Let me just say that he didn't show a tremendous amount of regret or remorse when we told him Ivory was dead."

Scott Hampton seemed to be his own worst enemy. "And you've determined, beyond all doubt, that the shank belongs to Hampton. Again, I'll point out that someone could have put it in the saddlebags of his bike."

"Someone could have, but we don't believe that to be true."

"Prints?"

"None. It was wiped."

"How many times was Keys stabbed, and where?" Coleman knew I could get all of this information from Doc Sawyer, the man who would perform the autopsy.

He sighed. "Stabbed in the chest. Three times."

"Anything else?"

"He didn't die instantly." He hesitated. "And that's all I'm going to say about the actual crime."

He'd been fair in giving me as much as he felt he could. I felt a flurry of anger as I realized how much I'd come to count on Coleman's fairness.

"So robbery is the motive?" I snapped back into professional mode.

"Ivory had Hampton tied up in an ironclad contract at Playin' the Bones for the next two years. Hampton has developed quite a reputation, and he'd gotten some big offers from other clubs. His career could have been on the rise, except he was legally tied to Keys."

"So you think he killed his benefactor for the money or to escape his contract?" I'd learned a few things in my brief stint as a P.I. Murder generally had one very specific motive. I wanted to know which one Coleman was going to try to prove when it came to a trial.

"We're still investigating."

"What about bond?" Ida Mae said she wanted Scott out as soon as possible.

"Friday. Judge Hartwell." His mouth hardened into a thin line as he said the name. Hartwell was only a justice court judge, but he had a reputation for rash and prejudicial behavior. "It's going to be high." He put the pencil down and placed his hands on the desk. "Let this one pass, Sarah Booth. It's going to get ugly. A lot of old scabs are going to be ripped off here."

His advice was meant as a kindness, but I wasn't in the mood to accept the crumbs of his generosity. The least he could have done was tell me himself that he was going back to his wife.

"Can I see Hampton?"

Coleman's eyebrows lifted at my tone. "Sure." He picked up a pencil and twirled it in his fingers, but his gaze held mine. "Is there something bothering you?"

"Not a thing." The wall of pride had erected itself with amazing speed. We had never spoken of our feelings for each other, so there were no words to take back.

"I've been meaning to come out to see you," he said. His gaze fell to the blotter on his desk. He seemed fascinated by the scribbling there.

I could have helped him out, but I wasn't in a charitable frame of mind.

"Connie and I are gonna give it one more try," he said, finally looking at me.

"I hope it works out." Thunderation, what did he think I would say?

For a split second, he registered surprised regret. Then he caught himself and nodded. "I'll have Dewayne take you back to see Hampton." He stood up and walked past me.

I could have put out my hand and touched his arm. The smallest gesture would have stopped him. But I had no right to make that move, and I let him walk past me without a word.

SCOTT HAMPTON WAS everything I expected. His face, undeniably handsome, seemed fixed in a permanent sneer. His blond hair was gelled back, à la Elvis, giving him a strange dated appearance that was at odds with his eyes, which said he was a man of the moment.

"Mrs. Keys has hired me to prove you didn't kill her husband." I didn't bother to hide the doubt in my tone. Scott Hampton sat on his bunk, rocking slightly to a beat I couldn't hear. He didn't inspire compassion or confidence.

"Tell her to save her money." He stood up and walked to the bars.

I had not been aware of the full measure of his sexuality until he moved. He was a jungle cat, a predator. It was in his walk, in the way he held me with his eyes. He was a dangerous man, and he liked knowing that I knew it. The first hint of a smile touched his lips.

I held his gaze until mine slid down his body, exactly as he wanted it to. The tattoo on his left arm caught my interest. The skull and crossbones looked professionally done, though the black ink spoke of decoration acquired in prison.

"I can't help you if you won't help yourself," I said, finding the words from a million old television shows.

"I don't want your help," he countered as he lounged against the bars of the cell. "Give Ida Mae back her money and leave me alone."

"For some reason, she wants to believe you're innocent," I told him. "Maybe she's crazy, but that's what she believes."

"Do you make a living taking advantage of old folks or is this a special case?"

I felt as if he'd slapped me. "Listen, Hampton, if it were up to me, I'd just as soon walk away from this. The sheriff is pretty certain you're going to Parchman prison for a good, long stretch. You may have done time in Michigan, but that's kindergarten compared to Parchman."

"So I've heard. Do they still work the inmates in the cotton fields? I might come in handy, singing the blues. Back to the roots of the music, you might say."

I was suddenly tired. Scott Hampton was a man who buzzed with electricity. He sucked at my energy level. "This may be a joke to you, but I'm not working for you. You can help me or not. Either way it's up to Mrs. Keys. I'm going to tell her that I think you're a waste of time, but she decides what happens next."

"Make her decide to drop this thing," Scott said, his voice even but his eyes sending all kinds of warnings. He tried to hold my gaze, but a breeze outside the jail caught the branches of an old magnolia tree that stood not far from the statue of Johnny Reb, the bronze image that memorialized all the men who'd given their lives to noble ideals enforced with foolish violence. My gaze locked on the rope that swung so lazily from the graceful branches of the tree, a hangman's noose on the end.

Scott knew that I saw it and a sound, almost animal, came from him. "Keep Ida Mae out of this. Give her back her money," he ordered.

"Who put up the noose?" I asked him, my voice only a little shaky. The South is filled with symbols—neon crosses, snakes and their handlers, bedsheets, flags, magnolias, and mockingbirds. But there is none more potent than the noose. Someone had sent Scott a very explicit message, and he knew it.

"Stay out of it," he said.

"Did you see them?"

"No."

"Have you told the sheriff?"

"No." He grinned, daring me to ask more.

"Coleman will find out who did this," I said. It didn't matter what Coleman thought about Scott Hampton personally. Someone had broken the law, and in doing so had stirred up the horror and hatred of the past. Someone would pay for that.

"My best advice to you, Ms. Sarah Booth Delaney, is that you keep your nose out of this, and don't take Ida Mae's money. She doesn't have much and she's going to need what she has to survive this."

"Tell me one thing, Mr. Hampton," I said, finding that cool, level voice that I needed. "Did you kill Ivory Keys? If you say yes, I'll take that answer to Ida Mae and advise her to let it go. But until you confess, she isn't going to drop this."

He walked to the window and looked out. Following his gaze, I saw deputies Dewayne Dattilo and Gordon Walters outside, removing the hangman's noose with great care. Someone had finally seen it and reported it.

When Scott came back to the bars, his face was hard, his mouth a thin line. "I'm tried and convicted. If they don't kill me before the trial, I'm going to Parchman. Some amateur private detective isn't going to change that at all."

"Nice dodge. Did you kill Ivory Keys?" I repeated. The least he could do was confess and let Ida Mae off the hook.

His hands grabbed the bars so fast I involuntarily stepped back. The smile that touched his face held satisfaction. "It's a good thing to be afraid of me," he said. "A very good thing."

Ivory's life when they were in prison together. He saved his life *and* his left hand. Ivory called that his boogie hand." A fleeting smile softened the pain on her face. "In repayment, Ivory taught Scott how to play the blues. You see, they both owed each other their very existence."

She walked over to an old upright piano that was missing the front panel. Trailing a finger, she glissaded down the keys. "My husband had a dream, Miss Delaney. A big dream. And he and Scott were making it come true."

"What kind of dream?"

She turned back to face me. "That music could heal all the old wounds and bring people together. Ivory said there was a power in the music that Scott played. It made people forget if they were black or white or poor or rich. It spoke to the bones and to the spirit, and it taught folks how to live with sorrow and joy. He believed that if folks could forget color for the length of a song, they could forget it for an hour, and then a week, and then a month. You get the idea. My husband and Scott were going to change the world, and they'd made a good start on it. That's why I know Scott Hampton is innocent."

She walked over to the coffee table, picked up the check, and stuck it in the pocket of my camp shirt. "Prove it. The worst thing that could happen to me would be to see Ivory's dream torn down like this. I can stand him dying, because I know it won't be long before I'll be with him for eternity. But here on earth, I can't let his dream be killed. Scott didn't kill my husband, and I want you to find out who did."

4

SO I'M A SUCKER FOR A WOMAN WITH CONVICTIONS. THE CHECK was still in my pocket, and I was still working for Ida Mae Keys. It was time to bring my partner in on the case.

I turned down the long drive to Hilltop, a locale I normally tried to avoid. At the sight of Oscar and Tinkie Richmond's Tara-like estate, a tidal wave of guilt slammed into me.

One night, not too long ago, I'd hidden in the bushes beside the house and waited until Chablis Richmond came prancing outside to do her doggy business in the grass. As soon as the little fluffball was in reach, I dognapped her. It was the ransom money Tinkie Richmond (née Bellcase) paid to me that saved Dahlia House from the auction block, and it was dognapping Chablis that eventually led Tinkie to hire me for my first case.

I'd taken Tinkie in as a partner in my P.I. business as penance for that act, but the cold truth was that it was one of the best moves I'd ever made. There were times when Tinkie saved the day—not to mention my life. She was the perfect partner, and it was time I filled her in on Scott Hampton.

The minute I rang the doorbell, I heard the excited yipping of Chablis. The Yorkie was spoiled, pampered, sun-glitzed by a professional colorist—and lovingly embedded in my heart. As I listened closer, I heard a distinctive baying.

Tinkie opened the door on a gentle reprimand for the dogs to be quiet. She was nearly knocked down by a big, brindle-colored hound that came bounding onto the porch, baying like she was on the trail of a deer.

"Sweetie Pie!" I groped for her collar. "What are you doing here?" Sweetie was my dog, and the last I'd seen her, she was snoozing under the kitchen table at Dahlia House.

"Chablis and I stopped by for breakfast and you weren't home, so we brought Sweetie Pie to play. Chablis wanted some company."

A dark suspicion clouded my brain. "You're not thinking of taking Sweetie to the poodle parlor again, are you?" Tinkie had taken Sweetie to a doggy salon and given her a new look, changing her from a brindled red tic hound to a vibrant shade of redbone. The color, after repeated washings, had finally faded away.

"It's the Canine Cut and Curl, and I promised you I wouldn't dye her ever again." Tinkie's lips pushed out into a provocative pout.

"That's wasted on me," I told her, walking toward the kitchen. "You can bring grown men to their knees with that pursed-up mouth of yours, but it doesn't have any effect on me."

"What's going on?" She opened the door and let Chablis out for a romp with Sweetie.

"I was just in the neighborhood." I sauntered slowly toward the kitchen. It was always better to let Tinkie get really hungry for details. I could hear the tippy-tap of her stiletto house slippers right behind me, and once again I had to admire her quick ability to move from one mood to the next. It was pure Daddy's Girl; a lesson in survival tactics. When a pout doesn't work, try a smile. But with Tinkie, the smile was always sincere, even if the pout was manufactured for effect.

My footsteps clomped and Tinkie's tapped across the imported tile of her kitchen floor. The place was a cavern. Huge. The walls and counters were lined with all the latest culinary tools, most of them used only by Margene, the cook. Tinkie could make coffee, and she did so with dispatch.

As she brewed, I filled her in on the Scott Hampton case. I didn't have to see her face to know she was distressed. Her posture told it all. When she did turn to face me, her eyebrows were drawn together.

"Sarah Booth, I heard about that killing, and I have to say, this is going to be a mess. All those damn Yankee reporters will be down here trying to make this 1964 again. We just got that fool Byron dela Beckwith convicted and all of that finally put to rest. We don't need this."

Truer words were never spoken. Mississippi was still stained by the blood of the past. Good people as tainted as the bad. While enormous prejudice and horrid acts of violence were committed in every state, Mississippi had served as a lightning rod for the attention of the rest of the nation.

"Need it or not, we're going to get it," I said. "We might as well face it head-on."

"I don't want to face it head-on. I went down to The Grove this morning to pick up Margene because her car's at the mechanics. She wouldn't ride with me. She told me to go home, that she'd find her own ride." There was hurt in Tinkie's face. "Margene's cooked for us since Oscar and I got married. She didn't want to be seen with me."

There was little I could do to take away the sting Tinkie was feeling, but I had another theory. "She may have been afraid to be seen with you." I told her about the noose.

"I hope Coleman finds those yahoos and puts them under the jail."

I doubled her sentiment. "I have to say, Scott Hampton isn't doing anything to help his case."

"Can't you just let this go?" she asked, sighing.

"I tried. I went to Ida Mae Keys' with the sole purpose of turning the case down. *You* go talk to that old woman and see if *you* can quit."

She shook her head slightly. "Why is she doing this?"

I had thought a little about that on the drive to Tinkie's. "Ida Mae knows what's going to come down here. Her husband's death has the power to divide the entire community again, and she doesn't want that to happen, because *he* wouldn't want that. Mr. Keys had some idea that music could heal the wounds of both races." I could see Tinkie thought I was nuts.

She put the coffee on the counter and slipped onto a stool beside me. "So tell me about Scott Hampton," she said. "He's incredibly hot. When he plays that guitar, it's like he's making love to it." She bit her bottom lip, sucking it in slightly and then letting it pop out. It was a habit of Tinkie's that made a drooling idiot out of even the most confident man. On occasion, I'd borrowed the mannerism, but I could never perform it as effectively as she did. "How did he strike you, Sarah Booth?"

"He's a total ass," I said, recalling his insolence and contempt. I had no desire to acknowledge his sexual appeal or admit that he frightened me a little.

Tinkie lifted an eyebrow and I could see her brain buzzing. "So how are we going to approach this?" she asked.

I grinned. Tinkie was in. "With great caution. I don't know that there's anything we can do. The evidence points to Hampton as the killer. But I told Mrs. Keys we'd try."

"Yes, *we'll* try, but there is one condition." Tinkie gave me a look that said she knew she had me.

"What?"

"An old school chum of Oscar's will be in town tonight. Go out to dinner with him."

"A banker?" I had nothing against bankers.

"Former banker. Independent investor now. I think you might find him interesting."

Tinkie was being coy, but she failed to realize that I happened to really like blind dates. Gambling, as far as slot machines, cards, or bingo, had never been one of my vices. But the old roulette wheel of romance piqued my interest. My theory was that a blind date could go either way, but no matter the outcome, I never ended up empty-handed. Either I had a good date or a good story to tell.

"Sounds perfect. What time, where, what to wear?"

My capitulation surprised Tinkie. "Tonight. The Club. I'll get back to you with the details. Aren't you even going to ask who it is?"

"Surprise me," I said as I walked to the door. "Now for your part, I want you to pump Oscar about the financial status of Ivory Keys and Playin' the Bones. Find out everything Oscar knows." I didn't give her a chance to ask another question. I whistled up my hound and left.

I'D GIVEN TINKIE her assignment. Oscar, her husband, was on the board of directors of Zinnia National Bank. In a small town like Zinnia, bank officials knew all the data. And Tinkie had incredibly effective ways of making Oscar talk. He didn't just talk, he gushed. By afternoon, I'd know whether Playin' the Bones was in the red or black and what the financial future had looked like for Ivory and Scott.

For my part, I went home to my computer. As much as I hated learning technology, I'd found the Web to be a place of many free facts. Even so, I wasn't prepared for the surfeit of information on Scott Hampton.

Especially not the kind of information I found.

While Scott dominated a lot of the blues Web sites, he was also listed on five neo-Nazi sites. Call me naïve, but I was shocked at the violence and racism rampant in those sites. I had just opened the third Aryan Nation site when I was brought up short. A skull-and-crossbones tattoo, an exact replica of the one on Scott's arm, was perfectly rendered on the screen.

The organization was the Bonesmen. An elite branch of the Aryan Brotherhood formed totally of convicted felons. The Bonesmen were one of the most violent of all prison gangs. Their listed enemies included blacks, Jews, Indians, both native and eastern, Asians, Hispanics, and Eskimos. They pretty much covered everyone who wasn't "white."

And guess who their poster boy was—Scott Hampton.

There were several links to music sites, and dreading what I'd find, I clicked through. Scott had an impressive body of work in the blues, but there was another side to his musical career. The titles of these songs, all produced by White Victory Studio, made my stomach knot with dread. The "N" word was in abundant supply, most frequently coupled with a violent verb or a sexual slur. Downloading the songs would take a while, so I went to the kitchen to rummage through the refrigerator.

I couldn't remember the last time I'd cleaned out the fridge, so I called Sweetie Pie in for help. If she sniffed at anything with disdain, we threw it away. After half an hour, the cupboard was looking bare, while the garbage was growing into a mountain. I was eyeing a container of what appeared to be macaroni and cheese. That was impossible. I hadn't made macaroni and cheese since I'd returned home to Dahlia House. I poked the container with a meat fork, seeing if anything moved inside.

"Fine time to clean the refrigerator."

Startled, I banged my head on the refrigerator door opening. Jitty was standing right behind me, crowding in close. I backed out and stood up straight.

"You've been harping at me for weeks to clean out the refrigerator. Now that I'm doing it, you don't like it." Having a nagging ghost on your heels twenty-four-seven can make a girl cross.

"You ought to have your head in that closet, pickin' out a dress to wear tonight. Or findin' one that fits."

That was it. I grabbed the container in question and tossed it at the garbage can. "I can wear everything in my closet," I said. "I'm tired of your cracks about my size."

"Your mama never gained an inch in her waist. She did a lot of walkin'. Some would have called it marchin', I suppose."

Jitty was wearing a navy, polka-dot skimmer, conservatively cut just above the knee. The dress was out of current character, but not nearly as much as the anger in her eyes.

"What's wrong with you?" Jitty would give me no peace until I heard her out.

"Your mama wouldn't be proud of what you're doin'."

I didn't even have to ask what. I knew. "I'm doin' what I'm doin' for Ida Mae Keys. She believes Scott Hampton is innocent, and she believes it enough to write a check for five grand."

"It's wrong. That man is bad, and he belongs in jail. Killin' Ivory Keys was a bad, bad thing. And don't go taking that innocent-till-proven-guilty attitude. You think he did it, too."

I sat down at the table. Jitty wasn't saying anything I didn't think. "What if he's innocent?"

Jitty paced the kitchen. "He's not innocent. He's a racist and a dope head. More than likely, he's a murderer. Coleman thinks he's guilty."

"Everyone thinks he's guilty, except Ida Mae Keys," I pointed out. "Right now, she's the one that counts."

"She's grievin' and tryin' hard to hang on to what little bit of her husband is left: his dream. That don't make it right for her to spend her money on that bad man. Don't make it right for you to take it."

I was going to hear this argument from a lot of people. I might as well hone my defenses on Jitty. "I'm only looking into the case. I won't take Ida Mae's money if it looks like I can't help."

"Help how? Help get that trash back out on the street?"

That, indeed, was the crux.

"Go listen to some of his *music*. Not the blues, but that other stuff," Jitty pressed. "Then you tell me he needs to be set loose on society."

Jitty's eyes were black chips of anger. I closed the refrigerator door and walked back upstairs to the computer. Three songs later, I lay down on my bed. My head was pounding and my stomach churned. Based on the recordings of White Victory Studio, Scott Hampton was one of the worst musicians I'd ever heard. His early rap songs were backed up by a band called the Brown Shirts, and the sick, racist rants never even came close to what I considered music. He was a vile man with a vile message. No matter how he'd reconfigured himself for public consumption in Sunflower County, Mississippi, he had once promoted hatred, racism, and violence with a passion that sickened me.

I had really stepped in it now.

I TOOK A long, hot bath and tried to think my way out of the predicament I found myself in. In my last case, I'd gone up against a mountain of circumstantial evidence *and* a signed confession from Lee McBride. But Lee was a person I'd known my entire life. She was someone I respected and knew to be good.

Based on my further Internet research on Scott Hampton, I learned he'd been on a quest for self-destruction for several years before he'd been arrested. He hated everyone and everything that wasn't white and male.

I'd found several sites that gave a brief history of the man. He was born into the very wealthy Hampton family of Detroit, Michigan. His grandfather had owned twenty Dodge dealerships in the area, and his father had increased that to thirty-one. Hampton Dodge was the name for Dodge vehicles in Michigan.

Scott was an only child, heir to fabulous wealth. But he'd squandered his initial inheritance. At the age of twenty-one he'd come into a million-dollar trust, and he'd taken the money and left.

Two years later, he was in serious trouble with the law. By the time he was twenty-five, he'd been convicted twice for possession of cocaine. By twenty-eight, he was arrested and convicted of possession with intent to sell. He was on the road to the Michigan Big House.

Six years later, he was out of prison and in Sunflower County, Mississippi, playing blues in a black man's high-end juke joint. In the past twelve months—since coming to Mississippi—Scott Hampton had cut two albums. The first was his rendition of Mississippi blues classics, drawn from the music of B. B. King, Mississippi John Hurt, Muddy Waters, and the mysterious Robert Johnson, who died of drinking whiskey poisoned by a jealous lover. The second album was compiled of original music written and performed by Hampton. Both had received critical acclaim. Scott was building a solid reputation, and I couldn't help but wonder how, based on the awful rap music I'd downloaded. It was a conversion that ranked close to a miracle.

How had a talentless rapper—and even I could judge he was talentless—become a master of the blues? What had happened to Scott Hampton during his prison term and his year in Kudzu?

An article published in a national blues magazine out of Helena, Arkansas, charged Hampton with following in the footsteps of Tommy Johnson. Johnson was one of several blues musicians said to have traded his soul to the devil for musical skill. I knew the legend, and had even traveled to several crossroads in north Mississippi where Johnson and Satan might have negotiated the bargain.

As the story went, Johnson had played the local juke joints with no apparent talent. And then he'd disappeared from the Mississippi scene for a while. When he returned, walking through the dark Delta night to the light and laughter of a club, he'd climbed up on the stage and delivered the blues with such power that his audience was stunned.

It wasn't hard to draw the same conclusion about Hampton. He'd come out of prison with a talent that no one could explain.

A cool breeze whispered across my skin, and I looked up to see if Jitty had entered the bedroom. But I was alone, and it was only the legend of a bargain made between an ambitious musician and a dark stranger on a hot summer night that was giving me the chills.

Before I turned off the computer, I went to an on-line music store and ordered both of Scott Hampton's latest CDs. I'd heard his old stuff. Now I wanted to judge his talent with the blues. I clicked next day freight. Before I made any decisions, I wanted to listen to the music that had made women melt and men forget their prejudices.

5

SINCE I'D CLEANED THE REFRIGERATOR AND NOTHING REMAINED inside it except a questionable hunk of cheese wrapped in green cellophane—I hoped the cellophane was green—I decided to drive to Millie's Café and "do" a late lunch.

Although she was in her fifties, Millie was my thumb on the pulse of Sunflower County nightlife. Or at least the nightlife outside The Club, which was where the Daddy's Girls and their fathers and future husbands, the Buddy Clubbers, partook of liquor, dance, character assassination, and general bitchiness.

My stomach growled a warning that a serious caloric disaster was in the offing as I drove through Zinnia's main street, called, appropriately, Main Street, and parked the Mercedes in the crowded lot at the café. I was thinking of several of my stick-thin contemporaries who frequently claimed that they "just flat forgot to eat lunch."

My own body was far better organized. In the thirty-four years of my life, it had never forgotten a single meal.

Millie hailed me with a shout and a wave as she whipped

through the café pouring iced tea and coffee. She could handle both at once, a pot in one hand and a pitcher in the other. She served only sweet tea and regular coffee. She didn't mess around with unsweetened tea or decaf.

I took a seat at the counter, put in an order for fried chicken, turnip greens, fried green tomatoes, fried okra, and corn bread.

"Why not change the turnip greens to French fries and make it a totally brown meal?" Millie teased.

"I'll put some catsup on the plate and balance the entire thing out," I assured her.

She plopped an iced tea down in front of me. "I'll be back."

She was, within ten minutes. The main lunch rush was ending, and the place was clearing out.

"What can you tell me about Playin' the Bones?" I asked as I stabbed several crisp okra morsels.

"A year ago, it was closing down. That man who was murdered, Ivory Keys, was a great pianist, but he couldn't get a singer. The club band was good, but they didn't have the necessary youth appeal to bring the thirty-somethings into the club. Then Scott Hampton started playin'." She arched her eyebrows. "I heard him last Memorial Day." Her mouth opened slightly as she was caught in some memory. "Wow. That's all I can say."

"Hot?"

"Honey, he had every woman in that place ready to play nasty right there on the stage."

"What about his music?"

"If you closed your eyes, you wouldn't know he was a white boy from the North. During part of the show he was using an old bottleneck slide, and I swear, it could have been Mississippi John Hurt or Sun House. He could make that guitar talk sweet and promise a lot of pleasure."

"As well as pain," I said, almost under my breath.

"As well as pain," she agreed. "That's life, Sarah Booth. Life *and* the blues."

"So what's the gossip around town regarding the murder?"

She glanced around the café to make sure all of her customers were chowing down. Leaning closer, she spoke softly. "There's a lot of high emotion around Ivory's death. Folks loved Scott's music, but they didn't much cotton to the man himself."

I waited for more, though I fully understood what Millie was talking about. With his arrogance and seemingly permanent sneer, Scott could rub a saint the wrong way.

"Ivory Keys set a great store by Scott. They shared some prison experience that bonded them together. I've heard two or three versions of the jail story," she shrugged, "but the bottom line was that Scott and Ivory were like blood kin. They both had a love of music and a dream of a different kind of future."

"Do you really believe that?" Millie was nobody's fool. She was a fine judge of character.

"It would break Ivory's heart to see what's happening now. I heard this morning some of the roughnecks up around Blue Eye community are planning on some retaliation for the noose at the courthouse. The fool thing is they all think Scott is guilty, too, but they're angry that blacks would have the audacity to threaten a white man with hanging." She shook her head.

That news troubled me, too. Hatred spread like gas fumes and it was just as volatile. "Do you have any names?"

"No. They're all too cowardly to step forward and say this in public. It's all secret meetings, anonymous threats." Her mouth showed her distaste.

"So why do you think Scott would kill his friend and benefactor?" I got back to the issue I had to resolve.

"That's a good question." Millie patted my arm as she picked up the coffeepot and made a quick circuit of the remaining crowd. She could pour with one hand and scoop up a ticket and payment with the other. After a dash to the cash register and a few moments to lay out change along the countertop, she was back.

"Some folks believe Scott is just a bad seed," she said, one corner of her mouth quirking up. "I can't say as I subscribe to that way of thinking. There's a lot of difference between drugs and murder."

"Coleman might say that one leads to the other," I pointed out.

"Coleman might say that, but even he doesn't believe it. Scott was involved with coke, but I really believe he gave it up." She gave me a hard look. "If everyone around here that dabbled in a little coke went right to murder, you'd be surprised at who was killin' whom in Sunflower County. The membership roster at The Club would be a lot shorter than you might expect."

I knew better than to ask for any names. Millie often helped me on my cases, but she wasn't a gossip. If cocaine use became pertinent to my case, she'd spill the beans. But not one second before. I decided on a different tactic.

"Scott has an extremely racist past. And he wasn't much of a guitar player until he came out of prison." I pulled Millie's pen out from behind her ear and began to draw the skull-and-crossbones symbol on the back of my ticket.

"So I've heard." She made a face. "His rap music was pure-D-raunch."

"Nasty," I agreed, working on the design. I was surprised that Millie knew as much about Scott as she did, but I shouldn't have been. Millie had a far more active social life than I did, and lately she'd been dating an antiques shop owner from Greenwood. They'd been to Memphis dancing and to Nashville to hear Lucinda Williams, but the blues was still her favorite.

"Folks can change," she said. "That's a fact."

"They can. And sometimes they can *pretend* to."

"True enough." She looked at me, worried. "You're working for Scott Hampton, and you don't believe in him at all. Why'd you take the case?"

"How'd you know I took it?"

"Cece called me."

I rolled my eyes. Cece Dee Falcon was the society editor for the *Zinnia Dispatch*. Formerly Cecil, Cece had spent her family fortune on a trip to Sweden and a change of gender. She was the best journalist I'd ever met, and she knew the dirt on everyone in town, including who was wearing panty girdles under summer sundresses and who'd had liposuction to avoid the horror of binding underwear.

"Cece's at the jail right this minute trying to get an exclusive interview with Scott. Some big music magazines are there, too. Coleman isn't in a good frame of mind." Millie cleared the counter as she talked.

"I can imagine." I tried not to visualize Coleman behind his desk, blue eyes seeking to catch my gaze. *I'm going back to Connie. We're going to give it another try.*

"You heard Coleman and Connie are back together?"

I kept my face perfectly blank. "Yeah, I heard."

"Fat chance that'll work out." She shrugged. "But you gotta give the man a blue ribbon for trying."

I stood up and pulled a wad of ones from my pocket. "If you had to say someone other than Scott Hampton killed Ivory, who would you name?"

Millie didn't hesitate. "Emanuel Keys would be my first suspect. I'd put him at the top of my list way before Scott. In fact, I'll bet you a steak dinner in Greenwood that Emanuel's the one behind that noose in the magnolia tree."

"Emanuel Keys? The son? He's alive?"

Millie acknowledged my surprise with a knowing look. "To hear Ida Mae talk about him, you'd think he was dead. But he isn't. And he's back in town just in time for his daddy to get murdered."

I recalled the gist of Ida Mae's limited comments about her son, and the sorrow and loss in her voice. Small wonder I'd assumed he was dead. "Tell me about him." I could see a real complication if Scott had become the "adopted" son.

Millie hitched one hip up on a barstool. "I think they found that boy under a cabbage plant. Or maybe a hemlock tree. He has poison in his veins—has ever since he was a little thing. He's just downright mean, and he treated his daddy like dog poo on the bottom of his shoe."

"Where is Emanuel?"

"He's back in the area. I know because I've seen him. He moved off to Atlanta in some big job as soon as he graduated from Notre Dame. He let Ivory and Ida Mae pick up the tab for his education and then told them he was too smart to come back to Mississippi. Then he came home about three months ago." She picked up the ticket I'd been drawing on. "What's this?"

"Scott's tattoo. Ever see that symbol anywhere?"

"Funny you should ask. I saw it Tuesday."

"Yesterday? Scott Hampton was in jail."

She lowered the ticket, her face puzzled. "It wasn't Scott. It was those other two."

I felt a pulse quicken. "What other two?"

"The bikers. They were in here for breakfast."

"Locals?" Sunflower County was small, with a minimal population, but there were all kinds in the mix. Even bikers.

"Not local. Hard to tell the difference sometimes, though. All that black leather, bandana head rags, sunglasses, black T-shirts. They all look alike."

"The uniform of the nonconformist." I knew what she was talking about.

"Exactly. Anyway, they came in for breakfast and they were talkin' hot and heavy about their preference in music, particularly Scott's music. Real connoisseurs, if you know what I mean." She rolled her eyes. "That's the first I heard of Scott's rap days. They were discussing some of the lyrics, if you can call that stuff lyrics, but I put a stop to it. I told them if they wanted to finish eating, they had to shut up." She made a sound of disgust. "Just a little more powder for the keg, if you ask me. Coleman ought to lock them up. Emanuel, too. Try to keep this place from going up in flames."

"Did they say they were friends of Scott's?" I was liking my client less and less.

"I doubt you could call those two friends of anyone, but they implied that they knew him."

"Did they happen to mention where they were staying or how long they'd been in town?" I picked up my car keys from the counter.

"No, I think their sole purpose in life is to stir up trouble. I'd stay away from those two, Sarah Booth." She saw I was getting ready to leave. "By the way, Cece's looking for you," she said as she picked up my plate.

"Thanks for the warning."

"She wants a quote for her story. It wouldn't hurt, you know. Publicity would be good for the Delaney Detective Agency."

"I'll keep that in mind." I had no intention of giving Cece a quote about Scott Hampton. In fact, I wasn't clear how I felt about Scott as a client—or a human being. I had my own soul-searching to do before I gave an opinion on anything.

6

WHEN I GOT BACK TO DAHLIA HOUSE, SWEETIE PIE WAS IN A deep doggy coma on the front porch, overcome by the morning's play with Chablis and the heat. Beside her was a message from Cece, written in her signature purple on eggshell vellum and topped with her initials in a gothic swirl. Cece took the Southern thing way over the top.

"Call me the instant you get home." Cece excelled at directives.

I crumpled the note and went inside, sighing as the coolness of the big old house swept over me, a haven from the blistering temperatures outside. On the short walk from the car to the front door, I'd worked up a sweat. I hit the switch for the ceiling fan in the parlor and stood under the whir of the blades. The rush of air created a chill on my damp skin, and I felt that prickle that could be either cold or a tingle of apprehension.

"Do you believe in the basic laws of nature?"

So it hadn't been the ceiling fan. Jitty was standing beside the horsehair sofa. I knew instantly that this wasn't going to be a casual conversation about something she'd seen on *Wild Kingdom*.

"Why is it that I feel this is a trap?" I asked, avoiding an answer. I headed to the kitchen to find some ice cubes and something cold to drink.

Following right behind me, Jitty didn't give any quarter. "It's a simple question. Can a tiger change his stripes?"

"What you're really asking is, can a wild animal be domesticated?" It was a feeble dodge, but I was wary of Jitty and her linguistic tricks.

"Would you put a Bengal tiger in with a herd of sheep just because the tiger had spent a few years with humans and seemed to be tame?"

"I suppose it depends on how hungry the tiger might be." I hated these philosophical arguments. Jitty had an agenda, and she was good at moving me into a corner to prove her theory.

"So the element of safety for the sheep depends on how hungry the tiger is?"

"I suppose." My stomach growled loudly, and I was sorry I'd said anything about hunger. I'd just downed at least five thousand calories, and if Jitty got close enough, she'd be able to smell the fried chicken on me.

She sat on the edge of the table, and for the first time, I noticed that she looked exactly like someone off the cover of one of my mother's old albums. The Shirelles, one of the original girl groups, came to mind. She had on a powder-blue tent dress of layered chiffon, powder-blue satin pumps, and her hair gelled or ironed or something so that it swooped into a French twist–beehive kind of do. I missed the *Star Trek* outfits she'd been wearing only a few weeks before.

"So a tiger can change his stripes as long as he doesn't get hungry, then he's goin' back to bein' a tiger, right?" She laid it out for me.

"It could work that way," I said, draining a glass of ice water.

"Scott Hampton is a racist, Sarah Booth. He may have hidden it while Ivory Keys was feedin' him, but he finally got really hungry, and he went back to bein' what he always was."

I refilled my glass and turned to face her. She deserved my full attention. She'd raised an issue that was troubling me, too.

"It may look that way to me and you, but Ida Mae Keys believes differently."

"Ida Mae *has* to believe that Scott's innocent."

"Why?" I was curious to hear her reasoning.

"If he's guilty, then she should have seen it comin'. I'm sure she knows all about Scott's past. She probably knows more than anyone, except her dead husband. And she let Ivory convince her that the tiger was defanged. She let that tiger into her home, up to her table, and walkin' beside the man she loved. Now that man is dead and the tiger only did what it was in his nature to do all along. She's got to bear the blame of that if Scott Hampton's guilty."

Jitty's words were chilling. Faced with a choice between belief in someone and such a burden of guilt, I could see what Jitty meant.

"Scott *looks* guilty," I conceded. "But there are other possibilities."

"The man who killed Ivory Keys is guilty of something a lot worse than murder," Jitty said. "Ivory had a big dream, and the power of that dream was the power to heal. The man who killed him destroyed that dream."

I saw a tear in the corner of Jitty's eye, and the panorama of all she'd witnessed passed through my mind. We'd both seen far too much loss. "Other men with dreams have died violently, and death didn't destroy the power of what they envisioned."

"No, but it sure knocked progress back in the ditch for a long time."

I couldn't argue that. I'd wondered more than once what would have happened if Martin Luther King Jr. had lived. Without his leadership, the movement for equality had faltered badly and never fully recovered.

"Ain't nobody risen up to take Martin's place," Jitty said, echoing my thoughts. "There are rare men—and women—who have the power to lead through the worst times. They don't come along ever' day."

"But the dream doesn't die," I insisted. "Maybe it gets stalled, but it doesn't curl up and die."

We stared at each other, both acutely aware of the long history that bound us so intimately together.

"If this guitar man killed Ivory Keys, he's done a terrible wrong. You can say the dream survives, but Playin' the Bones is closed, Ida Mae Keys is at home cryin' for her man, and the people who were beginnin' to believe that Ivory had a true vision are doubtin' all over again. If Scott Hampton walks out of this, not only will Ivory's dream die, but faith in the justice system will be destroyed." Jitty slowly stood up. "That's a heavy burden, Sarah Booth. You'd best shoulder it with a lot of thought."

She didn't pull a fading act, which was her usual exit when she thought she had the last word. She walked out of the parlor and disappeared up the stairs. I was left wondering how in the hell I had gotten myself into such a mess.

The answering machine light blinked urgently, and I played back my messages. Coleman had called saying he'd heard I had visited Playin' the Bones, which he had no doubt read as my decision to accept the case. He wanted a word with me "at my convenience." Good, I'd wait until tomorrow for a lecture. Besides, the thought of seeing Coleman made me nervous, angry, and sad. It was a dangerous cocktail of volatile emotions that I didn't trust myself to imbibe in public.

The other message was from Tinkie. My date was at seven sharp with a Bridge Ladnier, Memphis entrepreneur and investor. He was tall, handsome, and loaded. We were going to dinner at The Club, followed by dancing. Tinkie and Oscar would be there—close enough for an emergency, but far enough away to let "nature take its course." It was a date scripted from the Daddy's Girl Handbook of Red Letter Evenings.

I tried to sneak up to my room, but Jitty had heard the message from Tinkie and was waiting for me at the top of the stairs.

"A rich man, huh?" she said, and for the first time that day I saw a spark of the old devil I knew so well.

"Tall, handsome, *and* rich." I rubbed it in.

"Entrepreneur and investor," she said.

"Former banker," I tossed out.

"Tinkie's friend."

"Oscar's school chum." I was determined to have the final word on this. He was, after all, my date. Jitty and I were eye-to-eye.

"He's got all the financial credentials he needs, but can he cut the mustard or does he live up on Dead Pecker Ridge? Lots of men turn to makin' money when they can't make a woman grip the sheets and scream." Jitty was grinning, but she was also very serious.

"I didn't ask Tinkie for his Dun and Bradstreet *or* a report from his urologist." I was exasperated. Jitty could talk dreams and visions of a future, but for her it all boiled down to the tiny fusing of one sperm and one egg, all taking place in my female plumbing and ending up attached inside the Delaney womb. "Look, stay out of my social life." I gave her a hard look. "Why aren't you organizing a march at the jail or something?"

"If I could carry a sign, I'd be out there picketin'. Now forget about haranguin' me and go pick out what you're gonna wear tonight. Maybe that green halter dress with the full skirt."

Drat! It was exactly the dress I was thinking of. I hurried up the stairs and opened the closet. I wasn't a clotheshorse, but I loved a good bargain. During my tenure in New York as a failed stage actress, I'd happened upon a number of terrific secondhand stores. My wardrobe boasted big names at cut-rate prices.

I pulled out the green halter dress. It had a distinct 1940s look, with three big black buttons on the bodice, a pointed collar, and a completely bare back. The skirt was full and swingy, perfect for an evening of dancing to a big band, which was what The Club always offered. In fact, it was the same band from the 1940s. Wearing the same burgundy blazers with the gold lettering of The Club embroidered on the right lapel. Even the bubbles that churned from the hidden machine smelled vaguely of mothballs.

"Perfect," Jitty said. "That pale green matches your eyes. Wear those gold earrings Cece brought you from New Orleans. And those wicked black heels with the three sexy little straps."

Though she was an aggravation, Jitty had terrific taste in clothes. I couldn't help but wonder what she was doing, looking like a forgotten girl groupie, but I knew better than to ask. I had a date to prepare for, and at my age, it was going to take at least a full five hours to wash and condition my hair, put on a mud mask to shrink my pores, do my nails and toenails, pumice my calluses, lubricate my skin, pluck my eyebrows, shave my legs, and the host of other beautifying acts that every woman knew was a prerequisite to a Big Date. I would be exhausted before Bridge Ladnier showed up.

"If you went out more than twice a year, you'd be more caught up on personal maintenance," Jitty said. "What about that bikini line?"

"You make me sound like a car," I pointed out, choosing not to go into the fact that Bridge Ladnier wouldn't know if my bikini line was waxed or not.

"Well, you ain't no classic, so you'd better buff yourself up as much as possible. And remember to use that wax."

I sighed. There was no point in arguing with Jitty when she was on a tear.

I SIPPED A Jack on the rocks and watched the Jaguar pull up to the front of the house. The man who got out of the car was a perfect match for the clean, elegant lines of the auto he drove. Bridge Ladnier had arrived in style.

I saw his features clearly in the light of the porch. He had the look of a British aristocrat: deep-set brown eyes, a face toughened by the outdoors and touched with a hint of interesting lines, posture so perfect that it came across as casual. He rang the bell, adjusting his designer Picasso tie as he waited for me.

"Mr. Ladnier," I said as I opened the door. "Please come in."

He followed me into the parlor and took a seat on the horsehair sofa.

"Would you care for a drink?" I hovered by the bar, my Aunt LouLane's schooling in the caste of Daddy's Girl taking over before I could stop myself.

"Scotch and soda," he said, his gaze finding the old turntable where Marva Wright's powerful voice went deep and dirty. My mother had an extensive blues collection. "I saw Marva in New Orleans five times. She can bring a house down," he said as he accepted his drink.

Surprised, I poured Jack over ice for me. "You like the blues?"

"*Like* may be an understatement," he said with a slow smile. "I love them."

"We share that in common," I said. "I like a lot of music, but the blues are my favorite."

"Is that why you're defending Scott Hampton?" he asked.

The question caught me off guard. Somehow I hadn't expected Bridge to be interested in local happenings. "No, it isn't about the blues." I hesitated. "Mrs. Keys asked me to help Hampton."

"You seem a little hesitant. Can he be helped?"

I avoided a personal opinion. "The evidence is strongly against him, but many innocent men have appeared guilty."

"And if he is guilty, then he's done a terrible thing." He watched me closely. "You haven't become a hired gun yet, have you?" His smile was warm. "I somehow don't think you will. That says a lot about your character."

Bridge Ladnier obviously had heard a lot of details about Ivory's murder. "This is a case where it's hard to know the right thing to do," I conceded.

"Yes, our justice system is built on the ideal that every man deserves a fair trial," Bridge said, swirling his drink so that the ice clinked in the glass. "It's a case that's going to get a lot of publicity. Might be good for you, in the long run." One eyebrow lifted. "Now that's strictly a bottom-line assessment."

I started to laugh. "I never considered whether this case would be good for *me* or not."

"Then you should, if you want a successful business, Sarah Booth. In fact, that should be one of your primary concerns for all future cases. 'What can I gain from it?' and 'How will it impact my reputation?'"

I could see where he was a good businessman. "I have a hard enough time trying to decide what's right and what's wrong in cases this convolved. Future impact of publicity may be too complicated for me."

He gave a wry smile. "I lived up North too long, I suppose. I forgot that Southern belles don't worry their pretty little heads about business."

His remark caught me off guard, and then I caught the twinkle in his eye. "You're right," I said. "That was a ridiculous thing to say. I have to think about the business side of this, whether I want to or not." I finished my drink and rose. He did the same.

"You're beautiful and smart, Sarah Booth. Never ridiculous. Business is not something a person knows intuitively. It has to be learned, and if you ever need any help, I'm available." He took my arm and leaned to whisper in my ear. "Gossip down at the bank is that your business will be a whopping success. They say you have a knack for solving cases."

I was still flushing with pleasure when we headed out into the night. While the Jaguar hummed over the long, straight roads that cut through the whispering rows of cotton, Bridge spoke of his reasons for returning to the South. He had family in Memphis, but it was a longing for the culture that had pulled him back to Mississippi.

"That, and I have this crazy notion that I might be of use."

"Of use?" Bridge didn't strike me as the kind of man who would relish being used in any way.

"I know it sounds like I'm some seventeen-year-old still wet behind the ears and filled with dreamy ideals, but Mississippi has made great strides to overcome the past. I want to see it move forward even more. We've got good people, bright and talented people. I can convince my associates to invest down here, bring in some good jobs. I'm not talking about chemical plants or textile mills where folks work for minimum wage and the environment pays the ultimate price."

I watched Bridge's profile in the pale glow of the Jaguar's dash.

He was passionate about what he was saying. I felt something inside me stir, the brush of an old memory, and I realized that I'd heard the same powerful emotion from my mother as she talked about Mississippi and her love for it.

"Just because you have ideals doesn't make you naïve," I said. "I like people who dream."

Bridge chuckled with a hint of self-consciousness. "That's enough serious talk." He pulled into the parking lot, got out, and handed me out of the car. As I tucked my hand through his arm, he pressed my fingers, teasing the back of my hand as he let go. "Tonight we dine, drink, and dance. We'll save the serious discussions for daylight. It would be a pity to waste that moon," he said, pointing to the sky, where a pale moon hung on the horizon, gilding the surrounding cotton fields with silvery leaves.

He led me into The Club and proved that his word was good. Oscar, wearing a white dinner jacket, rose and waved us to a table. Before I could even sit, my napkin was in my lap and my champagne flute filled.

Tinkie was especially lovely in a pale orange swing dress and matching heels. She and Oscar hit the dance floor for a rumba, and I watched with amazement as Oscar's hips swiveled and his face was alight with fun. In his official capacity at the bank, he was a stoic and reserved man. Tinkie was the fuse that lit him, and I felt an unreasonable swelling in my heart for the two of them.

"No marriage is perfect, but those two do get on," Bridge said, giving voice to my thoughts.

"I'm really beginning to respect Oscar," I admitted. "But don't tell him, he'll get the big—"

I didn't get to finish. A shadow fell over my plate and I turned to find Marshall Harrison standing over me, a glower on his face. Marshall was a decade older than I and I knew him only because he owned the local fast-food franchise.

"You shame all of us," Marshall said, his words slurred with too much alcohol.

"I think you should walk away from the table," Bridge said levelly. He didn't rise, but his body was poised for action.

"I'm talking to Miss Delaney," Marshall said, putting a sweaty hand on my shoulder. "Your mother was a troublemaker and now you've taken up the flag. Decent folks around here don't like it and we won't put up with it."

Bridge had intervened once, as is a gentleman's right, but I was no lady. "Take your hand off my shoulder now," I said, turning in my chair so I could look at him.

Instead of removing his hand, he squeezed. "Hampton is white trash. He's going to get what he deserves."

I had a sudden thought that Emanuel Keys may not have hung the noose at the courthouse. There were factions, both black and white, that wanted violence. I drew back my elbow, prepared to land a blow where it would do the most good.

To my surprise, Marshall's knees buckled and he almost dropped to the floor. Oscar had stepped up behind Marshall and held his other arm in a viselike grip, levering it up behind his back.

"Take your hands off the lady," Oscar said.

Marshall's hand instantly fell away. "Excuse us," Oscar said calmly as he steered Marshall toward the exit. Bridge excused himself and followed. I started to go outside, but Tinkie caught my hands as she sat down at the table.

"Let the men handle it," she said.

"It's about me and I should see it through," I insisted.

"This is only the beginning," she said sadly, holding my hands in her lap so I wouldn't get up.

"Why?" I asked, still a little stunned. "What's this case to Marshall Harrison? I doubt he ever went to Playin' the Bones or even knew who Ivory Keys was, much less Scott Hampton. What does my mother have to do with this?"

Tinkie released one of my hands long enough to drain the rest of her champagne. "It doesn't matter, Sarah Booth. That's what I tried to tell you. The scabs are coming off the past now. The guilty and the innocent will be swept up in this. There won't be a winner, no matter what the outcome."

"There never is a winner when someone is dead," I said bitterly.

Bridge and Oscar returned, neither with a hair out of place. Oscar ordered another bottle of champagne, and Bridge leaned over to whisper in my ear. "It's important that we act as if nothing happened. And it didn't. The man was drunk and stupid."

When the waiter brought the champagne, we ordered dinner, and through the wit and manners of the men, Tinkie and I were able to put the evening back on track.

We laughed and danced, and in the quiet moments, I found myself surrounded by the ghost of memories of my youth, when I'd sat with my parents and watched an older generation of belles dancing with their handsome dinner dates.

Bridge offered me a bedazzling view of what my future might have been, had I not wanted to become an actor. Had my parents not been killed when I was a teenager. Had my mother not been a socialist and indoctrinated me into the ways of the independent female during my formative years.

Before the evening was over, I couldn't help but wonder if perhaps I'd made a serious mistake by chucking out the baby with the bathwater.

As we rode back through the soft night to Dahlia House, I kicked off my shoes and tucked my throbbing feet under me. I had paid the price of wicked shoes without a whimper.

"You're quite a dancer." It was an understatement. Bridge, for all of his upright posture, could move. In his life of privilege, he'd somewhere learned to salsa with just enough hip action to make a girl think of other activities.

"Thanks. You're a good partner." He glanced over at me. It was the most intimate action he'd committed all night. Bridge Ladnier was a very careful man.

"Will you be in Zinnia long?"

"I'd planned to leave Sunday. Although I'll be doing a bit of work here in Zinnia, my base is in Memphis. But I think I'm going to change my plans." This time his glance lingered on me. "Will you have some free time in the next few days?"

Bridge had mastered the art of making his intentions clear without applying pressure. It was a surefire lure to an independent woman. "I'll have some free time in the evenings."

He reached across and touched my hand, gathering it into his. When we were dancing, I'd noticed how long his fingers were. He had the hands of a musician. Rather like Scott Hampton's.

"Is something wrong?" he asked.

He was acutely sensitive, too. "No. I was just thinking about tomorrow."

We pulled up in front of Dahlia House. He got out, opened my door, and walked me to the front porch.

"Tinkie was right about you."

"Really?" I forced a smile. There was absolutely no telling what Tinkie had said about me.

"She said you were smart and talented and entertaining. 'A rare speciman of Southern womanhood' is the way she phrased it."

Relief swept over me. "It could have been a lot worse. Tinkie knows too many of my secrets."

"She adores you, Sarah Booth. And I see why."

Bridge was smooth. Another compliment, no pressure.

He stepped closer to me and put his hands on my shoulders. "It was a lovely evening. I'd like to take you to dinner Friday night."

My dance card was woefully empty, but I didn't want Bridge to know that. Coleman Peters tried to pop into my brain, but I firmly shut him out. "I'd like that."

"Good. I'll pick you up at seven. I'll make it a surprise evening, but dress comfortably. Wear something that makes you feel like reclining on soft cushions in the glow of a dozen candles." He leaned down and brushed a kiss across my lips.

I'd wondered for the past thirty minutes what it would feel like to kiss him. Pleasant. When I didn't pull back, he kissed me again, this time with more intimacy.

His arms circled me, holding me firmly yet without pressure. I closed my eyes and gave myself to the wonderful sensation of being held in a man's arms, of kisses that hinted at passion but didn't demand.

Lifting his lips from mine, he stepped slightly away from me, holding me long enough to make certain I'd regained my balance.

"I think I'm going to owe Tinkie a lot," Bridge said as he brushed his fingertips along my jaw, lingering just a second on my chin. "Good night, Sarah Booth. And don't give up on Scott Hampton. He could be your ticket to a lot of publicity and that's how you'll get bigger, better cases in the future. I don't think you'll have any more trouble from the likes of Marshall Harrison."

He walked back to the Jaguar and drove away. I leaned against the front wall of Dahlia House, feeling the summer heat baked into the old bricks.

"Get in the house and get into that bed," Jitty ordered from the foyer.

I opened the door and went in to find her sitting on the foot of the steps. Pink flowers decorated the baby-doll PJ set she wore, making her look all of about thirteen. I hadn't seen baby-doll pajamas since I was eight.

"Cute," I said, stepping around her.

"Honey, now that Bridge Ladnier is my kind of man. Smooth, charming—"

"Rich," I interrupted. "Darn, I forgot to ask if he was shooting blanks."

"The answer to that question is no."

Jitty said it with such authority I hesitated. "How can you be so sure?"

"First there's the name. He's carryin' the weight of a name that needs handin' down. Then there's the man. He knows that progeny is the only way to make sure of his place in the future. He knows the rules, Sarah Booth, even the ones you refuse to learn. Now that's the man for you." She stood up. "Get some beauty rest, girl. I have a feelin' it won't be long before he comes a-callin' again."

I didn't bother telling her our second date was already set. I took myself up the stairs and into my bedroom, wondering if the strange hot feeling in my gut was anticipation for my next meeting with Bridge, or revenge against a badge-wearing man who suffered from a waffling heart.

7

THE POUNDING ON THE FRONT DOOR WAS SHARP AND IRRITAT-
ing. It was, yet again, the familiar pitter-patter of little fists. It was
bright and early on a Thursday morning, and Tinkie had come
calling. She would be hungry.

My first thought, irrational though it was, was to pull the covers over my head and hide. I'd been in the middle of a complicated
dream that was backlit by smoky pink neon, rotating stage lights,
and a huge clock/calendar that kept running backwards until it
stopped in 1965. Someone was moving out of that smoky pink
neon toward me. A man who walked in a way that made a
woman think of making love in the middle of a hot afternoon
with the windows wide open and a breeze teasing the curtains.

"Sarah Booth Delaney, get your butt out of bed!" Tinkie beat
on the door with a rat-a-tat-tat that meant business.

I rolled out with a groan, threw on a T-shirt, and went to open
the door. The three bottles of champagne that had seemed like
such a fine idea the night before were now a bitter memory aggravated by a pounding headache.

"Sarah Booth," Tinkie cried, giving me a disgusted look. "It's nine o'clock, and you're still in bed. I thought you were going to see Coleman this morning."

A visual of Coleman at his desk flashed through my brain on jagged streaks of hangover pain. I could see him, blue eyes unflinching, as he questioned me about Playin' the Bones and my little visit there. "I am, but—"

"How late did you stay out with Bridge?" Tinkie shifted positions so that she was in my face. Chablis, who was tucked in her arm, hurled herself free and onto my chest. Luckily, my reflexes weren't affected by the bags under my eyes, and I was able to catch her.

"We were dancing and we got carried away. The night was—"

"You didn't!" Her face was stricken. "Sarah Booth, no man wants a woman who's *ee-a-zy!*" In DG lingo, the three-syllable pronunciation of easy has only one meaning—a desperate woman who drops her drawers at the first attention paid by a man.

I was annoyed. "Tell that to Jitty," I snapped before I thought.

"Who?" She was like a rat terrier. "Who's Jitty? What are you talking about?"

I shook my head. "Part of a dream," I said. "Let me put on some coffee." I stumbled toward the kitchen knowing that the only thing capable of diverting Tinkie's attention was the smell of bacon sizzling in my big, old cast-iron skillet. To that end, I threw a half dozen slices of thick-cut Smithfield into the pan.

Tinkie settled at the table, not even blinking an eye when Sweetie Pie picked Chablis up by the neck and carried her out through the doggie door. Not so long ago, such a sight would have given Tinkie a stroke. Now she'd grown to love my big old hound dog, and she knew Sweetie adored Chablis.

The bacon was sizzling and the coffee was perking, as was Tinkie's curiosity. "So, how was Bridge?" she asked. "I mean, I completely disapprove of sleeping with a man on the first date. It goes against all the rules, Sarah Booth. It's . . . cheap." She pulled a moue and tried to restrain herself—unsuccessfully. "How was he? Pitiful, adequate, or . . . divine?" She was leaning so far forward that only her chest kept her from sprawling on top of the table.

"Very athletic," I said. "And just a little kinky."

The look on her face was worth the lie.

"Sarah Booth! Bridge is a highly respected . . ." She caught the glint in my eye. "That was mean! For a minute you had me worried. I mean, you really can't throw yourself at a man like him. Women do it all the time, and that just makes them look like a Kleenex tissue—something to be used and tossed away. A man like Bridge likes to pursue. Or at least think that he's pursuing. That's the whole art—to run just fast enough to keep him thinkin' you can't be caught."

"Yes, lesson forty-nine in the Daddy's Girl book of 'How to Catch a Man,'" I said with a heaping dose of sarcasm.

"You may not want to admit it, but there's a lot of truth in the things our mamas taught us." She gave me a long look. "Well, maybe not your mama. She was a little different."

"Bridge was a lot of fun," I said, tired of deviling her. "I had a good time. We're going out Friday night."

That was all it took. She shot me a million-watt smile that made me just a little ashamed. Tinkie really wanted good things for me, and she put herself out quite a lot to see that they happened.

"Now, about this bluesperson." The smile was gone. "Sarah Booth, everyone in town thinks he's guilty as sin. Marshall Harrison is just the tip of the iceberg for what's going to happen. Is Scott Hampton really worth this?"

I wanted to argue in Scott's defense, but I couldn't. "I tried to quit the case. Really. Ida Mae made me feel guiltier for trying to quit than everyone else makes me feel for taking the case." That was the crux of the matter.

"I talked to Oscar this morning before he left for work." Her lips turned up at the corners as a memory struck her full force. "This detecting business has inspired me. I don't think Oscar ever enjoyed a shower quite so much."

Tinkie was one helluva partner. "What did you get? Aside from the obvious."

Ignoring the flush that touched her cheeks, Tinkie cleared her throat. "Playin' the Bones has been in dire financial straits for the past five years—*except* for the last six months." She reached in her purse and pulled out a notepad. "Ivory borrowed fifty thousand to refurbish the club and get it up and running. Now that was 1998. In the next three years, he missed two notes and was late on six more. Then in 2002, he nearly lost it back to the bank. But things changed in the last six months. He's been making double payments and putting money in two other accounts. The club has become very profitable." She saw I was holding up an egg. "Over-light this morning, please."

I cracked the eggs in the skillet. Tinkie's information was exactly what I expected to hear. Scott Hampton had begun to pull in a crowd, and gain a national reputation. He was the ticket to good times for Ivory. And it didn't take a rocket scientist to see that Playin' the Bones, at least in Scott's opinion, might have gone from life raft to prison.

WATCHING TINKIE PULL away from the front of Dahlia House, I could only marvel at modern technology. The air conditioner in her Caddy was so powerful, Chablis' shag-cut ears were blown straight back from her head. In contrast, Tinkie's perfectly swept-back "do" didn't even quiver. She knew every secret of hair spray in the book. Emanuel Keys, her next assignment, would be putty in her hands.

I, on the other hand, had Coleman to confront. A strange churning began in my gut. I tried to pinpoint whether it was anxiety, anticipation, dread, or relief. Or perhaps none of the above. I bathed, dressed, and headed to town.

I parked as close as possible to the courthouse, while still claiming a bit of shade, and started walking the half block to the north door of the building. The beautiful flowers of spring had given way to lush greenery and an occasional crepe myrtle. These hardy trees with their strange, smooth bark erupted in clusterlike swags of fuchsia, lavender, watermelon, white, and a deep purple that was my favorite. They were the only blooms tough enough to withstand the August heat, and the tiny flowers littered the ground in places.

Once, when I was seven, my mother and I had gone hunting for wild grape vines called scuppernongs. Her goal was to make wine, while I loved to suck the pulp out of the thick hulls and eat it.

In our travels, we wandered onto the old Lassfolk place. Overgrown with weeds, the driveway was lined with white crepe myrtles that had grown huge. We were walking down the choked drive when a sudden gust of wind shook the white blossoms free and they cascaded down around us, a snowstorm in August. "Mississippi magic," my mother said. I recalled that memory as I walked toward the courthouse and Coleman.

I heard the music first, a gut-tickling riff on a guitar. Then Scott Hampton's signature raw voice sang a line that made me stop in my tracks. I was stunned by the power, skill, and talent I heard—in contrast to the awful rap music I'd listened to earlier. I was also horrified by the lyrics.

"I went down to the corner, murder in my heart. He saw the shank I carried and said, 'Son, that ain't too smart.' But the devil gripped me tighter, oh, yes, he told me what to do. Now I'm headed straight to Parchman prison to sing those low-down, murderin' prison blues."

If a man could be said to have sung himself into a capital murder charge, Scott Hampton would be that man.

Scouting the area, I saw the big black boom box that was the source of the music. I started toward it, determined to unplug it or stomp it to death. The boom box was running on batteries, so I knelt beside it, searching for the power button.

"Hey! You! Stay away from that. That's private property!" A woman came out from behind a big azalea bush holding a sign that read "Free Scott Hampton."

It was only as she drew closer that I recognized her. Sort of. She bore a distinct resemblance to Stuart Ann Shanahan, known throughout high school and college as Nandy. But this was a Nandy I'd never seen before. This was Nandy after a long season in hell. She came toward me like a pit bull on the attack, then stopped. Recognition lit her heavily lined and mascaraed eyes.

"So, it's Sarah Booth Delaney, Zinnia's answer to Mickey Spillane. It's about time you were out of bed and working. You have to make them believe Scott's innocent."

I heard the words, but I was focused on the earring that had somehow crept from her shell-shaped ear to her eyebrow. A blue stone had been expertly cut into the shape of a record album—a blues album. How unbearably cute! And how incredibly expensive.

Helped by a shaft of sunlight, I saw a matching ring in her navel, exposed by her designer jeans cut to hang perfectly on her prominent hipbones. Topping off the effect were pumiced and manicured toes painted what looked like that nearly impossible-to-find shade of Snow White red.

"Nandy?" I wasn't certain it was really her. My last sighting of Nandy had involved a chiffon gown and tiara when she was crowned Sweetheart of Sigma Chi at Ole Miss.

"You were expecting Lord Darnley?"

I'd read enough historicals to catch her reference to the murdered husband of Mary, Queen of Scotts, and I also knew her family's obsessive fixation with the beheaded queen. They'd named their sprawling Delta holdings Holyrood. I ignored the Darnley remark and zeroed in on the pertinent issue. "What are you doing here?"

"Since no one else seems to care, I decided to start the protest movement. Scott is more than a musician, he's a god." She thrust the sign at an elderly gentleman who was headed into the court-house. "They have Scott in jail. Can you believe it? They've locked him up like a common criminal."

"He's charged with murder," I pointed out, still trying to adjust to this new Nandy.

"What a crock of shit." She wiped at some perspiration beneath her eye and smudged thick black mascara over to her temple. She wasn't wearing waterproof cosmetics!

"How do you know Scott?" I asked.

"I'm head of his fan club. The Blizzard Heads."

"I see." But I didn't. Nandy had preferred the soulful sounds of Barry Manilow. I'd gone through her CDs in college once, and she'd even had a couple of Perry Como's, as well as three albums of bagpipe music.

"The pigs won't let me even visit him in jail. Can you do something about that?"

"Would you turn that music off?" Aside from the fact that the lyrics were incriminating to Scott, I was positive the idea of a Blizzard Head broad playing loud music and holding a protest sign on the courthouse lawn was not helping Hampton's case.

"I'm not going to stop playing Scott's music, and I'm not going to eat until they let him out." Her lips thinned into a straight line that I remembered well from college. Nandy got what Nandy wanted—or else. But in the past, she'd never been one to deprive herself of anything.

"Nandy, the music isn't helping."

She ignored me. "Can you believe Coleman Peters is sheriff now?" she continued. "He was nothing but a stupid jock all through high school. Did he even go to college? Maybe some trade school. Something like Troughville State, where all the best pigs are trained."

I was wasting precious time. "I'll talk to you later." I stepped past her and started up the stairs. Nandy had transformed her exterior, but there'd been no corresponding renovation of her soul.

Her fingers clutched my upper arm in a grip of surprising strength. "Are you going to talk to Scott?" The look in her eyes told me a lot more than I wanted to know. Even though she obviously knew I was working on his case, she was jealous of the fact that I could talk to him.

I could have eased her mind by telling her he didn't want to talk to me, but I didn't. "I'm going to talk to the sheriff."

"Tell him he'd better let me see Scott."

I didn't say anything for several seconds. Nandy had gone from asking for my help to demanding that I deliver her messages. "For

Scott's sake, turn off the music," I said, hurrying up the steps and inside the courthouse.

Coleman was at the counter, and the dispatcher's chair was empty. Little Bo-Peep had gone to round up sheep. Or with any luck, she'd gone for a shearing herself.

"You went out to Playin' the Bones. You're on the case." Coleman wasn't asking.

"I took a look around."

"You're making a mistake, Sarah Booth." His voice was terse. "You don't need this, and neither do I."

"What, exactly, do you need, Coleman?" I heard the heat in my own voice.

"I don't know," he said, and he turned his profile to me.

Neither of us were talking about the case. But it was the only thing I could, legitimately, talk to him about.

"Any new developments with Hampton? What about that noose? Any idea who hung it?"

Coleman shook his head. "They were smart enough to use an old rope, so we can't trace it back to where it was purchased from. There's really nothing forensically that we can determine. We're trying to find witnesses."

"Do you have any suspects?" I pressed.

"When I make a charge, you'll be the first to know."

"What about the evidence against Scott? Anything new?"

"The coroner puts the time of death at between two and four o'clock in the morning. Hampton claims he left the bar at midnight."

"Maybe he did." I was at a real disadvantage since my client wouldn't talk to me.

"I have a witness that says otherwise." He put his palms on the counter.

"A reliable witness?"

"A *strange* witness." He turned back to face me, putting both hands on the counter as if to steady himself. "Nandy Shanahan."

"Nandy?" I couldn't hide my shock. "She's out there on the

courthouse lawn raising hell because he's in jail. She's president of his fan club."

"Right. The Blizzard Heads." Coleman looked at his fingers instead of at me. "She signed a statement that she saw Scott come out of the club at exactly two-twenty that morning." He looked at me. "Unfortunately for you, that makes Hampton a liar *and* the man I believe committed Ivory's murder."

I sighed. "You believe Nandy?"

"Do you believe Hampton?" he countered.

"He hasn't really talked to me," I confessed. This case was looking more and more like a quagmire.

"You'd better get something out of him. Linc's going to push this as hard as he can. He's having visions of the governor's office, and Scott Hampton is going to be his step stool to jump there."

What he was saying was true. Lincoln Bangs, the Sunflower County district attorney, was a very ambitious man. It was an unfortunate fact of life that the route to the governor's office, in any state, was often littered with bodies, the guilty and the innocent.

Coleman pushed off the counter. "So how was your date?"

I wasn't prepared for that question but I stepped right up to the plate. "Bridge Ladnier is a very interesting man."

"I'm sure he is. And successful." Coleman's hand had gone to his gun belt. He fiddled with his holster. "He belongs in places like The Club, by birthright as well as bank account." There was a flatness in Coleman's eyes I'd never seen. "I'm glad you finally found a social peer, Sarah Booth. You deserve that and a whole lot more."

He walked into his office and closed the door.

8

Deputy Dewayne Dattilo let me back into the jail. My greeting there was almost as warm as the one I'd gotten from Coleman. Scott reclined on his bunk, one leg crossed over a knee, and watched me as if I were some odious reptile.

"We need to talk." I wasn't in the mood for his attitude.

"*You* need to leave." His foot began to beat a rhythm as he tuned me out completely.

"Listen, Hampton, your ridiculous bad-boy posturing is wasted on me." I was angry and he was stupid. "James Dean died a long time ago. You might think you're a rebel without a cause, but you're really just a racist rich boy with a little talent and a long history of making seriously bad life decisions." I took a deep breath. "So cut the crap. Coleman has an eyewitness that puts you at the scene of the murder at the time Ivory Keys was killed."

He sat up suddenly, and in half a second he was across the cell and standing before me. He moved in so close I could feel his breath on my fingers where they gripped the bars.

"I know about the witness," he said, each word a hard, fast

little bullet of anger. "Stuart Ann Shanahan. That crazy bitch wanted to visit me here."

"You admit you know her, then?"

"I know her. She's the girl who's been stalking me for the past six months. It's a bit ironic that my biggest fan would put the nail in my coffin, isn't it?"

"Stalking? She's president of your fan club."

"And hell has swimming pools and ice-cold beer." He glared at me. "That girl is a stalker. She's broken into my house three times. She sits on my bike when I park it somewhere. She's always jumping out of shrubs and bushes, trying to get me to fuck her. And she tails me like a hound after a raccoon. I told the sheriff not to let her near me."

I nodded while I thought it through. "What you say about Nandy may be true, but she's put you at the murder scene, nonetheless."

"Who's going to believe a crazy bitch like her?" He challenged me with his eyes.

I kept my tone factual. "Most of Sunflower County. Stuart Ann is from a well-to-do family. Most jurors, if it comes down to it, will take her word over an ex-con drug addict's." I meant to make him angry, and I was rewarded by the snap in his eyes. Yet he held his tongue and his temper. That impressed me.

"We might balance Nandy out with some background about your family." I'd done my homework. "Your mother is head of the United Way Drive each year, and your father single-handedly started the drive to build a new shelter for abused women. That should count for something."

"Leave my family out of this," Scott said in a way that let me know he'd divorced them long before they cut the umbilical on him.

"How old are you?" I asked.

He hesitated. "Thirty-five. How old are you?"

His question caught me off guard, as did the curiosity in his gaze. He was really looking at me. "A woman never reveals her age." I didn't want Scott to have a lot of personal information about me.

"Did you give Ida Mae back her money?" he demanded.

I was tired of his attempts to wrest control of the conversation from me. *I* was helping *him*. "If you're so worried about Ida Mae and her money, why don't you call your own family for help? They're loaded."

His laugh was bitter. "They gave up on me a long time ago. The only reason they'd trouble themselves to come down to Mississippi would be to tell me they told me so."

His past wasn't my problem. His future was. "Then it looks like you have no choice but to accept Ida Mae's largesse." I leaned toward the bars. "So I suggest you get cooperative and quit wasting that old woman's money and my time. And you'd better pray she doesn't hear any of that music you wrote and sang in the early nineties. I don't think Ida Mae would be a big fan of the Brown Shirts."

My words were like a slap. He recoiled but he didn't lash out. I was again impressed. I'd heard Scott had a bad temper, but so far, he'd been able to control it. That indicated he might be able to avoid the classic "crime of passion," where a man's temper overrode his reason and his self-preservation. On the one hand, that was a good thing. On the other hand, that might put Ivory's murder as premeditated.

"I don't want anyone's help. Least of all Ida Mae's." He rubbed both eyebrows with the thumb and forefinger of his right hand.

"Guilty conscience?" I jabbed.

He stared at me. "No. I don't have anything to be guilty about. I didn't kill Ivory."

I was watching him closely when he spoke. "And you didn't lie about what time you left the club?"

He turned so suddenly that I stepped back from the bars. At my reaction, something flashed across his face. Surprise, or shock, I couldn't be certain. The hand he'd raised dropped to his side, as all of the energy seemed to drain from him.

"I wasn't going to hit you."

I didn't deny that was what I'd thought. "Did you lie to Coleman about the time you left the club?"

"Yes," he admitted. "What would you have done? I was the last person to see Ivory alive, except for his killer. I was with him until nearly two in the morning. We were arguing. We argued a lot." He shrugged one shoulder in more of a jerk than a gesture.

"Argued about what? Money?"

He shook his head, a strand of hair falling over his forehead. "Never about money."

"About what?"

"Things." He gave me a searching look. "We talked about lots of things."

"And you argued about . . . ?"

"We argued about music. Nobody would understand but another musician."

"Try me," I said, wondering if one of those musical things they argued about was the two-year contract that tied him to Ivory and the club.

"There are things that can be done to make money in a club. Things that are just good business."

I was intrigued. The anger had dropped out of Scott's face, and he spoke with unintentional passion. "Such as?"

"In a club, entertainment is the draw. The money comes off liquor sales. I wanted Ivory to bring in more acts, different things like hip-hop and rap. Something to draw in the younger folks. He wouldn't even consider it. He said that stuff wasn't music and he didn't want any part of it. For Ivory, it was the blues or nothing. He was hardheaded as a mule, but he was a man of principle."

With each conversation about Ivory, I garnered another fragment of who he was. The picture that was coming to life was of a man who bent into the wind.

"In a way, Ivory was the luckiest man I ever knew," Scott said, almost as if he were talking to himself. "He had such a strong belief in his music. No matter what went wrong or how hard he got set back, he never lost his belief. It must be wonderful to believe in something—anything—that much."

Scott's words struck home with me. Once, long ago, I'd believed in a lot of things. "So on the night Ivory was killed, what time did you leave the club?"

"I'm not certain. Sometime around two o'clock. I knew someone killed him not long after I left, so I lied about the time I left the club because I knew I'd be the primary suspect. I'm an ex-con. So you tell me, Miss Private Investigator, what would you have done in the same circumstances?"

I had not always walked hand in hand with the truth, even when the stakes weren't nearly as high as they were for Scott. But my decisions weren't on trial; my life wasn't at stake. I didn't have to admit to anything. "You've only made yourself look more guilty."

"And you think I don't know that? I may be an ex-con, but I'm not an idiot."

That was true. "Look, I see where you might have felt it was smarter to lie about the time. We can explain that to Coleman and—"

"The high sheriff has already convicted me."

"Scott, you need to get this once and for all. This isn't about your martyr complex. The evidence has put you in jail, not the sheriff. Coleman's a fair man."

His shoulders sagged almost imperceptibly. "I was guilty of everything I was convicted of in Detroit. Everything and more. I never pretended to be innocent. But I didn't kill Ivory."

There comes a moment between two people when trust is either established or destroyed. Against all common sense, I found that I believed what Scott was saying. I didn't have a hope he could convince a jury of his innocence, but if music was his talent, charisma was his charm. He'd won me to his side.

"Who would want Ivory dead?" I asked, striving for a professional tone that hid all personal emotion.

He didn't answer immediately. He weighed what my question

meant. When he finally spoke, his voice was calmer. "I don't know."

"Whoever killed Ivory went to a lot of trouble to make it look like you did it. The place was robbed and nearly three thousand in bloodstained money was found in the saddlebag of your bike. They'll know if it's Ivory's money before much longer." I didn't have to add that if the blood tests came back positive, it would be harder than ever to prove Scott's innocence.

"If I'd killed Ivory and robbed the place, would I have been so stupid as to leave the money in my saddlebag?"

It was a good point, but it led me to another. "So who would want you back in prison, or the gas chamber, badly enough to kill a man?"

Scott's mouth thinned. It wasn't a pretty sight. "A whole lot of people, Miss Delaney. I missed the Dale Carnegie seminar on how to win friends. I'm more adept at making enemies."

He did seem to have a knack for pissing people off. "My suggestion to you is to put your thinking cap on and come up with some names, Mr. Hampton. I can't help you unless you're willing to help yourself."

He didn't get a chance to respond. The door to the jail opened and Deputy Dattilo walked toward us, keys jangling on his belt.

"You've got visitors, Hampton," he said, making it clear he didn't like it. "Fifteen minutes."

Behind Dattilo, two men entered the narrow hall between the cells. They walked abreast, laughing and punching each other as they approached.

The light in the jail wasn't the best, but I caught the image these men wanted to project. They wore tight jeans, leather jackets, bandanas tied around their heads, gold hoop earrings in one ear, and one man had on dark sunglasses.

"Hey, man!" The one without sunglasses brushed past Dattilo and stepped in front of me. "We'll have you outta here in no time flat. These yokels can't keep you locked up."

Scott, too, seemed to have forgotten that the deputy and I were in the vicinity. He reached through the bars and grasped the biker's hand. That's when I noticed the tattoo on the newcomer's hard-muscled arm. It was exactly the same as the one Scott had on his arm. Crossed bones and a skull.

The one with the sunglasses stepped up for the secret hand-shake. "They won't get away with this," he said. He held out a wadded-up paper sack. "We brought you some beer, but the law-and-order man wouldn't let us bring it in here. He confiscated it. I guess they don't pay him enough to buy his own."

Scott laughed and nodded his head. When he finally remembered I was there, he gave me a cool look. "That's all for now," he said, dismissing me.

I was about to give him a piece of my mind when I felt Deputy Dattilo's hand lightly touch my arm. He nodded at me, and I followed him out of the jail and into the main office of the sheriff.

"Who are those guys?" I asked.

"Trouble."

I wasn't going to argue that.

"Your client, there, has friends in low places. Couple of ex-cellmates. They go by the names Spider and Ray-Ban. They actually tried to walk in here with a six-pack. Cute, huh?"

"I'm charmed." These were the guys Millie had told me about.

Dattilo closed and locked the door to the jail. "Those two rode into town yesterday, and we've had three complaints on them already. They've been riding through The Grove, gunning their motors, yelling, throwing beer cans at kids. That kind of stuff. As soon as we can catch them in the act, they'll be in the cell beside their buddy."

The Grove was a part of Zinnia that was predominantly black. "Does the word self-destructive come to mind when you look at Scott Hampton?" I asked, disgusted with my client. He'd greeted the two bikers like long-lost brothers.

"The word guilty comes to mind," Dattilo said. "Guilty and not nearly as smart as he thinks he is."

9

SITTING ASTRIDE REVELER, I GREETED THE SUN FRIDAY MORNING
as it nudged against the water oaks along the banks of the
Tallahatchie River. In August, the heat provides a half-light in
those hours before true sunrise—a time when past and present
mingle in shadows and whispers.

A thick mist hung over the cotton fields that grew right to the
edge of the river. The fields stretched into the fog, and as I stared,
I saw the silhouettes of slaves walking the rows, checking the
plants for insects and fungus, pulling the weeds.

They moved silently, intent on their tasks. Harvest would come
in mid-fall. The pickers, long sacks dragging behind them, would
bend to the white tufts of fiber that burst from the boles. A fast
picker could harvest up to three hundred pounds in a day.

Reveler stomped his hoof in impatience to be moving, and
Sweetie Pie came bounding out of the Tallahatchie, shaking the
cool water from her fur. My horse, my dog, and I were the present, but there was another presence in the fields. The past seemed
to rise from the dirt and blend into the fog, creating shapes and

images down the rows of cotton. One of the distant shadows craned his neck to look at us. He turned back to his work, singing as he did. The low, mournful sound seemed to wind itself into the mist, hanging in the air.

Farther away, another shadow answered, and the song spread across the field. It told a story both joyful and sad. Like the history of this land that I loved, the blues were a contradiction.

The sun topped the trees and sent a shaft of light into the misty field. The silhouettes of the men and women evaporated, and I was alone again.

Those images still in my mind, I nudged Reveler into a canter and raced through the last cotton field. Ahead, Dahlia House rose solid and real against a pink-and-mauve sky. I dismounted in the front yard, intending to walk Reveler cool.

"Red sky in the mornin', sailors take warnin'," Jitty said from the porch. "We'll have rain this afternoon."

She was wearing a sleeveless orange shift and matching pumps. The way she stood, determined yet vaguely unsure, she reminded me of a young woman setting out for her first job interview.

"So now you're a weather forecaster," I said, hoping to make her smile. My own thoughts were troubled by both the past and the present.

"Your great-great-grandma used to say that about the sky. She was more often right than wrong. Back then, bein' able to predict the weather meant survivin' for another day. Maybe for a season, if a crop was at stake."

"Did you ever harvest cotton?" I asked Jitty.

Instead of answering, she looked down at her hands. They were long and elegant, the palms soft. "We've both done hard labor, Sarah Booth. I'm more interested in what you're gonna do today than what I did yesterday."

"Scott's bond hearing is this morning." I walked Reveler the length of the porch, turned, and circled back toward her.

"Do you really believe he's worth helpin'?" Jitty asked.

I pondered her question. Yesterday, in his presence and under the full blast of his charisma, I'd believed him when he said he was innocent. This morning, I was having second thoughts. "I can't be sure."

"A man like Scott Hampton can make a woman believe just about anything he wants her to believe."

I looked at Jitty and realized that she knew I was attracted to Scott. I hadn't even admitted it to myself until that moment. It was an attraction fraught with paradox. He worked on me in a strange way, making me wary of him and yet wanting more of him. In that way, he, too, was like the blues.

"Scott isn't interested in making me believe anything," I told her.

"You can lie to yourself, but you can't lie to me." She stood so still. I'd never seen Jitty so static.

"What if he is innocent and I just walk away?"

"Is he that big a part of *your* future?" Jitty countered.

I started to repeat to her what Bridge had said, about how Scott could be my ticket to big-time cases.

She held up a hand and stopped me. "This isn't about future cases or the cover of *Rolling Stone* magazine. Watch yourself, Sarah Booth. A person can recover from hard work, but there are some mistakes that can't never be undone. Don't let Scott Hampton be that for you." She walked through the front door and was gone.

THE COURTROOM WAS jam-packed when I got there. Scott was seated at the defense table, to the left. Beside him was a young man I recognized as a court-appointed attorney. As I recalled, he'd gotten his law degree two months before.

True to her vow, Nandy was still outside the west-wing door, boom box blaring. She'd made more signs, all of them proclaiming Scott's innocence. One had declared his godhood, but I'd surreptitiously yanked that one out of the ground and hidden it in the camellia bushes. Nandy was not helping matters at all, and I had begun to seriously wonder about her motives. I intended to point out to Coleman that if she'd seen Scott at the club, she was there, too, and was therefore also a suspect.

Ida Mae Keys was in the fourth row behind Scott, seated alone. I slipped in beside her. She nodded once to acknowledge me, then turned her attention to the front of the room as the judge entered.

Coleman stepped into the room through a side door that led to the jury deliberation room. Tinkie was right on his heels, and they both stopped beside the door. Coleman's gaze found me immediately, but I could read nothing on his face.

He bent down to Tinkie, who was giving him an earful about something. His gaze shifted to Ida Mae, brushed over me, and then returned to my partner.

Judge Clarence Hartwell gaveled the room to order. He was a middle-aged man who was popular in town. He'd been a football coach at the high school and was known for his rapid—as in reactionary—judicial decisions. For the first time since I'd known him, he was wearing a robe. On closer examination, I saw it belonged to the First Baptist Church choir.

Lincoln Bangs was at the prosecution table, dressed in a suit that must have cost an arm and a leg. No doubt he had a date with the television crews that were setting up on the lawn. Judge Hartwell had ordered them out of the courthouse. There were several reporters I didn't know sitting across the room beside Cece Dee Falcon and Garvel LaMott from the *Zinnia Dispatch*. I was only a little surprised to see Cece on the case. High society was normally her beat, but I guess she'd managed to stretch her territory to include high celebrity.

Lincoln gave a brief summary of the evidence against Scott, including the fact that they now had a blood match between the stains on the money found in Scott's saddlebags and Ivory. It was devastating news that drew the intended gasp from the audience.

The young man, who was obviously Scott's lawyer, stood up and stated that the evidence was circumstantial. Linc countered with the fact that Scott had no ties to the community and a criminal record. Judge Hartwell set the bail at five hundred thousand dollars. It was over in less than ten minutes.

The bailiff came to lead Scott back to the jail, but Ida Mae was quicker. She was out of her seat and at the defense table in a matter of seconds. She put one hand on Scott's shoulder and squeezed. The face he turned to her was cold.

"Stay out of this, Ida Mae," he said.

"I can't." Her reply was carved in stone.

"I don't want your help." Scott walked away from her, following the bailiff out of the room as a hubbub of noise broke around him. Ida Mae came back to me, ignoring the reporters that sprang in her wake. Her cool fingers touched my wrist. "I want that boy out of jail," she said. "He thinks he can run me off with that bad attitude, but it won't work. I saw Scott sit with my husband and argue about Ivory's reputation in the black community and how he was damaging it by hiring a white, ex-racist ex-con. Scott loved my husband. I won't abandon him now."

"I'm not so sure he wants out of jail," I said. "It might be best if he stayed put." The image of a bloodthirsty lynch mob and the bitter ironies implied by such were racing through my mind.

"Mrs. Keys! Mrs. Keys!" A reporter who was wearing a name badge from *Rolling Stone* magazine came up to us. "I'd like to schedule some time to talk," he said.

"I've got one thing to say, and that's all. Scott Hampton didn't kill my husband. He's an innocent man, and Miss Delaney is going to prove it."

I was still recovering from the shock of that bold statement when the reporter leaned in closer. "Your son tells me that Hampton is guilty and that he's got some hold on you. He says it's voodoo."

I could see the insult in Ida Mae's eyes. "Some *hold* on me like voodoo." She was furious. "I'm a Christian woman and voodoo holds no sway with me. My son is mistaken, as he is in so many things."

"Emanuel Keys said Hampton deceived both you and Mr. Keys."

"My *son* said these things about me and his father?" It was asked gently, but even the reporter caught the hint of anger.

"That's what he said. If you'd like to refute his statements . . ."

"It's Emanuel who's deceived," Ida Mae said. "He's let hatred and ugliness eat away his soul."

She turned abruptly and walked out of the courtroom, ignoring the other reporters that ran after her. I looked up to find that Coleman had gone, and Tinkie was talking with great animation to Cece.

I walked over to them, catching Tinkie's baleful glare.

"That Emanuel Keys is the rudest man I have ever met," Tinkie fumed. "Next time you want some information from him, you can go get it yourself."

Cece's perfect white teeth were revealed in a Big Bad Wolf smile. She shifted her weight from one hip to another in a way that made several courtroom spectators glance up and then down her shapely legs.

"What happened?" I asked.

"I finally tracked him down yesterday evening. When I asked a few questions, he told me to mind my own business. Then he called me a parasite, a bloodsucker who lived off the misery of the poor. And then he told me to tell Oscar that he was looking into filing a lawsuit against the bank."

"A lawsuit?" That was even more than I'd imagined.

"A class action suit. He said that Oscar and my father used race as a qualifying factor in giving out loans." Tinkie's tiny fists were clenched at her sides, and she stomped one Gucci-clad foot for emphasis. "The nerve of that man."

"I don't think his mama likes him any better than you do," I allowed.

"I told you this case was going to rip the community apart. I told you, but nothing would do but that you put us right in the middle of it."

"Tinkie, you and I both know Emanuel doesn't have any grounds for a lawsuit." I intended to soothe her.

"To hell with the lawsuit!" She was speaking so loudly that several people had stopped talking to watch us. "He can sue till he's blue in the face, for all I care."

"Tinkie!" I put a hand on her arm. "Calm down." She was genuinely upset, and tears glistened in her eyes.

"I don't want to calm down," she said. "Oscar's worked hard to give everyone in this county as much of a break as he could. Black, white, it doesn't matter to him. Dammit." She wiped at a tear that slipped down one cheek. "I hate this, Sarah Booth. I just hate it."

She turned away from Cece and me and left the courtroom by the door she'd entered. She could at least avoid the reporters that way.

I looked at Cece. "Let's go get her. I hate to see Tinkie this upset."

"Let her go," Cece said, shaking her head. "She'll calm down in a bit."

"I wouldn't have sent her to talk to Emanuel if I'd had any idea he would upset her so."

"It's not just Emanuel."

I waited for her to explain, but since I didn't have her favorite bribe—a cheese Danish—I wondered if she'd be cooperative.

"Margene threatened to quit today."

"Margene!" I couldn't believe it. No wonder Tinkie was so upset. "Why?"

"Margene said she wasn't going to work for anyone who defended the man who killed Ivory Keys." Cece had a way of laying it out on the line when she wanted to.

"But—" I sighed. "Scott hasn't been found guilty yet."

"Not by a jury, but if it was left to the community, he'd be swinging from that magnolia tree out on the lawn," she said.

Her words eerily brought back the memory of the noose swinging from the tree. Someone had already made that point quite clearly. "Look, Margene loves Tinkie and Oscar. She loves Chablis. She won't quit."

Cece waited patiently for the truth to penetrate.

"Will she?" I asked.

"Yes. She may not want to, and she may regret it, but she will. Sarah Booth, you have to remember that Ivory was the most successful black man in this county. He stood for a lot of things to a lot of people."

"Ivory was successful *since* Scott Hampton came to play in his club," I said with some force. "Before that, he was sucking wind big-time."

She nodded. "Scott was the draw. But Ivory was the man they loved. He was a man that everyone could look up to."

I couldn't deny that. I didn't want to. "Ida Mae believes Scott is innocent. Didn't you see her just ten minutes ago?"

Cece nodded. "I saw her, and I intend to use that in my story. But most folks think Ida Mae has been taken in by Scott."

I saw the fine hand of Emanuel Keys in that rumor. And I wondered what kind of son would paint his parents as stupid and deluded just to win points.

"What, so people think Scott put a spell on Ida Mae?"

Cece's eyes narrowed. "That's exactly what they're saying. Rumor is that Scott sold his soul to Satan to learn to play the guitar like he does. And now he's used his power to convince Ida Mae he's innocent."

I took a long, slow breath. With rumors like that floating around town, things could only get worse.

10

IF IDA MAE WAS GOING TO GET SCOTT OUT OF JAIL, SHE WAS
going to have to come up with ten percent of the bond—a cool
fifty thousand, cash. That was good only if a bond agent would
stand in the remainder. According to the facts Tinkie had pumped
from Oscar, there was money in the Keys bank account, but the
mortgage on Playin' the Bones was steep, and it would come due
every month whether the club was open or not. I didn't think Ida
Mae had the scratch to just drop fifty large. Not on top of the five
she'd given me, which was once again sitting in the pie safe at
Dahlia House.

Since I didn't want to think about Tinkie, or Scott, or
Coleman, I was thinking dollars as I left the courtroom. The blare
of the loud music stopped me in my tracks. Then I heard the bullhorn.

"Scott Hampton is an innocent man. Let's hear it now. Free
Scott! Free Scott! Free Scott!" Nandy Shanahan's voice roared
through the amplifying system, but as closely as I listened, I didn't
hear a crowd joining in. No big surprise there.

I walked out to the south side of the courthouse, which was nearest the jail. Nandy had moved her headquarters there in the hopes of gaining a glimpse of Scott. Maybe she *was* a stalker. Heck, anyone who'd been brought up in a household devoted to a headless queen would be bound to have some emotional scars. One of the rumors from high school was that Mr. Shanahan had taken every photograph of everyone in his household and had them digitally altered to reflect the Stuart nose. Holyrood—the real one in Edinburgh, not the fake one in Zinnia—boasted a gallery of portraits with that very same nose. The portraitists had been ordered to paint the Stuart nose on everyone, to physically reflect their claim to royal blood.

Nandy lifted the bullhorn and turned sideways. I caught a profile, curious to see if she'd done anything with a scalpel to her own schnozzola. Though she'd poked holes in numerous body parts, she'd left her stubby little nose alone.

She was pacing the steps with her bullhorn, exhorting the crowd of six white farmers to take action to save Scott. The only action she got was when one of the men leaned over to spit tobacco on the grass.

"Okay, now all together. Free Scott! Free Scott! Free Scott!" She worked the megaphone. None of the farmers responded. They simply stared at her like they might a two-headed chicken. As she lowered the bullhorn and glared at the men, I recognized the sign of an impending emotional storm. She shot laser beams with her eyes at them and they passively stared back at her.

"I told you to chant with me." She put her hands on her hips and shook back her two-toned hair. "I know you cretins can't read, but surely you can talk."

"We can talk," the one wearing a long-sleeved shirt and overalls said. "The trouble is, you talk too much. Ivory Keys was a good man. He was murdered and robbed, and the person who did it is going to pay. Right now, that guitar man you seem so intent on savin' looks like the murderer to me." He grinned, but it wasn't humorous. "I'd leave that boy in jail if I were you. Bad things might happen if he was out and roamin' around."

The men all laughed and turned away, walking toward Main Street where they'd gather for lunch at Millie's or the competing diner, Arlene's.

"Redneck creeps," Nandy said. She pulled a tube of expensive skin lotion from her pocket and began to rub it into her hands. "Assholes." There was a five-second pause. "Cow fuckers!" she yelled at their backs.

They turned around in unison to stare at her. These were men who were slow to anger, but Nandy was beginning to wear on them.

One of them stepped forward. "Ma'am, that's no way to talk. You sound cheap."

"You wouldn't know cheap—"

I'd seen the black Mustang round the corner. It was a model from the eighties, and it showed its age. A slender black arm came out of the passenger side and lobbed a rotten tomato that landed at Nandy's feet, the red pulp spattering on both her and the farmer.

"Come on, you white assholes," one of the blacks in the car taunted. "Come on!"

Another tomato sailed through the air, landing a foot from the farmer, the pulp flying up from the hot sidewalk.

The farmer turned slowly and stared at the car. "There's only so much of that a man will take," he called out. "You boys go on home before things get out of hand."

"Boys! We aren't boys!" the youth jeered back.

"No, you're total asswipes," Nandy screamed out. "Get out of that car and come fight like men." She laughed at them. "Cowards!"

The door of the courthouse swung open and Dewayne and Gordon came spilling out. The black Mustang peeled rubber as it drove away.

"You okay, Sam?" Gordon asked the farmer.

"Sure enough, but if someone doesn't get a handle on this, there's going to be trouble. Tomato washes out. Blood is a little harder."

"I'll have those young men rounded up and brought in," Gordon promised him. "I know who they are."

The deputies and farmers parted, going their own way. I was left alone with the source of trouble.

"Nandy." I tapped her shoulder and stepped back when she whirled around so rapidly I thought she might slam into me.

"What the hell do you want?" she snapped.

"They set bond at five hundred thousand." I was hoping to enter the conversation with a tidbit of fact that would serve as a white flag. Such was not to be the case.

"Oh, big news! Like I haven't heard that thirty times already. Where are you going to get the money to get him out, that's what I want to know."

"Maybe your folks would loan it to him." I pretended it was really a possibility.

"They hate him," Nandy said with more than a little anger. "They blame him for the breakup of my marriage."

"You were married?" I hadn't heard a word about it, but then I hadn't kept up with the upper-crust gals. In fact, I couldn't remember Nandy seriously dating anyone in college. "Do I know him?"

"Yes and no. Yes I was married and no you never met him. Thank goodness." She rolled her eyes. "It was another brilliant maneuver by my father."

"Did you marry a local boy?" How had Cece failed to fill me in on this important issue? Nandy had been married. That probably left me as the only spinster in my entire peer group. All of this time, in the back of my mind, I'd had Nandy as my safety net. Now the cheese stood alone.

"Not local. From Edinburgh. Robert Pennington McBruce. Father almost died and went to heaven when he heard the name. Robert could have been a toad with warts. It wouldn't have mattered. It was arranged exactly like a royal couple. Letters, dowries, assurances of religious practices, and even a clause that the children would be raised Catholic." She pulled at the ring in her eyebrow, stretching the skin out until I wanted to slap her hands away. "He might have been a McBruce, but he wasn't anything like the Highland lord I imagined when we became betrothed."

I felt my eyes widening. "You were engaged to him before you met him?"

She gave me a withering glance. "Of course. Our parents arranged it. The agreement was airtight and perfect."

I needed a crash helmet, but I was going to ask anyway. "So why did you leave him?"

"He had a little dick and he whimpered in his sleep."

"Nandy!"

"Don't go all wide-eyed like a gigged frog, Sarah Booth." She gave me a contemptuous smile. "If Robert hadn't been such a little sniveling toad, it would have worked out fine."

"You're divorced?" The question I wanted to ask was if Robert was still breathing. Nandy had always taken the most efficient route to getting what she wanted. Robert might well be planted somewhere.

"Of course not! Divorce isn't acknowledged in the church. I simply walked out. Robert whines about it whenever he can track me down, but he doesn't have the balls to stop me."

Now I had a much better understanding of the Nandy transformation. She was pissed as hell at her folks, and she was getting even.

My Aunt LouLane had an old, wise saying: Don't step on a scorpion's tail if you don't want him to sting you. I took a baby step back from Nandy. I had a funny feeling she was just about to sting.

"Have you got a plan for getting Scott out of jail?" she demanded.

Her tone was high-handed and offensive. I didn't want to be stung, but I wasn't going to be bulldozed by a punked-out former debutante. "I have a better question. Why did you tell Coleman that you saw Scott leaving the club at two in the morning?"

"It was the truth."

"It's one of the main pieces of evidence that tie Scott to the murder."

"So I've been told." She pulled at the ring again and the sapphire caught the sunlight, winking blue.

I had a sudden insight into the twisted inner workings of Nandy Shanahan's mind. "You *knew* that when you told Coleman. You knew you were putting Scott right in the middle of a murder scene." I was astounded.

"Look, if Scott will only talk to me, I can give him an alibi. I can say we were together, behind the club."

She smiled, and tiny little chills slipped down my back.

"I can save him, Sarah Booth. All I have to do is say he was with me, making love to me. I can save him, if he'll let me."

FUNNY HOW COLD can creep through a person's bones even with the mercury hovering at 102 degrees Fahrenheit. I was still shivering when I got behind the wheel of the roadster and headed toward The Grove. I wanted to talk to my high school friend, Tammy Odom, better known these days as Madame Tomeeka, psychic. Tammy and I went back a long way, and I knew I could count on her to tell me how the black community was reacting to Scott and the two goodwill ambassadors from Scott's prison past. There was also the little matter of my dream. Tammy had no formal training in dream analysis, but she had something better. She had a gift.

There was a big Expedition in Tammy's front yard, so I parked half a block down the street and waited. In less than ten minutes, Vergie Caswell came out of Tammy's, her face hidden by a huge golf umbrella that sported the logo of The Club. She peeped out from under the umbrella, casting glances left and right, then scurried into her SUV and tore off down the street like the Hound of the Baskervilles was in hot pursuit.

I hustled up to Tammy's door and gave it a knock. She was frowning when she opened it, but her lips did a reversal and ended up in a smile as soon as she saw me.

"I didn't have another appointment today, and I was pissed off that someone just dropped by. Folks think they can come in whenever they take a notion." She held the screen open for me to enter. I caught a whiff of something good cooking, and I almost ran over Tammy as she led the way to the kitchen.

"What is that?" I asked, sniffing. My acute olfactory abilities led me straight to the oven.

"Sarah Booth, you know good and well I'm baking a roast." She was getting plates and silverware out as she talked. "Would you like to stay for lunch?"

"Oh, I don't want to be a bother."

She threw a dishtowel at me. "Sit down. Or better yet, make us a couple of glasses of iced tea."

I did as she instructed, and in a few moments, we were seated across from each other, plates heaped with food and big glasses of iced tea sweating in front of us.

"I saw Vergie hightailing it out of here." I was dying of curiosity. Vergie Caswell was four years older than me, but she'd been a prominent figure in my development. In her senior year, she'd been drum majorette, class beauty, campus queen, most popular, cutest, and most likely to succeed. That left friendliest and most athletic for the rest of the female population to thrash it out over. Vergie had married a landed Buddy Clubber and they were raising hounds, horses, and hoodlums about five miles west of town.

"She looked better as a brunette," Tammy allowed. She lifted a piece of tender roast to her mouth.

"Tobias junior isn't in trouble again, is he?" Last I'd heard, the fourteen-year-old hellion had hot-wired the SUV, driven across the Delta to Mississippi State University at Starkville, broken into the university's experimental agricultural station, and stolen ten top-grade marijuana plants with a potential street value of close to twenty-five thousand dollars. When he was captured, he'd only said that for a cow college, State grew damn good dope.

"Would you pass the butter?" Tammy said.

"Vergie looked upset. I hope it isn't her health."

Tammy pointed to the salt and pepper. "I should have put just a little more garlic on the roast, don't you think?"

I sighed. Tammy was worse than a priest. She never talked

about her clients. I was wasting my breath. "I need some advice," I said, handing over the condiments to her.

"As long as it's about your business and not someone else's." She smiled, but she was dead serious.

"My business. And Ida Mae Keys'."

The smile slipped off her face. "I was so sorry to hear about Ivory. He was a good man."

I nodded. "Everyone seems to think so."

"I know you make your living investigating cases, but this is one I wish you'd stay out of."

"That's not an original opinion," I noted.

"So what do you want to know?"

"How the black community feels toward Scott. I—"

"Angry. Folks are angry. They feel Scott stabbed Ivory in the back. Literally and figuratively. They think he's a no-good, racist user."

"Don't hold back," I said.

"You know about Scott before he came here?" she asked me. "About his so-called music?"

"Are you referring to his rap music?"

She snorted. "I don't call that noise music, and neither do most of the people around here. It's all there, on the Internet. He can't deny it."

"I don't think he'd try."

"Because in his heart, he's still a racist Nazi!"

I reached across the table and gently touched her trembling hand. She was very upset. "No, that's not what I meant. I just don't think Scott would try to deny what he's done in the past. I'm not saying he believes it was right. I'm just saying he wouldn't try to lie about it."

"It's going to take a real makeover artist to paint that man as noble," Tammy said bitterly.

Tammy normally wasn't a woman who let emotion rule her. I decided to shift the conversation slightly. "Have you seen those two motorcycle guys?"

"You mean his two cellmates?" She pushed her plate back, her food barely touched. "It's a good thing my grandbaby Dahlia isn't here or I'd be worried they'd run her down."

Dahlia, named after my own home, wasn't toddling yet. But I got Tammy's point. "Those two make me nervous."

"They've come here to defend their *brother*. They ride down the street trying to start a fight." She clenched her napkin in her fist. "They want trouble, Sarah Booth. And if they don't stop pushing at us, they're going to get it."

There it was, the them and us. My own appetite died. "I'd like to find out more about them."

"It shouldn't be hard to find them. Just follow the trail of empty beer bottles."

I'd actually come to talk to Tammy about my dream, but now I had a bigger concern. "This case won't come between us, will it?"

She kept her gaze on her food. "Scott Hampton is a bad man, Sarah Booth. You know, my mama always said that if you lay down with dogs, you'll get up with fleas."

"I know he looks guilty. I wouldn't have taken this case if Ida Mae hadn't insisted."

Tammy lifted her dark eyes to stare into mine. "That poor woman. She's caught in the middle."

"By helping her, I'm caught, too."

"Are you sure of your own motives, Sarah Booth?"

I could have taken offense, but I didn't. "I'm sure that Scott doesn't want my help."

"Be careful. That's all I can tell you."

The slash between her eyebrows told me exactly how worried she was. "Can you see something in the future?"

"I see a world of trouble coming from this. For everyone involved." She hesitated. "And I see danger. There's not a clear picture yet, but before this is over, folks will see violence."

"I'll be careful," I promised her, determined not to let her see how her words affected me. Then I told her about my dream, about the clock/calendar that kept running backwards to the mid-sixties.

She shook her head. "Even your subconscious is aware that

we're about to repeat history. You're warning yourself, Sarah Booth. All I can tell you is to listen up."

A timid tap came from the front door, and Tammy slowly rose to her feet.

"I thought you didn't have another appointment today."

"I don't. I'll tell them to make one and come back."

I stood up. It was time for me to leave. There wasn't anything left to say between us, for the moment.

I walked with her to the front door. When she opened it, I had an impulse to step back into the kitchen. Connie Peters stood at the screen, her round face thinner than I'd ever seen it. Her sundress hung from shoulders that were sculpted and thin. She must have dropped thirty pounds since I'd seen her last.

"I know I don't have an appointment," Connie said, pressing the knuckles of one hand with the other. "I have to talk to you, Ms. Tomeeka. Please."

Tammy opened the screened door for her to enter and held it open until I took the hint and walked through it.

"Sarah Booth," Connie said, flushing. "I didn't expect to see you here. Getting some leads for your new case from the spirit world?"

She wasn't being snide. She smiled, and I was aware of the lines of tension around her mouth. I was also aware of the boulder of guilt that fell squarely on my shoulders.

"I'm just talking to an old friend," I said, walking down the steps. "Good to see you, Connie."

"Sarah Booth?"

I turned around to face her, hoping that my expression gave away nothing of what I was feeling.

"I know you and Coleman have become good friends this past year. I'd like to talk to you sometime, when you have time." She blinked, and I was suddenly afraid she'd cry.

"Sure. Give me a call." I walked back to my car and drove away, wanting more than anything to point the roadster in any direction other than the one I felt myself traveling.

11

IT WAS PROBABLY GUILT, ANGST, AND A DESIRE FOR PUNISHMENT that sent me out to Bilbo Lane at eighty miles an hour. I'd made the assumption that Scott's buddies from the Big House were probably camping at his digs. I saw the bikes as I turned down the driveway, which was sprouting a healthy growth of briars and weeds. The ditch was littered with beer bottles, and I wondered if Scott was a slob or if his friends drank all of their meals.

My wiser self attempted to send up an alert, and I even considered turning the car around and leaving. But then the biker I assumed was called Spider walked out on the front porch of the little cottage and saw me. To turn tail would have revealed my fear of him.

I drove to the cottage and got out of the car.

He looked me up and down, his gaze lingering on all of the places that made a woman feel violated. "Scott's developed some fine-looking friends since he left us," Spider said over his shoulder, and Ray-Ban, wearing his signature sunglasses, stepped out the door.

Spider directed his next comment to Ray-Ban, but loud enough for me to hear. "She sure don't look like those women who get off on fucking ex-cons. I guess you get a different class of woman when you're a big blues musician."

"Mrs. Keys has hired me to prove Scott's innocence," I said, one hand still on the fender of the roadster as if the car could protect me. The two men made me nervous, and the maddening thing was that they did it deliberately. They were all about demeaning and intimidation. Anger put a little starch in my spine and I walked up to the porch, casting a disparaging glance at the litter of hamburger wrappers, fried chicken boxes, and beer bottles.

"We'll have to clean this up before Scott gets out," Spider said. He turned to Ray-Ban and laughed. "He always was a neat freak. Kept his cell spic and span."

For some reason, that made me feel better. "You both claim to be friends of Scott. What you're doing around town isn't helping him."

"That's from your point of view," Spider said. He grinned, but his gray eyes were not amused. "I learned a long time ago that making folks understand there's a price to be paid for their actions is a lot more effective than going around all mealy-mouthed and pleasant."

"I don't know where you're from, but that doesn't work around here." I was angry, but I was also not an idiot. I had no intention of pushing these men too far.

"I'm from—" He took two quick steps down to the yard. He was beside me so fast I didn't have time to withdraw. "Hell. Or at least that's what these folks are gonna believe before I'm through with them."

On the porch, Ray-Ban laughed in one big hoot. He eased to the top of the steps.

I was very sorry I'd come here.

"You know anything about training dogs?" Spider asked.

"I didn't come here to discuss dog training. I—"

He cut me off. "You can treat an animal nice and sweet, and

maybe half the time they'll do what you say. But you put fear into them, you make them understand they don't do what you say and they're gonna suffer, then they'll mind. Not *half* the time. Not *two-thirds* of the time. But ever' time you open you mouth. That's the way you make *animals* fall into line."

"You're wrong about that. And we're not dealing with animals." His inference was too clear to ignore.

"That's a matter of opinion, Miss Sarah Booth Delaney of Dahlia House."

I hadn't told him my name, but he knew it. He wanted me to know he knew my name, and where I lived, and all that it implied.

"Scott's in serious trouble. A large portion of the community, both black and white, respected Ivory Keys. They want to punish the person who killed him. If they continue to believe Scott is that person, he's going to be convicted, or worse."

"I guess it's up to me and Ray-Ban to make the folks around here understand that if Scott goes to prison, there's gonna be some of that spontaneous combustion." The two men laughed loud and long. "There'll be some fires and some other accidents. Folks might even consider what's gonna happen as acts of God. A real angry God."

That set both of them off into spasms of laughter.

"That's a good one, Spider. Acts of God." Ray-Ban was about to fall down laughing.

"You aren't helping Scott." Repetition might work, but I doubted it.

"We're the only friends he's got around here. Everyone else wants to lynch him." Spider's eyes glittered. "I've heard the talk. Folks would string him up without a second thought. They won't give him a fair trial. He's tried and convicted right this minute. This trial is just a formality—just a way for that power-hungry D.A. to get his mug on TV. You know that and so do I. So just make it a point to stay out of our way. We're gonna help our friend the way that works best for us."

"You're going to help him right into a conviction." I was wasting my breath. "If you don't stop trying to terrorize people, you're going to end up in a cell right beside him. And then folks will say the three of you are thugs who need to be locked away. Your actions justify everything people think about Scott."

"Then let 'em think they're scared, because before this is over, they sure as hell will be."

It was pointless. Spider and Ray-Ban weren't going to listen to reason. Maybe Scott could talk some sense into them before the damage they did was irreparable.

MY GREETING AT the jail was rather like a dip in a Himalayan river. Frostbite began to set in three seconds after I got there.

"What now?" Scott asked.

"You need to tell your friends to settle down, or even better, get out of town."

He shook his head. "I can't do that."

"Why not?" I was genuinely puzzled.

"I don't owe you explanations."

I'd had it. "You don't owe me a damn thing, and I owe you even less. But your friends are making it worse for you and for Mrs. Keys. Why can't you simply tell them to hit the road? Things are complicated enough."

Scott watched me a moment, as if he was making up his mind about something. "Okay, I'll tell you. But you won't understand."

"Try me."

"Back in prison, Spider and Ray-Ban were the only two friends I had. We looked out for each other. And now they're here to help me. You don't order your friends out of town when they've come to give help."

"They aren't helping. They're hurting you. A lot. They're stirring up a lot of racial tension that isn't going to do anything but make it harder, for you and for everyone in this community."

"I told you you wouldn't understand." He came up to the bars and stared directly into my eyes. "In prison, a solitary person doesn't stand a chance. If you don't have friends or a group to back you up, you become everybody's bitch. That's just the way it is."

I swallowed but kept my mouth shut.

"I wasn't a badass, or at least not the kind that counted in prison. I hadn't killed or raped or done violence. I was in on a drug charge, and I was upper-class white. No one had to paint a target on me. Every man in that prison took one look at me and began to decide what service I would provide. Walking into that place, I knew I had to align myself with a stronger force, or I'd be shaving my legs and wearing perfume."

"And so you joined the Bonesmen? For protection?" Even I wasn't quite that naïve.

"There wasn't a bridge club available." His sarcasm was quick and angry. "The Bonesmen were a formidable presence in the prison. I couldn't join the Muslims or the blacks. I was from the wrong background. Believe it or not, racism isn't just a white thing. I joined the Bonesmen because they provided safety, and because I was a racist. *At that time.*"

"At that time?"

"That was before I met Ivory. That was when I was still reacting instead of thinking."

It was the first hint that there was more to Scott than hatred and meanness. "Tell me about your rap days."

He didn't answer for at least a full minute. "I believed what I wrote back then. I believed that everyone who wasn't white was inferior. That violence and laziness and a welfare-state-of-mind were innate characteristics of everyone except whites." His blue gaze was electric and strong. "I was wrong."

"I heard your rap songs. You were terrible." There was no nice way to say a man had no talent.

"I was," he agreed.

"What happened?"

"I met Ivory and he taught me how to play a guitar. Really play and understand that to get the most out of a musical instrument, you have to make love to it. You have to touch it, and stroke it, and arouse it, just like a woman."

I swallowed hard. The images he created were hard to ignore. I forced myself to continue. "So that was it? A little private tutoring from Ivory and you become this virtuoso?"

"It wasn't that easy." He stepped a little closer, and for the first time he really smiled at me. "You doubt that a great teacher and a lot of practice could change me?" His smile faded, and a dark light touched his eyes. "You've heard that I sold my soul to the devil, haven't you? That's what you're really asking about."

I wanted to deny it, but I couldn't. It sounded foolish, but so did a crash course in talent. Most musicians spent years becoming masters of an instrument. "You got a lot of talent mighty quick. How'd the rumor get started?" I didn't really believe Scott had met the devil at a crossroads and traded his soul, but there were a lot of ways of trading with the devil, or so I'd learned.

"I told Ivory that was a bad idea," he said softly. "But he was set on it. He said the rumor that a white boy had met Satan at the crossroads would put me in all the magazines." He exhaled. "And he was right. In many ways, Ivory was a genius."

"So you didn't sell your soul?"

"You want a flat confirmation or denial, don't you?" He was amused at me, yet the strange dark light lingered in his gaze. "I won't answer that outright, but I will tell you that I've paid a heavy price for my career. While you're pondering my pact with the devil, think about what you might give up to achieve your dream."

For a split second, he sounded like Jitty, and I wanted no conversation about my dreams or my sacrifices. "How did you learn to play so well so fast?" I pressed.

"It wasn't just that I learned to play the guitar. I became a different person. Scott the rapper died, and Scott the bluesman was born. It's that simple and that difficult. But once you let go of everything that defines you as a person—all the beliefs that hold you in place like a fly in a spider's web—anything is possible."

I considered a few choruses of a Buddhist chant I'd learned in New York, but I restrained myself. If Scott was shooting me a line of crap, he seemed to believe it totally. There was energy and passion in his face. If his soul hadn't been transformed, his features surely had, just by remembering it.

"That's what Ivory taught me. Sure, he taught me how to touch my guitar, how to whisper to her, and slide my fingers so light on her strings that she sighs."

As he talked, his hands moved involuntarily in the motion. His long fingers seemed to tremble with anticipation. I found it extremely difficult to breathe, and I put my hands around the bars of the cell for support.

"Ivory taught me all of that, but the most important thing was how to leave my old, pitiful self behind. That's why I'm telling you I used to be a racist. I believed what I wrote. But I honestly don't feel that way anymore. Now, those songs shame me."

"How did you and Ivory meet?" I'd heard a summarized version, but I wanted the whole story. Once again, in Scott's presence, I had begun to believe in his innocence.

"The Bonesmen had a prison band. Heavy metal is a kind way to describe it. It was the band that did all of the prison shows, and because of that, we had special privileges."

"Were Spider and Ray-Ban in the band?"

"They were backstage hands. Moving the speakers and such. They never played music. What happened was that Ivory had started a blues band. They were a whole lot better than us, and so the warden picked them to play one of the events. That was the wrong thing to do, to put a black blues band in the place of a white band. Especially a white band composed of members of an Aryan Brotherhood."

"The Bonesmen couldn't go after the warden, so they went after Ivory."

"Right. Four of them caught Ivory out in the exercise yard one morning. They dragged him back behind the laundry. They were going to sever the tendons in his left hand. Cripple him so he couldn't play."

"Were Ray-Ban and Spider part of this?"

He shook his head. "No, it was some other guys, but Spider and Ray-Ban knew it was coming down."

"I heard you intervened. Why?"

Scott took his time answering. "I'd heard Ivory play. He was better than good. He was great. He had a real talent, not like the guys in our band. I guess I just couldn't let them destroy such talent."

I could finally breathe easily again. "So you and Ivory became friends."

"Not friends. Not at first. He felt he owed me something, and he was determined to pay me back. He'd heard our band, too, and he didn't think much of our music or my playing, but he said he saw something in me. He said there was a chance I could be great."

"And he was right," I said. I hadn't intended to pay Scott a compliment. It just slipped out. He was a major talent, no matter what else could be said about him.

"Thank you, Miss Delaney. I didn't realize you were a fan of the blues."

"All my life." But I didn't want to talk about me, or music. Talking about music with Scott was dangerous. He made me feel too much. "We still have to resolve the problem of your two friends. I can see there's a bond between y'all, but they need to be controlled."

Scott shook his head. "They saved my life the same way I saved Ivory. That's one thing that old man and I had in common. We both admired loyalty. He understood why I couldn't just turn my back on the men who'd befriended me when I first went to prison. Even though they were part of an organization of men who would have crippled him, he understood that I owed them. And he had the same problem with his black friends when it became apparent we were growing close."

"You don't have to dump them as friends; you just have to get them out of town," I pointed out.

"They won't hang around here long. They'll grow tired of their games and head out when the beer runs out and it looks like they need to work. Just let them do it on their own time."

I didn't really have another option. Spider and Ray-Ban weren't going to take orders from me, that was a dead-certain fact.

THE STORM THAT Jitty had predicted was massed to the east. It hung over the horizon, a line of thick black clouds that moved swiftly toward the west. The sky beneath the clouds was a pale gray with a hint of yellow. Sailors and landlubbers alike would take warning from this storm. Tiny wisps of cloud hung down in several places, suggesting the potential for a twister.

I drove home and put the roadster in the shed. Reveler was eager to get in his stall and eat, and Sweetie barked from the porch, a reminder that she, too, wanted some chow and attention, in that order.

I went in the back door, expecting to find Jitty at the kitchen table. Instead, the house was deathly quiet. I hadn't felt so alone in Dahlia House since the weeks after my parents' deaths. I stood by the table and listened to the loud ticking of the kitchen clock. A wind gust kicked up outside and sent a tree branch clawing at the screen. Though I knew what it was, I jumped anyway.

"Jitty," I said, and to my shame I was whispering. "Jitty!"

I pushed through the swinging door, crossed the dining room, and went to the parlor. There was no sign of my ghost. Whatever Jitty was up to, she wasn't available to me. I would be left on my own to figure out my reaction to Scott and my overreaction to Coleman, who'd been absent from the sheriff's office when I left the jail. He'd been gone, but Bo-Peep had been there. She was quick to let me know that Coleman had taken the afternoon off. He and Connie had gone up to Moon Lake to spend the night.

To heck with Coleman and his marital problems. I had a date to get ready for. I trotted up the stairs, ran a bath, and went to the closet.

Based on the prerequisites that Bridge had set, I selected a pair of peach capri slacks and a peach and white checked bodice top. I had the perfect pair of sandals to wear with it.

The whole time I was getting ready, I kept looking over my shoulder for Jitty. A date was a big occasion for her to boss me around. It was strange that she didn't put in an appearance.

Just as I finished applying my Peach Perfection lipstick, a loud crack of thunder was followed by a terrific flash of lightning.

Dahlia House was plunged into darkness.

12

JITTY—HAD SHE BEEN AROUND TO COMMENT—WOULD HAVE SAID that getting dressed in the dark was one of my major talents. But she wasn't around, and I managed to ready myself for a romantic evening without the high-voltage companionship of Reddy Kilowatt or Jitty.

I was still wondering where Jitty had gone when the power came back on and Bridge arrived to whisk me to Zinnia. Though his main office was in Memphis, he'd rented an antebellum town house only a few blocks from Cece.

The residential section of Zinnia was not as old as estates like Dahlia House. This section of town had been developed for the merchant class, those men who made their living in commerce rather than on the land. The house Bridge had settled into was designed for lawn parties and entertainment. The exterior was all gracious Southern charm. Inside was a big surprise. Bridge had transformed the front parlor into a temporary Bedouin chamber. Pillows littered the floor, and candles glowed through layers of gauzy hangings, creating soft and intimate illumination.

I stopped in the foyer and simply stared. It had been a long, long time since a man had gone to this much trouble for me. "Wow." My statement was totally inadequate.

"Make yourself comfortable," Bridge said, dropping to one knee. He took my hands in his. "Do you trust me?"

"In what regard?" I wasn't exactly comfortable looking down at him.

"Close your eyes, Sarah Booth," he urged.

My Aunt LouLane always cautioned me that curiosity killed the cat. I was dying to know what Bridge was up to. I closed my eyes and felt his fingers at the straps of my sandals. In less than a minute I was barefoot and reclining in the middle of a sumptuous pillow while he'd gone to make drinks.

"I decided to forgo the goatskin filled with fermented grapes," he said, handing me a crystal martini glass. "I was more in the mood for cosmopolitans."

The pink drink was just fine with me. Jack Daniel's was normally my party companion, but I could shake up my habits when an opportunity presented itself.

Bridge had prepared—or had had prepared—a cold dinner of boiled and peeled shrimp, fruit, and crusty French bread. We nibbled and talked. Bridge had graduated from Ole Miss four years before I started. He and Oscar had been in the same classes, the same fraternity, the same social order.

I had a moment of concern, but it passed. Bridge obviously knew nothing of my college capers. He'd gone on to Harvard to pursue his master's by the time I arrived at Ole Miss. There were others who'd known me when I'd rejected sorority life, protested against the unfair double standards of class and gender, thrown in with the unorthodox theatre crowd, and generally disavowed my heritage and birthright.

Bridge might run into some of my old alumni, but I doubted they'd think to talk about me. Tinkie was the only friend Bridge and I shared in common, and Tinkie would never spill the beans. I certainly wasn't in a confessional mood, so I simply let him think we shared the same view of our college days—golden and fraught with unlimited earning potential.

We finished the shrimp, and Bridge cleared the food and dishes away. He made us fresh drinks, and when he settled onto the pillow beside me, I figured it was time to fish or cut bait. He was interested in me. Very interested. And I was at war with myself.

As if Jitty were sitting on my shoulder tweaking my libido, I felt the urge to shift a little closer to this man, to brush my calf across his shin, to let my fingers slide over his ribs on the way to holding his hand. These were all tiny gestures that gave a man the idea that he could take the next step without fear of being slapped. A very large part of me wanted Bridge to take the next step.

He was an eligible man, and I did desire him. He had wealth, good looks, social position, refinement, education, and a sense of humor. If his clothes weren't so obviously Italian, I would have suspected that he made them himself. In other words, he was perfect.

There were complications, though.

Tinkie's words danced in my mind. Bridge wasn't a man who liked an easy acquisition. He appreciated the game, the struggle, the challenge. An easy victory would eventually lead to boredom.

The idea that a man might grow bored with me was scalding. But that wasn't what was holding me back.

Coleman was the fly in the ointment. Ineligible, poorly paid, working in dangerous conditions, and married. This was the man who stood between me and "marrying up."

"What's on your mind, Sarah Booth?" Bridge asked. He leaned back on his elbows in the pillows, effectively relaxing *and* putting a little distance between us.

"I have a lot on my mind," I answered, which wasn't a lie.

"Scott Hampton?"

It was a logical assumption on Bridge's part. "When I'm talking to Scott, I believe completely that he's innocent. When I'm away from him and I think about the evidence, I have doubts." It was much easier to talk about Scott than it was about me.

"He's very charismatic. I bought some of his CDs yesterday. Shall I put them on?"

"Sure."

Bridge rose and started the music, mixing fresh drinks while he was up. When he settled back into the pillows, he offered his arm for me to lean against. "No pressure," he said. "I don't like pressure, and I suspect you don't either."

Add perceptive to his list of dazzling qualities. I shifted and leaned back against him, knowing that he was a gentleman. I sighed with pleasure.

"That's a girl," he said. "Relax. We'll never get to know each other if you feel on guard all the time."

I snuggled deeper into the pillow, and Bridge, and listened to Scott Hampton's wailing guitar take over the room. I thought I might be able to lounge back and enjoy the evening. But blues aren't the proper music for casual lounging. The blues get in the blood and move around the body. Pretty soon, the body's moving around, too. I didn't want that to happen, so I took a candle over to Bridge's music collection, which covered three shelves of a big bookcase. "You have everyone," I said, my finger tracing down the spines.

"About ten years ago I bought this map of Mississippi and it had the places marked where every blues musician in the state was born. I started collecting from there. Mississippi has produced some remarkable artists."

I sat cross-legged on the floor and let my index finger slide over the plastic covers. *Tick-tick-tick-tick,* all the way as far as I could reach. He had a vast collection. "Pinebox Simpson! My mother had an album of his."

"They redigitalized it and put it on CD. Better sound."

I slipped out a Wailin' Betty CD. One of the guest vocalists was Big Dumplin' Blues Mama. I'd caught her act in a seedy bar in New Orleans some ten years before. She was hot!

I felt Bridge ease down beside me. His fingers slid up my bare arm, resting on my shoulder. It was a gesture that could be taken as friendly, or something more. He was leaving it all up to me.

"Do you have anything with Ivory in it?" I asked.

"I have everything he's done," Bridge said, leaning forward so that his chest came against my shoulder. A very solid chest, I might add.

He pulled out a CD and put it on. As soon as the music started, there was no doubt the man on the piano was a master.

"Who's he playing with?" The lead guitar was good, but it wasn't Scott "The Blizzard" Hampton.

"Band called Mad Dog Blues. That was the band he was playing in before he went to prison."

"How come you know so much about Ivory?" I asked him, suddenly curious.

"I know about all of the Mississippi blues artists," he said. "But Ivory is local, and he was still very much alive and performing until recently. I took a special interest in him because I could see him perform live."

"Did you ever go to his club?"

"A couple of times," he said. "I haven't been home that much in recent years. I regret that."

"Ivory served time for murder." I let the statement hang out there.

"He did. I heard the story from a reliable source, but I never talked to him about it."

"Will you tell me what you know?"

"Of course." He glanced at my drink to make sure I wasn't running dry. "Ivory was a handsome man, by anyone's standards. He was tall and lean, with a neatly trimmed mustache. And he was a ladies' man. As you know, it's part of the blues."

I understood this on one level. The life of musicians, particularly the bluesmen of the past, was one of travel, long weeks on the road, and an abundance of easy women.

"Ivory made his living traveling around to nightclubs, playing music that made the folks listening want to abandon themselves to sin and pleasure." He shrugged. "Pain and death are always just around the corner, so better take pleasure where you can. That's the motto of the blues, Sarah Booth. Ivory played them with all his heart. He lived them, too."

I nodded. Temptation, for an average man or woman, is hard to resist. But give a person fame and charisma, put them on a stage performing down and dirty music, have the women in the room calling out invitations for sex and fun, and trouble is hovering in the air.

"It still doesn't make cheating on his wife right," I said, wondering how Ida Mae had finally put all this behind her.

"It doesn't," Bridge agreed. His hand swept under my hair, lifting it off my neck so that the air-conditioned breeze touched off a racy little chill. "Nothing makes cheating right. But I think you have to concede that a certain lifestyle leads one into temptation easier than another. A musician has a hundred chances to stray each time he plays live. That's a lot of temptation to resist."

I didn't say anything. Scott Hampton was on my mind. Women loved him. They got excited watching him play and perform. They'd lay down on the stage for him. I doubted he had much respect left for the entire gender.

"Ivory was playing up in Detroit. The band was a huge success and was drawing bigger and bigger crowds. There was a female vocalist by the name of Darcy Danton."

"I haven't heard of her," I said.

"Her career was short-lived."

"She was killed, wasn't she?" It was a guess, but a good one judging from the look on Bridge's face.

"I would call it murder. She was singing at the club, and she and Ivory became very close. The story goes that her husband was abusing her. She'd come into the club with bruises, black eyes, broken fingers. One night she came in after her husband had nearly strangled her to death. She couldn't sing. Couldn't make a sound." He paused. "Ivory moved her into his room."

Train wreck coming. I could see it clearly. "And one thing led to another."

"Exactly. What started out as comfort, friendship, and support ended up between the sheets. It didn't take her husband long to track her down, and he entered the room just about the time Ivory entered . . . well, you get the idea."

I did, and I was amused at Bridge's wry humor. "Ivory was caught *en flagrante*."

"The enraged husband knocked Ivory out, pulled Darcy from the bed, and began to beat her viciously. Ivory regained consciousness and got his gun. He shot the husband twice. Both times in the back."

"Self-defense would be hard to prove." I could visualize the scene where Ivory had done only what he had to do. But convincing a jury with two shots in the back would be hard.

"The man would have killed Darcy if Ivory hadn't stopped him when he did. As it was, she was hospitalized for a month. Brain damage. She was never really right after that. Her death was tragic."

I was certain I didn't want to hear this, but I had to ask. "How did she finally die?"

"She froze to death in an alley behind the club where she sang with Ivory's band. Story goes that she was waiting for Ivory to finish his set. She couldn't grasp that he was in prison."

"Well, shit." It was a tragic story. It seemed that Ivory's life, and death, had been closely twined with tragedy.

"I know. And now Ivory is dead."

"Murdered." I knew that certain people, take Spider and Ray-Ban for instance, lived in a world of violence and suffering. They chose violence. But Ivory hadn't been that kind of man. He'd been caught in one violent act. Yet it had followed him home to the Mississippi Delta.

"I've only met Mrs. Keys once. She seems like a very strong woman," Bridge said. "I guess she'd have to be. Ivory served a long time, and she waited for him. She forgave him and waited."

Greek mythology was filled with such women, and Ida Mae, indeed, was a mythic force. "She is remarkable," I said.

Bridge picked a silk string from one of the pillows that had gotten on my pants. "I don't want to be presumptuous, Sarah Booth, but what is Ida Mae going to do with the club now?"

"I don't know."

He cleared his throat. "As you can tell, I have a great love for the blues. I'd like to keep the club open, and I'd also like to help Ida Mae out of her financial pinch. Do you think she'd consider selling the club to me?"

It was an extremely generous offer. There was no guarantee Playin' the Bones could recover from what had happened there. Folks in Mississippi were still superstitious. A murder had occurred in the club. That fact alone might drive an audience away.

"I don't know what Ida Mae is going to do. I don't even know who inherits the club. There's a son, Emanuel." I tried to keep my voice level when I said his name.

"I know him, or rather his reputation," Bridge said. "He's a very astute businessman, but he hates the blues. I can't imagine he'd want the club, even if he inherits it."

I shrugged. "I know the club is important to Ida Mae because it was important to Ivory."

"Exactly. I have the money to keep it open and give it time to recover. I'd like to do that. Would you speak to her on my behalf?"

I was surprised. "Why don't you talk to her?"

He frowned. "I don't want her to think any pressure is being applied. There's a big mortgage on the place. Ivory did a lot of work on it." I nodded that I'd seen it. "I don't want Ida Mae to think I'm moving in like a vulture to pick the carcass. I just really want to help, and to make sure that the club remains open and the blues continue to be played there."

"That's very generous, Bridge. But maybe not the wisest business decision."

Bridge chuckled, and it was a low, masculine sound of amusement and confidence. I liked it immensely. "Perhaps I'm not the best businessman," he said, lifting both eyebrows. "A man should keep a little mystery about him or else the woman he's trying to impress will find him boring."

My eyebrows rose. "Don't tell me you actually have rules for hooking women."

"The young females of a certain social strata aren't the only ones with pressures. Men, too, have expectations put on them."

"Such as?" I prompted, delighting in my companion.

"To marry a beautiful woman who is not only a bauble on his arm but a good breeder, a good mother, active in the community, and not too demanding."

Even though I'd known this all of my life, I was still a little shocked to hear it verbally acknowledged by a man. "Someone actually *told* you this. I mean, like it's a rule."

"Sarah Booth," he said, shocked. "I thought you knew. I mean, the book has been in print for generations."

"What book?"

For the first time since I'd known him, Bridge frowned. "I really thought you knew. I should never have opened my mouth."

He rose quickly and went to make another drink.

Like a hound on the scent, I got up and followed him. "What book? There's actually a book of rules for men to follow in getting a woman?"

"A suitable woman. One who is of the same class and yet not too much . . . trouble."

He wouldn't look at me as he talked. I felt the heat rise to my cheeks. "Trouble! What's that supposed to mean?"

"A woman who accepts her responsibilities cheerfully and doesn't complain. One who works by a man's side but doesn't step out in front of him. A woman who wants to build a family and a certain style of life." He finally looked at me. "You know exactly what it means, Sarah Booth. It's no different than the rules you women have for trapping a man who can provide a good life with security, family ties, social standing, and all of that. Women of a certain socio-economic level have certain wants and needs. Why would you think men would be different?"

He was right, but it didn't matter. I was hot. "The whole thing is idiotic. Acting a certain way to trick someone is stupid. For men and women." I was hammering away at my soapbox with everything I had, rearing to climb on top of it and start preaching. "How long are you supposed to act? Forever?"

"The best marriages are built with certain deliberate false-hoods," Bridge said, one eyebrow cocked. "For goodness sake, Sarah Booth, Tinkie said you were sophisticated. She said you'd been around enough to know the truth. Men and women need the cloaking of certain social conventions to live together successfully. If both parties were brutally honest, there would be no marriage or family. It would be tribal. The men would live in one hut and the women in another, and they'd only get together for sex."

"For purposes of procreation, no doubt," I threw out in a caustic tone.

"Of course," he said, nodding. "It's only the truly lower-class women who actually enjoy sex."

I saw it then, the tiniest flicker of devilment. He hid it quickly, but not fast enough.

"Damn you, Bridge, you're putting me on," I said, punching his arm in indignation, anger, and embarrassment. "You did that just to get me wound up."

"You started it," he said, chuckling in that very masculine way. He handed me my drink. "You sat right on the floor and pretended that you were nothing but the sweetheart of Ole Miss, all roses, chiffon, and parties." He gave me a look. "I happen to know you were a liberal rabble-rouser."

Busted. Bridge had caught me playing the game I despised, and he'd had his fun with me. I had no right to be angry with him for setting me up. I shook my head. "I have no defense," I said. "Guilty as charged. I just didn't want to get into it."

He lifted my chin with one finger so I looked into his eyes. "You didn't want to pierce the veil of pretense," he said.

"Not because I'm ashamed of what I did or because I wanted to pretend to be other than who I am, but I promised Tinkie I wouldn't slap you upside the head with it right off. Trust me, I don't have the patience to pretend to be anyone other than who I am. The ugly truth would have come out."

Bridge put his arm around my shoulder and kissed my cheek. "Now *that* I believe. But not ugly, Sarah Booth. Just the truth. You are who and what you are, and I find you delightful."

I suspected he was teasing me again. "I'm not biting twice in one night."

He laughed. "I'm sure Tinkie told you I've never married. I'm equally sure you know that my family is hounding me to take a wife and have children."

"Boy, do I know that pressure," I said.

"I didn't realize you had family living," he said, puzzled.

I'd been caught in a pretense once, but even so, I wasn't about to explain my current family—one Jitty. "I don't need family to remind me of my duties. For a Southern woman, they're bred into the bone."

He laughed. "Yes, I see your point. What I was saying is that I enjoy your company, Sarah Booth. Exactly as you are. I have no interest in the type of woman who bends herself to my views. I happen to like independence."

I smiled at him. He was a remarkable man. "I'm glad," I said. "I will speak to Ida Mae for you."

"Thanks," he said, brushing his lips across my cheek. "And now I'd better take you home. My tactic is to tantalize you, to make you want me as much as I want you."

I swallowed. He was very direct with his plans.

"Is it working?" he asked, and I knew he was teasing me again.

"Absolutely," I said, picking up my sandals from the floor. "That's why I'm going home. Before I spoil all of your hard work."

Laughing, he walked me out the door and into the hot Delta night.

13

I AWOKE TO A DARK SHADOW ACROSS MY EYES AND A BODING sense of disapproval. I forced one eye open. Jitty sat on the edge of the bed staring at me.

"Another opportunity lost," she said in a tone as serious as cancer.

"Go away." I threw a pillow at her, but it simply slammed into the wall.

Jitty grinned wickedly. "If you'd played your cards right, you could be incubatin' the heir to the Ladnier fortune right this minute."

"I'm not a chicken hatchery." I pushed myself up in bed and opened my eyes wide, the better to see her with. I closed them instantly.

"With that man's money, we could spend the next year redecoratin' Dahlia House. 'Course you'd need to hire help. You don't have a lick of decoratin' ability." Jitty was wearing a navy-blue suit with Kelly green piping. A little green polka-dot kerchief was tucked in the pocket. She wore a pillbox hat and navy-blue pumps.

"Why are you doing this to me?" I asked, making the sign of the cross with my fingers and holding them out at her. "You look like the Church Lady."

She only laughed. "This is a replica of a suit worn by one of our greatest first ladies. She knew the value of carrying an heir. She gave it her all. She had class. She carried herself like a lady at all times, even under the worst of circumstances. She knew her *duty*. Which is more than I can say for you. Duty is bein' a partner to a good man, Sarah Booth. That's the way you build a future. You look for values. That's what life is about. Like Jackie. She put up with a whole lot, but her values were right where they should be."

"What the hell are you babbling about?" I asked her.

"Jackie."

"Who?"

"Jackie Kennedy."

I took a deep breath. My mother's admiration for a woman who'd lived through the worst that life could hand her must have rubbed off on Jitty. I gave her attire a long look and recognized the suit from a photograph of Jackie in an old *Life* magazine. We had a huge stack of them in the attic.

"Why are you dressed like that at nine o'clock on a Saturday morning?" I asked. "State luncheon?"

"State funeral," Jitty said solemnly. "Ivory Keys. Services at ten." She checked a slender watch held on her wrist by a thin gold bracelet. "That gives you about twenty minutes to get ready and twenty minutes to drive there. Are you taking Tinkie?"

"Yes." I hadn't actually planned on taking Tinkie, but it was a brilliant idea. I threw back the light spread and got out of bed.

"What are *you* wearing?"

I ignored Jitty as I went in the bathroom and ran my bath. What did one wear to the funeral of a musical icon? Cece would know.

I called the newspaper and caught her just as she was preparing to leave for Blessed Zion Independent Church. She wanted some preliminary photographs and didn't trust Garvel LaMott to make the right choices. I didn't blame her there. Garvel wasn't bright, but he was ambitious. Not a good combination for a partner.

"Oh, dahling, one can't be overdressed. The hat is the important accessory. Vital. Something with flash. But not too much flash. You should have thought of this ages ago, Sarah Booth. If you simply throw your wardrobe together at the last minute, then you look like you're thrown together."

I rolled my eyes. "I don't have a hat. At least not one like you're thinking of."

She sighed. "Wear blue and I'll bring a hat for you. Navy is always totally appropriate for a funeral."

"It's August," I reminded her. My only wardrobe rule was never to wear anything dark on a summer day. Mosquitoes were attracted to dark colors, and so was sweat.

"August, Schmaugust. Wear navy, black, or purple. Which will it be?"

"Navy," I conceded, thinking of a linen dress I had with white buttons. It was sleeveless and ankle length. Sedate, yet as cool as navy could be.

"I have just the hat," she said. "Meet me before the service. And don't be late, Sarah Booth."

"Right." I hung up, called Tinkie, and told her I'd pick her up on my way. She, of course, had no wardrobe qualms. She was state-funeral perfection when I pulled up in front of her door. As was Chablis. The little Yorkie had on a black hat and veil that was a tiny duplicate of the one on Tinkie's coiffed head.

"Tinkie?" I frowned at Chablis. "Are you sure?"

"Drive," she said, getting into the car. "Ivory would be honored to have Chablis paying homage at his funeral."

I wasn't going to argue that. I was just going to let her out in front of the church and park the car while she entered.

We arrived at Blessed Zion fifteen minutes early, and Cece was as good as her word. The navy straw hat with a cubic zirconium-encrusted veil was perfection. I allowed her to twist up my brown curls and secure them under the hat. I was transformed from seri-ous summer brunch to solemn church event.

"Thanks," I said.

"Someone has to keep you from embarrassing yourself," Cece said, but not unkindly. "Did you hear that Scott Hampton will be here?"

"At the funeral?" I was surprised.

"Yes. Ida Mae talked Coleman into it. Can you believe it? She said if he wasn't allowed to attend, it would prejudice his case." She swept her hand around the small churchyard. "That's why all the deputies are hanging around. Volunteers from Bolivar and Alcorn counties came in. More are coming from Hinds and Tunica."

I hadn't really noticed the extra uniforms, but now that Cece had pointed them out, I added up a total of ten deputies sitting in their sun-baked cars or standing at the side of the church. They were all in uniform and all wearing guns and radios. I didn't see Coleman, Dewayne Dattilo, or Gordon Walters. What I did see was a cluster of black men standing at the side of the church. They were dressed in suits, but the Sunday clothes didn't hide their anger. That anger seemed focused on us.

"Coleman's inside with Scott," Cece said. "I knew it was im-portant to get here early for photos. I got one of Scott at the coffin. It's going to make the national wire. That Garvel was drag-ging his feet. I swear, he makes one want to do something drastic. One day when he's asleep with his feet propped up on his desk, I'm going to wax his hairy legs."

"Cece!" I wasn't shocked at the idea of waxing legs, but Garvel's legs were repulsive. He had pasty white skin and black curly hairs. It had been a subject of much disgusted commentary even in fifth grade.

"Don't act so prim and proper," Cece warned. "You'd like nothing better than to tear Garvel's leg hairs out by the roots and you know it."

I didn't answer. Several cars had pulled into the churchyard, and men and women were gathering on the church steps. Cece, Tinkie, Chablis, and I stepped to the side. We were not the primary participants in this ritual. A black limo pulled up to the church and a tall, slender man walked around and helped Ida Mae out.

"That's Emanuel," Tinkie whispered in my ear. He had the look of a zealot. He was not a man who found joy in many things. His angry gaze swept the churchyard, surveyed the clump of men, and landed on us. Abruptly he dropped his mother's arm and stormed toward us, the other men flanking him.

"Get out of here," he said, waving his left hand angrily in our faces. "This is no place for white people. You came here to gawk and make money on my father's death. You've harvested enough profit from the blood of the black man—"

"Yeah, go away," one man said, waving his hands like he was shooing chickens.

"Emanuel." Ida Mae cut him short as she walked up. She put a hand on his arm. "Go inside. These people are my friends, and they're welcome here."

"They didn't know my father."

Ida Mae withdrew her hand but held her gaze steady on his. "Neither did you, son. And you had many opportunities."

"You're just like my father. You always side with the enemy."

"Emanuel, this isn't the time or place—" Ida Mae started.

Emanuel turned abruptly and stomped up the steps, his cohorts right on his heels. The church door was flung back against the cement-block wall.

"Forgive my son," Ida Mae said, and I knew it was a phrase she'd had a lot of practice saying. "He's hurting and he's mad at himself because it hurts. He'd convinced himself he didn't love his father. I'm sure the river of feelings that washed over him has caught him up in a wild current. He's scared."

"Scott Hampton's inside," I said. Emanuel had been merely rude to us. What would he do to the man accused of killing his father?

"Thank you. I'll—"

The sound of a loud chopper cut the still August morning. It was abrupt and explosive, and I knew that the rider had been laying in wait somewhere nearby. A second engine fired and the two motorcycles came flying out of the cotton field not twenty-five yards to the south of the church.

"Yee-hah!" Spider cried as he pulled the bike onto its rear tire and walked it across the front of the church not ten yards from Ida Mae.

"The only good jigaboo is a dead jigaboo!" Ray-Ban yelled as he repeated Spider's performance.

I saw the deputies coming from all directions. They had not drawn their firearms, but their hands were ready, fingers splayed just above the gun butts.

The two bikers wheeled around, headed back our way. Spider punched something on his bike and the strains of "Dixie" began to play.

Beside me, Ida Mae drew herself up tall. Every person who'd come to the funeral stood rooted to the spot, eyes on Ida Mae, faces showing horror, embarrassment, and sorrow.

Ida Mae took a deep breath. ". . . land of cotton, old times there are not forgotten, look away, look away, look away, Dixieland."

Rich and filled with sorrow instead of the jaunty march of soldiers, Ida Mae's voice saturated the summer morning.

"I wish I was in Dixie, hooray, hooray, in Dixieland I'll take my stand, to live and die in Dixie. Away, away, away down South in Dixie."

The officers had caught up with Spider and Ray-Ban. In ten seconds the bikers were restrained, the motorcycles' engines turned off, and the music stopped. Cece started the applause, and it spread over the gathering.

Ida Mae ignored everyone. She walked up to Spider and stared him dead in the face. "I know what you're trying to do, and it won't work. That's not your song, son. It's a song that belongs to everyone who lived through hard times in a land they loved. You can play it and you can try to defile it, but it doesn't belong to you, and your stink won't rub off on it."

She turned away from him and walked into the church just as Coleman came walking out. They exchanged a few whispered words.

"What should we do with them?" a deputy asked Coleman.

His mouth a tight line, he stared at Spider as he spoke. "Take them in, charge them, have the bikes towed."

"We ain't done nothin'!" Spider said. "No law against riding our motorcycles and playin' songs. That old black bitch wasn't hurt." He tried unsuccessfully to shake free of the two deputies who held him. "I can ride around this church till hell freezes over if I want. You got an innocent man locked up for a crime he didn't commit. Until you let Scott go, we're gonna be a wart on your backside, Sheriff."

The right corner of Coleman's mouth took a downward slant, and I couldn't tell if he was going to laugh or was angry. "Take them on," he said to the deputies.

"You can't do that!" Spider put a hand on his handlebars, but it didn't stay even a split second when the deputy stepped closer.

"Watch me," Coleman said. "You boys can reclaim your bikes at the sheriff's office. Tomorrow or the next day."

I started up the steps to speak to Coleman, but he was already walking into the church.

"I've got to get this film back to the newspaper," Cece whispered in my ear. "I can make the afternoon paper if I hurry."

"What about the service?" Tinkie asked. She was clutching Chablis to her as if the bikers wanted to dognap the little fluffball, which wasn't as far-fetched as it might sound.

"Garvel can stay here. This is a national story and the competition is too keen." She nodded at a young redhead who was scribbling furiously in a notepad as television cameras panned the reporter and the church. "*Entertainment Today*," Cece whispered.

I heard the strains of an organ, and I nodded at Tinkie that it was time to go inside. Together we walked into the church and took a seat in the back.

Throughout the service, my attention strayed from Scott to

Coleman. One sat beside Ida Mae and the other stood against the wall, not twenty feet from where I sat. Emanuel was sitting all the way across the church from his mother and Scott. If looks could kill, Scott would be skewered and charbroiled.

The service went without incident. Glowing tributes to Ivory were paid by friends and relations. To my surprise, neither Ida Mae nor Emanuel spoke. The church was crowded to overflowing, and many of those attending were strangers. Judging from the expensive and unconventional attire, several were prominent in the music field. Their attention was on Scott. But his was on Ida Mae and on the plain pine coffin that dominated the front of the small church.

It was a brief service, and I was relieved to walk outside into the bright humidity. Tinkie and I stood out of the way as Coleman led Scott to a patrol car. He would not be allowed to go to the cemetery.

"Let's go home," Tinkie said.

"Sure." I was worn out.

"What's next?" Tinkie asked. She unpinned the hat from Chablis and the little Yorkie gave her chin a slurpy lick of appreciation.

"I don't know," I said, getting behind the wheel. "I honestly don't know."

14

I DROPPED TINKIE AND CHABLIS AT HILLTOP, AND I WENT ON TO town. I stopped at the bakery and bought sandwiches, oatmeal-raisin cookies, and two large cups of fresh coffee. Doc Sawyer was my next target, and I wasn't going to risk the stuff in his coffeepot again. Perhaps he was conducting an experiment on bionic caffeine. The same brew had been in that pot for at least nine months.

Main Street was bustling as I drove through town. Traditionally, Saturday was market day, and the fruit stand at the end of town was jammed. Hand-painted signs advertised boiled peanuts, satsumas, the last of the season's Vidalia onions, tomatoes from Joe Cramer's farm, early turnips, and a vibrant selection of the first fall mums. Pickup trucks were parked in a jumble as people wandered among the produce and plants.

I had my attention on a display of plump scuppernongs when out of the corner of my eye, I saw Connie Peters. And Coleman. He was holding two pots of yellow mums, walking about five paces behind his wife. I kept driving until I turned into the hospital parking lot.

Doc Sawyer was in his office, and he frowned as I walked in.

"You look like you need a good dose of castor oil," he said, eyes lighting up as he saw the bakery bags in my hands. "What'd you bring?"

"Nothing for you." I was fond of Doc, but I didn't like his diagnosis.

"You look peaked," he said, refining his earlier statement. "What's wrong? You got a stomachache?"

"No." I didn't want to pursue this line of questioning. It wasn't what I'd eaten but what I'd seen that had upset me. "Turkey or ham? Coffee or coffee?" I held out both bags.

Doc cast a glance at the coffeepot in the corner as if I might have hurt its feelings. That coffee had been around long enough that it might have developed feelings. "Ham," he said, taking the bag with the sandwiches.

I sat down in the chair in front of his desk, and he took a seat behind it. I was busy unwrapping my sandwich when he spoke again.

"How are you, Sarah Booth? Really?"

I pushed the tomato back inside the bread and licked my finger before I answered. "There are days when I feel like I'm about thirteen. Emotionally." Doc had tended my broken collarbone and removed my tonsils. He knew a lot of my foibles.

"Arrested adolescence," he said with a nod of his head. "A man must be involved."

I didn't deny it. Instead I took a big bite of the sandwich.

"Your appetite's still good, so I guess it isn't fatal." He chuckled as I threw him a black look. "I can't imagine a man who wouldn't throw himself down at your feet, Sarah Booth. What's this fool's name?"

I shook my head. While Doc knew many of my secrets, he wasn't the repository for Coleman's. "You're right, it isn't fatal, so let's forget about it."

Doc sipped his coffee, nodding. "This is good."

"Yeah, it's fresh," I hinted.

"I heard Tinkie had fixed you up with a blind date."

Drat Tinkie's hide! I didn't like everyone in town looking at me like some kind of social charity case. While I enjoyed blind dates, most folks looked on them as a last-ditch effort to have a social life.

"Don't look like a thundercloud. Cece told me about it in the strictest confidence. She hinted that blood tests might be in order. Is that why you're here?"

"Hold on a minute," I said, almost spilling my coffee as I leaned forward. "No one's said a thing about a wedding."

Doc grinned, pleased at his ability to get a reaction out of me. "So why are you here?"

"Ivory Keys."

The smile slipped from Doc's face. "That was a terrible thing. I meant to get out to the funeral this morning but I got tied up with Kelly Webster. Her son broke his leg. Fell out of a pear tree in Mrs. Hedgepeth's yard. I thought I would have to treat her for apoplexy. She was mad as a hornet."

If Doc was trying to divert me, it wasn't going to work. "Coleman told me Ivory died between two and four in the morning. Can you tell me anything else?"

"Stabbed three times, one piercing the heart."

"Was he beaten before he was stabbed?"

He gave me a long look. "He was."

"What else can you tell me?" Doc was being unusually reticent. Normally I didn't have to pry information out of him.

"What did Coleman tell you?"

I knew then that there was something significant I hadn't been told. Coleman was doing his job, but I still felt the white-hot tingle of fresh anger. We'd always been square with each other. Or at least he'd always been square with me. Until now. "Coleman didn't tell me anything. That's why I'm here, Doc. Ida Mae Keys has paid me to find out the truth. I owe it to her to do that, and I can't when everyone is keeping secrets from me."

Doc chewed the last bite of his sandwich and reached for a cookie. "Coleman has his reasons, Sarah Booth."

"No doubt. But if Scott Hampton is guilty, that's what I'll find out."

"I never realized private investigators were bound by the truth," Doc said, not bothering to hide his skepticism.

"Ida Mae believes Scott is innocent. If I can't prove that, I'll tell her so."

Doc wadded up his sandwich wrapper and tossed it in the trash. When he leaned forward at his desk, light from the window caught the fine white hair that fluffed out around his head. "There was a symbol cut into Ivory's back." He turned slightly away, tossing the lid to his coffee in the trash.

"What kind of symbol?" My heart rate had jumped.

He got up and went over to his file cabinet and pulled out a folder. "I remember when you were a child, Sarah Booth. Your daddy would have shot me for showing you something like this."

I didn't say anything as I took the photographs he offered.

Ivory Keys was lying on his stomach on the floor of the night-club. His shirt had been ripped down the back and flung to either side. The symbol of crossed bones had been cut into the flesh between his shoulder blades.

"He was dead when this happened, wasn't he?" I worked hard to keep my voice level. In my past cases I'd seen death, but not this kind of gruesome disfigurement.

"Yes, the cuts were made postmortem."

I looked at the dozen photographs, which showed the body from different angles. The design was crude, but there was no way the symbol could be mistaken. It looked a lot like part of the tattoo that was on the arms of Scott Hampton and his "brothers." When I handed the photographs back, I couldn't meet Doc's gaze.

"Your father would be very angry with me."

I looked up at him. "No, he wouldn't, Doc. He would know that he couldn't protect me forever. Whoever did that to Mr. Keys deserves to be punished."

"Are you going to take Ida Mae's money?"

If Ivory had written his killer's name with his own blood, it probably couldn't have been clearer. But I had to wonder if the evidence wasn't just a little too convenient. "I won't take her money unless I believe Scott Hampton is innocent."

He walked around the desk and put his hand on my shoulder. "You've got a good heart, Sarah Booth. Don't let it, or the rest of you, go to waste."

"Thanks, Doc." I threw my trash in the garbage. I had one more question to ask. "Based on your experience, what does the way Ivory was murdered tell you?" I held his gaze with mine, willing him to answer. It wasn't a scientific question; I was asking him to move into the realm of opinion and he was resisting. "Just tell me what you think."

"You've already said it, Sarah Booth. The man who did this was cruel. Sadistic. Ivory was severely beaten. Then he was killed and brutalized."

"You're certain it was a man?"

Doc's mouth lifted at one corner, acknowledging my tactics. "It took a strong person to thrust a knife that deep. Three times." He demonstrated the motion, using a lot of shoulder. "Whoever did this was very angry."

"Angry at Ivory?" This was, at least, a lead—if I could find someone other than Scott who was known to argue with Ivory. Emanuel popped to the front of my mind.

"Maybe not angry at Ivory personally."

I knew then that Doc recognized the significance of the crossed bones. "Angry at Ivory for what he represented."

He nodded. "A strong woman could have done it, but I'll wager you that the killer is a man. A strong man." He paused. "A young man."

Those last three words hung between us. I'd asked for his opinion. I nodded. "Thanks, Doc."

Leaving the air-conditioned hospital, I stepped into the August afternoon. I might as well have booked time in a sauna. Sweat popped up on my forehead, and my auburn hair frizzed. As I walked across the parking lot to my car, I could feel the heat of the asphalt through the soles of my shoes.

Damn. It was summertime. And the cotton was high. But the living wasn't easy. Not by a long shot.

COLEMAN WAS THE man I needed to see next, but I knew better than to go looking. The last I saw of him, he was snuggled in the bosom of domesticity. Well, that was a good place to hide, but I'd find him eventually. I was furious with him for withholding the fact that Ivory's body had been used as a canvas. It was a vital piece of evidence. Against Scott.

Or maybe not. Both Spider and Ray-Ban wore the same insignia.

I considered driving back out to Bilbo Lane to ask Spider and Ray-Ban a few questions, but my safety and the fact that it would be a wasted effort convinced me not to go.

Saturday night loomed ahead of me. Another dateless evening. Sunday through Thursday, being a dateless wonder wasn't so bad, but come Friday and Saturday, it was another story.

Instead of moping around Dahlia House and listening to Jitty point out my faults, I decided to drive out to Kudzu and talk to Ida Mae. I was sure she knew about the symbol cut into her husband—and if she didn't know, she needed to—yet she continued to support Scott. I needed to know why.

Driving through the cotton fields that surrounded Kudzu, I felt the past crowding around me. It was in those fields that so much wrong had occurred. Yet the land was innocent. It nurtured any seed pushed deep into its loamy fecundity. The thigh-high cotton plants were testimony of that.

The rows and rows of green plants flashed past the car window, creating an optical illusion. The land and the cotton were the same, only the humans had changed. This harvest, there would be no bowed backs and bleeding hands pulling the tough boles. Combines would harvest the cotton. The huge mechanical tractors would crawl over the land, doing the work of thousands of laborers.

The plain steeple of Blessed Zion Independent Church rose out of the cotton. I was nearly at the intersection. Playin' the Bones was on my right. The navy BMW parked in front of the club gave me pause, and I swung into the parking lot.

The sound of my tires crunching the gravel brought Emanuel Keys to the door, and the expression on his face let me know I was trespassing. I killed the motor and got out of the roadster.

"Mr. Keys, I'm Sarah Booth—"

"I know who you are. You're the one taking my mother's money for a lost cause."

Emanuel was a handsome man who took pride in his appearance. His trousers were sharply creased, his white shirt immaculate, French cuffs fastened by onyx-and-gold cuff links, designer sunglasses in his hand. Looking at him, though, I saw nothing of either his mother or his father. Though he had his father's high cheekbones and his mother's nose and lips, his expression denied any kinship with his parents.

"I give you my word that I won't take Ida Mae's money unless I can do what she wants me to do." I didn't feel that I had to defend myself, but I wanted to make it clear to this man that I was not the parasite he wanted to believe me to be.

"Why waste your time, then? Scott Hampton killed my father. The sooner he's tried and convicted, the sooner my mother can begin to put this behind her."

"Is your concern for Ida Mae or yourself?" He'd set the tone for this conversation.

"Get off this property," he said.

"Is the club yours now?" I held my body relaxed. "Are you the one who benefits from Ivory's death?"

I'd often heard the expression that eyes could shoot sparks. Emanuel brought that phrase to life.

"Mother hasn't allowed anyone to read my father's will, yet. I can promise you, though, that this club will be razed."

His hatred of everything his father stood for was palpable. It was also like sticking my finger in an electric socket. I was fried.

"Don't you have any respect for what your father accomplished?"

"Respect? For this?" He waved his hand at the club. "My father was a dreamer. He believed the races could get along. He was just an Uncle Tom with a club. He thought seeing the whites in his place was a sign that things had changed. He was too stupid to realize they were using him still."

"Your mother loves this club."

"My mother loved my father. She loved him enough to even love his foolish dream. But she'll see the truth. Once Scott Hampton is convicted of killing him, she'll see that my father was tricked by another white man."

Doc's words came back to me—Ivory had been killed by someone who was very angry. Someone who viewed Ivory as a symbol. I found that my mouth was dry. Fear had slipped up on me. My body had understood the danger before my brain had put it together. Unfortunately, my tongue wasn't as frightened as the rest of me.

"Your mother still loves your father. She loves his memory *and* his dream. And you're the only one left who can hurt her more than she's already hurting."

"What would you know about pain?" he asked, moving suddenly up to me. He grabbed my arm. Not hard enough to bruise, but with enough force for me to feel his fury.

"You aren't the only person who ever lost a parent," I told him.

"I never had one to lose. I never had a father. I had a blues musician and a woman who loved him. I can still see them sitting out on the porch, Daddy laughing with his friends when they'd stop over to visit. It wouldn't be long before they'd be inside, him at that damn piano, playing while sweat rolled down his face and the women laughed and danced. Then I didn't even have that. I had a jailbird for a daddy. But I had a lot of privileges. I got a good education, and I learned that I could take care of myself. So don't try to tell me about who I can hurt and how much I can hurt them." He dropped my arm and walked back into the club.

I got in my car and drove away.

15

IDA MAE'S YARD WAS A KALEIDOSCOPE OF COLORS, REMINDING me of lollipops and a game I'd played as a child. Candyland. A veil of hummingbird vines covered part of the front porch—and Ida Mae. She was sitting in a rocker watching the dozens of butterflies that darted around the delicate coral flowers of the vine. A slight breeze stirred the bottle tree, setting the glass to tinkling.

Ida Mae's voice came from behind the vines. "Butterflies. Look at them. They're just the color of fresh-churned butter, aren't they?"

There was sadness in her voice. I walked up the steps and took a seat in the rocker she indicated. "I haven't had fresh butter since Aunt LouLane passed away. She had a friend—"

"Ronald McRae." Ida Mae chuckled. "I knew him well. And I knew your auntie. She had her hands full with you."

I was surprised, but I shouldn't have been. Everyone in Sunflower County knew everyone else. Aunt LouLane would have been older than Ida Mae. But not by much. Ida Mae just didn't show her age.

"I knew your mama, too." Ida Mae reached over and laid her hand on mine, giving it a gentle squeeze before she withdrew it. "She was a woman ahead of her time. We didn't go to school together. Back then, blacks and whites had separate schools. But we knew each other. You and Emanuel were born the same year. He came in April, and you were right after that in May. Doc Swain delivered both of you. Of course, Emanuel was born here at home."

Now I was stunned. How was it that I'd never known a boy my age? The Sunflower County public schools were integrated in 1967. "He didn't go to school with me."

Ida Mae spoke so softly I leaned toward her. "No, he didn't. It was about the time Emanuel was to start school that Ivory got sent to prison up in Michigan." She cut her eyes at me.

"I know the story," I said, hoping she wouldn't ask me *where* I'd heard it. Now that I knew Emanuel's intent to destroy the club, I hoped Ida Mae would consider Bridge's offer.

"You know he was defending a woman against her husband's brutality, then."

I nodded.

"Ivory didn't deserve to be in prison. He didn't. But he went, and the talk was all over Sunflower County about him killing a woman's husband because he was running around with her. I didn't want Emanuel to hear that kind of talk about his daddy, so I sent him up to my sister's in Tunica. He went to grade school there, and he was so smart, he got accepted into a private school in Nashville. Brentwood Academy. He got a full scholarship."

Not all the money in the world could buy admittance into that caliber of private school. Emanuel was undoubtedly a genius. "You must be proud of him." This wasn't exactly where I wanted to go regarding Emanuel, but I decided to ease in that direction.

"Proud of him?" Ida Mae gave me a long look. "No. I'm not proud of my son. That's a sin I was guilty of years back. But I've given a lot of study to who Emanuel is and how he came to be that person, and that fancy grade school may have been where I made my first mistake."

"How could that be a mistake, to give your son the best education possible?"

"Maybe he didn't see it that way. Children don't think, they just feel. Maybe that school wasn't an opportunity to Emanuel, but a punishment."

"Surely he can understand you were trying to do the best for him that you could."

She rocked slowly back and forth. "No, I don't think he understands that, and I think deep down inside, he's still that six-year-old boy being sent away from home to live with strangers because of his daddy."

As much as I hated to admit it, what she said made sense. "And you think that's why Emanuel hates Ivory so much?"

She rocked a bit before she spoke. "Feelings aren't rational. Emanuel can intellectually grasp that his father went to prison for defending a helpless woman, but somehow it's all tied up in his head with music. I think he feels that Ivory always put music ahead of him. Just think for a minute, Sarah Booth, what it would have felt like to you if your daddy loved the law more than you."

"But he didn't," I pointed out.

"You said that mighty quickly. That shows how much it means to you. Ivory loved Emanuel. He loved me. Music was his job, and I was never jealous that he loved it, too. He made a mistake, and he paid for it. We all paid. But I'm thinking Emanuel paid more than anyone else."

Perhaps Ida Mae had put her finger on Emanuel's problems, but she'd failed to engage my sympathy. And I doubt hers would last long if she knew what plans Emanuel had in mind for Playin' the Bones.

"Ida Mae, I spoke with Doc Sawyer. Why didn't you tell me about the bones?"

She stopped rocking. "That doesn't prove anything except the killer knew about Scott's tattoo."

I figured she might take this approach, and I'd already beaten her there. "Did a lot of people know about Scott's tattoo and what it meant?"

She shrugged. "Who can say? I knew what it was because Ivory told me."

"When he performed in the club, did he wear long sleeves?"

"Most of the time. But he was around the club during the day, wearing T-shirts and short sleeves to move cases of liquor and supplies. Anyone could have seen that tattoo."

"How well does Emanuel know Scott?" So much for subtlety.

Ida Mae seemed to swell with air. She kept her focus straight ahead, as if she were watching the tan Taurus that seemed to float among the cotton. I didn't recognize the car but it was headed our way.

"Emanuel's been home eight weeks. He knew Scott. They argued a lot when Ivory wasn't around. They hated each other."

"Who inherits the club?"

"I haven't turned in Ivory's will yet. I've been holding on to it, waiting."

"For what?"

"I don't know," she said. "Just waiting."

"Who inherits?"

"Emanuel gets the club. Ivory wants him to continue with it, but he won't. He'll sell it or maybe burn it down. He hates it."

So Ida Mae already knew Emanuel's plans for the club. "Bridge Ladnier, an investor from Memphis, has expressed an interest in the club. In fact, he asked me to make an offer to you."

Ida Mae didn't look at me. "Ivory wanted Emanuel to have the club."

"Emanuel doesn't want it. He wants to destroy it. Bridge assured me that he would like to keep the club open and continue with what Ivory started."

At last she looked at me. "And you trust this man?"

Now that was a pertinent question. "I don't know him well, Ida Mae. I know he loves the blues. He has a tremendous collection. He's followed Ivory's career for years. I can only tell you what he told me—that he wants to keep the club running."

Ida Mae stopped her rocker and simply sat. Her gaze was locked on the tan Taurus that seemed stalled in the midst of all that cotton. Distance was hard to judge in the Delta. What appeared close could often be miles away.

"I'll speak to Emanuel." She pushed herself out of her chair, the first sign I'd seen of her age. "I'm tired. I think I'll go inside and make me some supper. Would you care to stay to eat?"

The idea was appealing. I could cook, but I didn't. It had been a long time since my turkey sandwich with Doc.

"Ida Mae, why does Emanuel hate Scott so much?"

She turned slowly to look down into my eyes. "He hates white folks, not just Scott. But he hates Scott the most. He claims it's because Scott is a racist. He says a leopard can't change his spots and that Scott joined the Aryan Brotherhood because that's what he really believes—that whites are superior. But Emanuel belongs to his own secret club, the Dominoes. He doesn't have a tattoo, but his heart is branded with their hate-filled dogma, and that's worse. Now I'm tired of talking about hate. Let's get us some supper."

She started to walk to the house just as the tan Taurus headed down the road in front of her house. We both walked to the edge of the porch to watch the car turn down her driveway.

"Now who could that be?" she asked.

I was wondering myself. When Deputy Dewayne Dattilo, complete with uniform and gun, got out of the car, I was as surprised as Ida Mae.

"Can I help you?" she asked, one hand resting on the porch column.

Dewayne nodded toward me. "I need to speak with Ms. Delaney, ma'am."

I felt Ida Mae's eyes on me as I walked down the steps to the Taurus.

"Sheriff Peters would like to see you," Dewayne said, his gaze grazing mine and then skittering away.

"He sent you out here to get me?"

"No, ma'am, I volunteered. I'm off duty, so this isn't official, you know."

I almost smiled. Deputy Dattilo was so sincere. "What does

Coleman want?" I needed to talk to the sheriff, but I wasn't certain I was in the proper mood.

"Scott Hampton's made bail."

"What?" I spoke louder than I intended. Ida Mae walked down one step, then paused.

"Someone put up the fifty thousand to bond him out. Sheriff wants to know who did it and he figured you'd know."

"I don't have a clue." I was trying hard not to sound as surprised as I was.

"Sheriff thinks you might," Dattilo insisted stubbornly.

"I'm busy."

"He'd appreciate it if you could talk to him right away." He looked over the top of my head as he talked. I could have felt sorry for him if I wasn't so aggravated.

"Then he should have sent someone to arrest me."

"Ms. Delaney, I told him I'd bring you back to town to talk to him. There wasn't any need to arrest you."

"Or any reason," I pointed out.

"It won't take ten minutes, ma'am."

He didn't say please, but it was in his voice. I took a deep breath. "Okay, I'll go. But in the future, you're going to owe me a big favor."

"Yes, ma'am." Relief was evident in his smile.

16

TEN PERCENT OF HALF A MILLION CAME OUT TO FIFTY THOU-
sand dollars, and not a lot of folks in Sunflower County could
command that kind of scratch for bond. As I drove in front of
Dewayne's Taurus, I went through the Rolodex in my mind trying
to figure out who could have bonded Scott out of prison. No one
popped into my mind as Scott's fairy godmother. Tinkie and
Oscar had the money, but they had no reason to want Scott free.
That same reasoning applied to all of my friends with large bank
accounts.

Dewayne escorted me to the courthouse and then went home; I
was left to face Coleman alone. My only consolation was that Bo-
Peep didn't work on Saturdays.

Stepping inside, my footsteps echoed on the linoleum tile. The
courthouse was empty, but my brain was not. Zinnia had one bail
bondsman, Yancy Pipkins, who ran a low-key operation out of his
home. I wondered why Coleman was leaning on me and not him.
In fact, as soon as I was done with Coleman, I intended to track
Pipkins down and find out who had bonded Scott out.

The front office was empty, and Coleman's door was, uncharacteristically, shut. I tapped.

"Come in, Sarah Booth," he said.

He had the phone to his ear but was obviously on hold when I stepped inside.

"Who came up with the fifty grand for Scott's bond?" he asked, and the deep furrow between his eyes let me know he wasn't in a patient mood.

I shrugged. "You tell me."

His knuckles on the telephone receiver whitened, as did the skin above his eyebrows. "I think you should just tell me," he said in a totally level tone.

"If I knew, I might." I was getting angry, too.

"Yancy said I was going to have to subpoena him to get him to tell. I don't want to have to do that. I want you to tell me."

I searched his face for any trace of warm feelings for me. Coleman acted as if we were strangers.

"I don't know. I don't know anything about the bond at all. Ida Mae doesn't have that kind of money, and so far, she seems to be the only person in Sunflower County who believes Scott is innocent." I ignored the chair he pointed at. "Do you have any other questions you want to ask me? Of course, it's just a waste of your breath since you don't believe a word I say."

He hung up the receiver and slowly got to his feet. "Having Scott on the loose isn't a good idea. For him or for me. If he hangs around, he's the perfect target for an act of violence by just about everyone in the state. The blacks *and* the whites hate him. He's a lightning rod for the kind of racial violence we haven't seen in this state in nearly thirty years. Now if you don't understand that, I don't know how to make it any plainer."

In all of the years I'd known Coleman Peters, he'd never assumed such a condescending tone to me or anyone else. I wasn't angry; I was furious. "Don't you lecture me, Coleman Peters," I said in a near hiss. "Don't you dare. I don't know who in the hell you think you are, but I won't be talked to in that fashion."

Coleman seemed to freeze. We stared at each other for a full minute.

"You honestly don't know who paid Scott's bond?" he asked, his gaze faltering at last.

"I don't know." I was too angry to add anything else. I wanted out of that room. I wanted to go home to Dahlia House. I needed to think through the wild rush of emotions that made me almost physically ill. I had been angry at Coleman for several days in matters unrelated to Scott Hampton. This was icing on the cake.

"I'm sorry, Sarah Booth. I owe you an apology."

"Is Scott out?" I was too hurt and too angry to accept it.

"No, he doesn't even know his bond has been made. I can hold him until Monday as a formality, and I intend to do just that."

I swallowed. "Are we done?"

He walked around the desk and stood only inches from me. "No, we're not done. We've been friends too long to treat each other this way." He hesitated. "I thought we were maybe a little more than friends."

This was the can of worms I didn't want opened. I bit down hard on my lip in an effort to control the tears.

"What's going on with you, Sarah Booth? With us?"

"That's a fine question!" It came out angry, and I was spared the humiliation of crying. "You've gone back to your wife. You're a married man. There's nothing going on between us."

My angry words seemed to slam into him, but he didn't flinch. Instead, he spoke calmly. "All summer you avoided me like I had a social disease."

"You don't have a disease, Coleman, you have a wife. And you've gone back home in an effort to save your marriage. I can't argue with that."

"Would you like to?"

"What am I supposed to say to that? Yes I want to do my best to break up your marriage, or no I don't see myself in the role of home-wrecker today?"

"Just tell me the truth, Sarah Booth. Tell me what you want."

My anger at him hit a new level of heat. "What I want doesn't matter, Coleman. I don't have a right to have any wants in this situation. If you don't understand that, you're not the man I thought you were."

I ran out the door and slammed it as hard as I could behind me. I was halfway across the office when I heard a low whistle. I whirled around to find Bo-Peep sitting at the desk in a pair of Daisy Dukes and a red-checked halter top tied under her breasts.

"Forgot my billfold," she said, leaning forward until her breasts almost spilled out of the skimpy top. "It's nice to know you rich girls have so many morals. You just left that man in there ripe for the pickin', and I'm here to enjoy the fruit."

Before I could answer, she swished past me, her hips swinging like a pendulum. At the door to Coleman's office she turned, one hand on the knob and the other fanning out her gnarly blond locks. "Thanks, Sarah Booth, I owe you." She opened the door and slipped inside, shutting it firmly behind her.

IF HOME IS where the heart is, it's also the place you instinctively run to to lick your wounds. I sped to Dahlia House and the comforts of my home and hound.

Sweetie Pie met me at the door, her tongue licking all exposed areas of my body. I went straight to the sideboard in the parlor and made a stiff Jack and water before I headed into the kitchen. Sweetie's bowl was empty! Another failure. I couldn't catch a man, and I couldn't even keep food in my dog's bowl. I refilled the bowl and sank into a chair at the table, my elbows on the table and my head in my hands. I'd just made a total ass of myself. Until my encounter with Coleman, I had been able to pretend that I'd never exposed my feelings for a man who was off limits. Now, to satisfy my anger, I'd sacrificed my pride. *In front of Bo-Peep!*

I felt the cool chill of Jitty's entrance and looked up to find her standing at the opposite end of the table. She wore an orange, sleeveless tent-dress that barely covered possible, orange hose, and white go-go boots.

"Where are you going?" I asked, noticing the heavy eyeliner and false eyelashes. I peered closer. There was a psychedelic flower drawn on her cheek.

"Your man done done you wrong." It wasn't a question, it was a statement.

"He wasn't my man, and he hasn't done anything wrong. I made a fool of myself."

"No reason to be all down. You should know from experience that doesn't kill you."

I mustered a glare. "I don't need you making me feel worse."

"I'd say that's about impossible," Jitty said. She turned to look out the kitchen window, her huge gold-hooped earrings jangling. "You're already so down I'm surprised you aren't six feet under with the rest of your kinfolk."

She was staring out at the family cemetery. Everyone who'd ever cared about me was out there.

"Maybe you should go ahead and call the funeral home. Make your arrangements, 'cause I know you ain't made no will and I can't be responsible for gettin' you planted." She sat on the edge of the table. "Just imagine how much fun ol' Fel's gonna have when he gets hold of your body."

"Stop it!" Fel Harper, the former coroner, had a real grudge against me. The idea of him doing anything to my body—even if it was dead—was more than I could abide.

"Yessir, that's gonna be some scene."

"Jitty! Just stop it!" I stood up, hoping she'd take a hint and evaporate.

Instead, she grinned. "That's better. You still got enough spit left to wanna protect your . . . assets. Nothin' like the fire of pride to burn off de-spair."

"Thanks for nothing." But the truth was, the little burst of horror at the thought of Fel's hands on my body had diminished my black slump.

"I been thinkin' about your case," Jitty said, slipping off the table and beginning to pace the kitchen. "Sarah Booth, this is a big deal. If Scott didn't kill Ivory, who did?"

"That's the million-dollar question," I said. "If I had a viable suspect, I could put him"—I thought of Nandy—"or her forward."

"The money stolen from the club was in Scott's saddlebags." She stopped and looked at me. "That was the only thing stolen from the club?"

"As far as anyone can tell," I said, feeling an itch of excitement. Jitty was onto something.

"If Scott didn't do it, then whoever did it got absolutely nothin' out of it, except the satisfaction of killin' Ivory Keys."

"A personal enemy!" I had been over this ground, but Jitty made it a lot clearer.

"Someone who hated Ivory," she said slowly, "or who hated what he stood for."

"That gives me three prime suspects: Spider, Ray-Ban, and Emanuel. And those are the same three suspects I've always had." Suddenly I was back to square one.

"Or someone who hated Scott."

I turned to look at her. I hadn't even considered that possibility. And I didn't think anyone else had. "Excellent, Jitty." And I meant it. "Who would hate Scott?"

"This involves the two j's," Jitty said, her wide grin revealing her perfect teeth. How was that possible? They didn't even have toothpaste back in the 1800s.

"The two j's?" I said, supplying the obvious question.

"That's right. Jealous and jilted. One or the other might account for the motivation of the killer."

"Stuart Ann Shanahan," I said softly. "She was at the club when Scott left."

"Very true," Jitty said.

"But is she strong enough to stab Ivory three times?" That was the fact that had allowed Nandy to slip from the suspect list, at least in my mind.

"Crazy folks sometimes get mighty strong," Jitty said. "Endorphins."

I gave her a long look. "What do you know about endorphins?"

"I can read," she said with a sniff. "You the psychology major. You should know the body produces chemicals that can make it do powerful things."

She was right. I'd studied such cases in my quest for a college degree. In a crisis situation, folks with brains in the normal range could produce adrenaline that gave them extraordinary strength. Then there were those folks considered abnormal. Their brains produced chemicals that allowed their bodies to commit amazing feats.

"Is Nandy crazy or is she just rebelling?" I asked out loud.

"A good investigator would have the answer to that question before sundown. Or, you could just sit here in the kitchen and mope."

I rolled my eyes. Jitty was a harsh taskmaster.

"I'd find out what's goin' on with Nandy *before* Scott gets out of jail," Jitty said sagely.

Great. I was headed to the courthouse again. I could only hope that Coleman and Bo-Peep were gone.

But not together.

NANDY WAS SITTING on the balustrade on the south side of the courthouse. The side closest to the jail. At her feet was the boom box, and Scott's voice came out of it, wild and lonely, the guitar riff beneath his voice pulsing and hot.

"Sarah Booth," Nandy said, not bothering to hide her disdain. "Some investigator you are. Scott's still in jail."

"How long have you been back in town?" I asked, trying to make my question sound casual.

"What's it to you?"

She lifted her foot up to the balustrade and examined her toenail polish. She'd changed from Snow White red to a bright pink. Baby Doll, if I wasn't mistaken. Nandy, for all her eyebrow piercing and grunge hair, had all the classic nail colors.

"It's nothing to me," I said, pushing my hair back. "I was just trying to be nice, since it's so obvious Scott can't stand you. I guess I was feeling sorry for you." I hit pay dirt. Nandy was on her feet, her cheeks flaming with color. It was a fine time to remember she was a natural redhead.

"Don't you dare feel sorry for me," she said. "Scott loves me. We were together when Ivory was killed. I'm his alibi. He just doesn't want to involve me in all of this."

"Right," I said. She really was crazy.

"Don't take that tone with me, Sarah Booth Delaney."

"Grow up, Nandy. Scott can't stand you. Whatever little scheme you have spinning around in your head, forget it. Scott didn't kill Ivory, and he doesn't need your lies to prove his innocence."

Nandy walked slowly toward me. "He needs me, and he's going to recognize that fact."

"You forget one thing, Nandy," I said slowly. "You put yourself at the murder scene. That makes you a suspect. Maybe you aren't protecting Scott. Maybe you need him to say he was with you to give you an alibi." I walked back down the steps and to my car. Turning to look back only once, I saw Nandy standing on the steps, her fists clenched at her sides and her face red with fury.

I also saw Scott's face framed in the jailhouse window. One hand lifted and his thumb came up.

17

As much as I wanted to talk to Scott, I didn't want to risk seeing Coleman. Or his sheep-girl. Instead, I decided to pay a visit to Yancy Pipkins.

The day was ending, but the air was thick with humidity. I put the top down on the roadster anyway and drove into the sunset. The breeze blowing against my face was hot, but I needed to feel it. My hair was already a frizzy mess, so a little wind wouldn't make any difference.

Yancy lived in an older part of town, near the city park. By the time I got to his house, the church bells at St. Lucy's were ringing for the seven o'clock mass. The August night was only moments away. Already a few stars were scattered across the eastern sky, peeking through the oaks that were the pride and joy of Zinnia's park. I pulled into the drive, got out, and knocked on the front door.

Yancy was a quiet man. And thin. He had a head full of thick brown hair and gray eyes surrounded by laugh lines. He didn't fit the picture of the typical bondsman.

"Why, Sarah Booth," he said, smiling. "Come on in here. What brings you calling?"

I followed him inside, glad to see that his wife wasn't around. "I need to talk to you."

"Care for a drink?" he asked. "I was just about to make me a little cocktail. Reba's gone over to Greenwood to check on her mama, and I'm batching it tonight. I've got the grill going and a big rib eye marinating."

"I don't want to interrupt your supper," I said, even though I had no intention of leaving. It was the polite thing to say.

"No, you're not interrupting a thing." Yancy was equally polite, though I'm sure he was wishing I'd take a hint and depart. "What'll you have?"

"Bourbon and water." I took a seat on the sofa.

He was back in a moment with a drink for me and one for himself.

"This is about Scott Hampton, isn't it?" he asked. "Coleman's been trying to track me down all day. I gave him the dodge for a while, but I can't keep running."

"Who made Scott's bond?" I asked.

He cocked his head and studied me. "I can't tell you."

"Why not?" I wasn't surprised that he was keeping his mouth shut.

"The person who put up the money asked me to keep it confidential." He sipped his drink, but his gaze never left me.

"I'm working on Scott's behalf. I really need to know."

He shook his head. "I can't tell you, Sarah Booth. I can't tell anyone. I gave my word."

"You'll have to tell Coleman."

"No, ma'am. Not unless he subpoenas me into court. By that time, it won't matter a bit."

He was right about that. It would be Christmas before the wheels of the justice system could grind any information out of Yancy. "Scott's life may be in danger. This person may want him out of jail so that something bad can happen to him."

"This person just put up fifty thousand dollars to guarantee Scott would be at his trial," Yancy pointed out. "I don't know many people who would do that just for revenge. Especially when it seems pretty clear he's going to prison for the rest of his life, if he isn't gassed."

He had a point. "Coleman thinks Scott is safer in jail, and I'm not sure I disagree with that."

Yancy shook his head. "Hampton doesn't have to accept the bond. But look at it like this. If Hampton's out of jail, he can play at the club and keep it open. That would help Ida Mae."

That I couldn't argue with, but what I couldn't tell him was that as soon as the will was read, Ida Mae wouldn't own Playin' the Bones. "If he isn't killed by some redneck or racist," I pointed out. "That *won't* help Ida Mae."

"You wouldn't be talking about Emanuel, would you?" He was staring into his drink, refusing to look at me.

"He is a racist, and he hates Scott." I wasn't willing to go any further than that, but I wondered if Yancy would. As a bondsman, Yancy dealt with all kinds of people. I couldn't help but wonder what he might have heard.

"Emanuel's the most angry man I've ever met," Yancy said, finally catching my eye. "In my business, I've seen a lot, but I never thought Emanuel would gain a following here in Sunflower County."

I remembered that my father told me once that hatred was an elixir for those who felt disenfranchised because of their own limitations. "Emanuel is passionate." I wanted to remain noncommittal so Yancy would keep talking.

"Passionate. That's another way of looking at him. He spews hatred, and he's poisoning some of the younger men. They're ganging up. I saw about twenty of them up at Devoe's Barbecue last night. They were tormenting this teenage girl."

"Why?"

"Best I could tell, it was her choice of friends. White friends. They were saying she was betraying her race. Just really nasty."

"Emanuel is breaking his mother's heart."

"I'd make it a point to stay away from him. And Hampton should, too. Both of them are trouble, and if you get caught in the middle, Sarah Booth, you're going to get hurt."

"Do you really believe Emanuel is capable of violence, or is he all talk?" I pressed.

"About two months ago I had a client, a young black man from Tunica who was just passing through Sunflower County. Not necessarily a good risk for me. You know I hate it when I have to go chasing after someone who runs. Anyway, this young man, name was Lamond, had ties to Emanuel. In fact, it was Emanuel who made his bond."

"What had the man done?"

"He cut another young man. A white man who happened to be driving a pickup truck with a Confederate flag on it. You might know him. Kenny Bristow." He watched me as he waited for a response.

"I know him." I'd gone to school with his eldest brother, Teddy. The whole family was short on brains and big on mouth. It was no surprise to me that Kenny would be driving around town looking for trouble.

"The two of them got into some sort of altercation in the Piggly Wiggly parking lot. Name-calling led to action. It ended up that my client was armed and the other man wasn't."

"How bad was it?" I didn't have to stretch my mind to picture the entire scene.

"Kenny would be dead except that one of the deputies showed up. Gordon Walters saved that man's life. My client was about to gut him like a fish."

"How did Emanuel get involved?"

"Apparently, Lamond was in town to see Emanuel. They belong to some sort of organization. They made a big point out of how they were more than brothers and how they'd promised to look out for each other and for their cause."

"Their cause being—?"

"Teaching white folks a lesson, as best I could tell. There's a whole lot of anger and hatred there. It's not like the sixties, when good folks wanted to work toward equality. This is just plain hatred. They don't want to build anything. They just want to tear things down." Yancy drained his drink. "We've had the vote on the flag issue, but it isn't over. Not by a long shot."

"Thanks for telling me that," I said, finishing my drink and putting the glass down on a coaster on the coffee table. It was time for me to get moving.

"There's something else I can tell you," he said, rising and starting toward the door.

I followed him and then stepped in front as I went out the door. He was going to make sure I was out of the house before he opened his mouth. On the top step, I turned to face him.

"Someone else showed up to make Hampton's bond." He said it so calmly he knew he was dropping a bombshell.

"Someone else offered fifty grand to bond Scott out?" I didn't even try to hide my shock. "Who?"

"Fella name of McBruce. He had an accent. You know him?"

It took a moment for the brain cells to fire, but when they did, I felt my mouth drop.

"You do know him, don't you?" Yancy said with a hint of amusement. "Now it's your turn to share a few facts."

I didn't see the harm in it. "He's Stuart Ann Shanahan's estranged husband."

"No kidding." Yancy grew thoughtful. "Why would he want Hampton released? His wife's up at the courthouse twenty-four/seven making a total fool of herself."

"Now that's an excellent question," I replied, my own brain spinning with possibilities. "Did he act clandestine in any way?"

Yancy's eyes narrowed. "Not what I'd call clan-*des*-tine. But he had cash money on him. That's a lot of dough to be hauling around. It made me nervous as hell for him to sit here with it."

"He came here personally?" Somehow I'd thought he had called.

"In the flesh. Big fellow. Dark red hair, burly. If you saw him, you'd know who he was. And if he opened his mouth, you'd know without a doubt."

"He had a brogue?"

"If that's what you call talking like his throat was clogged."

"Thanks, Yancy. You've been a great help."

"My pleasure, Sarah Booth. You know, I was just a kid when I started out in this business, and your father was always fair with me. He kept me from making a few bad mistakes." He grinned. "You can pass all of this along to Coleman. I'm sure he'll be asking what you learned."

"He doesn't know I'm here."

His grin widened. "I sort of doubt that." He nodded and looked behind me. When I turned, I saw the brown patrol car parked just under the big oaks in the park. Coleman was waiting for me. An icy chill fluttered through my stomach.

"Good night, Sarah Booth." Yancy stepped back inside and closed the door.

As I turned to head to my car, the lights of the patrol car snapped on and I was caught in the beam like a possum on the highway.

WITH ENOUGH TRAINING, a Daddy's Girl can ignore a pie in the face. In times of embarrassment and indignity, such as a trip to the gynecologist, this tactic is invaluable. Staring at the ceiling on the doctor's table, knees in the air, there is no way humanly possible to acknowledge what is actually going on. The only response is to pretend that something else altogether is happening.

Blinded by Coleman's headlights, I decided to adopt this tactic. I walked to my car as if he didn't exist. If he wanted to talk to me, he was going to have to come over to my car and speak.

I had just slid behind the wheel when I felt his hand on my shoulder.

"Sarah Booth, we need to talk."

"Yancy is right inside his house. You can get any information you need straight from the horse's mouth." My hand went to the ignition, and Coleman's fingers on my shoulder tightened. Not painfully, but close to it.

"Please. I want to talk to you." He released the tension on my shoulder.

I put both hands on the wheel as if I were driving, and tried to breathe deeply. My lungs had shrunk. There wasn't enough room for air.

"What is it?" I asked, my focus straight ahead.

"Let's go for a ride."

"No." I didn't want to be alone with Coleman in the August night. A million stars were scattered across the sky, and I remembered several moments Coleman and I had shared in the dark.

He opened the door and began sliding into the seat. He was a solid man, and I remembered, unwillingly, how comforting I found his arms. I had no choice but to move to the passenger's side, though it meant a slightly humiliating scramble over the console.

Coleman started the car and eased into drive, circling around the park and then heading out County Road 16 toward Opal Lake. The lake was a well-known parking spot for teenagers, and on such a lovely summer night, there were bound to be dozens of lustful couples parked along the shore. I slunk down in the seat and decided that silence was the weapon of choice.

The warm August night kissed my face as we drove down the lonely road. Coleman made no effort to talk until we turned down the rutted lane that led to the lake. We passed four cars and two pickups before we parked beneath a tallow tree that gave a lot of privacy but allowed a good view of the silvery lake.

"Did Yancy tell you who bonded Hampton out of jail?" Coleman didn't look at me as he spoke.

"He did not. You could get all of this information from Yancy. He said he didn't have to tell unless he was called into court."

"He doesn't have to tell anyway," Coleman said. In the light of a three-quarter moon, he was grinning slightly. "I already know."

"You do?" I regretted the question as soon as it popped out. It made me sound way too impressed.

"You should know this, Sarah Booth. Bridge Ladnier put up the bond money for Hampton."

"Why would Bridge do that?" I asked, trying to hide my surprise. But Coleman saw through me and he had his answer. Anger washed over me. "So I didn't know the man I'm dating bonded Scott out. Just another shining example of all the things I don't know about men. So sue me."

Coleman's hand touched my face, a whisper of electricity. "My God, Sarah Booth, you make me want to risk everything."

My anger, my only weapon, evaporated. I wanted him to fold me into his arms, to kiss me until I had no reason. I wanted him in that age-old way of women and men. Yet I knew that such an hour of wantonness would destroy us. We would end up hating each other and ourselves.

"Take me home," I said in a whisper. "Please."

It was the please that did it. Coleman started the car and drove, very fast, back to his patrol car. He got out of the roadster and started to walk away, then he turned back.

"This isn't something we can continue to ignore," he said softly.

"I don't have any answers." I was sick with conflict. My body, my heart, and my brain were all at war, all clamoring for a different resolution. There were things I knew were wrong, and tempting a man out of his marriage was way high on the list. But there was no satisfaction in taking the moral high ground. Damn!

"I'm the one who has to find an answer," Coleman said. He hesitated, his strong hands clenching and unclenching at his sides. "I'm not trying to interfere in what you do, Sarah Booth, but I'm worried. Be careful with Bridge Ladnier. Fifty grand is a lot of money to risk on a whim. I don't want to see you used. And I don't want to see Scott Hampton dead, and that's likely what'll happen if he isn't in jail. Every faction in the county wants to kill him."

I slipped over the console, got behind the wheel, and headed for the safety of home.

BY THE TIME I got to Dahlia House, I was numb. Coleman had slapped me with dire warnings that Scott Hampton was likely a dead man if he left the protection of jail, and the ugly possibility that Bridge's motives weren't pure—which called to mind what Coleman's motives might be in doing that. To complicate matters further, Tinkie had left a message on the answering machine saying she had gone to New Orleans with Oscar on a business trip. Drat! Just when I needed to grill her a little about the man she'd picked out for me.

As I hurried up the stairs to my bedroom, I couldn't decide who I was angrier with—Coleman or Bridge. Why in the world had Bridge interfered?

There was only one way to find out and that was to ask him directly. I picked up the bedroom phone and dialed his number. After fifteen rings I had to admit he either wasn't home or wasn't answering.

"You callin' that man 'cause the one you want ain't available?"

I almost dropped the telephone. Jitty had slipped into my bedroom and nearly startled me to death.

"I'm calling Bridge on official business," I pointed out. She was wearing a Nehru jacket and slim-cut black jeans set off with high-heeled boots. It was a magnificent outfit, but a little warm for August. Then again, ghosts didn't suffer from temperature extremes.

"Men are stupid, but even the dumbest ones catch on eventually, Sarah Booth. You mad at that sheriff, and you're calling up Bridge for consolation."

"I am not! I have a question to ask Bridge." What I said was true, but Jitty was also on the mark.

"What is it you want?" Jitty asked, and all of the needling was gone from her voice.

"I don't know." That was completely honest. I didn't know what I wanted. I was attracted to Bridge on many levels, but in some strange fashion, I'd hooked myself to Coleman. Certainly not in a physical way, but emotionally. Then there was the troubling Scott Hampton. He was a sexy man with no other redeeming qualities.

"You have to know what you want to get it," Jitty said.

"I don't want to be a home-wrecker."

"No, you don't," Jitty agreed. "The trouble with you is that you know what you *don't* want, but you don't know what you *do* want. You got to get your priorities in order. Look at Tinkie. She had her list—security, social position, a man who would be good to her—"

"That's fine for Tinkie, who is vacationing in New Orleans while I'm stuck here working." I didn't add that the idea of Oscar made me want to join a convent. There was nothing wrong with Oscar, except he viewed Tinkie as a possession. Sure he was good to her. He gave her everything her heart desired, materialistically. What he couldn't give her was respect. He loved her, but he didn't even have a clue who she was beneath her beauty, charm, and the façade of the Daddy's Girl.

"No man is ever goin' to know who you are, Sarah Booth." Jitty's voice was dark with warning. "Now get that idea out of your head right now. You the only person who knows you inside out." She sat down on the edge of the bed. "You the only person can stand knowing all of that."

"A man doesn't have to know me inside out, but he has to have a clue. He has to want to know."

"That's asking too much." Jitty shook her head. "That's a dream, Sarah Booth."

"Just like equality is a dream," I fired back at her. It was a direct hit. Her eyes widened. "Not two days ago you were telling me how important it was to have a dream. Well, I have one, too. I want a man who knows me, or at least tries to. I want a man who'll put the same energy into me that I'm willing to put into him." I picked up the telephone receiver again. "And the only way I'm going to find that man is to spend some time looking."

"It's nearly ten o'clock on a Saturday night," Jitty said with a hint of sadness in her voice. "I shouldn't have to point out that it's another Saturday night and you ain't got nobody."

She was gone before I could respond. Jitty had pulled her famous vanishing act while lambasting me with a line from an old Sam Cooke song.

18

SOMETHING WET AND WARM SLURPED ACROSS MY FACE. I opened my eyes to sharp white teeth and a long pink tongue that swept over my right cheek.

"Sweetie Pie," I mumbled as I focused on the bedroom window. It was late Sunday morning. I'd slept for almost twelve hours. Jitty's harangue the night before had exhausted me.

I threw off the cotton sheets and swung my feet to the floor. From out in the pasture I heard Reveler's whinny. Rushing to the window, I saw the sun was well over the horizon. Dang! It was already hot outside. Normally I got up early to ride.

I put on jeans, a sports bra, a sleeveless T-shirt, paddock boots, and a tractor hat with the logo "Cowboy Hardware."

Hurrying outside, I realized I was going into the world without the benefit of even one cup of coffee. The truth was, I didn't want to hang around inside Dahlia House. I didn't want to see Jitty. I was still sore at her from the night before. It was fine for her to have her grand dreams of world peace and equality for all, but I couldn't have a personal dream of relationship happiness. Right.

Reveler came willingly. When I held out the halter, he put his head in it. He loved our morning rides. Lee, my friend who bred the finest horses in the world, had loaned me an old Stuben saddle. It weighed almost nothing as I lifted it onto Reveler's sleek back. In less than twenty minutes, we were curried, brushed, tacked up, and ready to ride. Sweetie spun circles beside the horse's legs as she waited for me to mount up.

The three of us headed out through the cotton fields of Dahlia House. One of the equestrian benefits of cotton fields is the lack of fencing. The entire county is virtually wide-open. As long as I kept to the edges of the fields, no one seemed to care that I rode on their land.

Reveler had a trot that could eat up the miles, and I let him set his own pace, feeling my body relax into the rhythm of the post. Riding was pure joy.

We left my land and continued across the fields, picking up one of the straight dirt roads that seemed to go nowhere and do nothing except cut through the middle of rows of cotton.

My stomach growled a complaint that I'd left home without sustenance, but I promised it angel biscuits, sausage, eggs, and grits when I got home. I was headed vaguely north—I had no destination. I merely wanted to ride.

It wasn't until we came to a small yellow creek that cut through the fields that I realized I'd ridden for at least twelve miles. The sun was burning down on me, and I could feel the heat in my arms. A new crop of freckles was incubating, and probably something worse. This was the century with a hole in the ozone— suntans were out.

Sweetie flopped in the creek and wallowed, and Reveler, too, stepped into the cool water and took a long draught. It was a little late to think about something for me to drink.

The creek was bordered on both sides by trees. The farmer who owned the land had wisely decided to use the tallow and birch trees as a windbreak. The Delta wasn't often hit by high-wind storms, but when they did come around, they could blow off a foot of valuable topsoil.

I let Reveler meander up the stream for a ways. It didn't matter that I wasn't sure where I was, because home was due south. With the sun shining, I could hardly lose my way.

We came to a small bridge that was too low to ride under, so we ambled up the bank. There was something vaguely familiar about the area. When I recognized it, I felt a chill. Bilbo Lane. I was only about a quarter of a mile from Scott Hampton's rented cottage.

It was a little past noon on a Sunday. If Spider and Ray-Ban were around, they were probably still asleep. If they were out and about, I might ask them one more time to leave Sunflower County. Especially now that Scott's bond had been met.

Reveler took up an easy trot and we were at the driveway in only a few moments. Sweetie was right at my side, which made me feel a little safer. She looked harmless enough, but she'd saved my life more than once.

The first thing I noticed was that the fast-food wrappers and beer cans were gone. Spider and Ray-Ban had obviously heard that Scott was getting out of jail and they'd busted their butts picking up their trash.

There was the sound of chopping coming from the backyard. I nudged Reveler forward. As we turned the corner beside the cottage, I saw a lean, bare back and jean-clad buttocks. My mouth went even drier.

Sweetie Pie gave a soft bark and ran forward just as Scott Hampton turned around. His chest was covered in sweat that glistened on well-developed muscles.

"Ms. Delaney," he said, lowering the axe he was using to chop wood. "What a surprise to see you." But his gaze didn't linger on me, it traveled over the horse. "He's a fine-looking animal."

"Thanks." I was about to call out to Sweetie, but she ran forward, tail wagging, and accepted the hand he put on her head.

"Nice dog, too." He looked back at me. "You're just full of surprises, aren't you?"

"Not nearly as many as you. When did you get out of jail?"

"The sheriff cut me loose this morning. He said my bond had been paid. In fact, my bail was made Saturday, but no one bothered to tell me. I'd still be sitting in that cell if some reporter hadn't called my attorney." He lifted the axe effortlessly and then let the handle slide through his hand until he was holding it at the head. "You wouldn't know who paid my bond, would you?"

"Coleman didn't tell you?" I looked around, expecting Nandy to jump out of the bushes at any second. If Scott was out of jail, why wasn't she on his trail?

"I didn't give the sheriff much of a chance to explain anything," Scott said. "I was pissed off."

"So, you showed him your charming side?"

"I lost my temper. He said he thought it would be safer for me to stay in jail. That wasn't his call to make. After our conversation, I guess he didn't really care if I was safe or not."

"You would be safer in jail." I couldn't shake the sense that Nandy or someone was lurking in the underbrush that had taken over most of the backyard.

"It isn't his place, or yours, to decide about my safety." Scott stepped closer.

He had a point, so I decided to shift the focus of the conversation. "Your benefactor is a man named Bridge Ladnier. You have a right to know this. Bridge wants to buy Playin' the Bones, and I know he's hoping you'll stay and play at the club if he buys it. More to the point, though, someone else attempted to make your bail. Robert McBruce. Nandy's husband. I'd be on the lookout for an ambush."

His reaction was similar to my own. His mouth dropped. He snapped it shut. "Why would Nandy's husband want to bond me out?"

"I can't begin to imagine. Everyone in town knows Nandy has been up at the courthouse like a dog in heat." I glanced down at Sweetie, who was sitting at Scott's feet. "Sorry, girl."

Scott knelt down and patted Sweetie. "She didn't mean it," he whispered in her long, silky ear. When he looked up at me, his smile was unexpected.

"You look hot," he said, rising to his feet in a smooth motion. "How about some iced tea? I just made some."

Sweat was rolling down my back. I could hear the compressor of an air conditioner. "That would be great." I slid to the ground, taking a moment for my feet to adjust to my weight.

"Ms. Delaney, who is this Bridge Ladnier? Should I know him?"

"He's a very wealthy entrepreneur, a local man, sort of. And he's a blues aficionado. I have to say he has one of the best blues collections I've ever seen, and he's a big fan of Ivory's work. And yours, of course."

Scott thought, then shook his head. "I can't be certain. There were a lot of folks in the club who loved the blues. Why would he make my bond?"

"Like I said, he wants to buy Playin' the Bones. I suspect his motive was twofold. To put him on Ida Mae's good side and to tempt you to stay on if he should manage to get the club."

"To obligate me?" Scott asked sharply.

I shrugged. "I can't say. I haven't talked to Bridge. But I will, and I'll ask that question." I stroked Reveler's neck. "Bridge honestly doesn't strike me as the kind of man who would try to use that leverage, but I don't know him all that well. I will ask."

"Thank you, Ms. Delaney." He pointed to a pasture that was field-fencing on three sides and split rail on the one facing us. "We can put your horse in that field," he said. "There's a little creek. He can drink and cool off."

Scott Hampton was being social. More than social—courteous and concerned for my animals. "Thanks," I said, unbuckling the saddle. Before I could do anything else, he was standing beside me. He lifted the saddle off Reveler's back and put it on the top rail of the fence.

I walked Reveler through the gate and removed his bridle. He gave me one headshake and two bucks as he ran around the pasture before he dropped to roll in a patch of dirt. I latched the gate and leaned on the fence rail to watch him.

"Healthy animal," Scott said with admiration as he walked up beside me and hitched a boot on the bottom rail. A cowboy boot, I noticed.

"Do you ride?" I asked. It wasn't something I expected of a Yankee bluesman.

"Used to. There was a time when I wanted to be a cowboy." He grinned at my startled look. "I was taught to ride English, though. Cowboys were frowned upon in my family. Just about everything I was interested in was frowned upon."

There was humor in his tone, not self-pity. "I wanted to be an actress. Lucky for them, my parents weren't alive to see that fiasco."

He laughed. "From what I've heard around town, they would have supported you if you'd decided to be a sword-swallower." His smile was rueful.

In that second, I was completely charmed. The man had complimented my parents *and* achieved a rueful smile. He was also charged with murder, unemployed, without family or references, and had friends who should be under a jail somewhere. He spoke to my heart.

"That's a slight exaggeration, but they would have supported me in *almost* anything." He'd also ignited my curiosity. "Who was talking about my parents?"

"Ida Mae, for one. She had great respect for both of them. She said something about baby clothes. You were a girl, so your mother brought some boy baby clothes she'd gotten to Ida Mae." He looked over at me. "And the sheriff spoke of you. He urged me to cooperate with you."

"He did?"

"He said you were the only person in town willing to give me half a chance and that I should work with you. He said you were my only hope."

I didn't want to think about Coleman. "Why do you think Robert McBruce wanted to make your bond?"

He shrugged. "Let's get that tea. I'm about to die of thirst."

Sweetie Pie and I followed him up the back steps of the cottage and inside. The kitchen was spotless. A pitcher of tea waited on the counter. He got a bowl from the cabinet, filled it with water, and put it on the floor for Sweetie. She lapped gratefully, splashing water all over the floor.

"I'll clean it up," I said. The floor, until our arrival, had been freshly mopped.

"Forget it. It's only water." He cracked an ice tray, filled two glasses, and poured us tea. I took a sip. It was sweetened perfectly.

"You make good tea, for a Yankee," I said.

"For a Delta girl, you give good backhanded compliments," he responded.

"Touché."

He led the way into a living room that reminded me of magazine pictures of hippies. Madras throws covered the sofa. There was a brass incense burner on the coffee table, which also held a textbook on the local Indian tribes. Posters of blues musicians hung on the wall, and the floor was covered with a straw mat.

"Time warp, isn't it?" he said as he took a seat on the sofa beside me. "I always felt like I missed my era. I would have been great in the sixties."

"You would have been dead," I responded without really thinking. But it was true. "A white man playing the blues in a black club in Mississippi would have been a great target for the Klan."

"Am I a target for the Klan now?" he asked.

Scott wasn't kidding. It was a serious question, and one that deserved an answer. "I don't think so. The KKK was active in the sixties, but they were mostly thugs. They preyed on people who had no recourse, folks who didn't stand a real chance in the justice system. I don't really see you that way."

"Thanks, I think." He sipped his tea, then put his glass on a coaster on the table. He'd been brought up with good manners, and he took care of things, even if it was only a pine coffee table.

"Scott, who would want to frame you for murder?"

"That's a tough question. I didn't realize anyone around here hated me that much. They'd have to really hate me to kill Ivory just to get me."

For the first time I had an inkling of the scope of his loss. And the burden of guilt he carried. If his scenario was correct, someone had killed his friend and benefactor to set him up. He was, in a way, the instrument of Ivory's death.

"You think Ivory was just a tool to get you?"

He sighed. "What else could it be? The money and the shank were planted on me. The place was ransacked, and part of my tattoo was cut into Ivory's back. It looks to me like the entire thing was constructed to point the finger at me."

He was in anguish as he spoke, and I put a hand on his arm. "Even if that's true, it isn't your fault."

"Easy for you to say."

It was, indeed, easy for me to say. Of all the punitive emotions, guilt is the worst. And Scott was struggling under a tremendous weight of it. "You can't assume responsibility for other people's actions. Whoever did this was mean and depraved, but you can't take on their guilt."

"If I hadn't come here, this wouldn't have happened. I'm like a fatal disease. If I let anyone close to me, they suffer and die."

The pain in his voice told me as much as his words. A large part of Scott's coldness and rudeness was his desire not to be hurt, or to hurt others. "You and Ivory were great friends. You can't let what happened destroy that fact for you. The things that happened aren't your fault."

He leaned back into the sofa and closed his eyes. "That's all I think about. All I see. They beat Ivory before they killed him. He was an old man. Who would do such a thing?"

"That's the question we have to focus on. Now, I've got three suspects."

He opened his eyes. "Who?"

He wasn't going to like this, but he had to hear it. "Spider and Ray-Ban and Emanuel Keys."

"Emanuel wouldn't kill his own father. That kind of talk could destroy Ida Mae."

I was surprised on two fronts—that Scott defended Emanuel first, and that he defended him at all. Scott's stock was rising rapidly in my eyes. "I disagree. I think Ida Mae had already come to that conclusion."

He pushed his blond hair back from his eyes. When he looked at me, he was troubled. "Ida Mae loves Emanuel. She may not like him, but she loves him. And there wasn't an empty spot in her heart. Ivory was all over it. To think that her son killed her husband? That's the worst thing I can imagine for her."

"If he did it, he deserves to be punished." I sounded like Coleman, but I couldn't help it. I hadn't known Ivory, but I had met Emanuel. It was hard for me to find a soft spot for him or what he might have done. "But what about your... friends? Where are they, by the way?"

"I came home and when I saw this place, I hit the roof." His grin was a little shamefaced. "I have a temper."

"So I've seen . . . and heard." I motioned him to continue.

"I told them to leave." He looked down at his hands. "They'll be back. They just don't understand why I don't want to live like trash. It was the same in prison. I kept my things neat."

"It might be best if they didn't come back," I said.

"Maybe, but that's not what's going to happen. They'll come back. They think they're helping me. Showing support, protecting me. That kind of thing. They think they're doing good. Besides, they're the only friends I have."

"Scott, could they have killed Ivory?" I held my breath, waiting for his temper to ignite.

He leaned forward onto his knees. "I just don't see that. Why? Why would they do that? They have no reason to frame me."

"Are you sure?" I wasn't, and I didn't try to hide my doubt.

"Sarah Booth, I know you don't understand it, but there's a code in prison. Spider, Ray-Ban, and I went through some rough times. We became brothers. More than brothers."

"I've heard about the code in prison, but I've also heard about another code. 'There is no honor among thieves,' " I quoted him. "Maybe they aren't thieves, but the sentiment still applies."

"And what about me? Am I honorless, too?"

I considered that. "Scott, you got into some trouble. You said you paid your debt to society, you weren't bitter, you saved a man's life in prison—the very life your *brothers* were going to ruin, I might point out—and you made something of yourself. I just don't see you in the same light I see them."

"I had advantages they didn't have. I had an education. I—"

"Don't hand me that crap." I spoke more harshly than I intended, but he'd hit a hot button. "There's not a person in this country who can't get an education if they really want it." I lifted my eyebrows, daring him to contradict me.

"*If* they believe they can get one, and that's a big if."

I started laughing. I couldn't help myself.

"What?" Scott asked. "What is it?"

I pointed at him. "You."

"I don't recall saying anything amusing." He was getting aggravated and trying hard not to.

"You sound like me," I said. "Bleeding-heart liberal."

He smiled, then, that electric smile. "I believe that some folks can't overcome the image of themselves they're given by their parents. You and I were lucky, Sarah Booth. Particularly you. Your folks loved you for who you were. Mine saw me as an extension of themselves. It wasn't until I was grown that I displayed my potential for disappointment. But as a kid, I had the belief that I could do anything. No one ever believed Spider and Ray-Ban would amount to anything except trouble. All they did was fulfill those expectations."

I admired him for his sentiments, and in theory, I agreed with him. But Spider and Ray-Ban were a real problem. Their behavior in the community was totally unacceptable, and their conduct at Ivory's funeral made me believe they might be causing trouble for Scott deliberately, and I told him so.

"They just don't know any better," he argued. "Like throwing trash all over the place. They don't think that's wrong."

"Don't cancel your friendship with them, just get them out of town." I had run out of steam. Scott wasn't going to be reasonable, and I didn't care if he agreed with me; I just wanted results. "Promise me."

"Let me put on some music." He got up and went to a Bose stereo system behind the sofa. I was prepared for B. B. King or

Mississippi John Hurt, but what came out of the speaker was an Alabama artist, Percy Sledge.

It was a song that never failed to move me. "When a Man Loves a Wo-man," Percy came down hard on the lyrics in a voice that held back nothing.

"He's a master, isn't he?" Scott asked.

"He is." My mother and father had danced to this song in the parlor. I had great memories of them holding each other tight, laughing and kissing. I hardly ever played the song because it made me so sad.

"Sarah Booth?" Scott was looking at me. "Are you okay?"

"Sure." I tried to brush away the emotion that had suddenly trapped me.

"A good memory or bad?" he asked.

"Good."

He held his hand out to me. I took it and he pulled me to my feet. "Pick out something else?" he suggested, leading me over to a massive collection of CDs.

"No." I didn't want to stop the song. "I'm okay."

His finger was gentle as it caught a tear just hanging on my bottom eyelashes. "Yeah, you're okay," he said.

His arms wrapped around me and he held me against his chest. "You're a little more than okay, Sarah Booth."

I looked up at him and met his lips. It started out as a kiss of comfort, but in less than five seconds, it was a lot more than that. My body was on fire. His fingers, light as a whisper, stroked the inside of my arm, sending shivers throughout me.

His other hand laced in my hair, tugging my head back to reveal my throat. His lips seared down my neck, moving slowly toward my breasts.

I had no desire to stop him. My own hands were busy, moving over his body, feeling the hard muscles that sloped down his lower back to his waist and then gently swelled out again over his butt.

When he broke away from me and took my hand, I let him lead me through the bedroom and into the bath. He started the shower before he undressed me.

It took only seconds for him to slide out of his boots and jeans. When he parted the shower curtain, I stepped in, turning so that the water beat against my back as I held myself against him.

With great care he washed my hair, then took a bar of soap and washed my body. I'd never imagined he could be so gentle. When it was his turn, I did the same, my hands moving over every hard inch of him. Without bothering with towels, we walked to the bedroom. Scott sat down and pulled me to him, my thighs between his knees. When he looked up at me, his eyes held fire.

"No regrets," he said.

"No regrets," I lied. There undoubtedly would be—after all, I was sleeping with my client, a man I didn't know at all. I was doing it with bright Sunday sunlight streaming through the window and falling on the cotton chenille bedspread. I was doing it without benefit of Jack Daniel's or even Folger's. I was doing it because I wanted him so much that I didn't care what the cost would be.

His hands clasped around my waist and he lifted me over him and into the bed. As our skin touched, toe to chin, I forgot everything except the way he made me feel.

19

I DON'T KNOW HOW LONG I'D BEEN ASLEEP. THE QUALITY OF light coming in through the window had changed. I closed my eyes. Scott was pressed against my back, one arm thrown across my waist. How I'd come to be in this position could only be attributed to the Delaney womb.

I stretched, pulling the cotton sheet over my thighs and breasts. There was nothing on earth I wanted at that moment. Replete is a very underrated word.

Scott had made love to me in a way that left every cell stretched, vibrating, and now lazily comatose. With a little more exposure to his methods, I could become an addict.

I let my fingers drift across his arm, and his hand slipped up to capture a breast. He held me with just the right amount of pressure. He was, indeed, a master. The sexuality that he projected in his music was the real thing. No wonder he drove women crazy.

"Do you need anything?" he asked, his voice warm and easy.

"Not a single thing," I replied, kissing his arm. "How about you?"

"Baby, I don't know if there's anything left of me."

I opened my eyes, judging the time of day from the sunlight. It was midafternoon. Though I wanted to spend the rest of the day curled in bed with Scott, I had things I needed to do. Namely talk to Bridge.

Regret wasn't what struck me at the thought of Bridge. The proper name for it was guilt. I was dining with Bridge and sleeping with Scott.

He must have felt me tense. "Are you sure you're okay?" he asked, leaning up on one elbow to whisper in my ear.

All thought of Bridge fled. Scott's whisper tickled my ear, sending shivers through my body and reminding me of just how well he knew how to excite me. I turned my head and offered my lips.

His kiss had just begun to deepen when we both froze. Sweetie had risen from her place at the foot of the bed. A low growl issued from her throat.

Scott broke the kiss and tilted his head slightly to listen. I sat up in bed so I could hear better. I looked at Sweetie, who was slowly walking up beside the bed, her tail straight and her teeth bared as she growled. I glanced up at the window and let a small gasp escape. Nandy Shanahan was staring in the window at us, and the look on her face held pure hatred. She said something, but I couldn't make out what it was through the glass.

"Dammit!" Scott was out of bed, jeans in his hand. As soon as he moved, Nandy took off, too.

Scott ran out of the bedroom while trying to step into his pants. I clutched the sheet to my chest and got out of bed, searching for my clothes. They were in the bathroom.

I heard the back door slam as I was pulling on my riding jeans, which were tight and still damp, and therefore clung to my thighs. Tugging with all my might as I hopped around the bedroom, I finally tripped on my paddock boot and fell sideways onto the bed.

"Nandy!" Scott was shouting in the backyard. "Nandy, get your ass over here!"

I jerked my jeans up, threw on my T-shirt, and ran barefoot out the back door. Nandy was in the pasture. She held something in one hand.

"You think you've accomplished something?" she screamed at me. "He sleeps with anyone who'll drop their pants for him. And plenty of women do. You're nothing special."

Her face was pale, and her liner and mascara had smudged. She looked like a rabid raccoon. And she looked just about as dangerous. I didn't want to chance a bite. I stayed back.

"Nandy, this is none of your business." I kept my voice calm. "If you don't leave now, you're going to be in a lot of trouble."

"You're the one in trouble, you idiot." She grinned and lifted the hand holding something beside her head. "You knew I wanted Scott. You knew it. I was the one holding a vigil for him. I was the one who helped him get out of jail. But you couldn't wait. Just because I wanted him, you had to crawl in his bed. You're just a dog in the manger, Sarah Booth. That's all you are, and I'm going to make you pay for this." She brought her raised hand forward with great force and a big clod of dirt whirled through the air and struck Reveler on the hip. He whinnied loudly and started running.

I watched in horror as Reveler came straight toward the wooden rail fence. He was bred to jump. At the last minute he wheeled and ran in the opposite direction.

"You're just like all the other women who chase Scott. I'm going to make you sorry for the day you were born." Nandy bent down and picked up another dirt clod.

"Nandy, stop it!" She was in a real state, but not nearly as bad off as she was going to be if I got my hands on her. Or possibly Scott. He was circling behind her, getting ready to move in for the kill. All I had to do was keep her focused on me, which wasn't hard.

In the background I could hear Sweetie Pie howling. She was shut up in the house, and I regretted that she wasn't with me. She'd show Nandy a thing or two.

"You're a conniving little bitch, Sarah Booth. You act like

you're a professional P.I., but you're just a slut. You took this case so you could jump in bed with Scott."

Now was not the time to agitate her further, but I'd had enough of her verbal abuse. "If Scott wanted you, Nandy, *you'd* be in his bed. Face the facts, he can't stand the sight of you and that won't ever change. If he's slept with so many women, why weren't you one of them?" It was a direct hit, but Nandy was still in her Daddy's Girl armor.

"He knows that I'm someone special. He knows he can't just jump in the sack with me and walk away, like he's going to do with you, you taco." Her lip drew up in a sneer. "You're just fast food for him, Sarah Booth. A little snack, eaten and discarded."

I raised my eyebrows. "You have part of it right."

That was the final straw. A sound like something tearing came from her throat. She dropped the dirt clod and picked up what looked like a rock.

"Leave the horse alone," I ordered. "If you've got a problem with me, take it up with me." Scott was almost on her, but I wasn't certain he'd be fast enough to save Reveler.

"My pleasure! I'm going to brain you." Just as she reared back to throw, Scott leaped at her. He tackled her hard, knocking her down and falling on top of her. I could hear the *whoof* as the air was knocked out of her.

Even with her lungs empty, she still struggled. She grabbed a handful of dirt and was getting ready to pull the classic bad guy maneuver when I stepped on her wrist.

"Nandy!" Scott eased up, but pinned her shoulders to the ground with his hands. He was still straddling her, and she was writhing as she tried to get air back into her lungs.

"You're . . . going . . . to . . . pay," she gasped, trying to buck her hips.

"Sarah Booth, call the sheriff," Scott said. "I'm sick of this, Nandy. I'm worn out with you stalking me. This time I have a witness."

I stood in the field. Reveler was fine. He'd calmed down and was grazing again, one eye watching the antics of the humans as he ate. The dirt clods wouldn't really have hurt him, but it was the danger that he'd try to jump the fence that had scared me. He could have gotten into a lot of trouble before I could catch him.

"Don't call Coleman," Nandy said, finally getting her wind back.

"Call the sheriff," Scott repeated, glancing at me. "I finally have proof that Nandy is stalking me, and this will go a long way toward invalidating her eyewitness testimony."

I didn't move. It was as if my body had gone numb. I didn't want Coleman to get in the middle of this. Nandy would be sure to tell him exactly what Scott and I were doing that had her so upset. At the thought of Coleman's possible opinion of me, I felt the first tidal wave of regret. Anger was the next emotion. Anger at myself. Why was I feeling guilty? Coleman was married and had publicly announced his intention to make that marriage work. I was a free agent. I could do anything I wished.

"Sarah Booth?" Scott was looking at me with confusion.

"Wait a minute," I said. "Let's talk this through."

Nandy instantly quit struggling. Her makeup was bad, but her instincts were razor-sharp. "She doesn't want everyone in town to know she was doing the wild thing with you, Scott. She has a little pride left. It doesn't look good to be one of a thousand lovers. Even someone as pathetic as Sarah Booth wants to feel special." She grinned. "Get off me, or *I'll* call the sheriff."

"Sarah Booth?" Scott was waiting for me to deny her charges.

"Look, Nandy can recant her testimony—that she saw you leaving the club around two o'clock. If she does that, then we won't tell the sheriff about this." There was a way Scott could achieve his goal without involving Coleman.

"And Nandy goes free?" Scott asked, obviously unhappy. "I don't think so."

"I won't recant, because it's the truth!" Nandy glared at me.

"You offered to recant if Scott would say he was with you," I reminded her.

"That was before. This is now. Since he's been in bed with you,

I don't want him to say he was with me. In fact, I would be humiliated if he said he was with me. Unlike you, Sarah Booth, I have family and pride. I don't want the Shanahan name smeared with sexual association with Scott." She started wiggling again.

Scott was still looking at me. When he finally released Nandy, he rose fluidly to his feet and stepped away from her.

"Get out of here," he said, "and don't come back. Stay away from me, and keep your husband away from me, too."

Nandy stopped all movements. She looked up at Scott. "What are you talking about? What about my husband?"

When Scott realized Nandy was clueless about her husband's attempts to make his bond, a slow grin passed over his face. "If you aren't gone from here in the next five minutes, I will call Coleman and Sarah Booth will back me up. Now stay away from me, Nandy. Don't come around me, don't call me, don't show up for my performances, and I suggest that you listen to Sarah Booth and figure out how not to show up for court."

"You can't tell me where I can go or what I can do." She was on her feet.

"Take a vacation, Nandy," I said. "I hear Scotland's really nice this time of year."

"You lowbred . . . bitch." Nandy had a new talent; she could speak with her teeth clenched together.

"Go," Scott said, pointing toward the road. "I'm counting to ten."

Nandy started walking sideways. "I had something important to tell you, Scott. I came all the way out here to deliver a message, but I guess you're not interested in hearing it."

"I'm not," Scott said, his finger still pointing at the road. "Keep moving."

"I had a little conversation with Emanuel this morning."

"I don't care if you talked with Elvis Presley, just keep moving."

"He's going to sell the club."

Scott's finger faltered in the air. "That's not my business. That's up to Ida Mae."

She shook her head. "No, it isn't. Ida Mae doesn't have a say at all. The club belongs to Emanuel. Ivory left it to him in the will."

Scott was obviously stricken by the news, though he was doing everything he could to hide it.

"Emanuel said he was going to raze the club and sell the land. But I told him I might be interested in buying the club, as it is. I told him I was thinking about opening a country-music joint. He said he'd think about it." She stopped. "So I might be the new club owner."

"Good for you, Nandy," Scott said. "Have a ball. Maybe you can find a yodeler who'll sleep with you."

"I could keep it a blues club. Once it's sold, Emanuel wouldn't have any say over what I did with it. I could keep it blues, and I could make you my partner. We could create the finest blues club in the United States."

Scott walked over to stand by me. His arm went around my waist and he drew me against him. "Not interested. I wouldn't work for you if you had the last club on the face of the earth."

Nandy was pale with anger. "By the way, Scott, you should know that no respectable man in Sunflower County will go out with Sarah Booth."

Scott's smile was slow and sexy. "What's wrong with them? They can't hold up to the kind of loving she gives? She is hot."

Nothing I said or did could have scorched Nandy more.

"The two of you are perfect for each other. A male and female slut."

That was her parting remark, and then she was gone. She walked down the driveway and disappeared behind a row of chinaberry trees and thick hedges.

"That isn't the end of her and she's going to make trouble for you now," Scott said. "I'm sorry. We should have called the sheriff. Why didn't you want to?"

"You have nothing to be sorry about. As to Coleman, I thought we would have better leverage on Nandy if we didn't call." My lie was halfhearted. I had other things on my mind. Like my most recent actions. "Let's just hope Nandy decides to forget what time she saw you at the club. But if she doesn't, that also makes her a suspect."

"Right." Scott gently maneuvered me toward the cottage. "She's crazy, you know."

"Crazy as a run-over dog," I agreed. "I need to find out a little more about her husband and where they both were the night Ivory was killed."

Scott opened the door and followed me inside. "You honestly think Nandy could have killed Ivory?"

"I think she's capable of anything." And I wasn't exaggerating.

MY FIRST ACTION when I got to Dahlia House was to call Cece. It was Sunday afternoon, and I was lucky to catch her at home. As the newspaper's society editor in a county that put social connections above all else, she was invited to every significant soiree—or the celebrators paid dearly. Her dance card was rarely empty, and those who questioned Cece's sexual heritage did so very discreetly.

"Sarah Booth, dahling," Cece said in a long drawl, "one might get the idea that one is being snubbed."

"I've been working," I said, having the grace to blush at my lie. Thank goodness she couldn't see me. Part of her journalistic skill was her ability to discern truth from fabrication. She knew where debutantes bought their dresses and how much they paid for them and doled out the inches on her page accordingly. She was never fooled by a knockoff. She had a gut instinct for genealogy that made the grande dames of Zinnia tremble. "I need to return the hat I borrowed."

"You obviously need something else, too."

She also knew her friends. "I do," I confessed. Cece kept her finger on the pulse of all upscale rentals in the county. "Where is Robert McBruce residing?"

"He's taken a six-month lease on the old Jackson estate."

Her voice betrayed her envy. The old Jackson place contained the finest chandeliers in the United States. There were even chandeliers in the bathroom. Cece loved the fire and ice of good lighting ornamentation.

"You wouldn't want to have to clean all that dangly glass. Besides, the chandelier would detract from you, Cece."

"You're absolutely right, dahling." She was done with envy. "I wonder if Nandy will be residing there with her spouse. It was quite a scene this morning."

"What are you talking about?" Had Nandy made it back to town and already started the rumor mill grinding my reputation?

"Dahling! You don't know?"

Cece was firmly in control of the conversation and she loved it this way.

"What have I missed?"

"McBruce showed up on the courthouse lawn this morning and physically removed Nandy from the premises. It was something to see. She was spitting and fighting and screaming."

"You saw it?"

"Indeed, dahling. My sources never let me down. I got a call just as the sun was pinking up the sky in that delicious shade of peach. I put on my Chanel housecoat and a pair of Gucci slippers and I went right over. That twit Garvel couldn't manage to get a camera there in time, though. By the time he dragged his sorry ass—excuse me, dahling, I'm still feeling a little hostile—his sorry self up there, McBruce had shoved her headfirst into his Land Rover. Charming man, he waved to me as he drove away. I've already written it for my Tuesday column. I'm calling it 'Courthouse Capers.' Do you like?"

"Perfect."

"What do you want with McBruce? I think it's a little late for condolences on his marriage. I can't help but wonder how a man with a heritage of clan lords could have tied up with Nandy. She must have been on heavy psychotic drugs. You know, they say Thorazine is a wonder drug for someone like her."

"It was an arranged marriage." Cece's gasp was gratifying.

Well, Nandy had spilled the beans on herself. And then she'd shown up at Scott's and was currently engaged in a campaign to ruin me. Tit for tat.

"But that doesn't explain what you want with McBruce." Cece was seldom thrown off the scent.

"Focus on the arranged marriage. If I can tell you the rest, I will." The fact that McBruce had tried to make Scott's bail had come from a bondsman. He'd told me in a friendly conversation, and I wasn't certain he'd intended it to become fodder for the newspaper.

"Arranged marriage. I wonder if the Shanahans had to pay McBruce to marry her?"

"Ask for a list of wedding presents. Maybe a wooden stake was included." What else was there to say? Nandy had had a very busy morning being dragged and driven around the county. I intended to make her life even busier.

"Good work, Sarah Booth. By the way, how is Scott Hampton?"

There was just enough edge in her voice to make me wonder what she'd heard about me. Perhaps I was getting ready to bleed from the double-edge of the gossip sword. "Scott's fine. I've got to go. Talk to you later, Cece."

Two calls later and I was set for the rest of the day. In my wildest dreams, I'd never envisioned my P.I. job as a means of playing Robin Leach, yet I had appointments to interview two of the richest men in the Southeast.

Bridge was first. To my shame, he sounded eager to see me and thrilled that I'd broken Daddy's Girl rule number six, *phonus abstentia*, and called him.

When I called McBruce, he didn't even ask why I wanted to talk to him. My evening appointment with him—drinks at six o'clock at The Club—would serve the secondary purpose of keeping me from lingering too long at Bridge's. Confession might be good for the soul, but it was not good for my future as a social companion with Bridge. I'd learned from hard experience that if my womb was wanton, my tongue was even worse. I had been known to blab my most personal secrets.

I had just sunk beneath the bathwater when I felt someone staring at me. I rose, water sluicing in all directions, to find Jitty sitting on the toilet beside the old claw-footed tub.

"Water can't wash away what you done," she pointed out. She
was wearing a sequined evening gown. Red. And her hair was
swept into a beehive. Even though she looked like Satan's daughter, she was giving off the vibes of Pollyanna.

"I'm a grown woman. I can do whatever I want." I spoke
boldly, but even the Delaney womb was a little uncomfortable.
The truth was, I did feel guilty. And the demon regret that Scott
had evoked was nibbling my toes. How in the world was I going
to face Scott the next time I saw him? He was my client.

"You sure can do whatever you want, but you're gonna have to
live with the consequences. And what if those consequences need
bottles and diapers?"

The bathtub was deep, and the water covered everything but
my neck and head. Still, I felt vulnerable. "Jitty, there are no consequences. So I slept with Scott Hampton. I didn't violate any
laws. Besides, I thought a baby was all you wanted. When I slept
with Hamilton Garrett V, you were bitterly disappointed when I
didn't get pregnant." Even to myself I sounded pathetic.

"Scott Hampton ain't Hamilton Garrett V, and you know it.
Besides, you stomped all over your ethics."

"What are you talking about?"

"I don't think it's such a good idea to sleep with a client.
Especially not a racist murderer."

There it was, the little thorn that was festering deep inside my
heart. Jitty had found it and managed to wiggle it in a little
deeper.

"Scott isn't a racist. And he isn't a murderer."

"We've been over this before. But let me ask you just one question: What are you gonna do if it turns out he's both of those
things?"

It was a good question, and one that I didn't want to contem-
plate. I had made my share of social mistakes. I'd slept with men
for various reasons that seemed good at the time but turned out

to be not so good. But if he was guilty of killing Ivory, Scott Hampton would be the biggest mistake of my ignoble romantic career.

"He isn't like that." My heart and my womb surely wouldn't lead me that far astray.

Jitty stood up. "I almost called in my backup singers, but I thought I could handle this alone." She put a hand on one hip and held the other out, palm facing me. "Stop, in the name of love, before you get yourself pregnant with a love child that's half-Yankee and half-racist."

She was gone and I was left sitting in a tub of cold, dirty water. "You don't even look like Diana Ross!" I yelled after her.

20

STANDING NAKED IN FRONT OF MY CLOSET, I HAD TO ADMIT that Jitty had done her work. She'd planted the seed of fear regarding a love child. I tried to convince myself that the tiny bulge of my abdomen had been there for the last three years, but I couldn't be certain. Perhaps a child was already incubating!

Dang Jitty! If it had been any other man except Scott Hampton, Jitty would have been ecstatic.

Then again, maybe not. She was in a new mode. Gone were the advice for the lovelorn from *Cosmopolitan*, the Stephen Stills lyrics of "Love the One You're With," and the find-you-a-man-in-cyberspace lectures. She was operating on a new set of rules, and they reeked of that transitional era, the sixties. Jitty had regressed! Again!

Sinking deeper into de-spair with every passing second, I snatched a pair of white slacks and a chartreuse sleeveless sweater out of the closet and onto my body. My mother's peridot-and-amethyst earrings were perfect, even though wearing my hair on my shoulders slightly concealed the earrings. I'd perfected the humidity "do." My hair was gelled and allowed to dry in natural curls. Then it was hair-sprayed to the consistency of sheet metal. If I didn't mess with it, it wouldn't frizz.

I had to get out of Dahlia House. And I had to get out of my present mood before I talked to Bridge. I had legitimate questions to ask him, and I could not go over there beating myself on the back with a cat-o'-nine-tails.

I left Sweetie asleep in the kitchen, one paw on her food bowl. Reveler was grazing happily in the back pasture, and I was wearing the color, according to Margaret Mitchell, that blondes dare not wear. It was time to gird my loins and get busy.

Bridge opened the front door before I could ring the bell. In less than a second I was folded into his arms and he was kissing me.

"Sarah Booth, I've been thinking about you all weekend." He was strong and he gave me an extra little squeeze. "They were very pleasant thoughts. And here you are."

In a matter of hours, I'd slipped from the exemplary conduct of an earnest investigator to the ditch of compromised ethics. I'd slept with the primary suspect, and I was kissing a potentially important player. "Bridge," I said, pushing against his chest.

My slightest hint of discomfort was enough. His arms dropped and he stepped back from me. "Forgive me, Sarah Booth. I didn't mean to presume. I was simply delighted to see you."

His feelings were hurt. Damn! And he didn't even know the half of it. I put my hand on his arm. "I'm here on official business, Bridge."

"Oh." He stepped back from the door to allow me to enter. "Thank goodness. I was afraid you'd fallen in love with someone else and had come to tell me."

He'd turned away to close the door and didn't see me cringe. I hadn't exactly fallen in love, I'd jumped in the sack. The quicker I got to this, the better. "Bridge, why did you make Scott's bail?"

If I'd hoped to surprise him, it backfired. He gave a fine imitation of the Cheshire cat. "Scott is free to play at the club now. He and Ida Mae can keep it open."

Was it possible a man could be so generous? It was my job to be skeptical. "Are you going to buy the club?" Keeping it up and running would only be good business for him if he bought it.

"Ida Mae never responded to the offer you made in my behalf. I know it must be hard for her to consider selling the club, and I didn't want to pressure her right now."

"I hear Emanuel's going to inherit the club."

A frown crossed his face. "That might complicate things. He won't keep it open, and he certainly won't let Scott continue to play, no matter what Scott's contract says. I wonder . . ." His voice trailed off.

"Wonder what?"

The bemused look on his face was replaced with a smile. "Just a business detail, Sarah Booth. Contractual obligations."

"What kind of obligations?"

"It's Sunday afternoon. Let me at least make you comfortable and fix you a drink before we talk business." He led the way into the front parlor.

There wasn't a remnant of our Bedouin evening left. The front parlor now contained a leather sofa and club chairs. I took a seat in a chair, wisely avoiding the pitfalls of potential couch contact, and waited for Bridge to return with the drinks.

Realizing that I might have melted a little in the hot car, I slipped into the bathroom to check my makeup. Despite Bridge's hug and kiss, my hair remained a perfect helmet. I pulled a comb from my purse and worked on making it look a little more natural, arranging the lacquered curls on my shoulders. Dang the humidity! I hated summer. I pinked up my lipstick and was back in my chair before Bridge brought the drinks.

"Jack Daniel's, I believe, is your preferred drink," he said, handing me a crystal highball glass.

My heart gave a little contraction. He'd taken the time to find out what I liked to drink. "Tinkie has been talking again."

Bridge only laughed. "You'd be surprised at the people who pay close attention to your habits, Sarah Booth."

He meant it as a compliment, but it struck me as a little chilling. I moved right on to the business matter he'd dodged at the door. "What contractual obligations were you referring to?"

"Scott is obligated to perform at Playin' the Bones for two years. If the club is closed, I'm sure that invalidates his contract."

"If Emanuel finds out about that, he may keep the club open just for spite," I pointed out.

"Very true. But Scott may not be obligated if the club is sold. Contracts are very tricky. The wording might allow him to leave even if Emanuel keeps it open."

"Because Ivory isn't running the club." I got his point, and it was an interesting one. "I'd like to see that contract."

"That makes two of us."

Bridge tilted his head as he looked at me. "You are a lovely creature, Sarah Booth."

Compliments are like cocaine—they make a girl feel like a million dollars, even when they aren't justified. "Thank you, Bridge."

"You have a special glow about you today. And there's just the hint of . . . satisfaction in the corners of your mouth. You're a very sexy lady, Sarah Booth."

I couldn't afford to mainline pretty words from Bridge. I was working a case, and I had to keep that foremost in mind. "If you buy the club, would you try to hold Scott to his contract?"

"I hadn't really thought about that," Bridge said, "but I'd hope he'd agree to play there. Of course, the club isn't worth much without Scott. He's the draw."

Bridge was a businessman, and a good one. No matter how generous his offer to buy the club, he intended to turn a profit on it.

"Would making Scott's bail have anything to do with that?" I asked.

Bridge shrugged, turning down a corner of his mouth. "I thought it might not hurt if he felt a small obligation toward me." He waited for my response. When I didn't say anything, he leaned forward and put his hand on my knee. "Sarah Booth, do you suppose Ida Mae would allow me to walk through the club? I need to get an idea of what's there and what it's worth. I want to make a fair offer."

"I'm sure Oscar could make the financial paperwork available to you."

"He has. But there's nothing like a physical inspection to answer a lot of questions. At least in my mind. I want a contractor to take a look at the plumbing, the wiring, all of that. See what it would take to add more bathrooms, maybe put in a kitchen."

"When would you like to go?"

He lifted his elegant hands. "This evening would be fine. If they plan to reopen the club, it might be best if I could get this done right away."

"You can find a contractor on a Sunday evening?" This was an amazing trick. I was impressed.

He dropped his gaze to the floor. "I'm willing to pay triple overtime. I think I can turn someone up. And if I can't, I know a bit about such things. I wasn't always an investor."

When he looked back up at me, there was humor in his eyes. I'd underestimated him again. He was merely letting me know that he was a man's man, capable of building and other such manly activities. I had to smile. "I'll keep that in mind."

"Please do, Sarah Booth."

I got a pen and scrap of paper from my purse and wrote down Ida Mae's number. I'd gotten the answer to my burning question about why Bridge made Scott's bond. And I was relieved to discover that Bridge had no hidden agenda—he wanted to help Ida Mae and keep the club open. It was good business if he bought the club. "I'd call Ida Mae first. Emanuel may not be as agreeable. I'm not certain how property is transferred in a will." When my parents were killed in a car accident, I'd been a child. My Aunt LouLane took care of all the details. Dahlia House had simply become mine.

"If Ida Mae gives me permission to have the club inspected, I think that's all I need right now."

I stood up. "Thanks for the drink." In truth, I was disappointed—and a bit relieved—that Bridge hadn't asked me to dinner or for a future date. His words were charming, but he was all talk. It was just as well. I had my hands full.

He walked me to the door, and as I was leaving, he put a hand on my shoulder. "I'll call you, Sarah Booth."

I smiled. "Good evening, Bridge."

The car was hot as Hades, but I got in and drove away. By the time I got to the end of the driveway, sweat from the hot leather seats had soaked my back.

I had half an hour to kill before I was to meet Robert Pennington McBruce at The Club for drinks, and I'd need every second of it to cool off.

On Sundays when I was a little girl, my parents and I would drive to the Sugar Shack and get ice cream cones. It was a Delaney tradition that I'd deliberately avoided since my return to Zinnia. I didn't need the ice cream calories, but the memory was comforting, and I needed chocolate. I headed toward Main Street and mocha chocolate fudge—a bolus of caffeine-laced chocolate.

On the way, I passed Millie's. Two large Harleys were parked in the asphalt lot. The hog owners appeared to be the only customers, and I had a tingle of concern. Millie could handle herself, but if Spider and Ray-Ban were back on the scene, it could only mean trouble for Scott.

I canceled my plans for ice cream and pulled into the café. Sure enough, I saw the two men sitting at the counter. Millie stood behind it with her hands on her hips and aggravation on her face.

The bell over the door jangled as I walked in and both men turned my way, their faces lighting with grins. "Well, if it isn't National Velvet," Spider said, his grin widening. "Although I think the girl in the movie rode around on her horse. Seems to me you've been riding something else. By the way, nice hairdo. Is it real?"

I fought the flush that wanted to creep into my face. I don't know how successful I was, but I did see Millie flash me a curious look, and it wasn't about my hair. I decided to take the high ground and ignore the innuendo.

"Velvet Brown is the character in the movie *National Velvet.*

The word 'national' comes from a prize she won—it is not her first name. Seems to me you don't have any of your facts straight." It was weak, but it was the best I could do. The two bikers had caught me flat-footed. How did they know I'd ridden Reveler over to see Scott?

"Right," Spider said sarcastically. "How's my man Scott?" Ray-Ban continued to grin, his gaze wandering up and down me in more than a suggestive manner.

"I thought you boys had left town," I said, ignoring his question. "Millie, I'd like a diet Dr Pepper, please. Large. Lots of ice." I didn't meet her gaze.

"We realized Scott needed us, so we came back."

"Where are you staying?" I addressed the question to Spider, since he seemed to do all the talking for both of them.

"Oh, around." They looked at each other and laughed. "Scott didn't like our housekeeping. He can be a real pussy about stuff like that."

"Yeah, I can't imagine a man who would insist on hygiene and cleanliness." I laid the sarcasm on heavy, deciding to take a page from the Daddy's Girl handbook and ignore their vulgarity.

"Baby, if we got cleaned up, would you come over to visit us?" Ray-Ban had finally found his vocal cords.

"I wouldn't visit you for any reason."

Millie put the drink on the counter in front of me. "I'm closing up." She pointed to the clock on the wall. "It's already after five. Finish up, pay up, and move on."

I put my money on the counter, hoping they'd follow suit. What I really wanted to ask them was how they knew I'd been over at Scott's. Millie, I could tell, wanted to ask me a few questions about that same issue.

"Tell us about that rich man who made Scott's bond?" Spider said, and there was a hungry light in his eyes.

"Nothing to tell." I shrugged. "He loves the blues. He's a big fan of Scott's. Now you tell me where you were the night Ivory Keys was murdered."

Spider laughed and Ray-Ban joined in. "She wants to know where we were," Spider said, winking at Ray-Ban. "She's interested in us, even if she don't want to admit it."

"I suspect the sheriff might be even more interested," I said.

"Too bad. We were in Greenwood. Big Daddy's. You know the place?"

I did. It was a redneck honky-tonk just off the two-lane that had the reputation of a knife fight every fifteen minutes. Perfect for the two of them. If they were really there.

"Now, you tell us why that rich man made Scott's bail. He wouldn't be interested in buying that old club, would he?" Spider pulled two dirty fives from his jeans pocket and plopped them on the counter. "You think he might need some muscle? You know, to keep things orderly. Keep those hot women from trying to crawl up on the stage after Scott." He winked at me. "You wouldn't like that, would you, baby?"

"Yeah, we could take them out back and settle them down some," Ray-Ban threw in, licking his lips.

"You can talk to Mr. Ladnier. I don't know what his needs might be in the way of muscle."

Millie put their change on the counter. "It's been fun, guys, but I have to go."

They rose from their stools. Ray-Ban picked up his iced tea and drained it, slamming the glass down on the counter so hard I thought it would break.

"We'll catch you later, Sarah Booth," Spider said. "We have a deal with Scott. When he gets tired of a woman, he passes her on to us."

My ready retort was blocked by a lump of disgust the size of Kansas in my throat. "Keep dreaming," I managed.

They punched each other on the arm and walked out laughing. Millie waited until the bell quit jangling before she hurried around the counter and locked the front door. "What was that all about?" she asked, headed back toward me.

"I was over at Scott's house this morning." I fiddled with my straw in the glass. I didn't want to lie to Millie, but I also didn't want to tell her the truth. "I rode Reveler around the county and happened up on Scott. He was outside chopping wood."

"Sarah Booth, you're not involved with that man, are you?"

I met her gaze and saw more concern than curiosity. "Now, that's hard to tell."

She shook her head. "He's one of the sexiest men I've ever seen, but I don't think he's a serious candidate for any kind of relationship."

"I think you're right about that." How could something that seemed so good six hours before turn into such an awful mistake?

Millie took pity on me and decided not to press the issue. "How did he get out of jail?"

I told her about Bridge, and about Nandy's husband. She was suitably impressed and sworn to secrecy. When I had her solemn oath, I stood up. "I've got to go. I'm meeting McBruce for drinks at The Club." I had a sudden, horrible thought. What if Nandy showed up, too?

"Good luck," Millie said. "And keep me informed." She brushed my hair back from my face and a frown touched her lips. "Where's your other earring, Sarah Booth? Those were your mother's, weren't they?"

My hands flew to my ears and I felt panic. I never lost jewelry. I seldom wore any, except earrings. No matter how hard I squeezed my lobes, my left one was bare.

"I combed my hair at Bridge's," I said. "It might be there. Or it could be in the car."

Millie got a broom and swept around the counter to be sure the earring hadn't fallen there.

"It's probably at Bridge's," Millie said, her smile relieved. "It's just like in the *National Enquirer*, when Barbra Streisand was led to James Brolin by a kind spirit. I read all about it. One of your spirit guides has fixed it so you can see Mr. Ladnier again. And just let me say that he's a far more suitable match than Scott."

Boy, was she ever right.

THE BAR AT The Club was dark, glittering with leaded crystal hanging from an overhead rack. I noted that the bowl of the martini glasses seemed to shoot more sparks than the others.

Bernard—he had a last name but no one ever used it—ran the bar seven evenings a week, and as far as I knew, had never missed a day. He was a fixture from the forties, like the bank and the music and the dancing.

"Miss Sarah Booth," he said when I sat down, elbows on the polished mahogany. "I haven't seen you in a long time."

"Bernard." I leaned across the bar and gave him a quick hug. "How are you?"

"Just fine," he said. "No point bein' any other way."

There was some truth in that. "How's Mollie?" His wife had been my baby-sitter on the rare occasions when my parents were gone and Aunt LouLane was unavailable. Mollie made cinnamon toast and hot chocolate for me whenever I asked. One day I asked five times.

"She's gettin' the arthritis in her hands. It's hard because she loves her sewin'. You know Trina, our grandbaby, is in the Junior Miss pageant and Mollie's been workin' on the prettiest dress for her. She's determined for Trina to have an original, even if it hurts her."

I was sorry to hear that. Mollie could take scraps of material and create masterpieces. Once, when she'd had some imported lace from Ireland, she'd designed a wedding dress for Jo Dee Bethea, a belle who'd fallen out of a cushy lifestyle and onto hard-luck row. Jo Dee was a sweet girl, and when she agreed to marry a local farmer from Blue Eve, she asked Mollie to make her gown. The dress was so exquisite that it even fooled Cece. Our local maven of society had pronounced the dress a Lucy Lu original and caused a scandal as to how Jo Dee had managed to pay for it. Mollie had come forth only when it looked as if Jo Dee were going to jail for theft.

The memory of Mollie's talent and generosity had me smiling. "I'd like to stop by and visit her."

Bernard's smile was brighter than the chandelier. "She'd like that, Miss Sarah Booth. She sure misses your mama. They were close."

"I miss Mama, too," I said. No matter how many years passed, the loss was always there.

"Your mama, Mollie, Ida Mae Keys, and Dub Renfroe used to go to Little Talika Creek fishin' for bream down in the hard part of the summer like it is now. They said they let Dub go to bait the hooks and pull the bream off once they were caught." Bernard laughed. "Mollie would bring those fish home and fry them up, and the others would show up with cole slaw and the likes. Those were some good times. Nothin' like a fish fry on a hot August evenin'. I can almost taste those tender little fish right now."

Me, too. My mouth was watering. For the fish and for the safe, loving memory he'd given me. In my mind I saw the three women and Dub, an older man who used to always give me nickels, walking out the backyard of Dahlia House toward the deep fishing hole on the creek that ran through the back of the property.

The women were wearing straw hats—Mollie's bright with a long, kerchief tail—and carrying cane poles. Dub carried the can of worms and the stringer for the fish as they were caught. I'd forgotten all about it until Bernard reminded me.

"What can I get you, Miss Sarah Booth?" Bernard asked, picking up a cloth and polishing a glass. Someone had come into the room. I knew it by the change in Bernard's attitude. I glanced behind me and saw a big, sandy redhead. His shoulders were wide and his body lean and muscled. I slid from my barstool.

"Mr. McBruce?" I held out my hand.

"Miss Delaney," he said, glancing around the bar. When he saw it was empty, he relaxed. "I've been wondering all afternoon why you wanted to talk to me." He glanced at Bernard. "I'd like Dewars on the rocks." He lifted his eyebrows at me. It was an interesting way to ask what I wanted to drink.

"Vodka martini." The sparkling glasses had lured me to abandon my regular Jack and water. Without waiting for me or further acknowledging Bernard, McBruce walked to a table in the corner and sat down. I had no option but to follow. I was beginning to get a hint of why Nandy had suddenly turned into a blues-guitarist groupie. In just glancing over an audience, Scott gave each fan personal attention; McBruce gave none.

"What is it you need to talk to me about?" McBruce said as soon as he was seated, his back to the wall.

"You attempted to pay Scott Hampton's bond. Why?"

His gaze was level and long. "You know my wife." It was a statement made in that strange rhythmic brogue. "You've seen her, up there at the courthouse. I thought if Hampton were free, Nandy could take her act to a more private location."

He had every right to be embarrassed. Nandy didn't care that her actions made her husband a fool and a public cuckold. She looked like a wealthy punk, and she acted like she was thirteen with a massive overload of hormones. Still, he'd offered to put up a tremendous amount of cash to benefit the man his wife was pursuing. "Why didn't you just get Nandy to stay away from the courthouse?"

The look he gave me was pure contempt. "I thought you knew her. She's Stuart Ann Shanahan, distant heir to the throne of Scotland, France, and England. Didn't you know? All other humans live to do her bidding."

That was a neat summary of Nandy. "Do you believe Scott Hampton is innocent?"

"Madame, I don't care. The man is a public bane to me. I'd hoped he might get free and decide to leave these parts."

"You'd put up bond money for a possible murderer?"

His smile was chilling. "Why should that surprise you? It's crossed my mind that I'm married to one."

McBruce wasn't a kind man. He enjoyed cutting people off at the knees. And either he was brutally honest or he hated Nandy enough to deliberately point the finger of accusation at her. I wondered if he hated her enough to set her up. "Do you think Nandy killed Ivory Keys?" I asked.

He swirled the ice in his glass and looked at me. "Murder is often an act of expediency. Nandy, in pursuit of a goal, lets nothing stand in her way."

"How would Ivory Keys stand in her way?"

"My understanding is that Keys and Hampton were friends." His grin was cruel. "Nandy doesn't like her obsessions to have friends. It gets in the way of their total focus on her."

He was describing a ruthless, self-centered, insecure person— Stuart Ann Shanahan to a T. But was she that ruthless? I had a visual of her trying to injure my horse to get back at me. Yes, she was.

"Why are you still married to Nandy?" I asked.

"That's none of your business," he said with that strong burr in his voice, "but I'll tell you anyway. Inheritance. Mr. Shanahan understands the old ways, where the inheritance passes to the wife's husband for proper management. Nandy isn't the queen of Scotland, but she's going to be an heiress in her own right."

"Is it worth it?" That question just slipped out.

"I thought so."

His answer implied a change of heart, yet he was still in Zinnia and Nandy was still out of control. "Have you talked with the sheriff about your . . . suspicions?"

He laughed out loud. "I have no intention of talking to the law."

"Did you see Nandy the night Ivory was killed?"

He motioned Bernard for a refill and didn't answer until he had it. "I didn't see my wife that night. I heard her come home about four in the morning, which wasn't unusual. She hung about that club like a bitch in heat."

"So you were home—"

"All night." He read my mind. "Alone. Without an alibi. I finished a book by Robert Davies, but I doubt that will stand in my defense in this godforsaken, illiterate state. But while I don't have an alibi, I also don't have a motive. Now, if it were my wife lying dead on the floor, that would be another matter." He polished off his drink.

"Did you ever meet Ivory Keys?" I asked.

"Never. I have no interest in aging musicians with a mission and a soapbox. I find them ludicrous and boring."

I found McBruce vindictive and calculating. "What about the murder? If it wasn't Nandy, do you have any ideas who might have killed Ivory?"

McBruce looked at me as if I were insane. "That's nothing to me. The man is dead. Whoever killed Ivory Keys doesn't matter to me, not even if it *was* Nandy. I merely want my wife to stop behaving like a public tramp. A tramp she is, but let her keep it off the courthouse lawn!" He stood up and walked out of the room.

It took me a moment to realize he'd stiffed me for the drinks.

21

THE NIGHT HAD PASSED WITHOUT INCIDENT. MY CALL TO Bridge regarding my lost earring had gone unreturned. If he'd gone out to Playin' the Bones to scope out the club, he must have stayed late negotiating with either Ida Mae or Emanuel. If the club was to be sold, I certainly hoped Bridge would get it and keep it open.

Though I'd halfway expected a late call from him when he got in, I refused to let my mind wander to the possibility that he had another date. Instead of thinking about that, I'd gone to bed with an author. Elizabeth George, to be exact. I'd left Zinnia behind for the world of DCI Lynley and New Scotland Yard. If I had troubles, Lynley was in dutch worse than me. He wanted to marry Lady Helen, but he'd had an affair with Deborah, who was now married to his best friend, Saint Simon, whom Lynley had crippled in a drunken automobile accident. Of course, Lady Helen and Deborah were best friends. The only thing that made it more palatable than my life was that Lynley and Lady Helen were titled and most of the screwing took place in family estates and historical sites, which somehow lent a little respectability to it.

When at last I'd fallen into a troubled sleep, it was Tinkie who saved me. I was dreaming of ghostly figures darting among the sycamore trees of my driveway when she called with urgent news.

"Margene tracked me down to tell me there's a meeting tonight at Rideout Funeral Home in The Grove. Margene says Emanuel's going to challenge the men to go out to Scott's house and teach him a lesson."

"Shit!" I threw back the covers and leaped from the bed.

"It gets worse," Tinkie said. "Trina Jacks was abducted last night by men in black masks. She was taken down by the Tallahatchie and given a mock trial. She was found guilty of consorting with white folks and told if she was seen with a white boy again, she'd be punished."

"Who is Trina seeing?" I asked.

"She dates Marshall Harrison's boy, Zeke. He's the lifeguard at The Club pool and a decent kid. I heard this was tearing Marshall up, which is probably why he was such a fool at The Club the other night."

I almost couldn't believe what I was hearing. I'd just been talking to Bernard about Trina and her prospects for the Junior Miss competition. "Is Trina okay?"

"Gordon Walters got a tip from someone and he found her wandering down the highway, hysterical with fear. She couldn't identify anyone, but Margene said she hadn't been hurt, just frightened."

Sometimes frightened was worse than hurt. "Between Emanuel and those two bikers, this town is going to explode." At least Margene hadn't quit working for Tinkie.

"I thought maybe we should go talk to Tammy."

Tinkie's suggestion was brilliant. "I'll meet you there."

"I'm going to run by Bernard and Mollie's house and make sure they're okay. I've got us an appointment with Tammy at nine."

I dressed in a rush, fed Reveler and Sweetie, and drove to The Grove. As soon as I pulled into Madame Tomeeka's driveway, I saw my partner. Tinkie was on the front porch in the most divine pale yellow skimmer. It simply reeked designer. As soon as Tinkie saw me, she darted down the steps and ran across the lawn. My gaze was fixed on her tiny little feet in five-inch stilettos. She seemed to glide over the carpet of acorns that littered the ground—until the last step. She hit an acorn that rolled and she slammed into me.

"Sarah Booth!" she said, flinging her arms around me. "I'm glad to be home. I didn't want to go at all, but Oscar needed me."

And I was glad to see her, though it had been only a few hours. "Are Bernard and Mollie okay?" I asked.

"They're fine, and Trina, too. She was drinking coffee and she said she was going to talk to Coleman again today to try and identify some of her kidnappers."

"Good."

"I sure am glad to be home," Tinkie said. "It seemed like I was gone forever. I just knew if I left town you'd get into some kind of trouble." She stepped in front of me so that I had to stop and look at her. I fell into the trap for a split second before my gaze darted away.

Her mouth opened to a little O, which she quickly covered with her hand. "You did get into trouble, didn't you?"

"Don't be silly." But my denial had no heart. Tinkie knew me too well.

"You didn't sleep with Bridge, did you?" she asked, catching up with me as I walked toward Tammy Odom's house.

"No." I said that with conviction.

She caught my arm, tugging me to face her again. "You slept with Scott."

It wasn't a question, so I didn't bother to deny it.

"Sarah Booth!" She gave a little squeal. "When you fall off the wagon, you land right in the ditch. No halfway measures for you. You're the only woman I know who can go months on end without even kissing a man, and then you do the mattress tango with a murderer-slash-musician."

"Accused murderer," I insisted. Her words were little needles of guilt, piercing and stinging. "Stop it, Tinkie. You're making way too much of this."

"Like this isn't a big deal. Like you just sleep with every client." She paused and a frown pulled her eyebrows together. "You didn't sleep with Bud Lynch, did you?"

"No."

She sighed. "At least you aren't a complete client slut."

"Bud wasn't my client. Lee was."

"Right," Tinkie said, undeterred. "But Bud was part of the case."

"Okay, okay. So I didn't sleep with him anyway." I knocked on Tammy's door. We were right on time, and I needed a cup of coffee, though I'd drunk a pot the night before while I worked on the computer researching the McBruce family. I hadn't found anything worth reporting.

Tammy opened the door at Tinkie's rat-a-tat-tat knock. "I've got some cheese grits on and biscuits in the oven," Tammy said. "Either of you interested?"

Tinkie was petite and precariously balanced on her heels, but that didn't stop her from taking the lead in the rush to the kitchen. By the time Tammy and I got there, Tinkie already had the lid off the grits and her nose sniffing the pot.

"Mmmmmm," she sighed. "Large bowl, please."

There was also fresh ham sliced on the counter for the biscuits. Tammy had prepared for our visit.

"What can I do for you?" Tammy asked, after we each had a bowl, saucer, and mug of coffee in front of us.

"You tell her, Sarah Booth. I just want to eat," Tinkie said, digging into her grits with a spoon.

"Ray-Ban and Spider are back in town." It was the best place to begin. "I'm afraid they're going to stir up trouble tonight at the meeting."

"If they're breathing, they're going to make trouble for someone." Tammy didn't bother to hide her contempt.

"Scott got out of prison Sunday morning. He's home now. He'll be a sitting duck for anyone with a grudge." I took a breath. "Tammy, I'm afraid Emanuel is going to rouse the black community and they're going to try to lynch Scott. They already put a noose in the magnolia tree."

"*Someone* put that noose in the tree," Tammy said softly, pointing out that Coleman had never determined who the culprit was. Tammy put her spoon back in her bowl of still-steaming grits. "Everyone in town knows Scott's out of jail and living in that cottage on Bilbo Lane. He could have stayed in jail, Sarah Booth. He didn't have to get out and put his ass on the line. If he's so dead set on being free, maybe he should go back to Detroit where he belongs."

I sat very still until she finally looked at me. "He can't leave town, Tammy. You know that. And just consider that he may be innocent," I said softly.

"She slept with him." Tinkie had perfect enunciation even though she had a four-ounce slab of ham and half a biscuit in her mouth.

"You what?" Where Tinkie had been understanding and maybe slightly envious, Tammy was incredulous. Then she was angry. "You are a fool, Sarah Booth."

"I didn't plan it," I said.

"You're getting old enough to plan that kind of thing." Tammy's mouth was a thin line. She glanced from me to Tinkie. "That man is in bad trouble here. There are folks who want to hurt him. Hurt him bad. And if you're not careful, Sarah Booth, you'll be right in the middle of it."

My own temper sparked. "If all these people are so certain he's guilty, why don't they just wait for the trial?"

"There's not a long history of justice for the black man in this judicial system." Tammy had calmed down so that her words were not accusatory, just fact.

"Things aren't like that anymore." Things had not always been fair in Sunflower County. They still weren't *always* fair, but it was primarily money that mattered now, not color. I took a breath. "My father was never like that."

"Judge Delaney was not," Tammy said. "But he could only preside at a trial. The jury made the decisions, Sarah Booth. If you doubt my interpretation of history, go check the records."

I didn't have to. She was correct. There had been injustice, but it cut both ways. Black and white had suffered. In cooler moments, Tammy knew that as well as I did. At the moment, though, the past wasn't really my problem; the future was. "Tammy, have you heard anything?"

She got up from the table and refilled our coffee cups. "Nothing specific. Lots of ugly talk. Lots of threats. But thank goodness, most of those are just big talk."

"Will you promise to call me if you hear anything that alarms you?" Even if Tammy believed Scott was guilty, she'd still do the right thing.

"I promise."

I could see the relief on Tinkie's face. She took the last bite of her biscuit and sat back in her chair. "What we came to ask, Tammy, was if you'd speak up for Scott at the meeting tonight."

"I'm not sure I can do that," she said, gazing from one of us to the other. "I don't believe Scott Hampton is a good man."

I had an idea. "If I arranged for you to talk to Scott, would you do it?"

"Me?" Tammy was surprised. "Why me?"

"Then you could honestly give your personal opinion of Scott." I knew I was taking a risk. Scott could be a total jerk. But I was counting on the fact that he wanted to live, and maybe even pick up an innocent verdict on the way.

"I don't have a thing to say—"

Tinkie set her cup on the table, hard. "You want fairness. You said so yourself. How fair is it not to even give him a chance?"

Tinkie was a master. I couldn't have done it better.

"Okay, I'll talk with him. But he can't come here." She looked around. "I'll meet him. Out at Dahlia House."

"Good," I said. "How about lunch?"

She nodded. "But you keep it quiet, Sarah Booth. Wasn't bad

enough we had to worry about the Ku Klux Klan. Now there's the Dominoes."

"Tell me about them." I'd researched the name on the Internet, but had no success finding anything except a few bland mentions—an exclusive club for black businessmen who wanted to play an active role in promoting black interests, blah, blah, blah. I'd begun to wonder if the organization was merely a local group of wannabe blacks with a yen for exclusivity and secrecy.

"The group is very elite. There's a scholastic requirement. MBA from a major university. There's religious elements—no Catholics and no Jews. And there's gender. Absolutely no women allowed."

"Great. Another group of bigots," I pointed out.

"And these bigots are fueled with a dream," Tammy said. "They want to separate the races so there's no contact at all. And they're willing to go to extremes to accomplish this."

"What kind of extremes?" I asked the question with great trepidation.

"Bullying, intimidation, economic punishment." Tammy paused. "And more, I've heard."

"Do they ride around in sheets?" I asked, making my point.

She didn't smile. "Not sheets and hoods, but about the same. They wear masks. The traditional black domino. That's where the name comes from."

I didn't believe this. After the bane of the KKK, how could a group that had once been victims of such tactics even consider using them?

"They don't target whites," Tammy continued. "At least not normally, but I get the impression they might make an exception for you, Sarah Booth. As a rule, they focus on other blacks. You know, keeping them in line and out of the Uncle Tom and Oreo molds. One particular target of their intimidation is young black girls. They don't want them fraternizing or dating white boys. The price can be steep if they're caught."

"Trina Jacks!" Tinkie and I said in unison.

"What?" Tammy asked.

Tinkie relayed what had happened to Trina, and I could see the anger building in Tammy. "That bastard Emanuel. He's behind this. He points the finger at those two bikers, and he's worse than they are."

I didn't want to say it, but Emanuel was looking more and more like the primary suspect for his father's murder.

Tammy poured us more coffee. "Trina got off lucky. I've heard that some girls have been abducted and held for days. During that time, they're verbally assaulted and harassed until they agree to date only their own race."

I knew Tammy wasn't making this up. By her tone, I also knew she found it as reprehensible as I did. "This organization is active in Sunflower County?" I'd never heard of it, and judging from the look of shock on Tinkie's face, neither had she.

"That's why Emanuel came home, as best I can tell. To organize a cell of the Dominoes. That's why he and Ivory fought so much. Ivory was bitterly opposed to the Dominoes and all they stand for."

"As any sane person would be," I pointed out. My heart was heavy for Ivory and Ida Mae. It would be a difficult thing to see your own flesh and blood become something you despised. "Does Coleman know about this?"

"I'm sure he does, but until someone files a complaint or until the group is caught in the act of doing something illegal, Coleman can't do a thing about them. He isn't the thought police."

"What does Emanuel hope to gain?" I asked.

"He has a dream, Sarah Booth. You and I both happen to buy into Ivory's dream of mutual respect and caring, regardless of race or religion. Just because we find Emanuel's dream to be repugnant doesn't mean others will. He's come home to start the foundation of a social battle, and let me put it to you plain. Scott Hampton, as the accused murderer of his father, is the perfect poster boy for racial justice."

Tammy's delicious grits had turned into a gelatinous lump in the pit of my stomach. I slowly rose from the table. "I don't want to put you at odds with Emanuel." The only decent thing to do was withdraw my request for Tammy's help. She had a daughter and a grandchild who counted on her emotionally as well as financially.

"I'm not telling you this so I can back down. I have my own dream, Sarah Booth. I dream of a community where there's a group of women, black and white, and they're friends who can count on one another. But you see, I'm one of the lucky ones, because my dream has already come true." She reached across the table and took Tinkie's hand and mine. "I'll meet Scott, and I'll speak out on his behalf, *if* I believe he's innocent."

In the face of such courage and friendship, the only thing I could say was, "Thank you."

Tammy shook her head sadly. "Connie Peters was back here Saturday asking if I thought she should go and talk to you. How deep are you going to sink yourself, Sarah Booth?"

22

I DROVE HOME, MADE MORE COFFEE, AND FINALLY PHONED SCOTT to set up the luncheon. To my sweet relief, he didn't answer the phone. I left a message, emphasizing the importance of his appearance at Dahlia House.

It seemed all of my time was being consumed with keeping one faction or another from skinning Scott alive. I'd made little or no progress on the actual case. Of course, if my client were hanging from an oak tree, I wouldn't have a case.

I made another quick call to Bridge. I'd checked out the car and there was no sign of my earring. It had to be at his house. When I got the answering machine again, I hung up without leaving a message. No man liked to be dogged by a woman, even if he did have her heirloom jewelry.

There was another matter I needed to attend to. Even as my hand dialed the number and I heard the first ring, I knew I was a coward.

"Sunflower County Sheriff's Office."

Bo-Peep's voice was low and sexy.

"Coleman, please," I said, though I wanted to ask her if she had her own 900 number for ba-a-a-a-ad sex.

"May I ask who's calling?"

"Sarah Booth Delaney," was what I said; though I wanted to say, "Your worst nightmare, bitch."

"The sheriff looks mighty busy to me. I don't think I should disturb him."

I swallowed in surprise. She had taken control of the phones. I kept my voice level but firm. "Please tell him I'm on the line."

"No, I don't think I can do that. He's terribly busy."

Whatever else I did, I had to keep my cool. "If Coleman asked you to screen his calls for him, that's fine with me." I hung up. Blood was pounding in my ears, I was so angry. My first desire was to drive to the courthouse and take the telephone and shove it someplace in Bo-Peep's anatomy where it ought to be mighty uncomfortable. Lucky for her, I was a lady—I merely imagined vile things, I didn't act on them.

I poured myself a cup of coffee and walked to the kitchen window. The view never failed to calm and settle me. In the midst of the heat—mine and August's—the Delaney family cemetery looked cool. The trumpet vine that Harold had bought and planted for me while I was recuperating from a gunshot wound back in the spring had taken firm root. The vine was climbing up the wrought-iron arch, and the magnificent orange blossoms, shaped like a trumpet, were hanging in abundance. Mother would have liked the vine.

"Your mother might enjoy the flowers, but she wouldn't be so happy with your choice of beau."

I closed my eyes on a smile. I'd honestly missed Jitty, even for just one evening. "Where've you been?" I turned around to confront a mélange of styles. Jitty's head was wrapped in a rich burgundy scarf that matched the paisley palazzo pants. She wore a sleeveless black velvet vest with gold brocade and frogs. And the shoes. Platform didn't begin to describe them.

"I had a gathering," she said mysteriously.

"Looks more like you walked off a fashion runway about forty years ago."

"True fashion is never dated," Jitty said sagely. "Do you have any incense? Sandalwood would be nice."

"The short answer to that is no. Would vanilla candles work?" So far I'd resisted the rush to aromatherapy, but the candles had been a gift, and I did enjoy them.

"Vanilla isn't quite what I had in mind." Jitty lifted her arm and golden bangles slid almost to her elbow in a jingle.

"Scott is coming to lunch and I want you to behave."

"You know I can't devil anyone but you. For all the good it does me to try and help you out, I can't even make *you* mind."

"Tammy's coming, too." It had occurred to me only after I'd agreed to have lunch at the house that Tammy, with her psychic gifts, might be sensitive to Jitty.

"You've enlisted Tammy to help protect Scott?" Jitty's eyes narrowed. "Does she know you're walkin' his lizard?"

"Where did you get that vulgar turn of phrase?"

"Call it what you like, you're bumpin' uglies with the man."

I rolled my eyes. Since Jitty wasn't wearing her schoolmarm shirtwaist, she'd taken the governors off her tongue, too. "Would it be possible to say we made love? Is that so hard to believe?"

Jitty sat down on the edge of the kitchen table where she could really study me. "You don't believe that any more than I do. You don't love that man. You wanted him. You desired him, and you got him. Maybe you felt a rush, but it isn't anywhere close to love."

My first inclination was to deny it, but deep in my heart I knew Jitty was right, and it was a distinction I needed to own. "I don't love him, exactly." My feelings for Scott were confused.

Jitty nodded. "So why did you drop your drawers for him?"

I found myself lightly chewing on my bottom lip as I gave her question some thought. "I didn't set out to sleep with him." Which was the complete truth . . . or was it? How long had I been harboring desire for Scott? My first encounter with him in jail, when he'd moved toward me, had been fraught with sexuality. I'd felt desire then, and it was a lot more blatant than a ladylike tingle. Perhaps Aunt Cilla, my libidinous relative who was sent to Atlanta to hide her sexual activities in the hubbub of the big city, had a lot more in common with me than I'd ever thought.

"He's the most sensual man I've ever met," I said, feeling my way into the explanation. I was determined to be honest. "I crave his touch." Addiction had been the correct diagnosis of my condition. Even speaking of Scott made me want his touch, his kisses. But it wasn't that simple. "There's something else about Scott. He has the ability to own his mistakes and to change. Not many people can really change. He's proven that he can."

"Girl, you're in a place of great danger." All of Jitty's posturing was gone. She walked over to me and reached out to gather my hands in hers. I felt only a cool breeze at her intended touch. "You've given up a dream for a hallucination. Scott Hampton isn't real. He can't be real for you. He isn't that kind of man."

Staring out the kitchen window at the graves of my kin, I wondered what kind of man it would take to "be real" for me. Perhaps Scott's true appeal was that he wasn't the kind of man to become permanent. He was transitory. He was a mover. His very mobility made me want him more. He was yin to my yang.

"Opposites attract," I pointed out to Jitty, but I did it gently. She wasn't needling me for the fun of it. She was worried. After all, her future hung on my conduct.

"Beneath all the sexual fizz, there has to be substance. You want him because he's here for the moment. You want him because you shouldn't. Look at the things he appeals to in you, Sarah Booth—all the flash and dazzle of a shooting star. But after that moment of light, it's gone."

I felt a wave of sadness slipping over my ankles, up my knees, over my thighs, and headed for my heart. "Maybe I don't trust anything more permanent than a starburst."

"Baby girl, that's not a good thing."

I wasn't feeling up to judgment calls regarding my choices. My last fling had been a man home for a split second from his life in

Europe. Now, months later, I had slept with Scott, who would never stay in Zinnia. He had "big time" written all over him. "Maybe I don't want permanence right now," I said. "I can always change my mind." That made me feel a little better.

Jitty shook her head. "Changing your mind isn't like changing your habits. I see a pattern developing here."

"Maybe you should just be glad my libido reared its ugly head. Only a few months ago, you suspected that the Delaney womb had died."

A hint of humor touched the corners of Jitty's eyes. "That's a point, but I don't have to tell you that Bridge Ladnier would be a far better choice for your libido to play peekaboo with." She jangled her bracelets, a soft tinkling that sounded like the wind chimes on the corner of the house. "I just want you to be happy. That's all your mama would want."

"I'm working on it."

"What's for lunch?" Jitty asked, bringing me back to the immediate problem. Food and the imminent arrival of Scott.

"I'd better check the fridge and see what can be salvaged."

"I'm off to a meeting." Jitty glided toward the door.

"What kind of meeting?"

"A discussion of dream interference and noncorporeal powers. I'll let you know what we decide."

I knew she was gone when a breeze blew through the tiniest crack in the kitchen window, tickling my face.

As soon as I opened the refrigerator door, Sweetie Pie came out of her doggy coma and charged through the doggy door. She had the intense hearing of a bat, which she applied only to the sound of food. An electric can opener could draw her home from the next county.

"Here you go, Sweetie," I said, tossing a chunk of cheese her way.

There was romaine lettuce, red bell peppers, pickled okra, feta cheese, cherry tomatoes that I'd had to buy since my own plants had perished from lack of love, and one purple onion. It was the start of a salad. I went through the freezer and found some chicken to broil. Then my gaze fell on a pork loin.

This was my first meal for Scott. While Tammy and I might enjoy a cool grilled chicken salad, Scott was a man. Meat. The more the better.

And I had a recipe that my mother used every time she needed to put my father in a receptive mood. Roasted pork loin and Jezebel sauce.

Wicked.

I pulled the meat out of the freezer and started the big thaw. From the spiffy pull-out tater bin beneath the counter, I gathered sweet potatoes. It was summer, and the living was replete with fresh vegetables, so I decided on crowder peas, okra, squash casserole, and corn bread. There is no finer cooking than Southern. Scott Hampton would be slain by the goddess of bodacious eatin'.

By the time I got everything in the oven and almost done, I had just enough time to "put on my face," as Aunt LouLane used to say. Even girls with a perfect complexion had to coat their skin with foundation. In my aunt's time, foundation was the byword for appearance in all its forms.

I decided that a little foundation wouldn't hurt me, so, along with Angel Beige number 5, I chose a lacy spandex body suit to wear under my little red dress with white piping on the neck and sleeves. It was the perfect casual dress for a summer luncheon. White strappy sandals completed the look. Even Cece would be proud of me, I thought, as I did a twirl in the mirror just as the doorbell rang. My only problem was my hair. Because the humidity was now permanent in Zinnia, I'd chosen a French twist, which reminded me that I hadn't recovered my earring from Bridge's bathroom. If he didn't call me before the day was over, I was going to fetch it anyway.

Tammy arrived first, and I was left wondering if Scott would actually show. If Tammy noticed my anxiety, she was kind enough not to mention it.

We took a seat in the parlor, and Tammy sipped the iced tea I offered her. To my extreme relief, the doorbell rang again and

Scott Hampton stood on my steps, clutching an armful of coral gladioli. My heart sang.

"They're beautiful," I managed, getting him and the flowers into the house without damaging either.

"Surprised, aren't you?" he asked, unable to hide his grin. "You thought I was going to be a jerk."

I was so relieved I didn't even try to hide it. "The thought crossed my mind."

He leaned close enough to my ear so he could whisper. "I was raised with good manners. I just use them when I choose to. And I choose to with you." Then his lips caught the lobe of my ear and gave a tiny little nibble.

I thought my knees would buckle. His hand caught my elbow as he chuckled softly. I realized then that I'd lost any chance of pretending he didn't affect me. I'd given him the upper hand in the relationship.

We walked into the parlor, and Tammy took her time assessing the two of us together before she stood up as I made the introductions.

"The flowers are lovely," she said, going to the sideboard to get a crystal vase since I had obviously lost all powers of movement. She took them from me and deftly arranged them.

"I love flowers," Scott said. "I always wanted a garden." He shrugged, laughing at himself. "Ridiculous, right? A blues singer who putters around in the impatiens."

Tammy was looking at Scott, but she handed me the vase, her eyes hot with emotion. "Water." She leaned down to my ear. "I need to speak to him alone."

"Right," I said. "Scott, how about some tea?"

"Perfect." He waited until Tammy took her seat before he found one himself. He had been trained.

I stayed in the kitchen, eavesdropping on their conversation. At first Tammy was cool, asking sharp questions about Scott, his past, his relationship with Ivory. I almost dropped the platter when I caught her next question.

"What do you know about past lives, Scott?"

"I've heard the concept."

"But you don't believe?"

"I don't disbelieve. My focus has been pretty much on this life-time." There was humor in his voice. "But I have some curiosity. Sarah Booth mentioned that you have powers."

Tammy didn't deny it. "You have a strong presence. In this life and in others. I think the power of the past is part of your charisma now. You've been many things."

Tammy was tempting him, teasing him into her world. I wondered if he would follow.

"What do you see?" Scott asked, with the same interest as if he were asking for a doctor's diagnosis.

"Let me see your hands."

I peeked through the door, fascinated. Scott stood up and went to Tammy, his hands held out, palms up. She took one, holding it as her fingers stroked his palm.

"Calluses," she noted.

"I play the guitar. If I didn't have calluses, I wouldn't be a very good player."

"You don't play the guitar with your palms," she pointed out.

He bent lower, examining his hands, too. "They've always been that way. Or at least as long as I can remember. But you're right. My palms don't touch the strings."

"What would callus your hands?" she asked.

His face opened and I was reminded of a schoolboy with the correct answer. I was charmed anew.

"I've been chopping wood. It must be the axe."

"Or chopping cane."

He looked stumped. "Sugarcane? There isn't anything here except cotton."

"I see you, standing in the field in the heat, skin darkened even more by the sun. You're an angry man, Scott Hampton, though you go by another name. You look up toward the plantation house, and you think of violence. And around you the sugarcane shakes like a fierce wind, bowing as the other slaves slash it with machetes."

Scott's hands had begun to tighten on hers. "Where is this?" he asked.

She shook her head lightly. "Not here. Not this life. Another life." She held his hands. "Think about it, Scott. How many people have asked you how you could play the blues like—"

"Like a black man," he finished for her.

She nodded. "Can you even imagine it?"

I held my breath. Tammy didn't expect everyone to buy into her belief system, but I knew this was important. She might view a rejection of reincarnation as a rejection of a possible black incarnation.

"It makes sense," Scott said. "It might explain why I hate the taste of sugarcane. Once I was in Louisiana when they were burning the cane stubble in the fields after harvesting. I got violently sick. Ivory had to take me to an emergency room, but as soon as we got into the city, away from the smell, I was fine."

"Perhaps it was just the smell. It's a little overpowering."

Scott now held her hands. "No. It was something more than that. It went so deep, way down to a place that was twisted with anger."

I had a question, but I wasn't invited to the little private séance that was taking place on my grandmother's horsehair sofa. I'd heard that a person could shift genders as they progressed through their lives, but races? I'd never considered it. But that would mean that white folks might once have been slaves, and, of course, the reverse. And Jews might have once been Nazis. And . . . it was endless. And wonderful. If people would buy into this concept, it would be impossible for any one race or religion or creed to claim the role of victim. It would mean we had to give up the grievances of the past and live only in the present, with a nod of hope to the future. It was mind-boggling. And as I peeped through the doorway, I saw that Scott and Tammy had caught onto the power that had just been unleashed.

Tammy slowly released Scott's hands, and he touched the palms together, considering. "I'll have to think about all of this." He knelt down in front of her on one knee. "Whether you know it or not, you've given me the first hope of absolution."

"I've never had the power to absolve anyone," Tammy said.

"No, but you allowed me to consider forgiving myself."

The moment was so intensely personal, I shut the door and turned to check the table settings in the dining room again.

When I finally took Scott his tea, Tammy was actually smiling.

"Ivory was a great man," she said. "You know my granny got arrested with his band when she was a young woman."

This was a story I hadn't heard, and I'd known Tammy's grand-mother. "Were they trying to sing in an all-white club?" I asked.

Tammy laughed rich and full. "Heavens, no. Granny was dating that harmonica player they called Hotlips, and they were all in Memphis for a gig. Well, they drank all night and the next morn-ing they were arrested in a park, drunk as Cooter Brown." Tammy was still laughing. "My grandmother wasn't really a drinker, so it was a big adventure for her. No harm came of it, and she had a story to tell for the rest of her life. They were just young and ad-venturous."

"Ivory was a great man and a great musician," Scott agreed. "Did you know he played with Elvis?"

Tammy shook her head. "I never heard that."

Scott smiled at the skepticism in her tone. "He really did. Back at the first. He put the left-hand boogie in some of Elvis's first ap-pearances. A few of the sessions were recorded, but, to my knowl-edge, none of them were ever released to the public."

"That's too bad," Tammy said. "I would have liked to hear that."

"Ivory told me once that he and Elvis shared the same views on music and race. Both of them thought music was the key to bring-ing whites and blacks together."

I laughed. "All Elvis managed to do was alienate the old folks." I swiveled my hips.

"That's not completely true," Scott said. "Elvis managed to

bring black elements of music into the mainstream. He actually made that first step that's always the hardest, and I believe Ivory was part of that. Some folks said Elvis was part black, and they weren't talking about a past life."

"Mahalia Jackson played a role in Elvis's life, as did Ivory," Tammy pointed out.

Scott gave her an appreciative look. "You know your stuff," he said. "Lots of folks forget about Mahalia."

"Mahalia and the Lord," Tammy said.

"Lunch is served," I said. They'd found common ground, and now I wanted to move the meal along. Tammy would help Scott. She was that kind of person.

23

TAMMY DID NOT LINGER AFTER THE MEAL. SHE DECLINED COFFEE but agreed to speak up on Scott's behalf. When she turned at the door, Scott took her hand and squeezed it.

"I did my best to run Sarah Booth off," he told her. "I didn't want help from her or anyone else. It seems like everyone who ever cared about me ends up hurt, or else hurting me. I'd decided never to let anyone close enough to hurt me again. In the days in jail, I think I came to some conclusions about the kind of man I'd become. Ivory was part of that. Despite all my vows, I grew close to him. Then he was killed, and the community thinks I did it. Accepting help isn't easy for me, but I need it, and I thank you for taking my part."

Tammy let him hold her hand. "You're very different than I thought," she said. "Why did you write those first songs? Those racist, ugly songs?"

My breath caught right below the hollow of my throat, and I made a wheezing sound, but neither of them heard me.

"I was raised with a lot of opportunities for an education, but tolerance wasn't in the curriculum. I'm not blaming my family. They're elitist, but they aren't racists. At least not like I became." A frown touched his forehead. "When it became obvious that nothing I cared about was important to them, and nothing I accomplished would ever satisfy them, I lashed out. Like most children of privilege, I couldn't rebel against the hand that fed me, it had to be something outside my world. So I targeted race. It was an area unimportant to my family. I could posture without striking too close to home."

"You never believed what you wrote?" Tammy was puzzled. I knew exactly what she was thinking. Then why? Why stir up such dark emotions? Tammy watched him intently as he talked.

"This is the worst condemnation of myself that I can confess. It was convenient to believe those lyrics. I found a certain acceptance that I'd never known in my own family."

"That's very sad."

"And inexcusable. If I could retract them, I would. Once something like that gets out of the box, though, there's no getting it back." He shook his head. "It would be fantastic to hear how Ivory influenced Elvis, yet those recording sessions are lost. My early songs linger."

It was his sincerity that finally softened the tightness of Tammy's mouth. "You were young, Scott. You were in your teens."

"And so are millions of other young people who don't do what I did." He put his free hand on my shoulder. "There's no excuse for it. After I met Ivory, I suffered so much shame. The only way I could accept his kindness was to make certain he knew the truth about me. I sat with Ivory while he listened to all of those . . . songs. I made him hear them before I came to Sunflower County."

"And Ida Mae?" Tammy asked.

"I don't know for certain. Ivory may have played them for her, but I doubt it. Not because he wanted to protect me, but because he wouldn't want that stain to touch his wife."

Tammy finally withdrew her hand. "Who did kill Ivory?" she asked. "My gift hasn't given me any answers to this question. It's my heart that tells me you're innocent."

"I don't know who killed Ivory," Scott said. "I've thought and thought about it, and I just don't know."

There was a long pause as Tammy looked at the two of us standing side by side in the doorway of my home.

"Thanks for lunch, Sarah Booth," Tammy said before she turned and walked across the porch and down the steps. "I'll let you know how it goes."

Scott's arm shifted around my shoulders as we watched Tammy depart. For a split second I allowed myself the luxury of believing the moment—Scott and I together seeing our friend off after lunch. But it was only an illusion. Scott was not the host at Dahlia House. He was my guest.

"Thank you, Sarah Booth," he said. "I've heard a lot of rumors. Folks are angry and upset, and a lot of it is directed at me. I know that meeting tonight is important. I think Tammy can inject a note of reason into some of the hot emotion."

"Maybe you should go up to the courthouse and stay in the sheriff's office." I didn't want to exaggerate the danger, but I didn't want to minimize my concerns.

"No, I won't run. Once they smell fear on me, they'll never stop. If I'm going to stay in Sunflower County, I can't afford to let them think I'm afraid."

I motioned him back inside. "Coffee?"

He shook his head, stepping closer and putting his hands on my shoulders. "I'd like a kiss."

It was my pleasure to oblige. I stepped into his arms and lifted my face for the kiss. At the first touch of his lips, I felt the tingle. As his hands slid over my shoulder blades and down my back, the tingle grew into heat. I wanted him. And in the cool protection of Dahlia House, there was no reason not to have him.

Leaving a trail of clothes behind us, we started up the stairs to my bedroom. My dress slid to the polished oak floor outside my bedroom door, and I was glad I'd spent the ten dollars extra to get the lacy body suit rather than the plain beige spandex.

Scott held me back from him. A lazy smile crossed his face

while he looked at me. "Very sexy, Sarah Booth. I thought you Delta girls were demure."

"You know better than that. You've had Nandy after you. I wouldn't call her demure."

"Demented is more the word. By the way, she's been calling and hanging up. About a hundred times."

I felt a pang of guilt. Scott hadn't gone to the sheriff because I'd dissuaded him. "Maybe you *should* call Coleman."

He shook his head. "If it's only the phone, I can deal with that. And she hasn't shown up again."

I told him about my encounter with her husband.

"I still don't get that one," he said. "It's bad enough being obligated to your beau for my freedom. I'd hate to owe Nandy Shanahan's husband."

We were standing naked, hips pressed together, at the side of my bed, and suddenly the moment was derailed. I'd brought Nandy into the bedroom, and Scott had dragged Bridge in right behind her. I looked down at the floor, suddenly embarrassed.

"It's okay, Sarah Booth," Scott said, lifting my chin. "I know he's the caliber of man you'll eventually marry. Someone who's made something of himself in business. Someone without a prison record. Hell, I can't even vote."

Words often inflict pain on the listener, but I hurt for Scott. "There is no 'kind of man' for me, Scott. I see who I want to."

He bent and kissed my temple and then led me to the window. "Look out there," he said, pointing across the acres of green cotton. "You were born and bred to this. It's a world that's never going to be within my reach."

I was stunned. "Your family is wealthy, Scott. I'm barely hanging on to this place. Don't be silly."

"It's not a matter of money." He shrugged. "I'll make plenty. Maybe millions. It's not money; it's all of the other things. The way you think, the way you treat people, the way you fit into a place, and how you care about others and they care about you."

"That's who I am, not where I was born."

He put his arm around me. "The first day you walked into the jail, I knew you were something special. I wanted you right then. You were something worth having in my life. I knew how far out of my reach you really were. And I tried my hardest to run you off so I wouldn't have to constantly be reminded of reality."

Such pretty words that cut so deep. I didn't understand his inability to see that he could have whatever he wanted—be whatever he chose. I understood so much about Scott then. My limited psychology was only a degree from Ole Miss, but even I could see how he'd spent his entire life setting himself up to fail.

Daddy's Girl rule number three—never, never tell a man he needs therapy, no matter how true.

Instead, I turned back into his arms, locking his gaze with mine. "I'm not out of your reach right now, Scott. I'm here. Standing right beside you." My hand lightly touched his chest, and I let my Red Alarm fingernails scratch gently down his sternum, the ridges of his torso, his abdomen, and lower. Whatever insecurities he had socially, he had none sexually. His arm braced my lower back as he bent me backward with a hungry kiss.

There was no more talking. There was no need for it.

IT WAS DUSK when Scott kissed me at the front door and slipped out. The roar of his motorcycle was muffled by the full greenness of the sycamore trees that lined the drive. I'd slipped into some shorts and a T-shirt and walked outside to feed Reveler. I'd planned on riding him this evening, but Scott had intervened. Even as I walked, I felt a quiver in my thighs. I was undone by that man.

Sweetie emerged from her nap under a huge camellia and joined me as I went to the barn and scooped up a half-quart of feed for my boy. With the good grass in the pasture, he needed no grain, but I couldn't resist giving him a little.

As he greedily ate the sweet feed, I groomed his coat and talked to him. I needed to sort through my feelings for Scott before I had to face Jitty. Reveler and Sweetie Pie were my sounding boards as

I came to the conclusion that I was falling in love with Scott. He was such a puzzle—so tough on the outside and yet so tender and vulnerable. And so willing to let me see that soft side. Of course he was an artist, a man who painted pictures with his words and then set them on fire with his guitar and his body. He was not a man who would be easy to live with. He would never belong completely to me—there was always his public to lay claim to him.

I'd known a few stars in New York, men and women who were more alive onstage than anywhere else in the world, and I'd wondered how their mates handled knowing that no touch or whisper or intimacy could compare to the electric charge of applause. But perhaps I misjudged Scott. He'd certainly given me his total attention all afternoon, and I'd never felt more sated.

When Reveler was finished with his feed, he was also done with me. Nudging me with his head, he left an imprint of dirty lips on my T-shirt and galloped off into the pasture to eat the tender grass.

Unwilling to go back inside to Jitty, I walked to the cemetery to have a talk with my mama.

I was walking through the gate when Sweetie Pie stopped in front of me, her body rigid and a growl issuing from her throat that sounded like the precursor to a visit from Linda Blair in her younger days.

"Sweetie?" I knew enough to stop and listen. Sweetie might look flop-eared and slow, but she was nobody's fool.

She walked slowly into the cemetery and around the stones until she came to the twin angels that marked my parents' grave. I circled to the front of the marker and couldn't manage to stop the small cry that came from me. Someone had defaced my parents' stone. Someone had spray-painted a skull and crossbones in vivid red paint.

At the sound of a twig snapping, I whirled around. It was only Reveler. He'd followed me to the cemetery. I looked in all directions, but there was no sign of anyone nearby. Whoever had done this awful thing had sneaked in and out; a coward.

I knelt down by the stone and touched the paint. It was dry. In the thick grass of the cemetery, there were no footprints.

My impulse was to get a wire brush and cleaner and set to work on the stone, but I walked back to the house and immediately called the sheriff's office. When Bo-Peep answered, I was ready for her.

"Put Coleman on the line and do it now, or you'll be drawing unemployment tomorrow morning."

My tone must have been enough to let her know I wasn't willing to put up with her games. Coleman picked up in less than sixty seconds. When I told him what had happened, he said he was on his way. I sat down on the front porch and waited for him.

In the ten minutes it took for him to arrive, gravel spraying from his tires and siren wailing, I had a few moments to attempt to figure out what I felt. The main ingredient was anxiety, a good three cups, unsifted. There was a measure of guilt, a dollop of hope. Even a pinch of joy at the prospect. That was spiced with a bit of malice and a whisper of revenge. The ingredient yet to be added was the sense of safety that came as soon as he stepped out of the car. Of all the men in my life, I knew Coleman could protect me. I'd never before realized the potency of that particular emotion.

I stood up slowly, and Coleman caught me in a bear hug. "Are you okay, Sarah Booth?" I didn't answer. I melted into the haven of his arms.

He was hot, a body temperature created by the sun, the interior of a car, and his anger. I could feel his rage humming beneath his skin. "This has been a real day for trouble. Someone set fire to Goody's Grocery in The Grove. Luckily, the clerk got out and no one else was in the store, but it went up like a torch. It's totally destroyed."

"Who did it?"

Coleman shook his head, finally looking at me as his hands moved over my back, comforting and checking. "They snuck up to the back, doused the old wood with gasoline, and lit it. We found a gas container and we're checking it for prints."

"Ray-Ban and Spider," I said.

"They would be my first suspects, but I don't have any proof. Yet."

"Can you bring them in and keep them for questioning tonight?" I wanted them out of the way. They were the fuse that could blow Sunflower County sky-high.

"We'll see. Now show me what they did to your mama's gravestone. I've got Dewayne and Gordon on the way with a fingerprint kit and some other things."

We walked around the house to the cemetery without talking. Coleman's gaze shifted here, there, to the camellia bushes that clustered so thick, to the huge mass of wisteria that I'd allowed to get away from me and was climbing a pecan tree.

When he saw the tombstone, a curse escaped. "Who would do this?" he asked.

"Someone trying to make me believe it was Scott." The words came out without any forethought. "Stuart Ann Shanahan."

"Nandy?" Coleman was genuinely puzzled. "She's Scott's biggest supporter."

"Right." I wasn't ready to tell him that Nandy now hated her idol because of me. "Her husband told me yesterday that she was capable of murdering Ivory because he diverted Scott's attention from her."

"Why would she do this? You're helping . . ." His words faded and he put two and two together and came up with sex. "I see." He looked past me. "We need to get some samples. We can check the paint, see where it was sold, track it down for sure."

I couldn't look at him. "How long will this take? I want to clean it."

"Dewayne and Gordon will be here soon."

I heard them coming around the house then. They walked toward us, and I saw Gordon's gaze shift from Coleman to me, then back to Coleman, then abruptly to the ground. If he didn't know something was between us, he surely suspected. He was wise enough to want to avoid it.

Coleman gave a few suggestions to the deputies. When he finally looked at me, forcing me by his silence to look back, there was distance in his gaze.

"As soon as the reports come in, I'll give you a call." He nodded, that crisp professional kiss-off, and he started walking away.

I felt a pure clean rage begin to burn away all other emotions. How dare he? He was treating me like a stranger because I'd involved myself with Scott. Yet he was sharing bed and board with his wife, "trying to make it work." A direct quote.

"Coleman." I spoke sharply enough that everyone froze. "You can act like a jackass if you choose, but I won't take it off that high school dropout secretary of yours. Bo-Peep is incompetent."

I caught Gordon's look of sheer bewilderment. He was obviously untrained in the strategy of Daddy's Girl warfare—when you couldn't risk a shot at the general, take out a foot soldier. It was a low method of fighting, but I couldn't take Coleman head-on. Not in front of the deputies.

"Maybe if you got off your high horse and quit calling her Bo-Peep. Her name is Cricket."

"Locust would be more applicable. As in plague of."

"That's the kind of comment that makes people upset with you, Sarah Booth."

"What kind of name is Cricket?" I had suddenly become expert in diversionary tactics.

"She can't help her name. Not everyone is born into families so proud of their lineage they convert last names to given."

Coleman was not so adept, but he had more bludgeoning power. My sternum was crushed, my heart exposed. I glanced at Dewayne and Gordon, who'd given up any pretense of working. They were following the action of the argument like a Wimbledon match. Coleman had scored match point.

"When I call you, she won't put me through. She says you're too busy to talk to me. She says you're too busy making plans with your wife."

The last three words hung between us. I'd stepped over the line and I knew it. So did Coleman. So did the deputies. They bent over the black case they'd brought and got very busy.

Coleman took several steps toward me, then stopped. His blue gaze, no longer distant, searched my face. I don't know what he saw, but his features didn't soften. He turned abruptly and walked away. I followed at a distance, my pride bloodied and my sense of shame flying like a tattered flag.

24

After the deputies left, I sat out on the front porch in the darkness drinking Jack on the rocks. I was in no mood for triflin' water.

In the tinkle of my ice, I heard Jitty's gold bangles. She took a seat on the porch railing. "Fine night for a pity party," she commented.

"Go away." I wanted only to be alone, which might well be my natural state.

"Only drunks drink alone."

"Fine, so I'm a drunk." I had reaped the rewards of argument earlier in the evening. I wanted no more.

"My, oh, my. Black is black."

"Jitty, please."

She shifted from the balustrade to a chair beside mine. "Why are you so upset?"

There was compassion in her question, not censure. "I slept with Scott, and I argued with Coleman about his wife in front of his deputies. I'm just a slut."

Jitty rocked softly. "Now what part's upsetting you? Scott or Coleman?"

I thought about it. "Not Scott. It was good with him. Really good." A tingle of the afternoon came back to me and I felt the despair lift a fraction of an inch.

"You saw things in him that you didn't expect?"

"I did."

"And Coleman. What about him?"

"He took up for Bo-Peep."

"Sarah Booth, what he said to you and what he says to her may be two very different things."

I hadn't really thought of that. Knowing Coleman, though, it *was* his nature to publicly defend his employees unless it was something illegal. The fact that in doing so he was tormenting me, was awful only to me. In other words, Coleman wasn't being deliberately cruel to me. But it still stung.

"Reality is hard on heroes," Jitty said slowly. "Seems like we build 'em up for the pleasure of tearin' 'em down. Look at Martin Luther King Jr. No man did more for equality, but we all wanted to know what he was doin' in the bedroom. We drew in our breath at the scandal and begged for more. And John Kennedy, too. Even Jimmy Carter. We couldn't just let him be a good man runnin' the country. We had to fault him as a bumpkin, tear at his public admission of religious principles." She shook her head. "Human nature is a sad, sad thing, Sarah Booth. You're just sufferin' from the common state of affairs for all mortals. You thought Coleman was more than a man. He can't be, and you can't expect it of him. He's just a man, like you're just a woman. You slept with a sexy bluesman. You want Coleman to leave his wife. You're selfish. News flash, Sarah Booth, so is everyone else. The difference is, and it's a big one, you didn't do anything to make Coleman break up with his wife. You could have and you didn't. So cut yourself some slack and quit drinkin' alone."

She stood up, shimmering. I thought it was the dazzling gold tunic she wore, with thigh-high boots, but it was her translucence. She was simply gone.

Headlights swung off the main road, and I watched the car coming toward me. Coleman? Tinkie? Scott didn't have a car. I waited.

The big Plymouth pulled up and J. B. Washington, the man who'd dropped this case in my lap, came up the steps. He noted the empty drink and the slump in my shoulders. "Let's go," he said, putting a hand under my elbow and levering me out of the chair.

"Where?"

"Scott's at Playin' the Bones. An impromptu performance. Ida Mae's going to sing with him."

I needed no further prodding. We were off into the Delta night.

AS FAR AS I could tell in the neon lighting of the club, all evidence of the murder had been carefully scrubbed away. I hadn't noticed when I was there in the daylight, but Ivory had blown some bucks on very hot neon. The bar was a hot pink, while cool blue slithered and sizzled over the booths. I loved it.

J. B. left me at a table right at the edge of the stage while he got his guitar ready. He, too, was playing. Scott was nowhere in sight, but Ida Mae came out of the back and I gasped out loud. She wore a tight, sequined gown of blood-red that hugged a body still ripe and curvaceous. Her hair, always so neatly pulled back, hung in curls down to her shoulders, and the white gardenia that had always been Billie Holiday's trademark bloomed beside her left ear. In the stage lighting, Ida Mae was ageless.

Word of the performance must have spread like wildfire. Folks, black and white, began thronging into the club. I remembered that Ida Mae had once been a club singer, but had given it up for the church. Judging by the buzz of excitement from the crowd, some folks had heard Ida Mae sing. I was in for a treat.

Scott came on stage with no fanfare. He instantly started playing and the band picked up. The spotlight found Ida Mae and stayed on her. This was her night, and the lights were making that plain. Still, my gaze was riveted on Scott. I knew his body so well, but I'd never seen it in the one-dimensional lights of a stage, where his leanness was made both harsher and sexier. His guitar was slung low against his hips, and he held it tight across the neck, his fingers working up and down the frets while his right hand made it growl and whine. After a thirty-second intro, he picked up the melody of a Holiday classic, "Lover Man."

At the first note, I gave up on Scott and transferred my attention to Ida Mae. I'd heard a lot of good female vocalists sing that song, but none like Ida Mae. She sang with heart and gut. I was blinking back tears when she finished.

Ida Mae sang five songs before she began to talk. "I'm glad to see all of you here. I know there are other things you could be doing on a Monday night." It hadn't occurred to me before, but I saw it then, Ida Mae was fighting the black community meeting. She was fighting back with Ivory's chosen weapon—the blues.

"I don't know the future of this club, but I do know how much my husband loved it. And how much Scott, here, loves it. I don't know if we can keep it open, but if we can, Scott has promised me he'll stay here for a while."

The applause was wild. Those in the club had obviously decided to believe Scott. I looked around. The mix was half and half, but even better, race just wasn't an issue. These were music lovers undefined by anything except that passion. It was a hopeful moment.

Like all dreams, though, it lasted too briefly. There was a hubbub at the front door that flowed across the room. At first I didn't recognize Emanuel as he blasted onto the stage. A half-dozen men were with him, clean-cut thugs in business suits. He snatched the microphone out of his mother's hand in a gesture that made two men beside me rise to their feet and step forward. Emanuel Keys was begging for an ass-whipping, and he was about to get it.

"Every black person in here should be ashamed. Goody's Grocery is burned to the ground, the hand of the white man reaching out and squeezing us again. While our community is being torched you're in here laughing and drinking! This club is closed!" He shouted the words, his face contorted with rage. "Get out! All of you, get out!"

There was the flash of a camera and his face was caught in that rictus of fury. I looked around to find Cece holding the newspaper's Nikon. She fired off another shot of Emanuel, momentarily blinding him.

"Give me that camera!" he ordered.

"Come and get it, dahling," Cece replied drolly. "I've been itching for a good First Amendment lawsuit."

"Emanuel," Ida Mae said in a voice remarkably cool and restrained, "stop acting like a total fool. Get off the stage so we can play."

"This isn't your club, Mother," he said harshly.

The two men beside me took another step forward. Emanuel was breaking one of the fundamental laws of the South—and probably everywhere else. Public ill-treatment of a woman, especially a mother, was not easily tolerated.

"It's not yours, either," Ida Mae said. "Not yet, anyway. You know that."

"I'll call the sheriff."

"Go ahead," Ida Mae said. "I checked with a lawyer. I'm within my rights. Now you get off this stage. Find a seat and sit down and enjoy the show. You can stay if you behave."

"Mama, you're letting them walk all over us."

"You're wrong, Emanuel. I'm doing what I love, what I want. What I denied because I knew you needed one parent who didn't sing the blues."

That was the final straw. Emanuel turned from Ida Mae to Scott. "You murdering bastard. I don't know how you have the nerve to stand up here with my mother."

"Your biggest problem, Emanuel, is that you're jealous of me. You're jealous because your daddy loved me. He loved me and I loved him. You hate me because of that. The awful truth is, Ivory would have given everything he owned for the chance to love you. You wouldn't let him. You threw it all away because there's no room for love in your heart. It's too filled with hate."

Emanuel's fist connected squarely with Scott's chin. Scott went down, guitar flying out of his hands. The two men beside me were on the stage, restraining Emanuel with a few side jabs to his ribs, while Scott got slowly to his feet, his hand to his jaw. "Feel better?" he asked Emanuel. "I hope so. But nothing has changed. Violence can't change any of it. Funny that I should know that so well and I'm the one accused of murder. Your daddy was a good teacher."

"Take him out," Ida Mae told the two men. "Make sure he stays out." She turned her back on her son and put a hand on Scott's face. "Can you still play?" she asked.

His smile was his answer. He took the guitar that someone handed him. There was the *click, click, click* of the drummer starting the count, and the band was playing "St. James Infirmary."

J. B. DROVE ME home around one o'clock. I was feeling no pain. I'd had several drinks and danced until my feet were blistered. From the doldrums, I'd ascended to the top of Mount Jack.

Just as we turned in the driveway I caught a flash of moonlit gold through the sycamores. J. B. slammed on the brakes as Reveler flew into the driveway out of the trees. We came within inches of hitting him.

"Shit!" J. B. gripped the wheel as I opened the passenger door and ran into the night, calling my horse. Reveler was gone. I could hear his hooves thundering through the cotton field to my right.

The loud report of a rifle split the night.

"Reveler!" I called his name but knew he was too panicked to listen.

J. B. gunned the car, spinning gravel as he headed toward the house. He didn't slow in front but drove around back. I had no halter, no feed, no way to entice or hold my frightened horse, but I had to prevent him from running into the paved road at the front of my property. I took off through the night, tearing through the rows of cotton, searching the darkness for a glint of ghostly dun in the moonlight.

When I finally saw him, he was standing still, blowing. His sides heaved with exertion and fear, his nostrils wide.

"Reveler," I said softly. "Hey, boy, it's me. Come on."

As I got closer, I could see that he was trembling. Someone had really spooked him, possibly injured him. I kept my fears and my anger tapped down. Reveler would sense both. It would only excite him more.

Step by step I drew closer to him until I stood at his shoulder. I laid my palm flat against his withers and spoke softly in a singsong whisper. I could feel him calm beneath my hand. When his muzzle came around to nudge against me, I knew he wasn't going to run away. Now I had to get him to follow me to the barn so I could make sure he wasn't injured.

When I started to walk away from him, he hesitated, then fell into step behind me as we both walked to the driveway and headed home.

We were halfway there when headlights swung down the driveway, illuminating us. After a moment, the lights went out. A car door slammed and there was the scrunch of leather on gravel as J. B. came my way.

"The sorry bastard got away," he said. "I chased him through the cotton field, but he gave me the slip."

"Did you see him?"

"Not good enough to tell anything about him, except he had a rifle."

Reveler blew a little at J. B., then accepted him as we all walked back to the barn. I slipped a halter over Reveler's head and J. B. held him while I searched every inch of his body. There were no wounds or injuries. If someone had been trying to hurt him, they'd missed.

"Best I can tell, the horse jumped the fence and took off," J. B. said. "The gate was still closed when I got here. The man was over there." He pointed to the side of the pasture. "I caught him in the headlights just long enough to see he had a gun. Either he was black or he was wearing a ski mask. He started running and I went after him."

"Thank you." Reveler had stopped trembling and was happy with the scoop of grain I gave him. I, on the other hand, felt like a lump of Antarctica had moved into my chest.

"Hey, he's okay, Sarah Booth." J. B. put an arm around me and hugged me close. Though I tried hard not to, I started crying.

"Ah, girl," he said, rubbing my back lightly. "No need to cry. The horse is fine."

"Someone tried to hurt him," I said between sobs. "The low-life bastard went after an innocent animal."

"I can't deny that's a coward's work. We'd better go report this to the sheriff."

We walked to the house, and J. B. made the call to the sheriff's office while I put on coffee. As soon as he was finished with the phone, I called Lee McBride. She'd given me the horse as payment for a case. As soon as I told her what had happened, she offered to let Reveler stay at Swift Level for a while. I declined, but kept the offer open. If someone wanted to hurt my horse, they could do it at Swift Level, and possibly injure Lee's horses as well.

It didn't surprise me when Gordon Walters showed up and did the investigation into the shooting. The fact that the intended victim was a horse would greatly lessen the potential charges, Gordon warned us, but J. B. insisted that my life and his had been endangered, which notched things back up again. I didn't ask Gordon to call Coleman, and he didn't offer.

Gordon dug a bullet from the barn wall and said it would go a long way toward solving the crime if we could find the rifle. Probably a 30.06, he said.

When we'd finished the preliminary search, I gave Gordon the biggest searchlight I had, and he went back to examine the area around the barn again. He didn't say so, but it was easy to see that he wanted to do his work without an audience. I stood at the kitchen door and watched the light working here and there in neat patterns.

J. B. drew me to the front porch, where we could sit in the rockers. It wasn't until I saw two cars careening down the drive that I realized what he'd done. While I'd been busy talking to Gordon, J. B. had sneakily called both Tinkie and Cece.

"You don't need to be alone," he said.

"Thanks," I said grudgingly, because I was glad that he'd called them. I didn't want to be a nuisance to my friends, but I sure didn't want to be alone.

"Dahling!" Cece cried as she leaped up the steps two at a time. She air-kissed me on each cheek, then did it again. "One shouldn't frighten one's friends." She was huffing hard, and I realized she was still dressed to the nines. "You had a date," I said, eyes narrowing. She'd left Playin' the Bones alone. Where had she found a man between Kudzu and downtown Zinnia at one o'clock in the morning?

"Men are a dime a dozen, dahling, but friends are priceless." She smiled.

Tinkie finally made it up the steps, and we all went inside and took a seat at the kitchen table. J. B. served us coffee and foraged around in the cupboard until he found a box of brownies, which he promptly mixed up.

I told all of them about the spray paint on my folks' tombstone and about Reveler, with J. B. throwing in his side of the story as he baked.

"Dahling, this is going to be front page," Cece said. "That Deputy Walters, acting like it isn't important because it was a horse. We'll see about that. This is Zinnia, Mississippi, not the O.K. Corral. I'd be willing to bet it's those two thugs who hang out with Scott."

I hadn't thought of Spider and Ray-Ban, but they did seem to be the most likely suspects, based on general attitude and character type. But why would they want to hurt me? I was helping Scott.

"I second that," Tinkie said, "though we need some hard evidence before we accuse them publicly." I couldn't help but grin. Tinkie had come a long, long way in a few months.

"I don't know," I said.

"It was just one man," J. B. threw in from the counter, where he was beating the brownie batter. "Do you have some pecans or walnuts?" he asked.

"Second cabinet, blue Tupperware." J. B. was implying that Spider and Ray-Ban were too cowardly to act alone, and I agreed with him. "Who would really want to hurt me?" I asked. "Even better, who would know that he could hurt me by hurting Reveler?"

"That's a good question," Tinkie said. "I don't think Ray-Ban and Spider are smart enough to figure that out. They would never love an animal enough to think to hurt someone else's."

"She has a point," Cece conceded. "But who?"

The door opened and Gordon Walters stepped into the bright kitchen lights. "Could you come outside with me for a moment?" he asked. His radio crackled and he spoke into it. "Yessir, Sheriff, I think you should come out to Dahlia House right now."

"What is it?" I asked.

He didn't answer but led the way across the lawn and to the barn. He went around the south side and we followed single file, Cece cursing once as her high heel slid in a pile of fresh manure.

When we rounded the corner of the barn, I stopped so suddenly that J. B. collided into me and Tinkie into him.

"Shit," J. B. whispered as he looked past me at the object framed in Gordon Walters' bright flashlight. Two large bones were wired together in the shape of a pirate's crossed bones. They leaned against the side of the barn, where the crude drawing of a human skull had been spray-painted above them. The bottom portion of both bones were manacled together by what looked like old leg irons.

"I don't suppose this was here yesterday, was it?" Gordon asked rhetorically.

"No," I said.

"The Bonesmen," Tinkie whispered. "I knew it was those low-lifes."

"I don't think so," I said softly. "There's something else here."

"The manacles," J. B. said. "I don't know a lot about the Bonesmen, but I know that isn't part of their thing. They do the skull and crossbones, the old pirate symbol." He knelt down and stared at the iron manacles. "This is different."

"We'll have them tested, but I'm pretty certain the bones are from an animal," Gordon said, kneeling beside them.

"That's a relief," Cece said. "I wouldn't want to be on the search party looking for the rest of the body."

No one heard Coleman as he slipped around the corner and came to stand behind me. It wasn't until I sensed him that I turned to find him staring at the evidence, an expression of pure anger on his face.

Standing in the night, both J. B. and I retold our stories, with Gordon throwing in what he'd discovered.

"Find Emanuel Keys and bring him in," Coleman said.

Tinkie, Cece, and I spoke simultaneously. "What?"

Coleman was in no mood to explain himself. When he spoke, his voice was terse. "I've been doing a little research on the Dominoes," he said. "They took the symbol of the Bonesmen and then took it one step further. The manacles, to symbolize their past history of slavery. I'm willing to bet this is the work of Emanuel Keys. He's been running amok all night, first at that blues club, then down at the black community meeting, and now here. We haven't found the evidence to connect him to Trina Jacks' abduction, but I'm sure he was behind it. Find him and put him in a cell."

The last was directed at Gordon, and Coleman walked away without another word.

Her gaze on Coleman's back, Tinkie put an arm around me. "What's eating him?" she asked.

No one answered.

25

TUESDAY DAWNED STORMY AND GRAY. WHEN A RAINSTORM MOVES into the Delta in August, the air is congealed. It lays on the skin like an unwanted touch. I woke up sweating, grumpy, and out of sorts.

I was drinking coffee when the phone rang. The sound of Bridge Ladnier's voice perked me up a little.

"I hear I missed the show of the year last night," he said. "I was in the middle of some serious business or I would have been there earlier. I missed the whole thing."

"It was terrific," I rubbed it in. "Ida Mae can pull from the gut. She's the real deal."

"I was talking to an old friend of mine, Mike Utley. He was a green kid working with Sun back in the early fifties. He said he recorded Ida Mae once or twice."

"No kidding." I was impressed. Bridge knew the most interesting factoids about the blues. "Any chance those recordings are still around?" I had heard Ida Mae sing. I would give anything to have a record of her.

"I doubt it. Mike does, too. He said they were never released. Ida Mae abruptly gave up singing the blues and devoted herself to church. She didn't want any recordings released. If they still exist, someone's got them under wraps or else they have them in an attic and don't know what they have."

"That's too bad."

"Mike was talking about some recordings of Ivory and Elvis. Has Ida Mae ever mentioned anything about that?"

"No, but Scott did. He said Ivory told him about them."

"From what I hear, it was quite an ensemble. Mike said it was one of the hottest sessions he ever got on tape. The sessions were so dynamic, they went direct to disk, which was highly unusual. Ivory was on piano, Kingfish Tucker on lead guitar, the legendary Hotlips Freeman on harmonica, and Elvis did the vocals. Can you imagine?"

I could. "I'd give just about anything to hear that."

"The story gets even better. During one of the recording sessions, a man burst into the studio. He was waving a gun and he began shooting wildly. He got Hotlips in the shoulder, but he was after Elvis. Ivory jumped up from the piano and leaped across to Elvis, tackling him at the knees and knocking him down. Ivory saved Elvis's life. They caught the man and it turned out his girlfriend said she was in love with Elvis. The guy was just a nutcase."

It was a great story. "I wonder what happened to those recordings?"

"Mike said he thought one of the band members may have ended up with them. There were twenty-two cuts in all. Mike asked if Scott or Ida Mae ever mentioned the possibility of someone having them."

"Scott didn't say, but I'm sure if Ida Mae had access to them, she'd bring them out. She could use the money."

"I'm sure. They'd be quite valuable, and for a private collector . . ."

He didn't finish. He didn't have to. Ida Mae could name her price.

"Sarah Booth, I'm sitting on the terrace waiting for Eunice to bring me some fresh orange juice and croissants from the bakery. I'd love for you to join me."

"Sounds like Sunday on a Tuesday," I pointed out. "I thought even entrepreneurs had to work."

"Money begets money. It's the first rule of finance. All you have to do is stand back and let it multiply." His voice lowered. "I'd like to share breakfast with you."

"I'd like that, too," I said, treading carefully. I spoke the truth, but I had no desire to lead Bridge on. Flirting was fine sport, if both sides understood the rules. I did enjoy it, but I was basically a one-man woman. "I think I left an earring in your guest bathroom."

"And I thought that was just a ploy to see me again. You disappoint me, Sarah Booth."

I laughed. Bridge was damn good.

"Shall I ask Eunice to set another place?"

It was tempting, but I had things I needed to do. "I'd better decline this time," I said. "Duty calls."

"Duty or destiny?"

It was a curious question, and I decided to dodge it, exercising my Daddy's Girl option number thirty-nine. In matters of the heart or the bedroom, a Daddy's Girl never has to be direct. In fact, subterfuge and prevarication are always preferred.

"Someone shot at my horse last night," I said instead.

"Sarah Booth, that's terrible. Do you know who it was?"

"Not for certain. The sheriff was interested in talking to Emanuel Keys. I'm headed to the courthouse to see if he was charged."

"Do you want me to go with you?"

It was a charming offer, and one that made me stiffen with alarm. "No, no thanks. It's best I do this on my own. It's my business."

He chuckled. "Yes, it is. Sorry. I didn't mean to sound like 1940."

Bridge was a remarkable man. He picked up on a cue like he'd been trained. "I'll call you later," I said, eager to get off the phone. Bridge had accomplished one thing. I was motivated to begin my day.

WALKING INTO THE sheriff's office, I was prepared for anything Bo-Peep cared to dish out. I was in my red Guccis with the block heel and crisscross straps and a red crepe skort set that was raffish and designer. Bo-Peep could bring it on. Denim and daisy dukes were no competition.

Coleman's door was closed. That was troubling; he never closed his door. "I need to speak with the sheriff. Privately," I said, crisply efficient.

Bo-Peep swung her hips from left to right and somehow made forward progress to his door. She tapped, stepped inside, came out, sashayed to the counter, and finally looked at me. I wondered how she kept her eyes open under the weight of all that mascara. Her thick hair hung in tresses down her back.

"The sheriff will see you now," she said.

"Thanks." I smiled. "There's something crawling in your hair." I made a face and drew back.

She squealed and began batting at her head.

"I use Show Sheen to get the tangles out of my horse's tail. You should try some," I whispered. I was smiling to myself as I walked past her and into Coleman's office. I closed the door.

"Sarah Booth," Coleman said, rising to his feet behind the desk.

Our gazes locked and held. I closed the door behind me, unable to look away from him. We stood like that, transfixed, for a long time. The anger seeped out of me, and to my shame I felt the sting of tears. Damn! I absolutely couldn't cry. What did I have to cry about? I was being an idiot. Still, a single tear balanced on my left eyelashes, then slowly crept down my cheek.

Coleman was around the desk in a flash. His arms were around me and he was hugging me close. "I've been so worried about you. I wanted to call you, but I just didn't know what to say."

His shirt was starched. Only Coleman would wear a starched

shirt in August. I breathed in the clean smell of the shirt, the sunshine, and Niagra. I felt his hands on my back, soothing and caressing. I was safe. The luxury of it was incredible. Held against his chest, I could shed my burdens.

My arms went around his waist and I held on, breathing in the clean, ironed smell of him. His hands moved lower. My tears dried up quickly in the sudden heat that he generated. He felt the change in my body and gently stepped away.

"Are you okay?"

I nodded. "Never better," I said to his sternum. In your arms, I wanted to add but didn't.

His fingers glided down my cheek, lifting my face. "My God, Sarah Booth. I've never wanted anything as much as you. You can't imagine what it's like, wanting you and trying to do the right thing by Connie."

I could imagine it, and it made me want to howl. It didn't matter what I felt. He was still a married man. He'd invoked his wife's name. He'd drawn the line we couldn't cross. And deep in my heart, I knew he was right. "I'm trying really hard," I said, the words rock-bottom honest.

"I know," he said slowly, his hand moving up to cradle my cheek. "We both are. We've both gone down a rocky path this time," he said, lowering his hand. It was a good thing he did. I wanted to step into his touch, to bask in the warmth that he generated in me.

"How is Connie?" I asked, the words sticking a little in my throat. I smiled to hide the pain.

"She's doing okay. We're in counseling. I guess I needed to hear some hard things about myself. In fairness to her, I haven't been the best husband. A woman can't come in at the bottom of the priority list all the time."

"No, she can't." I swallowed hard. My throat was parched, and there were words lodged in it. Words that would never get spoken.

"I never realized how it must seem to her. I was always on the job, always putting it first. I thought I was being a good provider.

Seems like I was hiding from my feelings by working all the time. I've learned that's a form of addiction. Work to avoid feeling. Connie hasn't been happy, but neither have I." He shrugged, embarrassed and guilty.

I couldn't lie and tell him that I hoped he worked it out. I just couldn't say those words. "I think counseling's a good idea."

"Yeah, women do."

I put my hand on his badge. "It'll make you a better lawman, and a better man."

"I could use a little of both of those, especially the latter," he said. He went back to his desk and sat down, motioning me to take a seat. "We brought Emanuel in last night but we had to cut him loose. He had an alibi for the time Reveler was attacked."

"Who was his alibi?"

"Three men. All members of the Dominoes."

I could tell Coleman didn't believe the alibi. "What about the bones and the manacles?"

"He admitted it was the sign of the Dominoes. He feigned surprise that it was left at your place. We got a search warrant and went through his car and his home. There was no gun, no other bones, nothing to tie him to the act."

"Whoever did it was trying to frighten me. It worked, too. It made me realize how vulnerable I am when it comes to the things I love."

"That's where we're all vulnerable, Sarah Booth." He made no move toward me. "I'm vulnerable where you're concerned because I love you. That's why you have to be so careful. That's why you have to promise me that you'll drop this case."

The air leaked out of me. I didn't sigh or gasp or anything. Suddenly, my lungs were empty. "I can't," I said simply. I breathed. Coleman loved me, and it did neither of us any good. It was just one more open wound we both had to try to protect.

"This county's going to explode," Coleman said. His voice was gentle. "Sarah Booth, you've put yourself in a position to be hurt by both factions. Please walk away from this."

"I can't." If I were a true Daddy's Girl, I would invoke the name of wife, pointing out that we both had things we just couldn't back away from. Coleman had his obligations and I had mine. But I wasn't a DG and Coleman wasn't an adversary. He was the man, under different circumstances, I might have married.

"Do you still believe Scott is guilty?" I asked him.

"It doesn't matter what I believe. What I can prove is what matters to the law."

I studied Coleman. I couldn't be certain what he really thought about Scott, or what he knew about the two of us, but he wasn't showing the edge of certainty about Scott's guilt that had been there earlier in the case.

"If it wasn't Scott, who else would want Ivory dead?" I asked.

"Ivory was a symbol to a lot of people. Symbols are always an easy target. His death serves a number of purposes, if you put it in a political perspective."

I nodded. "Where was Emanuel the night his father died?"

Coleman's hands were flat on the desk. He had large hands, the nails clean and neat, and they could be so gentle. But if I touched the palms, I knew I would feel the calluses that came from physical labor. While his job didn't require a lot of manual labor, Coleman liked hard work. When he didn't answer my question, I looked up at him.

"Emanuel was at the blues club until about midnight. He had an argument with his father. He went back to the club around four. He found his father's body."

"And you don't find that suspicious?"

"I do. But the shank and the money were found on Scott."

"Easily planted evidence."

"Scott had motive, means, and opportunity."

"So did Emanuel. And Nandy Shanahan."

There was a brisk tap on Coleman's door and he called out for Bo-Peep to come in.

"We have a 10–52 out on Bilbo Lane," she said, trying hard not to let me hear.

Coleman stood up abruptly. "I have to go."

I stood up, too. Bilbo Lane could only mean Scott Hampton. Coleman started out the back door and I was on his heels. He stopped so suddenly I slammed into his back, the butt of his gun jabbing my hipbone.

"Ouch!"

"You're not going," he said.

"What's a 10–52?"

"Assault and battery."

I'd mentioned Nandy's name, and she'd appeared, for it could be no one else. "Wild horses couldn't keep me away."

Coleman's grin let me know I'd responded exactly as he'd expected. "Hop in," he said as he strode to the patrol car.

26

WE TURNED DOWN SCOTT'S DRIVE AND INTO A SWIRL OF FLASH-
ing red lights. The muggy August air seemed to hold the light in a
long, red scream. Something tragic had happened.

Two paramedic units were there, and men in white shirts bus-
tled about the yard. They lifted a stretcher on Scott's porch and
ran toward the open back doors of the closest ambulance. I
couldn't stop myself from rushing forward. Coleman had told me
no additional details on the drive over.

The sight of Nandy's bloody face, surrounded by sandbags to
stabilize her neck, stopped me in my tracks. My gaze locked on
the place in her eyebrow where the blue sapphire record stud had
been. The flesh was split; the ring torn out. My stomach tightened
and flipped.

Nandy's eyes were closed, but she opened them and saw me.
One thin hand motioned me toward her. I had no choice. I
stepped close.

"You can have him," she whispered. "*If* he ever gets out of
prison." Her smile was that of the victor.

The paramedics loaded her into the ambulance, slammed the door, and drove away. I couldn't move. Not even a foot. Not even when I saw Scott on the porch, his torso and hands covered in blood. Coleman was talking to him. He was shaking his head, pointing to the porch floor. Finally, I forced my right leg to move, then the left. I walked to the porch.

"I heard something out here and when I came out, I found her, lying there." The place Scott indicated showed a smudged blood-stain. "I called 9-1-1, then I called your office."

"You didn't hit her?" Coleman was looking pointedly at Scott's hands, which were bloody.

Scott bowed up. Authority figures still rankled him. "I didn't hit her," he snapped. "I'm not an idiot, and I'm not an asshole who beats on women."

"Did you touch her?" Coleman asked with more patience than I expected.

Scott looked down at his hands and realized there had to be some explanation. "I couldn't tell how badly she was hurt. I was afraid she'd bleed to death, so I touched her. I tried to find where she was bleeding. But I never hit her." His tone had corrected it-self, and he sounded like the Scott I'd come to know.

"How'd she get in that condition?" Coleman asked.

Instead of getting angry, Scott shook his head. It was an effort I appreciated. "I know how it looks, but that's how I found her. I don't know how she got here or what happened. Could you tell how badly she was hurt?"

"I'll check at the hospital and let you know," Coleman said.

My face must have registered my surprise. Coleman wasn't ar-resting Scott. I was positive Nandy had accused him of beating her, but Coleman wasn't buying in to it.

Scott's face opened in relief. "That's it?"

"You're done," Coleman said.

Scott ran down the steps and scooped me into a hug. "Am I glad to see you," he said, squeezing me. "When I saw Nandy all bloody like that on the porch, I almost flipped out." He put his face in my neck, nuzzling into my hair. My arms went around him, holding him. My gaze went up the porch to Coleman, who stared back at me. If I'd ever doubted my power to hurt him, I didn't any longer. Neither did I doubt how unintentionally cruel life could be. I didn't want to hurt him, and I finally understood, completely, that his choices with Connie were unconnected to me, no matter how gravely they affected me. Wisdom is a bitter, bitter draught.

"I'll give you a call and let you know the results at the hospital," Coleman said to Scott as he walked past us, got in his car, and drove away. He didn't offer me a ride back to town. He followed the second ambulance out.

"Are you okay?" Scott asked, standing tall and holding me at arm's length. He examined my face, reading God-only-knows-what thoughts. I couldn't hide that I was upset.

"I'm shocked. What happened?"

He led me into the cottage and closed the door behind us. When I was on the sofa, iced tea in my hand, and he was beside me, he put his arm around me and held me close against him. "I've never felt I could tell another person that I was scared, but I can tell you, Sarah Booth. You won't judge me."

"How can I? I'm scared, too." It was so simple with Scott. For a man who put up a barricade of solitude, once it was breached, he was a candidate for *Oprah*. He had feelings, and he knew more about them than I did mine. Perhaps that was why he wrote such powerful music. "Tell me what happened."

He kissed the top of my head. "I heard something on the porch. I'd been thinking about you. Daydreaming, I guess you'd say." He gave me a wicked look that tingled the Delaney womb.

"Go on," I urged. I needed to hear the facts before we started in on the fantasies.

"I thought it might be you, coming to visit, so I opened the door, and there was this bloody thing lying on the porch. For just one terrible moment, I thought someone had hurt *you*. Then I realized it was Nandy. I knelt down and tried to see where she was hurt. She was moaning and she grabbed my shirt, pulling me down."

I could see it all clearly. Nandy making sure her blood got on Scott. I had no doubt she'd set the entire thing up just to pin it on him.

"Her face was bleeding where the ring had been in her eyebrow. It seemed all of the blood was coming from there. At least I didn't see any on her shorts or legs. Once I figured she hadn't severed an artery, I didn't look much beyond that. I tried to make her talk, but she wouldn't. She just moaned. When she grabbed me she was pretty strong, so I risked leaving her and called the paramedics and the sheriff."

"She's going to try and set you up for the beating." Judging from his nonreaction, Scott had already anticipated this.

Scott put a hand on my face. "It doesn't seem possible that I'm saying this, but I don't think the sheriff will believe her." He sought something in my expression. He sensed there was something between me and Coleman.

"Coleman won't believe her." He might *want* to believe Nandy, but he was a man who believed only evidence. At first glance, the evidence supported the theory that Nandy was trying to set Scott up. "No matter what Coleman believes, we need as much supporting evidence as possible. Where's Nandy's car? She had to drive herself here. There's bound to be blood in it."

"I hadn't thought of that. There's a bunch of trails that go back to the creek. I'll bet she parked it there and walked here."

"Let's go."

"Now?" he asked.

I nodded. "No time like the present. I want to find that car before anyone can tamper with it."

Working on the theory that Nandy would park as close as possible while still hiding the car, we went down the first trail that led back to the creek. We'd gone only thirty yards into the trees when I saw the BMW convertible. The top was up. I told Scott not to touch it, but we walked around it. There was a bloodstain on the headrest and one on the visor above the passenger's door. My best guess was that Nandy had parked the car and then ripped the ring out.

"Will this help?" Scott asked.

"I think it will clinch it if we have to go to court," I said. "Let's call Coleman and let him know."

Walking back to the cottage, I reached out and took Scott's hand. He'd washed the blood off, and the long, elegant fingers stretched out as I examined it. I looked at the other hand. "We should let Coleman see your hands. You haven't hit anyone." I looked up at Scott. "The hands I want to see belong to Robert McBruce. If anyone hit her, and that's a big if, I'll bet it was him."

His lips turned down at the corners. "I was hoping Nandy had moved on. She wasn't at the club last night, and I couldn't help but hope she'd left this area."

I'd also noted her absence and hoped she'd turned her warped attention to someone else. "If she accuses you, Scott, you'll have to file charges against her. False accusation, slander, whatever we can cook up. You were right. We should have gotten a legal injunction."

"Or a wooden stake. Why would she do this? Does she think I'll want her?" he asked, confusion in his voice. "I mean, does she think she can *force* me into wanting her?"

It went against my better judgment, but a smidgen of pity touched my heart. "Nandy never had a chance for normal thought processes. You know the story of her wacko family, all that Mary, Queen of Scots stuff. Then the arranged marriage. She was bred and trained for disaster." We were back at the cottage and Scott held the door open for me.

Inside, he paced the room. "She had money, opportunity, the chance to make something of herself. Just like I did. My family was just as screwed up as hers." Scott's laugh was bitter. "Try having a father who made a fortune selling Ram trucks, but who wanted to be a Bentley dealer. You can't begin to imagine. He'd sit in the middle of the showroom floor at night, a bottle of Scotch and a crystal glass beside him, crying because he'd inherited a dynasty, but it wasn't the one he wanted." Scott sat down beside me on the sofa, his forearms resting on his thighs and his hands dangling.

I'd never really considered how much background Scott and Nandy shared. "Perhaps a stint in Michigan State prison could redeem even Nandy." I meant it as a joke, a comment to lighten the moment.

"It wasn't prison. It was Ivory." Scott's head lowered. "I have so much to learn. We'd really just begun. Now I'm on my own again."

It struck me then, the state of adult orphanhood. Though I knew it intimately, it was a revelation. Everyone confronts this moment. It doesn't matter if we're six or sixty, we still long for the parent, the trusted guide. We never recover from the loss.

"It really sucks," I said, and a sad smile touched the corners of Scott's mouth.

"Well said, Sarah Booth. You could write lyrics for the blues."

"Somehow I don't see the word 'suck' as blues material. It's too graphic, too . . . crisp." I was glad I'd made him smile.

"Perhaps it is. But it's a very interesting word. So many applications." His gaze dropped to my breasts.

The heat was instantaneous. Marvelous how that worked. He looked at me with sexual intent, and I wanted him. We melted together, locked in a kiss that went from intimate to intense in less than ten seconds.

Our hands were on each other's clothes, working buttons and zippers, when we both heard the roar of the motorcycles in the front yard.

"Damn!" Scott stood up and went to the front window. "It's Spider and Ray-Ban."

"Tell them to leave." I understood male bonding, but Spider and Ray-Ban had two strikes against them. They were complete creeps and they had lousy timing. "Or better yet, ask them why they set fire to Goody's Grocery. Coleman's going to pin that one on them."

Scott ignored my ire. "Let me see what they want."

I rebuttoned my blouse and rose. "It's okay, I've got to go into town and check on some things."

"You aren't mad, are you?" He shifted one hip out. "I just can't throw them away. Everyone else does."

"I'm not mad." And I suddenly wasn't.

"Will you come back and have dinner with me tonight? I'll make you my specialty—pompano in parchment."

"Really? You can cook that?"

"Sure. Fish sticks in a cardboard box."

I couldn't help laughing. "Should I bring my own catsup packets?"

"No, I have a big bottle. Will you come? I'll make something special."

"I'd love to." I heard Spider give a rebel yell. There was the sound of glass breaking. My best guess would be a beer bottle. "Just don't encourage those two to hang around. If they're really your friends, they'll understand how much they can hurt you."

He shook his head. "I don't know if they can understand that, Sarah Booth. That's why I don't just send them away. They don't understand. They honestly think they're showing support for me."

Perhaps he was right. A two-celled organism couldn't be expected to understand.

SCOTT PLACED THE call to the sheriff's office, and I didn't wait for Coleman or one of the deputies to come out and examine Nandy's not-so-hidden car. I called Tinkie for a ride. On the way to the hospital, I filled her in on Nandy's ploy. Tinkie complimented my work in finding the car so quickly, but there was a hint of distance in her tone. She was worried about me. And annoyed that I was making her worry about one of my romantic peccadillos. And I wasn't confiding in her—or anyone else.

"I need some help," I said. "It would be best for everyone if Nandy simply confessed to trying to set Scott up for hurting her."

"Yes, that would be best."

Tinkie wasn't her normal, enthusiastic self. "Could you talk to

her? I think you'd be able to finesse her better than I could."
Which was the truth. My idea of finessing Nandy involved a
blackjack shampoo. Tinkie's thoughts didn't run to violence, at
least not at first.

"Finessing Nandy isn't the real problem," she said.

I took a breath. "Scott is more than a client to me. You know
that."

"Everyone in town knows that," Tinkie said. "I mean everyone. And we're all concerned for you. *You'd* know that if you
talked to us."

"I don't need to talk—I know you aren't thrilled. Look, my in-
volvement with Scott is going to make Nandy hate me even more. I
think you could make some headway with her. Will you try?"

"Sarah Booth, I care about you," Tinkie said. "Yes. I'll talk to
Nandy. I'd love to. But I wish you'd quit running out to Bilbo
Lane. At least until this is over."

"I can't promise that. But I will be careful."

We stopped by the courthouse and I got my car. By the time I
parked in the hospital lot, Tinkie was standing on the curb, waiting for me. She was well turned out in white slacks, sandals, and a
pale pink sleeveless sweater that rippled with every move she
made. It was stunning. She'd matched the muted pink perfectly
with Baby's Day Out nail polish and lipstick. Not everyone could
wear that shade, but Tinkie made it look easy.

We found Nandy on a stretcher in the hall. She caught sight of
me and sat up. The gash in her eyebrow was closed by three small
staples. I wondered if she liked them, since she had such a pen-
chant for metal in her flesh.

"What are *you* doing here?" she demanded, ignoring Tinkie,
which was a serious mistake.

"Checking on you," I said.

"Where's your husband?" Tinkie asked.

"What's it to you?" Nandy asked.

"I wanted to meet him. I just wanted to ask how much your
daddy had to pay him to marry you." Tinkie's lips were pink innocence.

"Don't worry about your car," I told Nandy as I started to walk away. "The sheriff's office is towing it in. They needed a sample of the bloodstains. Leather holds stains so much better than vinyl. There are benefits to money."

I didn't hang around to hear her bark. I went down the hall to Doc Sawyer's office. Even if he hadn't examined Nandy, he'd know exactly how badly she was hurt. The hospital grapevine was the most efficient in town. After seeing her car, I was willing to bet the entire damage involved her eyebrow.

Doc was brewing a fresh pot of coffee. I couldn't believe it. I'd been certain the coffeepot in the corner of his office was being used to incubate some rare new bacteria that would cure cancer, diabetes, and arthritis with one dose.

"Stuart Ann Shanahan," he said as he sat on the edge of his desk. "I remember the day she was born. Her daddy had a little tiara and a scepter that he wanted to bring into the delivery room. I put an end to that, but he managed to smuggle it into the nursery so she could have her first picture made wearing the tiara and holding the scepter. That child never had a chance."

I wasn't about to buy in to sympathy for Nandy. I'd had my moment of weakness with Scott. "She's trying to frame an innocent man for a felony battery charge."

"The ER doc told me someone had ripped an earring out of her . . . eyebrow." He cocked an eyebrow.

"Yeah, a sapphire stud. It was a made-to-order piece and probably very valuable." Nandy would also try to include robbery on the charges. I could see it coming.

"Lots of blood vessels around the eye. She had her own plastic surgeon come in, but I hear she bled a lot."

"She'll just replenish her supply by drinking someone else's."

Doc laughed. "That's a good one, Sarah Booth."

"Don't let her near your neck."

He laughed harder.

"Did you hear how badly she was hurt?"

"From what I heard, only the eyebrow."

"Could she have done that herself? Ripped out the ring?"

"She could have." He templed his hands in front of him. "Edgar, her doctor, said there weren't any bruises to indicate she'd been beaten. He wants to have her mentally evaluated."

That was good news. Still, if she made the charge against Scott, it would stir up the community even more. A lot of folks wouldn't wait to hear the whole story, they'd just see Scott as the man who killed Ivory Keys and beat a woman. "Edgar believes Nandy injured herself, doesn't he?"

"Yes."

"Did he tell her so and would he testify to that?"

"Yes, I believe so."

I nodded. With that background, I knew Tinkie could break her. Scott would never be brought in for questioning.

"Doc, can I see the photos of Ivory Keys again?"

He lowered his hands. The coffeepot gave its last gasp, and he got up and poured us both a cup. When he handed me the white Styrofoam, I swallowed hard. The coffee was thick and black and toxic. Yet it was a fresh pot. I'd watched it brew. When I looked at Doc, he was grinning. I didn't bother with creamer because I wasn't going to drink it.

Before he sat back down, he got a folder from his filing cabinet and handed me the photos. I hardened my expression as I quickly sifted through them, stopping on the shot of Ivory's back. The design that had been cut into his flesh was definitely crossed bones. But if it was representative of the Bonesmen, it was an unfinished work. The skull hadn't been included.

"What's that?" I asked, pointing to a place on Ivory's back just above the crossed bones.

"Another cut."

"Made at the same time?"

"No," Doc said, frowning. "It was made before he died."

I knew he'd been beaten. His face showed it, and even in death the dark bruises could be found beneath his skin. I hadn't realized he'd been cut, too. "Were there other cuts?"

"Three," Doc said. He shook his head. "The brutality of people. It sickens me."

"Where were the other cuts?"

"That one on his back, one to the left of his sternum, and two lower."

"Symbolic?" I asked him.

"More likely they were trying to frighten Ivory. I believe the killer went into that club intending to kill Ivory. I don't think there was ever a chance he was going to be left alive."

"Premeditated murder."

"That's what I would call it. Based on my experience, I'd say the killer was someone who had a score to settle."

I sighed, thinking of what Coleman had said about Ivory being a symbol. We humans did like to build them up just to knock them down. "But what about the club being torn up and the money stolen? Couldn't it have been a robbery that went bad?"

Doc finished his coffee. "I believe the robbery was an afterthought."

I put the pictures back in the folder and stood. "Thanks, Doc."

"Be careful, Sarah Booth. This county is like a powder keg. Emotions are high, and Nandy isn't helping matters."

"It might be best if she was sent somewhere for evaluation. Best for her and certainly best for the rest of us."

Doc nodded. "Her old man will buy her out of this, just watch."

"Coleman won't—"

Doc held up a hand. "Not Coleman. But Shanahan will bring in a name shrink, and they'll whisk Nandy off for 'treatment.' Then it will all blow over."

"You know, I don't care, just as long as she's gone from here for the next few weeks."

Tinkie was waiting in the hallway for me. I almost missed her. She was surrounded by white coats.

"I just think I'm a little anemic," she was saying to the handsomest of the doctors. Tinkie had a fetish for men who'd taken the Hippocratic Oath. She could talk about herself and her conditions without any holding back. "You know, it's just my inheritance from Grandmother Camilla. She was so delicate, and I'm just like her."

"Perhaps you should stop by the office. We could run a few tests, do a complete physical. . . ." The doctor put his hand on Tinkie's forehead.

She closed her eyes, her lips going into her famous pout, made even more sensual by that pink lipstick. "I feel better just letting you touch me," she said. "You have the most healing touch."

"I'll have my nurse call you with an appointment tomorrow," Dr. Haywick said. I checked his name tag. Gynecologist.

"Tinkie, if you're healed, we have work to do." I smiled at the doctors, who scattered as if I had the plague. I didn't inspire the need to heal the way Tinkie did.

"Isn't he a doll?" Tinkie whispered to me, her gaze following Dr. Haywick's back.

"You're married," I pointed out to her.

"He's a doctor," she whispered back. "That's the only fun married women get to have, Sarah Booth."

I decided not to answer. "What did Nandy say?"

"Oh, she was driving down Bilbo Lane when a wasp got in her car. She's terrified of wasps, you know. Very allergic. Anyway, she became panicked at the wasp and tried to kill it. In doing so, she caught the sleeve of her blouse on that stud in her eyebrow and yanked it right out. She was blinded by the blood that ensued. Half-crazy with pain, she realized the closest person she knew was Scott and she went to his house. He aided her and called an ambulance."

The entire time she was talking she looked straight ahead. When she finally looked at me, she was grinning from ear to ear.

"That's the biggest crock of shit I've ever heard," I said, grinning too.

"I know, but it's her signed statement."

"She signed a statement to that effect?" I was ecstatic.

Tinkie reached into her straw handbag and pulled out a typewritten sheet of paper that bore Nandy's signature. "I got one of the nurses to type it up. Nandy was very willing to sign it."

"How did you do that?" I was amazed.

"Oh, Oscar helped the nurse's husband get a loan for his lawn service business back—"

"How did you get Nandy to sign it?" I interrupted.

"Oh, that!" Tinkie's eyes twinkled. "I told her she could never get even with you for stealing Scott if she was locked up in a mental institution."

My grin faded. "You said that."

"Of course not! I was just kidding. I told her that I'd have a little talk with her father and explain the benefits of a trust administered by her husband. A mentally unstable person can't be trusted with large amounts of money. Nandy understood that if her husband was named her executor, she'd be his prisoner for the rest of her natural life. Not *exactly* historically accurate, but close enough."

"Tinkie, you are a genius!" I gave her a big hug before we parted in the parking lot and I drove home to prepare for my date.

27

I HELD THE WHITE RAYON DRESS IN FRONT OF ME AND STARED IN the mirror. It was perfect, except for the buttons. Faux pearl was just a little too dressy. I let the hanger slip from my fingers and reached into the closet for my favorite green skirt.

"Why bother with clothes? You won't keep 'em on more than five minutes."

I had been expecting Jitty, so I wasn't surprised when I heard her caustic voice. I looked behind me and she was standing there, arms akimbo, watching me.

"You're right," I said, frowning, "but I don't want to drive to Scott's house naked. What if I get stopped for speeding?"

"Honey, you're not just speedin', you're committing reckless abandonment. And it ain't behind the wheel I'm talkin' about." Jitty took a seat on the side of my bed and leaned back, her elbows supporting her. She was wearing a pair of low-slung jeans and a halter top made from a red kerchief. A strangely familiar outfit.

"Hey, those are Mama's clothes," I said. My mother had been

very comfortable in the 1960s. She'd had the figure for hip-huggers and navel-revealing tops.

"No, I'm taller than your mama. These are mine."

"You copied them."

"The highest form of flattery, or so they say."

Jitty wasn't about to be shaken by my accusations or criticism, so I decided to tell the truth. "You look very . . . mod." Sleek *and* mod. Being dead, she didn't resort to mashed potatoes, ice cream, grits, and other comfort foods.

"And *you* look frazzled," she pointed out. "I can see your problem. It's hard to know how to dress for this very special occasion. Let's see, what would be appropriate for fish sticks? Maybe something red, to hide the catsup dribbles."

"Ha. Ha." I still held the green skirt and went through several unsuitable blouses before I dropped it to the floor and pulled a pair of black jeans out of the closet. The old classic five-pocket design.

"That looks a little more realistic," Jitty said. "Try the red cotton pullover with the black buttons."

I knew before I got the top out of the drawer that it was the makings of a sharp outfit. Jitty had flair, and I had the perfect pair of black stack mules to wear with it.

"That's a much better ensemble," Jitty said, nodding. "You go prancin' over to his house in a skirt and stockin's, and he's gonna feel bad about the charred wiener he's servin' you on a stale bun."

"I believe the menu is fish sticks," I reminded her. Jitty was contrary as a cornered snake. She'd spent the last year nagging me to find a man. Now that I had one, she wasn't satisfied. I knew her objections. Scott was a bluesman. He was a Yankee. He was a convicted felon and charged with the murder of a symbol for racial harmony. But Jitty's concerns went even deeper than that. Scott wasn't going to stay in Zinnia forever. Probably not for much longer now that Ivory was dead. It was his potential for transitory behavior that had her agitated. Trying to hide my actions, I selected a pair of red lace panties and matching demi-bra.

"Wasted effort," Jitty said. "That man is used to groupies who don't wear undies. Ex-pedient is the byword you should use. You won't win Scott Hampton with Victoria's Secret. Fancy lace panties won't capture his heart."

I decided to take her head-on. "Tell me why you don't like Scott." I already knew all her reasons, but I wanted to make her say them. As she started to talk, I pulled the jeans over my hips, noting how easily they slid up. I'd lost at least five pounds. No wonder. I'd hardly had time to eat.

"It's not that I don't like him," she hedged. "It's just that he's an unknown, Sarah Booth. We really don't know anything about him, except what he's told you. He's not the kind of man to stay put in any one place. He could be gone tomorrow, and probably will be."

I saw it then. For all that Jitty harped on me getting bred and having a baby, she wanted the whole package. She was a true woman of the sixties—she wanted freedom *and* the security of a reliable man. But was that what I wanted? "The fact that Scott may move on isn't a problem for me. I don't believe in forever." I was testing the sentiment even as I said the words. "Maybe I like it that Scott won't stay here permanently." I zipped the jeans and gave a thumbs-up to my image in the mirror.

Jitty was suddenly hovering behind my shoulder. "That's what worries me. That ain't a dream, Sarah Booth. That's hidin' out from a dream."

"Pox on dreams." I was satisfied with my game plan, so why couldn't Jitty leave me alone?

"Dreams don't just happen. You have to work at 'em. I think you're afraid to dream, Sarah Booth."

"I have my dream and it's just fine." I liked the idea of independence. Scott was a man who wouldn't shackle me or try to pin me down. He was an artist. He understood the need to be free. He wouldn't try to define me or confine me like a lot of men.

"Tell me your biggest dream," Jitty said. Her voice was soft, not her usual disapproving tone.

"That would be the success of my detective agency." Ha! I had her there.

"At the sacrifice of everything else?" she asked, and I could see she was troubled. It was a strange twist of events. In the past, Jitty had deviled me endlessly, but I'd never been able to turn the tables. Until now.

"If Delaney Detective Agency doesn't succeed, I won't have this life, and neither will you," I pointed out to her. "I have to focus on making a success of this, above all else." I'd never realized before how true that was. If Scott stayed or left, I would continue with my new career. The detective agency was the constant in my life.

"Sarah Booth, don't squander your dreams on a job. Mortals don't realize how powerful they are. If you can dream it, you have the power to make it happen. You simply have to believe strong enough and focus hard enough." She held my gaze with hers. "You have to let other dreams fall away and choose only one. That's the secret. Now don't you have another dream?"

"I'm too busy on the first one."

Her smile was sad. "What about a family? Wouldn't that be a wonderful dream?"

"I had a family. I lost it." I was suddenly angry with her.

"I know," she said. "You lost your folks young, but now it's time you built another family, one with a steady man, not some blues-singin' guitar man."

"Family is *your* dream. You're the one who's always harping about an heir to the Delaney name." In the past, I'd bought in to Jitty's dream, but now I wasn't so certain.

"And you're the one who's gettin' laid tonight. Just remember, dreams can be suppressed but not destroyed, and I don't think you're tellin' the truth about what you want."

"What is that supposed to mean?"

"Not even Catholics use the rhythm method anymore."

"Taken care of," I assured her. And it would be. I had no desire to be a mother. None. I slipped on the red blouse and my shoes and took a turn in the mirror.

"Don't get serious with Scott. He won't stay here, Sarah Booth. You'll be alone again, and that'll do a lot more damage than you think. Guard your heart, and don't get careless."

"I won't, I will, and I won't," I promised her as I picked up my purse and keys and ran down the stairs. I was almost to the front door when Sweetie Pie came rushing out of the parlor and almost knocked me down.

She stood, tail wagging furiously. She wanted to go with me. "Okay, but no begging at the table," I warned her, knowing that she'd promise anything and then do exactly as she pleased. I opened the door and she shot out and jumped in the front seat of the roadster. I got her sunglasses and a scarf to keep the wind out of her eyes and ears, and we were off.

The night was hot, but driving created a wonderful breeze. Although I hated the heat, I loved many things about summer. There was the smell of fresh-cut grass and ripe watermelons. When I drove through a stand of pines on Bilbo Lane, I could hear the cicadas rising to a crescendo before they fell away to silence.

Turning down Scott's drive, I stopped the car in wonderment. The driveway was lit by at least a hundred candles in white paper sacks. Scott had created this magical starlit path just for me. For such a tough guy, he had a romantic streak a mile wide. I walked to the front door and found the porch alight with more candles. Even more flickering tapers beckoned me inside, and as I stepped into the front room, a shadow moved forward to greet me.

"Sarah Booth," Scott said, gathering me into his arms. "I've been thinking about you all day."

"This is beautiful," I told him. "Thank you."

He kissed me gently before pouring us both wine. The most enticing odor wafted from the kitchen. "What is that?" I asked, sniffing, wondering if I should have worn something with elastic in the waist.

"Prime rib. Not exactly Southern, but I think you'll like it."

"I think you're right."

Like Jitty, I'd halfway expected a "meal in a tin pan" that we didn't bother to eat, opting for bed instead. Scott had other ideas. He'd worked on the dinner all afternoon, and he'd put a lot of thought into the evening. We drank Merlot in coffee cups and ate off mismatched plates, and I'd never had a more elegant meal. As we ate, Scott told me anecdotes and gossip about the music business.

"I didn't realize you were such a host," I said, remembering my earlier fantasy of Scott standing beside me at Dahlia House, hosting an evening. He'd been born to money and gracious manners. He would be a perfect *guest* host.

"I haven't cooked in ages, but there was a time when I enjoyed having company. I'd like to do more of it, with you by my side. Things are going to start changing real fast once I'm found innocent of Ivory's murder. I think you'll really enjoy the music world, if you'll give it a try."

There was no aspect of the entertainment world that fascinated me more than the blues. It would be fabulous to sample it with Scott as my guide. Jitty was wrong. I had plenty of dreams. "I'd really like that," I said. "In between cases, of course."

"Of course," he agreed.

For dessert, he'd made a tart from the sand pears on the tree outside his door. I was impressed and told him so.

"Coffee?" he asked. "Fresh from the Folger's bean, roasted and ground only moments before you arrived."

"I couldn't turn that down."

When we both had steaming mugs, he reached across the table and took my hand. "Where are we going, Sarah Booth?"

I'd changed locations and conversational partners, but not the topic. It was as if Jitty was directing from the wings. "What do you mean?" I asked, stumbling into the conversation I'd never expected to have with Scott.

"I've never known anyone like you, Sarah Booth."

Sweeter words could never be spoken to a woman, but something in me had changed. I didn't want declarations of permanence. I wanted only this moment. I didn't want to think about a future. I didn't even want to know what Scott might be offering. What I'd said to Jitty was true. I didn't want a family—or any of the branches of one. At least not now.

I sipped my coffee, forcing myself to look him in the eye. "Do we have to be going anywhere?"

His pale eyes grew troubled. "You're the first woman I've ever seen a future with. Don't you want to be going somewhere?" He was puzzled by my reaction, but calm.

"I'm a detective. Not a wife. Not a mother." For the first time in my life, I had a crystal-clear view of myself, and for the moment it didn't involve a spouse. I had a sudden revelation—perhaps this was the appeal of Coleman. There, yet unattainable. And, in some part, Scott too. He would move on; it was inevitable.

"Don't you ever want to marry?" he asked.

"I don't know." My lack of a matrimonial direction was just another sign of my failing as a Daddy's Girl. Every DG knew from the first moment of consciousness where she was going. She had her eye on the shoreline, with a perfect vision of what her future would be. I was just drifting.

There was a long silence. "You're involved with the sheriff, aren't you?" he asked.

"No, I'm not." The denial was quick.

"Involved may not be the right word. You have strong feelings for him, don't you?"

Scott was a perceptive man. He'd seen more than I thought. "He's married."

Scott took my hand and held it. "And you wish he weren't."

There was no point denying that. Besides, I couldn't lie to Scott. I hated a liar. "But he is. And he wants to make his marriage work," I said gently.

Scott's grip on my hand tightened. "I'm beginning to fall in love with you. It scares the hell out of me."

"That's not very flattering," I said, wanting desperately to veer from this serious path Scott had chosen. We had a long stretch of smooth water in front of us where we could glide and drift together, without commitment to any particular course. Why couldn't we simply be? "I don't have a warning label, you know."

"Maybe you should, Sarah Booth. I think you could be lethal if you chose."

He dropped my hands and looked down at the floor. "It's

probably for the best. If I were lucky enough to have you love me, I'd just lose you. Everyone I've ever cared about is dead."

My heart didn't break, but it cracked a little. I knew how it felt to be left behind.

"People always think prison is bad," he continued. "Losing the people you love is much worse. That's my life sentence—whoever I love, dies."

"That's ridiculous," I said softly. "Nothing's going to happen to me." But I knew what he meant, and I knew how terrifying it was to feel that loss was first cousin to love.

"Tell me one thing, Sarah Booth, are you irrevocably in love with the sheriff?"

I picked up Scott's hand and held on to him. I could hedge the truth because my feelings for Coleman, whatever they were, would come to naught. But I owed Scott as much truth as I knew. "I don't know," I said, and it came out in a whisper. "I've been so very careful not to think about the possibility. It's wrong. Coleman is off-limits to me now and possibly forever. That's the reality. That's what I live with. How can I say if I love him when I haven't allowed myself the possibility?"

"Reality has nothing to do with emotions. All the facts in the world won't change how you feel. You just have to decide what you feel."

"Why?" I asked. "Why torture myself?"

"Because you feel what you feel, Sarah Booth, and that's important. Not naming those feelings is just a way of tricking yourself. And when you're doing that, you're—" He broke off suddenly.

I glanced toward the front door, where Sweetie Pie was moaning softly. She'd been a perfect angel all evening, begging only half a loaf of garlic bread and at least a pound of beef.

"What's the matter?" I asked her.

She gave a sharp yap and then growled deep in her throat. There was the distinct sound of footsteps running in the gravel of the drive.

"There's someone out there," I said.

Scott stood and put his napkin on the table. "I'll check."

"I'm going, too." I followed him to the door. As soon as we opened it, Sweetie Pie went flying out into the night. She didn't bother with the steps; she leaped to the ground and began to run, baying loudly.

"What the—"

Scott never got to finish. Something whizzed by my head and crashed into the front door. There was the smell of gasoline and the whoosh of flames. The explosion was like a sledgehammer in my back. Suddenly I was flying through the air. The last thing I remembered was hitting the dirt.

"Sarah Booth, you have to wake up. I'm tired of standing here in these heels, waiting for you to do something other than drool out the side of your mouth. Open your eyes, right this minute."

I cracked an eyelid open. Tinkie's face filled my vision, and though she was slightly blurred, there was no mistaking her. "Quit nagging at me," I said.

Her answer was a loud squeal that made me squint my eyes shut.

"Open those eyes," Tinkie ordered again.

When I did, Tinkie had been joined by Cece. The two of them were hovering over me. I thought of the Harpies, but I knew better than to say anything. I was already injured. I wasn't sure how or why, but my body was screaming at me in a thousand different places.

"Where am I?" I couldn't see much of my surroundings, but I wasn't at Dahlia House. Then I remembered. I'd been at Scott's. Something awful had happened. "Where's Scott?"

"He's okay," Tinkie said, putting a gentle hand on my forehead. "He's been released, minor injuries. Coleman took him in for questioning. You're the one that has everyone worried because you wouldn't wake up. Doc wouldn't let them take you to a room. You're in the ER, where he could personally keep an eye on you. He just went to make a phone call."

I tried to turn my head to glance around, but a warning pain convinced me to take it slowly. "What happened?"

"Someone tried to kill you, dahling," Cece said. "Molotov cocktail. But cheer up. You're going to be in the paper tomorrow. Rather a ghastly picture, though. Not your best side, what with your butt up in the air. We couldn't find an angle that made it look smaller." She shrugged. "Of course, those black stack mules on the porch show you have dainty feet."

"You were blown right out of your shoes," Tinkie said.

"Front page!" Cece said.

I glared at her. "Never let injuries to a good friend stand in the way of a headline."

"They arrested Emanuel," Cece responded, knowing it would derail my tirade.

"Emanuel Keys?" I was shocked.

"No, Emanuel Gable, Clark's illegitimate son," Cece snapped. "Of course Emanuel Keys."

"Why?"

"Because Coleman thinks he tried to kill you and Scott," Cece said with impatience. She was acting ornery because she'd been so worried about me. It was one of her least charming traits.

Tinkie frowned at her. "She's had her brain scrambled. Don't be so snappy."

"I was asking why Emanuel was trying to kill us," I said, rather irritated myself. My body was a jangle of pain. Even my fingers hurt.

Tinkie answered this one. "Coleman caught Emanuel speeding away from Scott's house. There was another bottle of gasoline and a rag in the trunk of his car."

"Wow." I was still a little confused on the details of what had happened. One minute I'd been drinking coffee with Scott, and the next, I was flying across the front yard. "How did Coleman get there so quickly?"

Cece and Tinkie exchanged glances. It took me a couple of seconds, but I worked it out. "Coleman followed me to Scott's, didn't he?"

Instead of answering, they stepped back. Coleman stepped into view.

"Sarah Booth," he whispered, putting the backs of his fingers against my cheek. "You've scared ten years off my life. When I saw you in the yard . . ." He shook his head.

"I'm okay."

"Doc said you were mighty lucky."

"Did you see Emanuel throw the Molotov cocktail?" I asked.

His smile was both sad and tender. "When you're on a case, you're on. That's a good sign. Mule-headedness is normal for you." He took a deep breath. "I didn't see Emanuel throw the bomb, but I was turning onto Bilbo Lane when I heard the explosion. About five minutes later, Emanuel passed me doing at least a hundred. I radioed Dewayne, and he caught him on the south side of town. Emanuel was running hard and had all the makings for another bomb in his trunk."

I wasn't surprised, but I suddenly remembered something more important than Emanuel. "Sweetie Pie! She was with me."

"She's fine," Tinkie said. "Coleman brought her to my house and she's playing with Chablis."

"Was she hurt?"

This time it was Tinkie and Coleman who exchanged glances, and I knew instantly that something wasn't right with my dog. "Was she hurt?" I asked again.

"She's fine now," Coleman said. "She got a few scrapes. She was hit by a car, but it was a glancing blow and she's fine."

I started to get up, but a sudden pain shot through my midriff. "Boll weevil!" I gasped. "How badly am I hurt?" I asked Coleman because he would tell me the truth.

"You're bunged up pretty good, but nothing fatal. Bruised ribs, lost a good bit of hide from your left arm, singed off a lot of your hair."

I thought of all the gel and hair spray I'd loaded into my hair. It was a wonder I hadn't gone up like a human torch.

"Can I leave?"

"As soon as Doc releases you," Tinkie said, "I'll take you home."

"Why would Emanuel do this?" I asked.

"I think he was trying to kill Scott. That would solve a lot of problems for him. With Scott charged with Ivory's murder, there's the possibility that the case would be closed without further investigation."

I knew Coleman well enough to know that that would be only Emanuel's fantasy. "I suppose I was just an innocent bystander?"

"I don't think there's any love lost on you from Emanuel's point of view," Coleman said. "Two for the price of one."

"Did he admit that he did it?"

"Hell, no, he's proclaiming his innocence." He leaned down closer, but not before I saw the grin on his face. "And he's asking to see you."

I didn't bother to hide my surprise. "Me? Why?"

"He says he wants to hire you."

EMANUEL WAS HOLDING on to the bars of his cell when I entered the jail, walking very slowly and carefully. Part of my caution was my battered body, but most of it came from the fact that I was wearing a pair of Tinkie's slacks. Any rash movement might split a seam. Tinkie had deliberately chosen the pale pink silk slacks that were capris on my taller frame. She'd known they would hug my butt like Saran Wrap. It was her method of showing disapproval for my "mule-headed" decision to talk to Emanuel tonight. She'd tried to refuse to drive me to the jail, insisting that I should be in bed. At the moment, she was sitting with Coleman in his office, discussing my "clinical stubbornness."

I watched Emanuel watching me with what could only be called contempt.

"Crime is obviously down in Sunflower County," I said, indicating the empty cells I passed on my way to Emanuel. "Except for attempted murder. Coleman said you wanted to see me."

"I didn't think you'd come," he said.

"That makes us even," I said. "I didn't think you'd ask for me."

He snorted, lowering his head as he held on to the bars. "Me and you can never be even. In case you haven't noticed, you're white."

"That won't work with me, Emanuel," I said with a bit of heat. "In case *you* haven't noticed, you're the man charged with trying to kill me, yet here I am, willing to listen to your story. And let me point out that I'm about the only person in town who's willing to listen to anything you have to say."

"Everything they're saying is a pack of lies. I didn't try to kill anyone. They've been trying to put me right here in this jail for years. Now they have me locked away on some trumped-up charge."

"Who is this *they?*" I asked. "Coleman? The law? The town? The county? Who, exactly, is it that has it in for you?"

"Why are you here?" he asked with some aggression.

"Because of your mother. This is going to kill her, having you locked up like this. And there's one other reason."

His eyes narrowed. "You believe I'm innocent?"

"No," I said, because it was true. Emanuel had enough hate to fuel an attempt to kill Scott. "What I want is to show you that not every decision in Sunflower County is made on race. I'll look into your *claims* of innocence. For your mother and because that's what I do."

Emanuel's hands tightened on the bars and I could only imagine that he wished it were my throat. "I didn't throw a Molotov cocktail. I'm being framed. Someone put that stuff in my car."

"What were you doing at Scott's?"

"I got a call. The man said if I wanted the evidence that would convict Scott, I should meet him on Bilbo Lane." He looked down, and I couldn't tell if he was lying or simply feeling stupid.

"You knew that was where Scott lived." I wasn't going to let him get away with playing dumb.

"Yeah, I knew that. I assumed Scott wouldn't be home and I wasn't going on his property. I figured the man who called would want some money. I was willing to pay."

"So you were driving along Bilbo Lane waiting to meet someone. How did the makings of a Molotov cocktail get in your car?"

Emanuel looked up at me. "The man told me where to park in the woods, and then I was supposed to walk down the road. He was going to meet me and give me the evidence against Scott. I did exactly as he said, but no one ever showed up. I was walking back to my car when I heard the bomb. I panicked. I ran back to my car, got in, and drove. I passed the sheriff, and I knew then I'd been set up."

"You were running," I said flatly.

He nodded. "I knew I was in big trouble. I was just trying to put some distance between me and whatever terrible thing had happened at Scott's house."

"I guess it never occurred to you that Scott might be badly injured."

He came at the bars so suddenly that I stepped back. "I didn't care. I don't care. I wish he was dead."

"That's exactly the reason you're behind those bars," I said as coolly as I could manage with my heart thumping. Emanuel frightened me. He was consumed with anger and hatred, and Scott had become the focus for a lot of it.

"Get out of here," he said through clenched teeth. "I knew you wouldn't help me."

"I'm going to see your mother," I told him, glad that the bars were between us.

"Leave her out of this!"

If he could frighten me, I could agitate him. "I would gladly leave Ida Mae out of this, but you made sure she was in the middle of it when you drove out to Bilbo Lane."

"I didn't throw that Molotov cocktail."

"Who is this mystery man who called?"

"He was a white man."

"You're certain of that? Or are you just being racist?" I'd discovered quite a talent in bruise-mashing where Emanuel was concerned.

"He was white, but he didn't sound like he was from here."

"How so?"

"Maybe like he was educated or pretending to be educated. Or like he'd been living somewhere else for a time."

"I'm sure Coleman will check your phone records. If this pans out, we've at least got a lead to pursue."

"You're taking my case?"

"No," I said with some satisfaction. "I can't. Conflict of interest since I'm already working for Scott. But I'll do what I can to find the truth."

28

"DON'T YOU DARE GO TAKING UP FOR EMANUEL. HE HAD THE makings of another Molotov cocktail in his car," Tinkie insisted as she drove me home. "He abducted and intimidated a teenage girl!" It was close to midnight and I was hurting and exhausted. Sweetie Pie, who was far wiser, was resting in the backseat of the Cadillac. Like me, she had lost a bit of hide. The big difference was that she still wagged her tail. Mine was dragging.

"He says he didn't do it—the Molotov cocktail, anyway. I didn't ask him about Trina," I felt obligated to point out.

"Yeah, like he would confess to the woman he nearly blew to smithereens. He can say what he wants to. The hard facts show he had all the ingredients for a Molotov cocktail in his car, including a box of detergent to make sure it would have some oomph. I guess when he saw you flying through the air, he figured he didn't need to throw the second one." Tinkie was talking with both hands and steering the big Cadillac with her knees. Luckily there were no other cars on the road.

"He says someone planted all that stuff on him. His finger-prints weren't on the wine bottle."

"There were *no prints at all* on the bottle!"

"Which is exactly the same scenario with the prison shank found in Scott's motorcycle bags." I found that significant, and Tinkie would, too, if she'd give herself half a chance.

"It was cheap wine." Tinkie sniffed. "He could have used *it* as an inflammatory instead of gasoline."

Tinkie's moments of snobbery were extremely rare, so I decided to ignore this one. "Other than the bottle of gasoline—"

"Stuffed with a rag," Tinkie pointed out.

"Was there any other evidence?" While I was talking to Emanuel, Tinkie had gotten the pertinent legal facts from Coleman.

"Emanuel was there right at the time the bomb was thrown. What was he doing hanging around Scott's house if he wasn't up to meanness? He's not a friend of yours or Scott's."

I repeated the story Emanuel had told me.

"Very convenient," Tinkie said, "especially since *I* think he killed his daddy."

I didn't say anything as I turned the facts I knew in all direc-tions. Tinkie was absolutely right. If Emanuel killed Ivory and was responsible for setting Scott up for the murder, this story that he was out on Bilbo Lane searching for evidence against Scott was a perfect cover for his own guilt.

"Is Emanuel deluded or is he putting up a smoke screen?" I asked.

"I vote for the second scenario," Tinkie said. She turned into Dahlia House. "What the hay!"

I looked down the drive and saw nothing out of the ordinary, until I remembered that I'd left my car at Scott's. My car! There it was, sitting right in front of Dahlia House.

It had been parked right by Scott's cottage when the bomb went off. I only had five more payments on the old classic, but more importantly, I loved that car. "Was my car damaged in the explosion?"

"The car wasn't hurt," Tinkie said soothingly. "We were a lot more worried about you and Sweetie Pie than the car, but Coleman looked it over carefully."

"Thank goodness," I said, surprised at my concern for a heap of metal.

"I just wonder how it got here. I . . ." Tinkie didn't bother to finish, since we were pulling up at the front door. Both her question and mine were answered when Scott stood up on the front steps.

"Here's your car. I would have brought it to the hospital, but the sheriff said he'd put me in jail if he caught me within ten yards of the emergency room. Must be nice to have the law protecting you like a little jewel."

"Scott!" I got out of the car and despite my wounds and Tinkie's skintight pants, I hurried over to him. He stepped back from me, one hand raised to chest level. I realized someone had told him about my ribs. "I'm okay. Just a few minor burns and bruises."

"Good for you."

I stepped to the left so I could get a better look at him in the dim light of the front porch. "What's wrong?"

"I brought your car back. If something happened to it, I didn't want it blamed on me." He pressed the keys into my palm and started walking away. I grabbed his sleeve. Only a few hours before, he'd been falling in love with me. Now he acted like I had head lice. "Scott! What's wrong?"

"Not a thing, Sarah Booth. Your car is just fine." He didn't even look at me as he spoke.

"What's wrong with you?" I didn't care that Tinkie was a witness to our first argument. There was a coldness in Scott that gave me a feeling of great urgency.

"Okay, you want to do this now, then we will. You're fired, Sarah Booth. I don't want you working on my case anymore. I don't want you anywhere around me. Every time you get within twenty feet of me, something bad happens and I'm in trouble again. The sheriff made it abundantly clear that you're his property, and that was how *you* wanted it. I finally understand. Just stay away from me."

A sharp pain caught me just below the sternum. "You can't fire me. You didn't hire me," I reminded him. "And I don't belong to anyone."

"Right. You're a free agent, an independent woman. Maybe you'd better tell that to Coleman Peters," he said with an ugly twist to his mouth. "I'll speak to Ida Mae and tell her she's wasting her money on you. You haven't done a thing to help my case. In fact, you've only made things worse for me. I'll make sure Ida Mae sees that."

"You go right ahead." I was finding it hard to breathe, and it wasn't due to my injured ribs. Something serious was happening around my heart. "Talk to Ida Mae. Her son is in jail for trying to kill you, and you're charged with the murder of her husband. That's peachy for her. Go ahead and load a few more things on her back."

Scott's pale eyes glittered. "Listen, that guilt crap won't work with me. In fact, nothing about you works for me anymore. For one split second, I saw something in you—or I thought I saw it. Then I got a reality check. You aren't anything special. You're mildly interesting in the sack, but I'm afraid I just lost interest. I don't need you hovering over me." He turned to Tinkie. "Keep her away from me, I don't need another stalker. Nandy was enough."

I watched him walk to the shadows beside the house. I hadn't noticed the motorcycle until he got on it. He stood with his foot on the starter. "Lucky for me I've got a few real friends who look out for me. Otherwise, I guess I'd have to walk home." He kicked the bike into life and scattered gravel as he took off.

"Charming," Tinkie said as she grabbed my elbow to lead me up the steps. "I can't believe you threw Bridge Ladnier over for him."

TINKIE LEFT ME with great reluctance, but when she was gone, I did exactly as Doc Sawyer had told me not to. I made a very large Jack on the rocks and I ran a very hot bath. After a fifteen-minute soak, I was no more relaxed. Scott's words continued to buzz loudly in my brain.

Pacing my bedroom and wondering where Jitty might be, I finally saw the red light of my answering machine blinking. There was only one message and it was from Bridge.

"Sarah Booth, the most extraordinary thing has happened. Someone has stolen my car. Please call me when you get home, no matter what time it is."

My heart was still blistered by Scott's harsh rejection, and Bridge was the perfect balm. He'd never say I was "mildly interesting." I dialed his number. After ten rings, his answering service picked up, but I didn't leave a message.

I found a book, crawled into bed, and lay staring at the ceiling for another fifteen minutes. What had happened to make Scott hate me so? No matter what Coleman might have said, Scott hadn't given me a chance to explain.

Finally, at one o'clock, I phoned Bridge again. Still no answer. The idea that Bridge might need my help with his stolen car came as a terrific relief. In less than five minutes I was driving toward Bridge's.

Zinnia was empty. The three traffic lights in town had been set to blink a red warning, but there was no need to stop. I cruised past the darkened businesses and took a left into the residential section. Passing Cece's house, I noticed the lights on. She was finding it impossible to sleep—or else she was writing copy for the next edition. She was a workaholic.

Bridge's house was dark, and his car was parked in the driveway. I was a little disappointed that he must have recovered it already. My help wasn't really needed, but since I was there, I knocked on the front door. When no one answered, I knocked again. It was possible he'd fallen asleep. I didn't want to go home and be alone.

My hand slipped to the doorknob and it turned with ease. The door opened without even a creak.

"Bridge!" I called his name softly, then louder. Surely he was in the house. The idea that he might be injured came as something of a shock. "Bridge!" What if he'd accosted the car thieves and they'd done something to him?

I crept inside and made my way through the house, room by room. He simply wasn't at home. Standing in the middle of his bedroom, I didn't know what to do next. My purpose in coming to see Bridge had been more about my needs than his. I'd come to him for solace. Now I was standing alone in the middle of his bedroom. Bridge either had good taste or an expensive decorator. Oak furniture in a sleek Scandinavian style kept the focus on a big brass bed covered in silk sheets and a brocade coverlet.

The only ornate note in the room was a mahogany chest sitting on top of the dresser. It was obviously one of the few family heirlooms that Bridge had brought with him to the rental house.

I started back to the front door when I remembered my earring. I could retrieve it now and leave Bridge a note. A search of the guest bathroom yielded no sign of it. I went back to Bridge's bedroom and the little ornate chest, which probably held his personal items. Feeling only a little guilty, I opened the top drawer. Credit cards, business cards, and several keys were scattered about. The second drawer was deeper, and in it were two watches, a couple of rings, and cuff links.

Bridge wasn't a man who wore a lot of jewelry, and I picked up the rings and cuff links, curious to see if my earring was mixed up in the jumble and also to see what his taste ran toward. As soon as I turned over the onyx cuff link, my fingers went numb. I held it up and kept looking at it, hoping that somehow it would change. But it didn't. The white ivory bones, crossed at the center, were a perfect contrast to the onyx.

In rapid succession, scenes flashed through my memory, where Bridge displayed interest and curiosity in my case, in Scott, in the club, in the legendary records. I'd thought he was interested in me. And he was, but for the wrong reason.

Very carefully I put Bridge's jewelry back in the chest, closed the drawer, and stepped back. Each movement took incredible effort. Crossing the bedroom, I walked through the door, down the hall, and to the front door. My arms and legs were stiff as I opened the door and closed it firmly behind me.

My mind was fast-forwarding through my various dates with Bridge. The blues had been a constant theme. We'd even talked about the symbolism of the crossed bones. Not once had he ever indicated that the symbol meant something to him. I'd thought him so philanthropical, wanting to buy Playin' the Bones from Ida Mae. But he didn't want the club as much as he wanted what he thought was hidden there. Those damn records. If they even existed.

But did he want them bad enough to torture an old man and kill him? Somehow, I just couldn't picture Bridge that way.

My roadster was parked farther down the drive, but I went to Bridge's car. He'd reported it stolen, yet here it was. I walked to the front of it and looked at the fender. There was just a small dent, and what looked like blood and hair. Someone had struck my dog and kept going. If this was Sweetie Pie's blood and hair, then it was Bridge. My stomach roiled. In the time I'd spent with Bridge, I would never have believed he was capable of murder, or even hit-and-run on a dog. But the initial evidence—Emanuel had said the voice on the phone sounded educated—showed I might be wrong about his character.

I'd learned enough as a detective to know I needed solid fact, not conjecture. As soon as I got to a phone, I'd call Coleman and get him to examine Bridge's car.

I swallowed hard to keep down the nausea. This wasn't the place to be sick. I had to get away before Bridge came home and found me.

THROUGH THE LONG hours of the morning, I sat out in the barn with Reveler. Sweetie stayed at my feet, occasionally licking my ankles. I studied each piece of the puzzle and tried to fit it into the new shape of Bridge Ladnier. It didn't seem possible, but the evidence told the story of Bridge's guilt. He had the opportunity to commit every act that spoke of guilt.

When dawn broke the eastern sky, I went in the house, bathed, dressed, put on a pot of coffee, and called Tinkie. She was barely awake, but when I told her about the cuff links, she woke right up.

"Bridge and crossed bones!" I could hear her tap-tapping across the floor in her high-heeled bedroom slippers. Even in a crisis, Tinkie didn't abandon the necessity of looking good. "I'm getting dressed."

"I'll put some bacon on," I said.

"Don't bother. I'm going to find Oscar. He went to the bank early this morning to get some papers straight for the auditor. If Oscar brought home a man who would hit a dog and then leave the scene, he's going to have some explaining to do. I'll swing by the bakery on my way to your house."

"Fine," I said, because it was the polite thing to do. In truth, I needed to be in the kitchen cooking. Southern women, and perhaps women all over the world, turn to cooking in times of high drama. I was ready for a grit soufflé with sausage crumbles. Whatever Tinkie brought from the bakery, the soufflé would be the perfect complement. And I needed to keep my hands busy, because my brain was in overdrive.

The soufflé was in the oven when I heard Tinkie tap on the front door and enter. There was something wrong, though. She was walking like an old lady. The swinging door opened, and Tinkie entered, Chablis and a bag of pastry in her arms. As soon as the pampered little Yorkie saw Sweetie, she leaped to the floor and the two dogs took off through the doggie door.

Tinkie put the bakery bag on the table and took a seat. "I had to threaten Oscar with a sexless future, but I got him to tell me about the cuff links." She stared at her perfectly manicured hands as she talked, her voice a monotone.

I got a cup of coffee for her. She didn't even touch it. She hadn't commented on the aroma of the baking soufflé—Tinkie was gravely depressed.

"What did he say?" I asked, getting a plate and dumping the bag of fresh crullers on it. I pushed the plate toward her, but she just shook her head.

"My stomach's in a knot. Sarah Booth, I don't know what to say."

"Tinkie, what happened?" My own stomach was twisting and churning. My friend was in pain. "What did you find out?"

"Oscar knew all about the cuff links because he has a pair, too. They're hidden in a special drawer in his desk at home. Both of them belong to a secret club for rich boys. Rich men, I should say. They joined the Skull and Bones Club at Ole Miss and they've been members all this time."

"And?" I prompted. I tried not to show any of the stampeding emotions I felt.

"They call it S&B for short, and the members are dedicated to becoming multimillionaires. A lot of very powerful men are members. Former presidents, world leaders, men who control oil and gas and other energy supplies."

"A secret rich-guy society," I said, immediately seeing the potential for a lot of unethical wheeling and dealing on a global level, not just in Zinnia. But it was the local application of the bones symbol that had me worried. Rich men were just as capable of murder as poor. But what if the symbols were somehow linked? Piracy seemed a common theme among all three of the groups I knew about: the S&B, the Bonesmen, and the Dominoes.

"Oscar has belonged to this organization for years!" Tinkie said in the midst of a rant. "He's gone to meetings and lied to me about what he was doing. It's like he's hidden a part of his identity from me. It's wrong."

I saw her point immediately. "Did he say why he lied to you?"

"They take an oath. Everything is secret, and the membership is all male, of course." She blinked away a tear. "Oscar never mentioned a word of this to me."

I went to Tinkie and put my hands on her shoulders as she slumped at the table. Tinkie was an all-or-nothing person. It was one of her traits that I loved best. She'd given herself to Oscar completely, and now she'd discovered that he'd held back this part of himself. She was devastated and feeling more than a little betrayed.

"I'm sorry, Tinkie." I rubbed her shoulders lightly.

"Oscar could have told me. I've never divulged anything he's ever told me in confidence."

"This isn't about you, it's about him," I pointed out to her. She turned around in her chair and looked up at me, eyes brimming with tears.

"Thank you, Sarah Booth." Her chin lifted. "Can you believe it? A secret club with no girls allowed. Talk about discrimination!" Color was coming back into her face. "One thing Oscar's going to learn the hard way. If he has secrets, I'm going to get a few of my own. What's sauce for the goose is sauce for the gander."

I was relieved to see her spirits picking back up, but more than a little worried. Tinkie had once considered having an affair, primarily because Oscar was ignoring her. But she wasn't the kind of woman to lie and deceive, not even when the code of Daddy's Girls allowed it. "Don't do anything rash, Tinkie," I counseled.

"I'll show Oscar rash! To hell with Oscar and his foolishness. Let's get on with the case."

Tinkie was sitting up straight now, a flush of anger on her cheeks. She picked up a cruller and bit it in half. "What's that wonderful aroma I smell?"

I gave her a hug and took the soufflé out of the oven. It was a perfect golden brown on top. When we both had a plate before us, I sat down. "What did you learn about Bridge?"

"He came to Zinnia to talk to Ivory Keys. He told Oscar he was going to make a lot of money. When he found out from Oscar that you were working for Scott, he asked Oscar to set the two of you up."

"Oh." My fragile ego turned black and shriveled to a crisp, but it was further proof of Bridge's guilt. He'd dated me only to find out what I knew. "What did Oscar say?"

"He thought it was great. Oscar likes you, Sarah Booth, and he thought Bridge would be perfect for you."

I'd make it a point not to let Oscar introduce me to any more of his friends in the future. "What did he say about the Bones symbolism?"

"He says the Skull and Bones has nothing to do with Ivory Keys' death. He insists the secret club is harmless. When I told him about Ivory being cut like that, he was very upset."

"Did he know if Bridge and Ivory had ever met?"

"He said Bridge was distressed when Ivory was killed *before* he got a chance to conduct his business with him."

"He never told Oscar what his business might be?" I asked.

"Maybe we should just ask Bridge what he's up to," Tinkie said.

"I doubt he'll confess to trying to bomb me and Scott to smithereens," I said dryly.

"Do you really think he struck Sweetie and kept going?" Tinkie didn't want to believe this. A doggie hit-and-run was obviously far more serious than trying to blow up me and Scott, but I didn't let it hurt my feelings. We were talking about Sweetie Pie, after all. "I'll bet those awful biker boys were on his payroll!"

"I don't know," I said, "but I don't think we can afford to just go and talk to him. I don't think he'll tell us the truth." But Tinkie's observation sounded right on. If Bridge was behind Ivory's death, it was very likely that he'd hired someone to do the dirty work. Ray-Ban and Spider fit the bill perfectly, and I didn't think they were smart enough to think up such a scheme on their own.

"What about Scott? He fired us."

"He can't fire either of us, but even if he could, he only fired me," I said. "He didn't fire you."

Her face lit up. "You're right, he didn't!"

"So what I want you to do is tell Coleman about the blood and hair on Bridge's car. I was going to call him, but it would be better if you did it."

"What are you going to do?" Tinkie was looking at the bandage on my arm with motherly concern.

"Just a little visiting." I smiled as convincingly as I knew how.

"You're not going to see that awful man, are you?" She was

referring to Scott. "He treated you terrible, Sarah Booth." She lowered her voice. "He said you were *mildly* interesting in bed. That rumor could ruin you!"

"I'm not calling on Scott," I assured her. And I wasn't. I might prove him innocent of murder, because it was my job, but I had no intention of ever talking to him again. He'd lashed out and hurt me without giving me a chance to defend myself.

"I'll talk to Coleman." She gave me a sympathetic look. "You're in a real romantic mess, aren't you? Coleman, Scott, Bridge." She counted off the names on her fingers.

Instead of answering, I served her the soufflé. She forgot about counting romantic mistakes and picked up her fork. "This is delicious, Sarah Booth."

"Thanks." I wasn't really hungry; I'd just needed to cook. Now I was ready to talk to Ida Mae.

THE DRIVE TO Ida Mae's did nothing to soothe my bruised and battered heart, not to mention my sore ribs. A vicious killer was on the loose, and I intended to ferret him out. I climbed the steps and knocked at Ida Mae's door. Wearing a navy suit, navy stockings, and navy pumps, Ida Mae held a navy hat in her hand. She was ready to go out.

"I heard what Emanuel did," she said. "I was headed to your house to check on you."

"I'm fine," I assured her. "Scott isn't hurt at all."

"Sarah Booth, I don't know what to say. I was wrong to hire you on this case."

My face must have reflected my pain, because she pushed open the screen and stepped out onto the porch to put her arm around me.

"I'm not criticizing your work, child, I'm trying to say I'm sorry you were hurt."

Relief made me smile. "It's only a few bruises."

"Come inside and tell me, did my son do this?" she asked.

I followed her into the living room and took a seat before I answered. "I don't know. To be honest, I don't think he did."

"He called this morning, wanting me to bond him out. I'm not going to. I think it best he stays in jail. When I told him that, he got very angry."

I could see where it would tend to make Emanuel mad. Ida Mae would have bonded Scott out, yet she wouldn't help her own son.

"I told him I was afraid for him to be out on the streets. Either he's going to really hurt someone, or someone is going to hurt him."

I saw the sorrow in Ida Mae's eyes, and I admired her more at that moment than ever before. How difficult it must be not to give a child what he wanted. Instead of trying to win Emanuel's love, she was trying to save his hide.

"I'll talk to him." He was one of the few primaries in the case I could talk to. "I'll explain."

She shook her head. "He won't listen, but you can try. If you don't think he did it, who do you think did?"

"I don't want to say, but I have a question for you. The recordings with Elvis and Hotlips that Ivory talked about, what happened to them?"

"Why are those old records suddenly so important?"

"Were they at the club?" I pressed.

She understood then. "You think Ivory was killed for those recordings?"

"I can't even guess at their value."

She stared out through the window at the bobbing sunflowers and thought. "I don't know where they are. The last thing Ivory said about them was that a lot of folks thought the blues was the devil's music, but that sometimes the devil's tune could lead a lost soul home."

"What does that mean?" I wanted an answer, not a riddle.

"I don't know for sure. The only thing I know is that those recordings meant a lot more to Ivory than money. They were part of his dream."

"When was the last time you saw them?"

"About a year ago."

"And he never mentioned them again?" I was astounded. Obviously neither Ida Mae nor Ivory had a clue how valuable those recordings might be.

"He said he'd cast them on the water hoping they'd multiply, but that it might turn out to be pearls before swine. That's the last I heard."

I knew instantly where the recordings were. "Thank you, Ida Mae." I stood up, almost running from the room. "I'll be in touch."

29

ON THE WAY TO THE COURTHOUSE, I USED THE CELL PHONE
Tinkie had badgered me into getting, to call an old friend, country
diva Krystal Brook. It took Krystal three phone calls and ten minutes to get me an estimate of the value of those recordings.
Between eight and ten million dollars.

I was still in sticker shock when I hurried down the jail aisle toward a waiting Emanuel Keys.

"Did Mama send you with the bond money?" he asked. "Is she
getting me out of here?"

"Where are those recordings?" I watched him closely. Confusion was quickly followed by gloat when he realized what I was
talking about.

"They're in a place where no one will ever hear them. That music is a sin. I'm ashamed that my daddy and the others were playing and singing with that rockabilly white man." His voice grew
bitter. "You should hear them, laughing and cutting up like
they're *brothers*." His mouth twisted. "It's disgusting."

I could barely breathe. What Emanuel had were live sessions, including all the horseplay among the musicians! "Those records are worth millions."

His features grew even harder. "It doesn't matter how much they're worth. Daddy gave them to me. They're mine, and I can do anything I want with them." His smile was an ugly thing to see. "I'm going to burn them. I've been waiting for the perfect moment. A big fire and everyone watching them melt, so they can see that principles are more important than money."

I wanted to reach through the bars and jerk his ears off. "You jackass, don't you realize those recordings are the reason your father is dead?"

I felt a lot of different things, but my primary emotion was complete fury at Emanuel. I no longer believed he'd killed Ivory, at least not physically. What he'd done was worse. He'd set out to deliberately destroy something his father loved.

"So you finally believe Scott killed my father." His breath was short. "Scott asked Daddy more than once what happened to those recordings. Scott probably killed him because he wouldn't say what he'd done with them."

"Who knew you had them?" I had no interest in his theories about who killed Ivory. It hadn't been Scott, but I did believe that whoever killed Ivory did it in an attempt to get those recordings.

"You still don't believe—"

"Shut up and listen to me." I had to clench my hands at my sides to keep from reaching through those bars and grabbing any part of his anatomy that would give pain. "Someone wants those recordings. They killed Ivory. They may kill Ida Mae if they think she knows where they are. Now tell me where they are."

Emanuel swallowed. "Let me out of here. I'll get them and tell everyone I have them. They can watch as I melt them."

I was so angry, my voice had grown deadly quiet. "I'll make a proposition. You tell me where those recordings are, and I'll prove that you didn't try to kill Scott and me."

"The sheriff will prove that. I don't need you. I was a fool to ever talk to you." He was cornered and mad—forced to rely on the justice of the white man he hated so much.

"I wouldn't count on Coleman." I stepped back. "The truth of the matter is, no one's hunting very hard to prove you're innocent. Coleman is delighted to have you here, out of harm's way and unable to stir up more trouble. You'll rot in here." I swallowed, knowing that I was defaming Coleman with my lie. "In the meantime, Ida Mae may be the target for someone who wants those recordings bad enough to kill. Again." I started out of the jail. "Live with that, if you can."

"Hey!"

I slowed my pace a fraction.

"Hey, Delaney, come back here and talk to me."

Panic was in his voice, and I felt a stab of satisfaction. "Bite me," I said, almost at the door to the sheriff's office.

"I'll tell you. Come back here."

Those were the only words that could have changed my course. I slowly walked back to stand in front of his cell.

"If you're messing with me, you may find yourself responsible for your mother's death. Where are those recordings, and who all knows about them?"

Emanuel's eyes grew unfocused. "Mama doesn't know where they are. Nobody does but me."

We stared at each other. I wasn't going to try and convince him. He had to decide if his hatred was more important than his mother's safety, or his freedom.

Time passed, perhaps a minute. Then he nodded. "Behind the old high school there's a dirt road. It leads to—"

"Wilbur Ward's house." I knew it well. I'd played hooky from school once or twice, and that was the escape route. Mr. Ward would be sitting on his front porch, rocking, watching us sneak away. He was older than dirt, but he knew how to keep his lip zipped. He'd never ratted on us a single time.

"There's a shed behind his house. In the shed is an old refrigerator. The records are in there."

"In a refrigerator!" I couldn't hide my dismay. With the temperatures in the high 90s, the records would be a blob of melted vinyl by now.

"I pay Mr. Ward's electric bill. He keeps the fridge cool for me."

I blew air out. "I'm going to get them now." I started toward the exit again. "I'll be back."

"Hey! You said you'd get me out of here."

"And I will. As soon as I get those records."

"How are you going to get me out?" He was yelling. "Tell me."

I didn't like Emanuel, but I owed him the truth. "My dog was struck by a vehicle at Scott's house the night the bomb was thrown. Your car was clean."

"Who threw that Molotov cocktail?"

"I'll tell you when I know for certain. The only thing that should concern you is that I know you didn't."

"What are you going to do with those records?"

The man had a one-track mind. "Use them," I said, and I couldn't hide the smile.

"Use them how?" He was growing belligerent again.

"For bait."

WALKING OUT OF the jail through the sheriff's office, I tried to keep my gaze focused straight ahead, but my eyes had a will of their own. They tracked Bo-Peep like prey. Dangerous prey. She was the proverbial mouse with fangs. She was leaning against the closed door of Coleman's office. The pose she struck was provocative and proprietary.

"You can't go in there," she said.

"Are you having to lock Coleman in his office so he can't escape you?" I kept walking.

"You screwed up real bad," she said so softly I had to stop to hear her.

"I believe this is the pot calling the kettle black."

She frowned. "I'm just pointing out that you could have had Coleman for the asking. You were too stupid to ask." She cocked her right hip out a little higher and her skirt hiked up a little more. Another inch, and what Aunt LouLane delicately referred to as "possible" would be on display.

I had a lot on my plate, but suddenly Bo-Peep took on top priority. "Have you had your vision checked lately?"

"What are you talking about? My vision is fine." She dropped the pose and struck another, hands on hips. "Don't you dare go around saying my vision is bad."

Boy, I'd struck a nerve. Inbreeding must have caused a lot of ocular problems in her family. "If you can see so good, how come you haven't noticed that gold band on Coleman's left hand?"

She snorted. "Wedding bands don't mean a thing. They slip right off."

"Are you talking from experience?" I'd always figured her for a home-wrecker, but I hadn't realized she was stupid enough to just point-blank admit it.

"There's no such thing as a married man who never strays."

"Coleman is the kind of man who takes his vows seriously. And so do I." The door to Coleman's office opened a tiny amount, paused, then continued to open until he stood in the doorway. Bo-Peep didn't realize he was behind her, because she was staring daggers at me.

"Coleman may think his vows are sacred, but no man is immune to good loving. Didn't your mama teach you anything?" She laughed. "You couldn't get any dumber if you cut off your head."

"There are men who put their word before gratification. I respect that, even if it isn't what I want." I was talking to Coleman now. Bo-Peep was of no importance, only she wasn't smart enough to realize that.

"There was a time when the sheriff was interested in you, but that time is past." She swelled her chest. "Now he's looking at me."

"I don't believe that. He's a married man, and he's not stocking shelves in anybody's store but his own." I handed her a shovel to dig her own grave.

"He isn't any more interested in that wife of his than I am. She's a cow. Nobility won't keep him warm at night. It won't be long before he's tired of trying. I'll be standing right here, ready and waiting."

"I don't think so," Coleman said softly.

Bo-Peep let out a little shriek and whirled around. Eyes and mouth wide, she clapped a hand to her lips.

"Get your things together; you're fired. Leave immediately." He didn't look at me—probably couldn't bear to see the I-told-you-she-was-a-bitch look on my face. He went back into his office and closed the door.

Bo-Peep spun back around to glare at me. "You knew he was standing there all along."

I couldn't help smiling. "I may be dumb, but at least I don't run off at the mouth like a leaky toilet. By the way, you've just been flushed."

GLEE RODE SHOTGUN with me as I headed for Wilbur Ward's little cottage. Tinkie was supposed to call me with the results of the tests on Bridge's car and where the Memphis entrepreneur was. I was a little uneasy that he hadn't been home when I went by his house.

Before turning behind the high school, I made sure no one was following me. I had become just a little paranoid after being tossed through the air like a sack of Sweetie's dog food.

Wilbur was sitting on his front porch, his pose unchanged for nearly two decades. As I got out of the car, he took his pipe out of his mouth and grinned, exposing one good tooth.

"They never caught ya skippin', did they?"

The man had a memory that would be of interest to science. "Never did."

His grin widened. "I always wondered where you was goin'. Thought I might like to tag along."

The idea made us both grin. "Emanuel sent me over to get something out of that refrigerator in the back."

He nodded. "It'll set my mind at ease once those records are gone. They must be worth a truckload a'money." He waved the hand holding the pipe toward the back. "Help yourself."

I walked through the bare yard to the back of the house. The shed was about thirty feet beyond that, the big refrigerator clearly visible. Emanuel's hiding place was brilliant. No one would ever think of that old rusty fridge.

I opened the door and saw the boxes of black vinyl records, all carefully wrapped in plastic sleeves. Most likely they'd have to be played on 78 speed. Aunt LouLane's old turntable was in the attic. The thought of hearing those recordings was almost irresistible. It took a little grunting, but I finally got them out of the fridge and loaded in the trunk of my car.

Wilbur watched the entire operation and offered no advice. It was a rare quality in a man. I went up to the porch and said my good-byes.

"Come see me," he said. "I'll be here awhile, yet."

Just as I got in the car, the cell phone started ringing. Tinkie had news.

"The tests are back on Bridge's car." I could tell by her tone of voice that the news was bad, for Bridge. "It's animal blood. They said they couldn't tell if it was Sweetie Pie's for positive. They said they didn't run DNA tests on dogs. Have you ever?"

She was indignant that Sweetie didn't get the same treatment as a human. I was right with her. "What did Coleman say?"

"He told me not to jump to any conclusions. He said you'd probably already jumped, but for me to hold you back."

"Very funny. Where's Bridge?"

"Coleman went to bring him in for questioning, but they aren't back yet. The Jag is still impounded, so Bridge doesn't have a car."

"Did Coleman say anything?"

"No, not really. He was very quiet, but I did read the report Deputy Dattilo made on the car theft."

Tinkie was worth her weight in gold. "Tell me."

"Bridge came into the sheriff's office around eleven o'clock and reported the car missing."

That was about half an hour after the bomb had been thrown at Scott's. Bridge would have had time to get back to town.

"After that, he said that he went to Cece's house." There was a long pause. "He spent the night and didn't go home, so he had no way of knowing the car was returned."

"Cece?" I was shocked.

"He met her at Playin' the Bones. You'd already gone home by the time he got there. From all accounts, he and Cece hit it off. It seems they're an item."

30

IT WAS EARLY AFTERNOON AS I DROVE AWAY FROM WILBUR'S. Even though I hadn't eaten in what seemed like a week, I wanted only to crawl into bed and pull the covers over my head. Exhaustion, near-starvation, and anxiety about what I knew I had to do next, put me in a dark mood. Passing by the high school, I wondered if the architect and contractor had been publicly hung. The 1960s building, flat roof and institutional windows that didn't open, looked more like a chicken hatchery than a place of learning. No wonder I'd skipped school as often as possible to go wading with my friends down at Cottonmouth Creek. What might I have been if I'd ever mastered trigonometry? Why was it that in our society, education often came at the price of freedom? I was just too tired to come up with a decent answer to either burning question.

As I turned down the long drive toward home, I slowed to look at the beauty of the sycamores in the sun. Dahlia House was so much more than my home. It was there that I'd known the meaning of family.

To save it, I'd stolen my best friend's lovable little dog. I'd almost married Harold Erkwell to keep the wolves at bay. I stopped the car and simply stared at the old white plantation house. In that house my parents had loved each other and me. My mother had played her blues records and tried to teach me right and wrong. My father had told me a bedtime story each night until he died. My Aunt LouLane had given up her private life to move in with me and attempt to raise me.

I'd done a bad thing, dognapping Chablis, but my twinges of guilty conscience were minor compared to the pain that would have come from losing my home. In saving Dahlia House, I'd stumbled upon a career that I'd never once dreamed of choosing. But in such a short time, it had become how I viewed myself. I was a private investigator. And a good one. I hadn't been lying when I told Jitty that being a P.I. was my first priority. It was. Scott Hampton had hurt me, but all of my essential parts were still intact. I'd survive.

Now my job was to prove that Scott did not kill Ivory Keys. To do that, I had to catch the person who did. I pressed the gas pedal and drove up to my home.

Sweetie Pie stood up from her nap on the front porch and greeted me with a mournful howl and frantic tail-wagging. After I brought the records in, I followed Sweetie to the kitchen and filled her food bowl and gave her fresh water. Reveler, too, had to be fed. When I was done with my chores, I dragged myself up the stairs to my bedroom, undressed, and crawled into bed. My eyes were closed, as were the shades, but I couldn't sleep and I knew Jitty had entered my bedroom.

"No lectures," I warned her.

"Tell me, Sarah Booth, is it your body that's hurt or your heart?"

"Whatever it is, it'll mend." My thought was simply to ignore all pain and let time work its miracle cure.

"You'll mend, but how much scar tissue will be left behind? How bad did he hurt you?"

I didn't need this conversation. Not now. My defenses were far too weak, and Jitty knew all my emotional bruises. I felt a tear leak out of my eye and slip down my temple. I tried to pretend I wasn't crying, but Jitty was on to me.

"I didn't think you really loved him, Sarah Booth," she said gently.

"I didn't either." Perhaps I didn't really love Scott. Only time would have told that story. "He was just so damn mean about it."

Jitty sat on the edge of the bed and I finally opened my eyes. The room was dim, but there was plenty of light to see her. She wore a paisley miniskirt and blue tank top. Her hair was in a short fro. "Where's Ike?" I couldn't resist.

"Cute," she said. "And here I thought you were hurtin'. You just want to mock me."

"No, that's not true. I really just want to sleep."

She gave me a sorrowful look. "That man turned his back on you, just like I warned. Cracking wise about it won't make it different."

She was right about that. Jitty couldn't resist an "I told you so," but she was also the only person I could be completely honest with. "I wasn't ready to lose him, and certainly not the way it happened. Scott and I would probably have gotten enough of each other after a few months. We didn't get a chance to let it burn out on its own. Or I didn't."

"At least you're acknowledging what you feel. That's a big step, even if you don't know it."

"And it doesn't change a thing," I pointed out. "So I've admitted I hurt. I still hurt. Big deal. I won't die. Now I need a few hours sleep before I initiate the plan that will bring Ivory's killer out into the open."

IT WAS THURSDAY when I opened my eyes to the white light of an August day in full swing. It was impossible. I'd slept almost eighteen hours. When I looked at the bedside table, I saw the phone knocked off the hook by a pillow. Still, it was a wonder that Tinkie hadn't sent a search party for me.

My body ached as I swung out of bed and stumbled down the stairs to the kitchen for coffee. It wasn't until I had a steaming cup in my hand and had slumped into a chair at the table that I saw the handwritten note.

"You were so sound asleep I didn't wake you. Call me when you wake up. It's nothing that won't keep for a few hours."

So, Tinkie *had* looked in on me. She was that kind of friend. There was no telling what might have happened since I'd clocked out of reality.

I checked my answering machine and found messages from Millie and Cece asking for some assurance that I was healing without damage. I intended to see them in person. It was more than telling that Bridge Ladnier hadn't called.

As I made some eggs and toast, I couldn't help dwelling on the fact that Scott hadn't called. Deep down, I'd hoped that he would.

Before I got cleaned up, I went up to the attic, a place of many treasures. I found Aunt LouLane's old phonograph packed in a suitcase. It was something out of the fifties, but it had three speeds—45, 78, and 33. And it worked. I got it and an old hand trolley that would prove useful.

My mood was grim as I took a bath, dressed, and prepared for my day. The thought I forced myself to hang on to was that Scott was innocent of murder. He might be a verbally abusive creep, but he wasn't a killer. That's what I'd been hired to prove, and I intended to do it. My pride was a cattle prod to action.

I loaded the records, put the top down on the roadster, and opened the passenger door for Sweetie. The sun was blazing down on us, and as we drove through the fields of cotton, I could almost see the plants growing.

We drove by the courthouse, but Coleman's car was there, so I kept driving. I had a plan that would prove Bridge Ladnier guilty or innocent.

The first place I stopped was Robert Pennington McBruce's rented estate. His car was gone and he didn't answer my knock.

There was no sign of Nandy, so I drove on out to Holyrood. I hadn't seen her mother since high school, and I could see that Nandy's antics had taken a toll on her. Mrs. Shanahan's hair was snow-white and her mouth bracketed by deep wrinkles.

"Go away," she said before I could ask a single question.

"May I speak with Nandy?"

"You're no friend of my daughter's. She told me about you. Jealous! You always were. Even when you were a little girl, you were envious of Nandy."

"Mrs. Shanahan, I need to see Nandy."

"She's gone, thanks to you. She won't be coming back."

I didn't believe her. Not completely. Nandy would turn up again, like a bad penny. "Could you tell me where she is?" I asked.

"Go to hell." She slammed the door in my face and I was left with only the option of retreat.

I was running out of time, but luck was with me. When I went by the courthouse the second time, Coleman's car was gone. I pulled in and gave Sweetie strict orders to remain in the passenger seat. She was wearing her sunglasses and scarf, definitely incognito.

Using the hand trolley I'd found in the attic, I trundled the records into the courthouse. I wheeled my cargo into the sheriff's office and noted, with satisfaction, the absence of Bo-Peep. Dewayne was acting as dispatcher.

"Coleman asked me to leave these in his office," I said, wheeling by him. He was too green to think to challenge me. In my previous visits, I'd noticed that Coleman's office contained a closet. That was my destination. Just in case things got out of hand, I didn't want anything to happen to Emanuel's records. I left the trolley, too, and a little something extra I liked to think of as the cavalry.

Walking back out, I stopped by the desk. "Don't mention I was here. It's . . . best." I hurried out knowing that Dewayne would never dare broach the emotional waters of my visit to Coleman.

Swinging by Dahlia House, I made sure Sweetie was inside and

Reveler in his stall. I wanted everything locked down. I'd learned the hard way that my most vulnerable point was the people and things I loved.

Dusk was falling on the Delta as I drove through the cotton fields. I pulled into the unpaved front parking lot of WBLK-FM radio station, a small white frame building that had been built in the middle of a huge cotton field. There was a solitary Mercury Sable parked in front of the door.

WBLK wasn't one of the top market stations. It wasn't powerful enough to extend much beyond the boundaries of Sunflower County. But it was the local blues station that competed with Memphis—and actually did a superior job. The evening-shift DJ was Doctor Lucky, an award-winning musicologist who hid his college education behind a lot of shuck and jive. Doctor Lucky was very interested in a little illegal blues medicine.

I carried one record in my hand and my Aunt LouLane's suitcase phonograph in the other. When I walked in the front door, Doctor Lucky was sitting at a soundboard, talking into a microphone.

"There's a little lady here tonight says she's got somethin' that's gonna make every single one of you loyal listeners want to get down on the floor and scream. If she has the real thing, you folks are just about to hear something you ain't never heard before. Now listen up to Keb Mo while I use a few muscles other than those in my tongue."

He started the music and then got up to help me. It took him only a minute to set up the phonograph. When he was done, he looked at me. "If this is some kind of a joke—"

"I swear. It's Elvis Presley and Ivory Keys. The cut was pressed back before Elvis was Elvis."

Doctor Lucky flipped the switch for the mike. "Folks, Miss Sarah Booth Delaney, our homegrown P.I., has found a real treasure, though I'm afraid the quality of the sound won't be the best. Funky old turntable piece of crap. But it looks like it works. So sit back and test your blues I.Q. Call in and tell me who's playin' on this cut."

He started the record as he held the microphone down by the phonograph speakers. "Holy shit," he breathed, looking up at me with big eyes. "It's Elvis. And Ivory Keys."

Only the first verse of the song had played when the phones lit up—all three lines. Doctor Lucky didn't bother answering it. He sat mesmerized, watching that old black record spin on the slightly warped turntable.

When it was over, he slapped on another song without even announcing it. "What are you gonna do with that record?" he asked in a voice that might have been used to refer to a religious icon.

"Catch me a killer," I said, snapping the lid shut on the phonograph. I walked out and got in the car.

My car radio was tuned to WBLK as I drove away. Doctor Lucky was fielding questions and comments as fast as he could. And every few seconds he mentioned that the record had been brought to the radio station compliments of Sarah Booth Delaney.

It was the perfect setup.

31

I WAS RIDING HIGH, SATISFIED WITH MY DAY'S WORK, WHEN THE cell phone rang. I hated the dang thing, but I carried it, when I remembered, because I'd promised Tinkie.

"Sarah Booth!" Cece was breathless. "I just got a call from one of my sources. Where did you get that record?"

"It's a long story," I said. This was going to be another one of those cases where my conscience was going to bother me for years to come, yet I had no choice. "Did you like it?"

"I can't believe you didn't tell me, dahling. It makes one feel left out."

Her voice was laced with genuine hurt that I hadn't confided in her. "I just got my hands on the record this afternoon," I reassured her. "I haven't told anyone, except Doctor Lucky, who insisted that I bring it right over."

"I've got to interview you, dahling," she said. "Do you have any idea what that record is?"

"I *think* it may be valuable."

Cece gasped. "Valuable? I think you'd better call Harold and tell him to get ready to enlarge the vault at the bank. Honey, that record is worth a fortune."

"There's not just one record. I have twenty-one more."

The fact that Cece was speechless said more than anything else could have.

"You know, Bridge told me about these records, but I didn't believe they existed," I said, talking as casually as I could. "Won't he be shocked?"

"He'll be very excited. He's mentioned them to me several times. Sarah Booth, where are those records?" Cece's voice had gone from enthusiastic to concerned.

"They're in my trunk. I'm taking them out to Scott's tonight. Technically, they belong to him."

"I don't believe you! Tinkie told me how cruel Scott was to you. *Mildly interesting*. Dahling, I'd put his dick in a splint. Talk like that could *ruin* your social life."

"Scott was awful." There wasn't any point lying about it. Tinkie would have told Millie, too. Not to gossip, but to prepare my friends to be ready to support me. "He was mean, but the records are his."

"I'm sorry, Sarah Booth. He may be one sexy man, but he's a skunk when it comes to women. And speaking of women, have you heard the latest on Nandy Shanahan? She's been put in an institution by her family."

"What, they thought she was trying to commit suicide with a self-inflicted brow mutilation? Are they going to let her wear her tiara?" I couldn't resist. "Hey, maybe she can marry a nutcase Napoleon and rule all of Europe instead of just Scotland."

"Sarah Booth!" Cece said, delighting in my wickedness.

"Do you know where her husband is?" I wanted to be sure McBruce wasn't around to spoil my plan. I didn't need any interruptions.

"I happen to know for a fact that Robert Pennington McBruce closed up his rental house and moved to Glascow the very day that Nandy attacked herself. Dahling, he may talk like he has a mouth full of cockleburs, but he isn't a glutton for punishment.

Not even the prospect of inheriting Nandy's family estate could convince him to linger. My sources tell me that he didn't bother to pack his things. He drove to Memphis and left his brand-new car in the lot. He called the bank from the airplane and told them to pick it up for repossession."

Cece's source could only be Oscar, via Tinkie. I had to hand it to my partner. Although Tinkie had never been at the top of the class in math, she'd demonstrated astute skills at cause-and-effect equations. She'd learned quickly that if she tugged one part of Oscar's anatomy, his mouth flew open. All kinds of interesting tidbits were liable to fall out.

"You're positive Nandy is in loony town?" What I wanted was a fix on the human boil. I didn't want her launching a sneak attack, and I had a slight misgiving that her *family* had put her in an institution. Only the enemy would imprison the queen.

"Honey, she's gone. The whole town is buzzing about her. McBruce went on a rampage at The Club just before he left and gave everyone who would listen a blow by blow of Nandy's eccentricities." Cece purred. "She has an entire closet of human-sized Barbie outfits. Dr. Barbie, Barbie goes shopping, Barbie goes to the beach. She'll only have sex when she's wearing her Barbie goes to bed pink peignoir. I'm sure she's gone, Sarah Booth. She can't show her face around Zinnia. She may not be in an institution, but she's not in Zinnia, I'm sure of that."

"Thank goodness." At least Nandy was one thing I could check off my list of toxic worries.

"You're not still worried about her and Scott?" Cece's voice held disapproval. In her view, Scott had trampled all over my tender heart *and* my reputation as a sex partner. To cling to any hope of having him was just plain dumb. Perhaps because she'd been one, she understood that reform was hard-won in most members of the male species. A man got one chance with Cece.

"After tonight, Nandy can have Scott." I meant it, too. My lesson wasn't from the Daddy's Girl Book of Conduct. It came from the Delaney handbook—wounded pride is the best preventative for continued romantic stupidity. For a few short days, Scott had held up an image of a sensitive man who cared about me. Last night the glass had shattered, and I saw once again the arrogant, selfish man I'd first met in the jail cell.

"What's going on tonight?" Cece asked.

"I have to take those records to Scott. Then I'm dropping the case. Scott has made it very plain he doesn't want my help."

"Bravo," Cece said. After a second's hesitation, she asked, "Are you still interested in Bridge? I know Tinkie tried to match the two of you up."

"I'm not romantically interested in Bridge," I said, wishing more than anything I could warn her that Bridge was now my number-one suspect in the murder of Ivory Keys. But I needed her to remain ignorant of my plan, to help me prove Bridge's guilt or innocence. My consolation was that Cece was in no danger. She didn't have the records that Bridge wanted so badly. I did.

"Thanks, girlfriend."

"Don't thank me," I said after I hung up. There was only one other loose end I needed to tie up.

MILLIE PUT THE bowl of turnip greens in front of me with a wary eye. "Are you sick?"

"No," I assured her as I picked up my fork.

"The fried chicken is hot."

"No, thanks."

"What about a hamburger steak smothered in onion gravy? Mashed potatoes?"

I shook my head.

"Sarah Booth, you must be sick. There's not enough grease in those greens to count for anything. You always eat grease. And catsup."

I took a long swallow of my iced tea. "I'm just not in the mood for anything fried."

"Are you in the mood for anything . . . Elvis!" She stacked plates piled high with mashed potatoes and chicken all along one arm. "I heard about your record on the blues station. You are something else, Sarah Booth. I'll bet your mama had that record, didn't she? Did you know about it all along? Be right back!" She wheeled across the restaurant, delivering meals to hungry patrons. She was back in less than a minute.

"The record's existence was a big surprise to me," I said. "So have you seen Spider and Ray-Ban?"

She made sure all of her customers were happy and then took a seat on the stool beside me. "I haven't. In fact, no one has seen them since Wednesday." At my concerned expression she asked, "That's good, isn't it? Scott will stand a better chance if they aren't running around pissing everyone off, right?" Her eyes widened. "Not that we want Scott to get off after what he did to you. He deserves to be locked up." She restrained herself from repeating the *mildly interesting in bed* remark.

I decided to let the whole Scott thing drop. To be honest, I was a little tired of being viewed as a victim of blighted romance. "I'd rather know where those two troublemakers are."

She nodded. "Have you asked Coleman? He may have run them out of town."

I dug into my turnips and didn't answer. I hadn't talked to Coleman since he fired Bo-Peep. But I was going to have to, and sooner rather than later. "If you saw them Wednesday morning, they were in town Tuesday night, which was the night someone threw a Molotov cocktail at me."

"I suppose. But I was calculating it on the story in *The Meteor* about Julia Roberts being abducted by aliens and possibly impregnated by Elvis. I bought that paper when I went to get some eggs so I could open the café Wednesday morning."

"I see," I said, hoping that Millie would never have to testify to the time element.

"Don't act so snooty. Everyone in town reads those magazines in the grocery check-out line. I'm just honest enough to pay for mine."

She was right about that. "Sorry," I said.

"Anyway, I was reading that story when the two of them came in. I remember clearly, because they were laughing about the cover with the Siamese twins cloned from one egg." She shook her head. "It was an awful sad story, those two little babies sharing one set of lungs, and those two fools were laughing about it."

I didn't have to point out that they were creeps. Millie knew it as well as I did. "Did they say anything that might be important to the case?"

"They said they were leaving town. The one with the sunglasses, he said that Scott had asked them to leave. He was pretty indignant about it, too. He said that Scott had broken the bond of brotherhood or some such foolishness. I pointed out right away that if they were really Scott's brothers, they would have left last week instead of stirring up hard feelings against Scott. Everyone in town knows they're the ones who set fire to Goody's Grocery. Coleman will get the evidence he needs to arrest them."

Millie didn't mince words, one of her better traits when it wasn't aimed at me. "Did either of them say where they were going?"

"They said they were going to the Gulf Coast." Her face brightened. "In fact, they said a specific place. The Golden Wheel bar in Biloxi. The reason I remember is because they said they were friends with the man who owned it, Jimmy John Franklin. You remember him. He did some time in Angola for a hit." Her brow furrowed with concentration. "He had some highway official killed when his construction company didn't get a contract for a stretch of Interstate 10. Remember?"

While Millie enjoyed the tabloids, she was also an avid reader of regular newspapers. "I have a vague memory," I said, not wanting to admit that it was so vague it couldn't really be labeled a memory at all. I would never pass a test on current events.

"Jimmy John Franklin just got out of Angola last year. It was a big stink in the papers when the state gave him a liquor license for his club, what with his criminal record and all. Maybe his wife applied for it." She shook her head. "I don't remember the particulars."

"Thanks, Millie." I finished the last of my turnips, paid, and walked out into the night. It wouldn't be long now.

32

INFORMATION GAVE ME THE NUMBER FOR THE GOLDEN WHEEL IN
Biloxi, and I placed the call, adopting what I hoped was a sexy
tone with notes of frightened dismay. Jimmy John Franklin came
on the phone without a decrease in the sound of the honky-tonk
jukebox.

"What?" he asked.

"That bastard has gone off and left me." I forced a desperate
sob. "He promised me we were gonna get married."

"What the hell are you talking about?" Jimmy John obviously
didn't like complications.

"I'm talking about Ray-Ban. I need to talk to him. Is he there?"

"Where'd you get my name?" Jimmy John was suddenly alert.
"Who are you?"

"Lana," I said, hoping his knowledge of older stars wouldn't
kick in. "Lana Taylor. Ray-Ban said you were a man who knew
the score. He said you were solid. I need to talk to him. Ray-Ban's
left me in a bad way, if you know what I mean."

"A likely story." His suspicions were somewhat alleviated. "I'll give him the message."

"Is he there? I'd like to speak with him."

"He's busy."

"I really need to talk to him. Would you please put him on the phone?"

"Honey, I said he was busy. I'll give him the message and if he wants to, he'll get back with you. But it looks to me like you need to focus on fixing your problem. I don't suspect ol' Ray-Ban's figuring on being a daddy."

I faked a sob. "Please. Just put him on the phone. Once he understands, I'm sure he'll do the right thing."

Jimmy John laughed. "You're not only pregnant, you're stupid. Ray-Ban ain't aiming to marry anybody. He's got his hands full with all he's got going on."

The phone clicked down.

Perhaps my years in New York City hadn't been a total waste. I'd never wowed a Broadway audience, but I'd just pulled the wool over the eyes of one Mississippi hoodlum. I'd ascertained the information I needed—Ray-Ban was in Biloxi. That meant Spider was there, too. The road was clear to set my trap—except for Tinkie. I had to make sure she didn't wander into the middle of the fray.

As I dialed her number, I made myself a stiff Jack on the rocks as a reward for my exceptional performance. I called Tinkie at home, and when there was no answer, I resorted to her cell phone. She loved the gizmo. Hers was a fancy flip version with a face that could be popped off at every whim and replaced with a coordinating color. Needless to say, she had more colors than Crayola Crayon.

Her cell rang several times, and I was about to hang up when she answered in a breathless rush.

"What's going on?" I asked.

"You've been all over town and haven't bothered to give me a call." She wasn't angry, but her feelings were hurt. "Coleman's arrested three men for abducting Trina Jacks. They're all members of the Dominoes."

"Did they incriminate Emanuel?" I wasn't surprised to find the Dominoes responsible.

She shook her head. "Not yet."

"Excellent work, Tinkie," I said breezily. It might work to my advantage if Tinkie was a little put out with me.

"Right. You can save that manure for somebody else. All I did was talk to Coleman."

"And I need you to talk to him again. To persuade Coleman into helping you dig up some information."

"What kind of information?" Her interest was piqued.

"Background on Bridge Ladnier and the Skull and Bones organization."

There was a silence. "Do you honestly think Bridge is capable of killing Ivory Keys?"

"My gut tells me it isn't true, but all the pieces fit." The evidence stacked against Bridge was high. He had as much means, motive, and opportunity as Scott.

"I don't think Bridge would kill for money. Is there another motive?"

Tinkie was becoming a proficient P.I. She was going to put me through my paces, and I didn't blame her. "There are twenty-two records of Ivory and Elvis playing together. I spoke with Krystal. She estimated the value in the millions, and that was before she knew that the records included a lot of banter among the musicians."

"And Bridge knew about these records?"

"He told me about them on a date. He offered to buy Playin' the Bones. I believe he thought the records were hidden somewhere in the club. Cash was stolen out of the register, but the place was also ransacked. Someone must have been hunting for something else of value."

"Bridge doesn't need the money," she pointed out again.

I took a deep breath. "He's a collector. I don't think it's the monetary value. Bridge wants the recordings."

There was a pause as she thought. "How would Bridge get a prison shank?"

"Even I could make one, and you know I'm not allowed to use sharp tools." Talking through a case with Tinkie helped me clarify my own thoughts. "But I think Bridge had some help."

"Ray-Ban and Spider," she said with conviction. "I knew they were trouble. They had to be the ones who hit Sweetie Pie and ran off. Bridge wouldn't do that."

"I hope it wasn't Bridge. The way I figure it is that Ray-Ban and Spider did the dirty work, including shooting at Reveler, and trying to make it look like Emanuel did it by setting up those animal bones. I know that wasn't Bridge because he was with Cece that night."

"What about the paint on your parents' tombstone? That had to be them, too."

"They were on the loose at the time. It makes sense that they did it. They like to intimidate. I'm willing to bet my fee that they did it."

"Me, too." There was a bit of hesitation. "Have you verified that Bridge was in Zinnia on the night of Ivory's murder?"

"That's what I need you to do." In her zest, Tinkie had created her own job. I could only be thankful.

"How can Coleman help me with that?"

"Go back through Bridge's statement about the theft of his car. There's something strange. Bridge reports his car stolen and then walks over to Cece's house, where he stays until morning. When he returns, violà, his car has been brought home. Cece is a very convenient alibi. My guess is that he hired Ray-Ban and Spider to throw the bomb and solidified his alibi by reporting his car stolen. I'm sure they burned Goody's, but I just wonder if that was a little freelance action because they enjoy torching things."

Tinkie sighed softly. "Bridge and Oscar have known each other for many years."

"I'm sorry, Tinkie, but all the evidence points to Bridge."

"And when you took the case, all the evidence pointed to Scott. What happened to that evidence?"

Tinkie had tremendous lawyer potential. She was argumentative and she had her facts lined up. "Convince me," I said. "Get with Coleman and go through all the facts and prove to me that Bridge couldn't have killed Ivory and he didn't hit my dog with his car."

"Okay," Tinkie said. "What are you going to do?"

"I'm going to return those records to Scott."

"Sarah Booth, have you no pride? I heard the way that man talked to you."

I didn't like the fact that all of my friends so quickly jumped to the conclusion that I would go back to Scott. "I'm only returning the records," I lied. "Then I'm going out to Ida Mae's. She's worried sick about Emanuel, though he isn't worth it. I'll work on proving that Emanuel didn't throw that Molotov cocktail at Scott's house, then I'm done with the whole thing. Just let me remind you, though, that Bridge didn't go to Cece's until after someone tried to blow me and Scott up."

Tinkie ignored that last bit of evidence. "Do you want to meet for a drink when we both finish?" she asked.

"I'm tuckered out. I'm going home and going straight to bed. I'll give you a call tomorrow. Better yet, come by for breakfast. I'm making French toast and bacon."

"Seven?"

"Perfect." I was about to hang up when emotion swept over me. "Tinkie, you're the best partner anyone could ever ask for."

"Are you okay?"

My sentimentality had stirred the hounds of suspicion. "One hundred percent. I just had a moment of weakness. I should know better than to hand out compliments. It goes against my character."

"I'll see you tomorrow."

"I can almost smell the bacon sizzling." I hung up before she could ask any more pertinent questions.

I went to the sideboard and made myself another drink. While I was in the vicinity, I went through my mother's records and pulled out B. B. King. Every year the town of Indianola celebrated his birthday with a big picnic. He and Lucille, his guitar, brought the blues home one more time.

With the music playing, I went up to my room and broke a half dozen fashion rules as I put on black jeans and a black tank top in August. Not to mention the black riding boots. I found my black leather jacket. So if I wasn't shot or knifed, I'd die of swelter. The life of a P.I. is rough.

I'd loaded my car trunk earlier and I was as ready as I'd ever be. Tape recorder in my hand, I started toward the bedroom door.

"Are you sure you know what you're doin'?" Jitty wore a somber black suit. The bow tie at her neck reminded me of the costumes so many women had to adopt in the early days of the feminist movement—severe suit softened by the *de rigueur* bow of white or tasteful pastel. We had come a long way, baby.

"I'm going to lure Bridge Ladnier out into the open and then I'm going to get him to confess."

"Exactly how are you going to accomplish that?"

I held out the small tape recorder, also compliments of Tinkie. I'd never used it before, but now it was going to make its debut. "Trick him."

"How?" Jitty held her hands clasped in front of her pelvis like a good little girl. Her pumps were sensible. Her hair sculpted into what served as a French twist. Then I noticed the hat. A black veil marred her beautiful skin.

"Where's the funeral?"

"Maybe right here at Dahlia House. Maybe yours."

That stopped me. Jitty was a haint, but she wasn't in the habit of offering up doom and gloom. "What's wrong with you?"

"Is Scott Hampton worth dying for?"

She'd taken up the litany of my friends. "This isn't about Scott. It's about the truth. He didn't kill Ivory."

"Did you ever consider that Coleman would figure this out if you stayed out of it?"

"Ida Mae hired me. I'm in it now. Besides, Bridge wouldn't shoot me in cold blood."

"If he killed Ivory, then he tortured him, too—or had him tortured. And you don't think he'd put a bullet in you?"

Jitty had hit the one point in my theory of Bridge's guilt that also troubled me. I couldn't see him torturing Ivory by beating and cutting him. That was why I'd gone to such lengths to make sure Ray-Ban and Spider were out of town. While I would set a trap for Bridge, I didn't want to catch the two bikers in it. That I would leave for the law.

"I think Bridge doesn't get his hands dirty, but his two henchmen are way down in Biloxi."

"I'm back to the how question. How are you gonna make that man confess?"

I had an answer for her, but I knew she wasn't going to like it. "Ego. I'll play dumb, and Scott can pretend to be his buddy."

She lifted the veil enough to let me see the contempt in her eyes. "Ain't no *playin'* dumb involved. You are a fool, Sarah Booth."

"If Bridge killed Ivory, he won't leave without those records."

"Now that's a fact. Even if he has to kill you." She stepped closer to me. "You better have a backup plan."

"I do," I said, picking up my keys. I sprinted down the stairs and opened the front door, hyped about the coming events. Connie Peters stopped me dead in my tracks. She was standing on the porch, hand lifted to knock.

"I need to speak with you," she said, and I could see that she'd been crying.

"Connie, I'm in a bit of a rush right now."

She slipped past me, and I realized how much weight she'd lost. She was bone-thin. Before I could stop her, she was in the parlor sitting on the old horsehair sofa.

"I know there's something between you and Coleman and I have to know what it is." Her hands were clasped so tightly in her lap that her fingers were slightly blue.

This was one conversation I really didn't want to have. "Look, I've got to be somewhere in just a few minutes." That wasn't a lie. I'd timed the whole thing out. I had to be at Scott's in the next half hour.

"I've only got one question. What are you to my husband?"

One question that might take me the rest of my life to figure out the answer to.

She leaned forward and stared at me. "I see," she said, dropping her gaze to her hands. "I should have realized this, but I was too busy nursing my grudges to wonder what my husband was so busy doing."

"Nothing has happened between me and Coleman." I didn't have an answer for her question, but I couldn't let her think that her husband had broken his vows. "Coleman isn't the kind of man to cheat on his wife. You have my word on that. Nothing has happened."

The ghost of a smile touched her face. "Thank you for getting rid of that horrible creature in his office."

My face must have shown my confusion.

"The dispatcher," she reminded me.

"Oh, Bo-Peep."

"That's a perfect name." Connie's laugh brought back a rush of high school memories. She'd been the best tumbler on the cheerleading squad. She'd had an infectious laugh that made it seem as if the girls leaping and yelling on the edge of the field were having more fun than the law allowed. I'd been keenly jealous of her, even then.

"Look, Connie, Coleman has always been true to you." I jangled my keys, hoping she would take the hint.

"As far as *you* know."

She could have slapped me and not shocked me more. "What are you saying?"

"I've been following you lately. Coleman doesn't come here, but he doesn't go home, either."

"Why don't you follow him?" So she had an infectious laugh. It might be because the sound resonated in her empty head.

She unclasped her hands. "Maybe I don't want to know the truth. Maybe I have to learn it bit by bit."

"Maybe there isn't any truth." I felt a headache coming on. "Look, sit here as long as you want. I have to go."

And I did. I walked out of my house, leaving the door wide open, B. B. King playing his heart out, and Coleman's wife sitting on my great-great-grandmother's sofa.

33

MY HEADACHE ONLY INTENSIFIED AS I DROVE THROUGH THE muggy night. Moonlight silvered the leaves of the cotton and turned the tight boles into ghost-shadowed buds.

No matter the outcome of this night, the land would continue to nourish its crop. That was only mildly reassuring as I drove to Scott's and what I knew Coleman would label as "abject stupidity," with a few more profane adjectives slipped in the middle. But I'd done the best I could to make sure this turned out right. My gut told me that Bridge would confess, especially if he thought Scott was getting ready to abscond with the records.

There was one bright spot in the evening. I could easily imagine Emanuel foaming at the mouth in his cell when he heard I had the records and that I was taking them to Scott. And I had no doubt he would hear it—I'd seeded the gossip clouds thoroughly.

Though my mind was on the case, I couldn't help but think of Connie. If I'd said I was sleeping with Coleman, what would she have done? Left him? Attacked me? Neither scenario seemed likely. So why had she come? I pulled my thoughts back to what lay ahead of me.

I checked my watch. It was almost nine. If I calculated correctly, I had a few moments to let Scott in on the plan for the evening.

The lights were on in his cottage when I pulled into the driveway. I stopped the car in front of the porch and got out. The front doorway held his silhouette, but he made no move to greet me.

My foot was on the step when he spoke. "I never realized you and Nandy shared the trait of showing up where you aren't wanted. I guess it's something in this Delta soil that makes the women stupid and desperate."

"There are some boxes of records in the trunk. Please bring them in." I steeled my heart and my voice. Though his words were daggers, I kept going forward.

"Get off my property, Sarah Booth."

"Get the records and quit acting like a prick. I'm not here to seduce you. I'm here to catch Ivory's killer. Now I need your help." I brushed past him and walked inside to survey the room. He had a portable phone and I picked it up, punched the number of my cell phone in the speed dial memory, turned the volume up to loud, and hid the phone in the pillows of the sofa. I put my tape recorder right beside it.

I was only slightly amazed when Scott walked in with one box of heavy records. "Get the suitcase, too." When he shot me a look, I glared back. "I'm not moving in. It's a phonograph. Bridge is going to demand to hear at least one of the records if he's going to pay for them."

Light dawned in Scott's eyes. It was perhaps the only satisfaction I would ever get from him again, so I drank it in. "You found the records," he said with some degree of respect.

"Emanuel had them hidden. I'm using them as bait to lure Bridge out. He's been after the records all along. When he gets here, you act as if the records are yours. I want you to slap me hard enough to knock me onto the sofa." I pointed to the place

I'd hidden the phone. "I'll pretend to be out. Then it's up to you to get him to tell you how he killed Ivory."

"Me?" Scott was ready to balk. "How can I get him to confess?"

"You convinced me that you cared about me. Charm him, Scott. Lie. Do what comes naturally. I know you can." My bitter words found a target. He stepped back from me before he got his expression under control.

"You've got it," he said, all ice once again. "Of course, since Bridge is a man, he may be a little harder to manipulate."

My first impulse was to slap him. Hard. Instead, I pointed to the door. "Get the rest of the records."

He walked out and I had a moment to compose myself. He was such a bastard. Had it not been for Ida Mae, I would have walked out right then. Ida Mae and the memory of Ivory Keys. I'd never known Ivory, but in working the case, I'd come to admire him and his dream.

After Scott brought the remaining records and the phonograph in, I showed him where to set it up. When I handed him the album, he held it as if it were the most valuable thing he'd ever seen.

"I was never really certain Ivory had the records. I suspected he had a line on them. I begged Ivory to sell them. He and Ida Mae could have lived their golden years in great comfort." When he looked at me, the hardness was gone from his eyes. I saw again how much he'd loved Ivory.

"Did he ever hint to you he gave them to Emanuel?"

He shook his head. "All he'd ever say was that music was a powerful weapon. He said one day the person who had the records might listen to them and realize that music didn't see color. He said that when that happened, a true miracle would be performed." Scott's gaze dropped. "I didn't believe him."

"Emanuel intended to destroy them in some sort of public testimonial to prove his hatred was stronger than money."

"Ivory believed there was good in everyone. That was actually what got him killed." His face darkened. "And you really believe this rich man killed him?"

I hesitated. The evidence led me to believe Bridge was the culprit. The night would give me an answer. "Killed him or paid someone to do it."

Awareness dawned in his eyes. For all of his years in prison, Scott had never considered that Ivory was killed by a hired gun. "No," he said, shaking his head. "Not Spider and Ray-Ban." He said it emphatically. "They're just easy targets, like me. They wouldn't do this. Not because of Ivory, but because of me."

"You're as naïve as Ivory ever dared to be." It was the pot calling the kettle black. I was among the sinners on that list, for once upon a time, I'd believed in a future with Scott. I ran down the list of reasons I believed they were implicated. He was still doubtful.

"They're involved in this, Scott. They were in town before Ivory was killed, weren't they?"

"They could have been," he said slowly. "I make you this promise: If they hurt Ivory in any way, I'll make them regret the day they were born."

I had no doubt about that.

"They're in Biloxi at Jimmy John's," he said. "He called them to come take care of something for him. I didn't ask questions. I was relieved to see them go."

Something niggled in my memory. Spider and Ray-Ban had told Millie that Scott had *asked* them to leave. So they were liars about everything, using their banishment in an effort to win Millie's sympathy. Not much luck there. "Coleman will get them, but first we have to get Bridge to confess. I believe your old prison buddies killed Ivory when he wouldn't tell them where the records were."

Learning the true nature of Spider and Ray-Ban was going to be costly for Scott. Though the two bikers would be caught and punished, Scott would never forgive himself. He'd given succor to the enemy.

"If that rich bastard doesn't confess, I'll beat it out of him." Scott's fists were clenched. He was ready to inflict pain on someone, because he was hurting himself.

I didn't bother to argue. That wasn't in my game plan for the night.

Further talk was stopped as headlights came down Scott's driveway. Halfway, when there had been enough time to see my car in the beams, the headlights stopped. A door slammed. In a few moments the boards of the steps creaked.

"Hampton?" Bridge's voice called out.

Even though I'd anticipated this, had planned for it, my heart sank a little. Though I believed Bridge to be guilty, a part of me had hoped for a different outcome.

"Who is it?" Scott's voice held anger. He was playing his part to the hilt.

"Bridge Ladnier. Is Miss Delaney there?"

"What's it to you?"

"I've come to negotiate with the two of you. I believe you have something I very much want."

"I'm not interested in selling the records. Beat it."

The porch creaked as Bridge came to the open door. He held a stack of hundred-dollar bills in one hand. "I want those records. I'm a collector." He tossed the money to Scott, who caught it with one hand. "Keep that just for talking with me."

Scott threw the money down on the table and grinned. "I like the way you do business. Come on in."

"Bridge, don't trust him." I stepped into the fray. "He's going to try and cheat you."

"Shut up!" Scott yelled at me.

"Sarah Booth," Bridge said smoothly, "I enjoy a challenging negotiation. It's the art of entrepreneurship. The win is no fun unless there's risk."

"Don't trust him, Bridge. He killed Ivory to get these records. I came here to get him to confess. I thought I could—"

"I'm not telling you again." Scott grabbed my arm so tightly that I almost dropped to my knees. His grip was the only thing that kept me standing.

"Hey!" Bridge started toward us.

"Stay out of this." His voice was threat enough to stop Bridge in his tracks. "This bitch has to learn who's running this show." He pushed me slightly as he released me. I stumbled against the coffee table but caught my balance. Scott was damn good at this. Almost too good.

"May I hear the merchandise?" Bridge asked.

Scott got the record I'd shown him from one of the boxes and put it on the old phonograph. There was some chatter among the musicians.

"Lord, we're gonna show the world that Mississippi is a place where music rules." Ivory Keys was talking.

"Put your hands on those keys and start us off." I would have recognized Elvis's voice anywhere. Even if I hadn't, the look of rapture on Bridge's face would have clued me in.

The music was red-hot and blue. Elvis's voice wasn't the slick Vegas drawl he'd perfected later. It was raw and moaning. Without a doubt it was some of his best work.

"What do you want for all of them?" Bridge waved at the records.

"Ten million." Scott didn't blink an eye. "And something else."

"What?"

"Don't listen to him. Bridge, I was wrong about him. He killed Ivory. He can't be trusted. He'll take your money and kill you." I stepped forward so Scott had a clear shot at me. He swung and came at my head. As his palm connected with my cheek, I felt almost nothing, but there was the sound of fist meeting flesh and I knew Scott had somewhere learned the art of wrestling. He'd slapped his chest while pretending to strike me. I let him push me back onto the sofa, and collapsed as if I were unconscious. I fell with my face and one hand right in the crack of the pillows where I'd secreted Scott's phone and my tape recorder. I could work both devices with minimal movement.

"Sarah Booth!" Bridge's voice was indignant.

"She's not hurt." Scott was matter-of-fact, as if he punched me out every day. "She's just quiet for a while. Now that she's not chattering on, let's do business."

As they talked, my fingers found the necessary buttons. I hit the speed dial button on Scott's phone and listened to the tinny ring buzzing in my ear. I'd left my cell phone in the boxes of records in Coleman's office closet. I counted five rings, and panic was setting in when Coleman picked up the phone and said hello. I didn't answer. I just inched the telephone so he could hear the conversation in the room, and I clicked on my tape recorder.

"I'll give you the ten million for the records," Bridge said. "Cash. Right now."

"That's a fair price, but I want something else."

"What?" Bridge was antsy.

"A confession."

"To what?"

"Don't play dumb with me. Sarah Booth thinks I killed Ivory, but I didn't. She came here offering those records she found, hoping to trick me into confessing. I told her what she wanted to hear, because I don't expect to hang around here for the trial. But I want to know who did kill him."

"Why are you asking me?"

"Because I think you killed him trying to get these records." Scott laughed. "It's a good thing you realize you can just buy them from me or I might be in danger myself." He laughed again. I had to hand it to the man, he had a flair for the dramatic.

"I would have bought the records from Ivory, no doubt about that. But he wouldn't admit to me that he had them." Bridge wasn't biting.

"Right. That old man was tough. It took me a long time to get him to trust me. I knew he had those records all along. That's what kept me hanging around."

Scott sounded so believable. And Bridge sounded so genuinely confused. I risked opening one eye. Their expressions matched their words.

"I didn't have a thing to do with Ivory's death. As a collector, I wanted these records. But I wanted to buy them. I admit, after he was dead, I tried to buy the club because that was the logical place he would have hidden them." Bridge shrugged. "But even that didn't work. And someone had already searched the place. It was trashed when I took a contractor over there in the hope of finding something. Whoever killed him knew a thing or two about tossing a place."

I opened my other eye. This wasn't going as planned. Not at all.

Scott walked over to the record player and picked up the record. He held it delicately. "Tell me you killed Ivory or I'm going to smash this record."

Bridge's face paled. "I didn't kill him. Please don't destroy that. It's invaluable to someone like me. I'll give you twelve million."

I started to sit up when there was the sound of a gunshot. A bullet splattered into the wall beside Scott's head. I ducked back into the pillows, but kept one eye open on the door. Spider and Ray-Ban walked into the room, and both of them held guns.

34

"I'LL TAKE THAT," SPIDER SAID AS HE STEPPED FORWARD AND took the album from Scott's hands. "We went to a lot of trouble trying to find those records. Where're the others?"

It was all I could do to force my body to remain limp on the sofa. Where in the hell had Spider and Ray-Ban come from? They were in Biloxi. Jimmy John had said they were there, but then I realized he hadn't. I'd simply assumed they were there. I had committed what might prove to be a fatal mistake.

"You killed Ivory." Scott's voice was without inflection, and I realized that not until that moment had he really believed his friends were guilty.

Spider gave Scott a contemptuous look. "That crazy old negro talked way too much. Everyone in prison knew he'd played with Elvis on some records. After you got out and came down here, we decided that we'd travel south and find what he had stashed away." He pointed to the three boxes of black records. "You being here and so tight with the old fool made it a whole lot easier on us." Spider's grin was wide. "When we showed up at the nightclub, he remembered us and wasn't all that welcoming. Then we reminded him we were friends of yours and took such good care of you in the joint. He loosened up, let us right in, and set up a round of drinks for us, talking about how everybody deserves a second chance." Spider leaned down and grinned. "Thanks, *brother.*"

Scott lunged at Spider, but it was an act of fury and not a planned attack. Ray-Ban deftly stuck out a foot and tripped him. Spider drew back the butt of his pistol and brought it down on Scott's cheekbone as Scott was falling. I heard the bone crack. Scott crumpled and fell on the floor moaning.

Instead of standing, I took a horizontal route to Scott, sliding off the sofa and scrambling on the floor. I was almost to him when I felt the barrel of the pistol pressed into the small of my back.

"So, *Miss* Sarah Booth Delaney, you don't look so high-and-mighty now." Ray-Ban had shoved his sunglasses up on his forehead as he leaned over and pushed the metal deeper into my back. It was the first time I'd actually seen his beady black eyes, and I looked away from the hate and malice.

"Stop that! Leave her alone." Bridge started forward to defend me. Though he was an athletic man, he was no match for Ray-Ban. In one swing, Ray-Ban swept the gun from my back to Bridge's jaw, connecting solidly. Bridge dropped like a sack of cement, momentarily stunned and in pain.

"Stay out of it, Moneybags," Ray-Ban said. He looked down at Bridge. "By the way, that's a nice ride you've got. Hope we didn't hurt it when we hit that ugly dog."

Rage boiled in my heart, but my brain was clear enough to know that if I hurled myself at the bastard, he'd simply cold-cock me, too. I took the opportunity to check on Scott. He was moaning and spitting blood. His cheekbone was definitely cracked and I could see chips of tooth in the blood he was spitting. "He needs a doctor," I said. I put a hand on his chest to hold him steady on the floor. If he tried to get up, they'd simply whack him again.

"Load the records. I'll keep an eye on them." Spider pointed Ray-Ban at the sturdy cardboard cartons. An ugly grin lit his face.

"Put them in the trunk of the Jaguar. Moneybags won't be needing that fine car anymore."

Ray-Ban hefted one box first.

"The records won't do you any good," I pointed out. "Everyone knows about them. No music company will buy stolen goods."

"Who needs a music company? I've already got a private collector lined up. He doesn't care where the records come from or how I get them."

Damn. Spider was a lot smarter than I'd anticipated. That was the flaw in my whole scheme. I'd never considered that the two creeps were smart enough to conceive of such a plan and execute it by themselves. I'd vastly underestimated them. "What are you going to do with us?" I asked.

"Kill you. I don't believe in leaving loose ends behind." Spider grinned, and I knew he was telling the truth. We were only moments away from a bullet in the brain. The cavalry should have ridden over the hill by now. Delay was the only tactic I had left.

"I thought Scott was your brother." I eased his head into my lap as he tried to rise up. His eyes were dazed with pain, but his fists were clenched.

"Scott broke the code when he sided with that old negro against his brothers." He made a face. "He should have understood that standing up for a black was something we'd never forgive. We got a name for someone like him."

"And I don't want to hear it." I had to keep them talking. "Why'd you try to kill my horse?" I asked.

"If I'd really been trying to kill him, he'd be dead. At first, we wanted to scare you off. We painted the tombstone and shot at the horse, but that was before you became a real pain in the ass. You kept snooping around, poking into things. Once you climbed in the sack with Scott, we knew you'd never give up trying to help him. So we decided the easiest remedy was to kill both of you."

"You're a real specialist with fire, aren't you?" I asked.

"I like my cocktails dry and hot," he grinned. "But the grocery store was more fun. It really burned."

Ray-Ban had loaded one carton of records. Our time was running out. "Hey, Ray-Ban. Maybe you'd better play some of those records. You might be in for a big surprise."

Spider was instantly alert. Still holding the gun on us, he walked over to the last box. Pulling up a black record, he examined it a moment before he threw it to the ground. "Glenn Miller!" He pulled out another one. "Frank Sinatra? What is this?" He threw the record against the wall.

"Hey, those are very valuable. They're collector quality." I didn't try to hide my smug grin.

The muzzle of the gun swung down at me. "Where are the Ivory records?"

His finger inched the trigger back, and I wondered how it was going to feel to die. Once I told him the truth, he was going to shoot me. Then again, he was going to shoot me anyway.

"Bite me," I said with the biggest grin I could muster in the face of death.

"You little—"

"I can make her talk. In fact, I'd love it."

All heads swung to the front door where Nandy Shanahan stood, all tricked out in a pink cloud of lace and nylon. She stepped into the room and I realized she was wearing pink acrylic glitter heels with a little pink-feathered pompon on each foot. She was also wearing Baby Doll polish and lip gloss, which contrasted nastily with her glossy red hair. The episode of self-mutilation must have ended with some type of psychiatric therapy and some mighty good drugs. Nandy was clean and polished. Despite the problem with her color choices, she'd been transformed from a grunge groupie to a strange kind of glamour girl—if peignoirs were your taste. The metal staples in her forehead gave her Barbie meets Bride of Frankenstein panache.

My big problem with Nandy wasn't fashion, but that she was standing in Scott's doorway. Once again, I'd assumed. I'd been told she was gone by two sources. I'd assumed it was fact. Twice in one day I'd violated the golden rule of a good detective. I might not live to break it a third time. I could see from his expression that Spider was not impressed with the latest visitor, no matter how bizarre her getup.

"You're that crazy bitch from the courthouse," he said, unfazed by Nandy's fashion flip.

"I can make Sarah Booth squeal, but you have to promise that you won't hurt Scott." Nandy looked at me with anticipation. "I would enjoy making her talk."

She was serious. "So, you came for one more shot at scoring with Scott." I pointed at her getup. "Everyone in town knows that you only have sex when you're wearing your Barbie peignoir set. I can't help but wonder what you wear to the shrink. Does Barbie have a cute little pink straitjacket?"

"When I see that big-mouth Robert again, he's a dead man." She was fuming.

Scott pointed at the door and mumbled something to the effect that she should get out.

Nandy rubbed her feathered pom-pom on his leg. "Baby, I'm the only one who can save you. You might as well accept it."

Scott tried to sit up, but I held him back. At this particular moment, Nandy was a good thing. The longer she diverted Spider and Ray-Ban, the better our chances were. I was positive Coleman had heard enough of the conversation to realize Scott and I were in grave danger, though not from Bridge. Surely Coleman was racing through the hot night at this second. I took a deep breath and tried to calm myself.

Spider and Ray-Ban exchanged glances. Spider stepped closer to Scott. "I don't need a crazy bitch to get anyone to talk." His booted foot pressed down on Scott's left hand as he gave me a victory smile. "You tell me where those records are or I'm going to crush his fingers. He'll never play again."

"Okay," I said, pushing his foot away. "I'll be glad to tell you."

"Don't trust her." Nandy stepped up to Spider. "She was a liar in the womb. Every time she's in a tight spot, she lies. In the sixth grade, she was caught drawing penises on pictures in her geography book. She pretended she'd never seen those pictures and then said that I'd borrowed her book the day before."

I'd forgotten all about the pen-and-ink penises. I hadn't actually accused Nandy, but now I realized how the teacher had figured out she was the guilty party. No one else in sixth grade would draw a penis with a tiara on it.

"She's a total psycho," I interjected. "She honest to God believes she's heir to the Scottish throne. Forget the fact that there hasn't been a Scottish throne in centuries."

Nandy's pale face flushed, and I noticed for the first time that when she was upset, the flush extended down her legs. It was a fascinating bit of science.

"That's a damn lie, Sarah Booth Delaney. I'm sick of you interfering in my life. I want him to kill you." She turned to Spider. "She took the records to the courthouse. I saw her."

Spider pushed Nandy aside with such force that she fell against the sofa and whacked her head against the wall. I could tell by the way she landed she was unconscious. It was the preferred state where Nandy was concerned.

"Where are the records?" Spider had a one-track mind and it was focused on me.

"Nandy's finally right about something. The records are in Sheriff Coleman Peters' office. In his closet." I pulled the telephone out of the pillows, pushing the off button as I handed it to him. "Call Coleman and ask, if you don't believe me." I wanted to call Coleman. I wanted to call him and give him a piece of my mind. Where in the hell was he? I'd designated him the cavalry, and he wasn't riding over the hill.

"You'd better be lying," Spider said as he lifted his boot.

I snatched Scott's hand off the floor. Then I realized he hadn't intended to stomp Scott. He was going to kick me.

Bridge had remained silent throughout the entire exchange. He chose this time to speak, though he didn't bother with words. With a loud roar he charged at Spider.

I watched in horror as Spider shifted the gun from me to Bridge. I saw his finger pulling the trigger back in slow motion. There was the sound of a gunshot. Bridge's body changed course in midair as he dove beside the sofa where Nandy sprawled. Spider turned slowly to face the door as he staggered and began to fall.

Then I saw the blood on his pants leg. The denim had erupted with splinters of bone, and blood was jetting out in bright crimson gushes. Coleman walked calmly into the room, ignoring Spider as he fell. Coleman pointed his gun at Ray-Ban. "Hand it over," he said.

Ray-Ban hesitated, but the look in Coleman's eyes convinced him to yield his gun. As deputies Gordon Walters and Dewayne Dattilo rushed into the room, Coleman took Ray-Ban's gun and picked up the gun Spider had dropped. Finally, Coleman squatted beside Spider, who was moaning on the floor, clutching frantically at his bleeding thigh.

"Damn, I hit an artery. Sarah Booth, call an ambulance," Coleman said.

"Coleman!" I'd never been gladder to see anyone.

"Give me your belt," Coleman said to Scott, who sat up and pulled his off. In a few seconds Coleman had fashioned a tourniquet and slowed the bleeding.

He stood and motioned Dewayne to hold the tourniquet. "Gordon, if anybody moves, shoot them. That means anybody, but especially her." He pointed at Nandy, who was now whimpering.

He grabbed my arm and pulled me up and out to the front porch.

"Are you okay?" His hands moved down my arms, then along my back as if he wouldn't believe my words.

"I'm fine. You got here just in time."

"Playing that record on the radio was stupid, Sarah Booth. This whole plan was foolish and dangerous. You knew the people who wanted the recordings had killed once."

His hands tightened on my arms and he pulled me into a hug. I didn't care that he chastised me. The only thing that mattered was that he held me.

"By the way, leaving your cell phone in the records was a good piece of work." He pulled the small phone out of his pocket and returned it.

His whispered praise made me smile.

"How did you know I would be in the office?" he asked.

"It was a risk, but where else would you be?"

He squeezed me tight and let me go. "When did you figure out it was Spider and Ray-Ban?"

It was on the tip of my tongue to tell him that my trap had been set for Bridge. But I remembered DG rule eighty-eight. Never admit to anything less than perfection.

"Did you hear their confession?" I countered.

"Heard it and recorded it. The quality of sound won't be the best, but it's good backup, especially since we have you and Bridge and Scott to testify."

Coleman walked me back into the room, his arm around my shoulders. I didn't feel it necessary at that time to tell him I'd recorded the whole thing, too—just in case.

Coleman stopped in the doorway, his arm possessively slipping around my waist. "Where did Nandy come from?" he asked.

"Hell," I answered.

We were both laughing when I looked at Scott. His jaw was swollen, but it wasn't pain from his injury that showed on his face. He truly cared for me. I saw it in the way his gaze slipped from my face to Coleman's arm around me. Right before we'd been bombed, Scott had been telling me that he was falling in love with me. And right before that, he'd admitted that everyone he loved got hurt. I knew then that the entire scene when he'd returned my car had been staged in an effort to keep me safe. He'd decided to run me off by treating me mean, rather than see me get hurt. It took my breath away.

Nandy, who had revived, saw her opportunity and knelt down beside Scott. "I told you she was fucking the sheriff," she said with great satisfaction.

The hush in the room seemed to suck all of the oxygen out. It was Bridge who moved first, getting to his feet and picking up the old black record from the coffee table. "So who actually owns the records, and are there more of them?"

"Emanuel Keys owns them. There are twenty-two, counting the one you're holding."

Bridge nodded slowly. "My offer still stands."

"As soon as I get back to the courthouse, I'll cut Emanuel loose—until we can prove he was involved in Trina Jacks' abduction," Coleman said. "Whatever deal you work out is between the two of you."

There was the sound of an ambulance headed down Bilbo Lane, and in a moment the flashing lights could be seen in the driveway.

At Coleman's direction, Gordon started leading Ray-Ban toward the door. I stepped in front of him. "By the way, that ugly dog you hit was mine." I lifted my knee with as much force as I had. The result was very satisfactory. Ray-Ban was still doubled over when Gordon put him in the patrol car.

"I'll take Scott to the hospital," I offered. I needed a moment to talk to him. There was no denying what he'd seen with his own eyes, but surely there was a way to soften it.

"I'll take him!" Nandy was reaching for his arm.

"I'll ride with Bridge," Scott said. "I want to talk to him about Playin' the Bones."

"I'd still like to buy the club," Bridge said as he and Scott walked out of the room.

Nandy glared at me. "See what you've done. You didn't even want him and you hurt him. Why is it that everything you touch suffers, Sarah Booth?"

Even though I knew spewing poison was her nature, the knowledge didn't keep her words from hurting me.

I turned away, focusing on the ambulance attendants who were loading Spider on a stretcher. He'd lost a lot of blood, but he'd managed to hang on to his meanness.

"I'll be out in a few years, and you'd better watch out," he said to me, his voice a low whisper. But not so low that Coleman didn't hear.

Coleman leaned down. "You tortured and killed an old man who only wanted peace and music. You burned a historical building that served a community as a grocery store. Now you're trying to scare a woman with threats of revenge. You won't be much of a threat with one leg," he said. "The bone is shattered. Amputation is your only chance."

Spider looked sick as the paramedics wheeled him away. I felt a little nauseous. "Is he really crippled?"

"Who knows," Coleman said. "I just thought he needed something to think about, other than you."

We walked out of the house together and watched as Nandy hurried to her car. I had no doubt she'd follow Bridge and Scott to the hospital. She wasn't the kind of woman who gave up easily.

Coleman and I stood on the porch alone. There were a million things I wanted to say to him. I looked up and put my hand on his cheek, feeling the stubble of a long day. We stood like that, letting our eyes do the talking. His head bent down to kiss me.

"Coleman." The voice came out of the dark, but I recognized Connie. "It's time to come home."

We were frozen together, Coleman's lips just above mine. I felt him ease back from me. Whatever pain I might have caused Scott, I felt it tenfold.

"I've booked us a cruise," Connie said. She was talking very carefully. "I want to try to save this marriage. I know how you feel about Sarah Booth, and I know that it's partly my fault. I didn't love you when I should have. But maybe I can make you feel what you used to feel about me. I want to try." She was crying. "Please. Coleman, I'm pregnant."

I stepped away from Coleman and walked down the steps. I got in my car and backed up, my headlights catching Connie and then Coleman. He was still standing on the porch. He hadn't moved an inch, but the light around him glowed in a shimmering halo. Or at least it looked that way to me, because I was crying.

35

I SWIRLED THE ICE CUBES IN THE GLASS OF STRAIGHT JACK AND watched as Tinkie's headlights swung down the driveway. Coleman had returned my cell phone, and I'd called her as I drove home. She was in a high state of miff. As she made the curve by the house, gravel slung and peppered the porch.

"Hold the bullets," I said, striving for a light note.

"Sarah Booth, I'm very angry with you." She got out of the car and marched toward me on five-inch leopard-print heels. She was in such a state that she allowed Chablis to jump to the ground and walk by herself. "I'm your partner and you didn't even give me a chance to help catch those two."

I patted the step beside me. "I could have used your help." That was true. Tinkie had her own way of handling things. If she'd been there, perhaps no one would have gotten hurt.

My admission mollified her somewhat, and she took a seat beside me. She leaned over and sniffed my glass. "That's not a very ladylike drink."

"I'm not a very ladylike lady." The bourbon was warm as it slipped down my throat. It was a very comforting sensation.

"Are you hurt?"

"Physically, I couldn't be better."

"And how's your heart?"

"Well, let's just say that it's taken something of a beating tonight, but it was not alone in the fray." I told her the whole thing, including Connie's unexpected appearance and her more than unexpected pregnancy.

"I'm sorry, Sarah Booth." Tinkie put her tiny hand on my back and rubbed it gently. "You're the only girl I know who could lose three beaus in one night without using a gun, automobile, or poison. That may be a Sunflower County record. Maybe even Mississippi."

"That makes me feel so much better." I took a long swallow of my drink.

She got up and went to her car. When she returned, she had a brown bag of fried pork rinds. "Margene's cousin made these," she said, holding the bag out. "Her name's Rachelle and she's thinking of starting her own business. Rachelle's Rinds and Renderings. It has a certain ring to it." She gave me a crooked smile. "Despite the name, the product is excellent. I'm going to talk to Oscar and see if he'll invest."

She rattled the bag until I took one.

She held a rind between her fingers as if she were studying it. "After Tammy talked to the community Monday night, Margene decided she didn't have to quit. We owe Tammy a lot. She stood up for Scott."

I crunched the rind. It was crispy, light, and perfectly seasoned. "We do. On the other hand, she could have told me that Connie was going to get pregnant."

Tinkie put her arm around me. "I'm sorry about Coleman, Sarah Booth. Bridge isn't a man to play second fiddle, especially when you made it pretty clear you suspected him of murder. What about Scott, though?"

I shook my head. "I screwed that up, too. I couldn't imagine that he would ever love me, but I think he really did. Tonight, he saw clearly that he wasn't my first choice." I'd solved the case, in a manner of speaking, but the cost had been high.

"What are you going to do now?" she asked.

"Look for my next case. No more sitting around and waiting for something to drop in my lap. Bridge was right about that. If I'm going to be successful, then I'm going to have to pursue my options." I nudged her. "*We're* going to have to pursue *our* options."

"We don't have to worry about finding cases, Sarah Booth. Every time you turn around, you're in the middle of something. I was asking what you're going to do about the men."

I wanted to ask her what my options were, but I already knew. "I guess I'm just going to keep on dreaming, and one day the right man will walk through my door. Jit— A good friend told me once that I had to find a dream and stick with it. I guess I've just got to find that dream."

Tinkie sighed. "You try so hard to be tough, Sarah Booth, but you're really a romantic at heart."

"Desperate is the more accurate description." I stood up. I was bone weary. "I think I'm going to bed. Maybe my dream will visit and I'll know what to hope for."

Tinkie advanced an extra step so she was closer to my height. From that vantage, she put her arms around me and gave me a hug. "At least this time you aren't wounded."

"Only internal injuries." But I was smiling as I hugged her back. There's something to be said for a friend who can always find a silver lining.

MY ROOM WAS filled with sunshine and my bedside clock showed nine A.M. when I finally realized the horrible ringing was coming from the telephone and not my head. Ringing wasn't necessary, my head was satisfied with severe pounding.

"This better be good," I said into the receiver, squinching my eyes against the pain of speaking.

"Sarah Booth, how much did you drink? I knew I should never have left you alone."

Leave it to Tinkie to assume the burden of guilt. "You couldn't have stopped me," I told her, and it was the truth. I was just that stupid. I'd consumed a considerable amount of my good friend Jack before I'd fallen unconscious into the bed.

"Guess what?" She must have realized I wasn't in the mood for games because she immediately answered her own question. "Emanuel is selling Playin' the Bones to Bridge. They're up at the bank right now."

"That's great." I was finding it very hard to believe. Emanuel wasn't the kind of man to do something sentimental and nice.

"He's also selling Bridge the recordings."

I opened my eyes and stared at the sun streaming in the bedroom window. It was a white light, pure and summery. "Are you teasing me?"

"He told Bridge he wanted the world to share the music. He said that while he was sitting in that jail cell he had some time to think. He said he heard that you'd played a record on WBLK and he listened to the way people were talking about his father and the music, and he realized Ivory was right."

This was almost more than I could grasp. "Emanuel had a conversion?"

"You could say that." Tinkie giggled. "I think the ten million dollars Bridge offered had a little something to do with it. He's going to split it with Ida Mae. You should see the two of them together, Sarah Booth. It just does my heart good. After all this hurt and pain, she finally has found her son."

Emanuel was still in trouble with the law. "What about Trina Jacks?"

"Emanuel wasn't with the three men who abducted her, but he accepted responsibility for instigating it. He's left the Dominoes and, for his mother's sake at least, he'll keep quiet."

Even though my face hurt, I grinned. "Sounds great."

"Ida Mae was up at the courthouse, and she gave the remainder of the fee to me." She paused. "I've saved the best for last. Ida Mae's going to work with Bridge in the club."

"What about Scott?" Even saying his name hurt.

"I don't know. He hasn't been around the courthouse or the bank." There was evasion in her voice.

"What are you doing for breakfast? I think I promised you French toast." If she came here, face-to-face, she'd tell me the truth about Scott, and there was no one I'd rather hear it from.

"No, thanks. I went to Millie's this morning with Oscar. I knew you wouldn't be in any shape to cook."

It was true. My stomach almost revolted at the idea of food, but I didn't want to be alone. My case was over and I had nothing to distract me from the fact that I had no one in my life.

"Sarah Booth, are you okay?"

"I'm fine," I said, rolling out of bed and standing up. After the first wave of dizziness, I was okay.

"I've got to go to Memphis with Oscar this morning, but I'll be back tonight. Would you like to have dinner with us? Margene's cooking shrimp and pasta."

"Sounds wonderful, what time?"

"Seven. Try to rest up."

"I'll be there. Tinkie, did you see Coleman this morning?"

She paused. "No. He's out of town." There was a long silence. "He and Connie went on a cruise."

The idea of morning sickness and seasickness came to me with a dollop of malice, but I managed to keep my mouth shut. "I'll see you tonight," I finally said before I hung up the phone.

I wanted to roll up and crawl back in the bed. I was about to do that when there was a banging on my front door. It wasn't Tinkie—not her style, and she was at her house.

"Damn." I got up and started down the stairs in my underwear, when I thought better of it. I didn't feel like dressing and I didn't have to answer the door. I was hungover and I was grown-up. I could simply ignore the pounding and go back to bed. I was almost in the bed when I heard Scott's voice.

"Sarah Booth!"

I owed him the opportunity to tell me what a fool I was. "Scott, wait. Please." I dragged on some jeans and a T-shirt.

Still barefoot, I rushed downstairs, feeling the need to hold my head with each step. He was standing on the porch. When I opened the door, he turned around. His right eye was black and his jaw was mightily swollen.

"Man," I said, wincing. "How bad is it?"

"Broken molar and a broken jaw. It's not so bad if I don't laugh." His eyebrows arched as he looked at me. "Wow, you look like you're in pain."

"Self-inflicted." He had no reason to feel sorry for me, but I wanted to cry just at the sight of him.

He shrugged, the gesture reminding me that he had some of the sexiest moves I'd ever seen on a human. "I knew you'd get hurt if you hung out with me. Everyone does."

"Would you like to come in? I was about to make some coffee."

He shook his head. "I'm leaving."

It wasn't unexpected, yet I still felt a terrible pain. "Where are you going?"

"I have a gig in Chicago, then Detroit. BAMA Records has offered me a real nice contract for two albums. Don't tell Nandy, please. She's still bird-dogging me." His grin was rueful. "Anyway, Emanuel has released me from my contract with Playin' the Bones. He was really decent about it."

"Congratulations." I tried to put some enthusiasm in it. "I always knew Zinnia was too small for you."

"There was a time I didn't think so." He wasn't going to let me off the hook so easily.

"You have a lot of talent. In more than music."

"Thanks." He reached out and touched my cheek. "If Spider, Ray-Ban, and the sheriff hadn't gotten between us, we might have made something of this."

"We might have." I was finding it hard to speak around the lump in the back of my throat.

He kissed me gently on the top of the head, turned around and walked away. I saw he was driving Bridge's Jaguar. Well, it was a fine car for the man whose family had made an empire of selling Dodges.

As Scott drove away, I knew something special had just left my life. Why hadn't I been able to love Scott completely? Was it because Coleman was in the way? Or was it because I could only love a man I couldn't have? Loving the unattainable was safe. That love could never be tested by day-to-day reality.

As I passed through the parlor, I saw Jitty's fractured reflection in the cut-glass decanter.

"Three men in one night, Sarah Booth. Tinkie was right. That must surely be a record." She was wearing jeans rolled up at the ankles, white canvas shoes, a cotton shirt, and a bandana on her hair.

"Looks like you're having a picnic," I said as I pushed through the swinging door into the kitchen.

"Looks like you're having a hangover."

"Nothing like pointing out the obvious, right?"

"It's obvious to me that you're a fool. Pick up the telephone. Call him. He'll come back."

I shook my head again. "Scott deserves a woman who can love him without reservation. I'm not that woman."

"And Bridge?"

I shook my head. "I'm glad he wasn't behind Ivory's death, but I don't love him."

"Pass some more time with him. A man like him has to grow on you."

"He's not a mold," I said, preparing the coffeepot.

"No, he's a rich man who's going to be spending a lot of time in Zinnia, what with his new blues club and all."

"He may be your dream, Jitty, but he isn't mine."

"Dreams are peculiar things, Sarah Booth. I don't think this is Ivory's exact dream, not the way he imagined it, but I think this may be the best outcome he could have hoped for. Emanuel saw the truth. Ivory would be proud of him."

I plugged in the percolator and turned to face Jitty. "Ivory would be proud. Of Emanuel and Scott both." It was something good from all of the bad things. "I wish he were alive to see it."

"Oh, he sees it, Sarah Booth. Don't you worry about that. He knows."

She spoke with authority, and who was I to question the wisdom of a ghost? I poured a cup of black coffee and started the long exercise of pulling my life back together.

"I'm sorry Scott is leavin' town. Now that he's gone and you aren't gonna run off with him, I can see he had the potential for makin' a mighty fine baby."

Babies were the last thing I wanted to think about. "Connie managed to snare a sperm."

"That's a mighty big assumption," Jitty pointed out.

I looked at her long and hard. It *was* a big assumption, and if nothing else, I'd learned my lesson about assumptions the night before.

"Sarah Booth, you didn't get the man you wanted, but you still have the dream. You got to remember that's the important thing. Just hang on to the dream."

I wanted to believe in dreams. Ivory had believed, and in the end, he had achieved nothing short of a miracle. His music would be heard by the world, his club would survive, and his son had been humanized by his love.

"Feel it, Sarah Booth. It's there. Your dream is still there. Where there's life, there's hope. It's a cliché because it's true."

Although my head was still pounding, I did feel better. I finished my cup of coffee and put the cup in the sink. Looking out the kitchen window, I saw my family cemetery. The tombstones were nearly white in the August sunlight.

"What're you gonna do?" Jitty asked.

I suddenly knew. I was going to put on my boots, saddle my horse, and ride. I would let Reveler gallop over the cotton fields, with Sweetie Pie by my side, and in doing so, I'd start the process of healing my heart. Whatever I'd lost, I still had Dahlia House and the land.

"I'm taking Reveler for a ride."

Jitty's smile took on a wicked glint. "Keep those thighs tight, girl, you never know when the right man's gonna walk into your life. When he does, you clamp those legs around him and make him scream for the Jaws of Life to cut him free."

"You're a bad influence, Jitty," I told her.

"Maybe so, but I'm the one who knows you best. And I know you don't need a man, you just want one."

She was right. I didn't really need a man. I might want one, but I could live without one. That would be small comfort when I climbed into my bed at night, but for the moment, with the hip-high cotton fluttering in a gentle breeze, it was enough.

"Come on, Sweetie," I said, picking up my boots from the back porch. "Let's ride."

ABOUT THE AUTHOR

Mississippi native Carolyn Haines, a former photojournalist, has written numerous books and was recently honored with an Alabama State Council on the Arts literary fellowship. She now lives in southern Alabama with her horses, dogs, and cats, including the real-life Sweetie Pie, where she is hard at work on the next Sarah Booth Delaney mystery, *Hallowed Bones*. *Crossed Bones* is her fourth mystery for Bantam Dell. Visit her website at www.carolynhaines.com.